Alive in the Merciful Country

a novel by

A.L. Kennedy

Saraband

Published by Saraband
3 Clairmont Gardens
Glasgow, G3 7LW
www.saraband.net

ISBN: 9781916812284

Printed and bound in Great Britain by Clays Ltd, Elcograf S.p.A.

1 2 3 4 5 6 7 8 9 10

For V.D.B

With thanks to Shelby White for her enduring hospitality.

Nous sommes si accoutumés à nous déguiser aux autres qu'enfin nous nous déguisons à nous-mêmes.

François de la Rochefoucauld

A person becomes what they need to be so they can meet their time. That's my theory. Of course, you need luck to make that work. And some people have no luck. That's why we're supposed to have mercy.

Exactly when you're reading this is a matter for conjecture. Still, I think that I'm safe in assuming very many things will be appalling and will remain appalling or become more appalling after that. More comfortable circumstances may not appear, because as a species we fail to impress.

Sorry about that. I don't know what we were thinking.

But also – perhaps we'll be thriving. Or perhaps we will be just about to thrive, all poised. Perhaps we will be learning and somehow living inside the fires we have lit, being happy and not consumed. Afterwards, we might walk out of the storm and into existing gently, building gently. We'll move on and rarely look behind.

That's the hope, or something like it. You do have to hope, don't you?

I read once about an experiment with mice confined in awful little tubes filled with water. Left to themselves, the mice would paddle and paddle to keep afloat, but it wouldn't take many minutes before they would be utterly exhausted and close to drowning. At which point, researchers observing what I have to assume was their idea of a reasonable and necessary experiment would have to fish the mice back out.

The funny thing was that when the terrifying researchers returned those same mice to the water torture tubes – because of course they did – the little creatures would swim and swim and swim, for twice as long, ten times as long and on and on. Somewhere in their tiny mouse brains they trusted that when they were desperate they'd be saved, and this let them endure. I am unable to say if this was good news.

Nonetheless, I do hope. And I also mean well. You need to, these days. If you are in any way thoughtful, you are obliged to mean and act really well, really forcefully, really every single day, because everything that's loudest and most rewarded is entirely the opposite.

And Oakwood School means well, too. We still all recite the Oakwood Primary Promise every morning before we do anything else, just as we would on a normal school day. We sit up proud at our computer screens with our various rooms behind us, our various wandering pets and our various chaoses, just out of sight.

We are friendly and helpful, we're kind and polite,
We mend and don't break things, we do what is right.
We grow every day in our beauty and light,
We learn and we're brave and we sleep well at night.

On any given day, almost none of this is true for me. I like to believe the kids are doing better. We're trying to make progress anyway. That's what matters.

Oakwood is a school where the fees paid by comfortable parents of comfortably disturbed and neglected children subsidise the wits' end parents of wits' end and embattled children and everyone mostly aims to do their best. There are also very normal kids here, of course, although normality levels fluctuate. Tony was rock steady and nowhere near any kind of drowning tube until last month. Then his grandad died alone and hidden inside the coma that doctors had slightly hoped would hide Poppa from death. No one was there to hold a hand or speak a word as he was leaving. His ventilator, doubtless, bailed away calmly throughout the process, because ventilators are machines and can't get upset.

It all gave Year Five a horrible lot to talk about. We got scared. We're rallying now, processing, but I can catch flickers of the darkness under glances. Things smear and press against our windows at night like maniac faces. Not that we often mention the possibly maniac things behind the faces in case they hear us say their names and then take an interest.

Everyone's becoming superstitious. I no longer kill even large and swift spiders. Just in case.

On Wednesday, Talha suddenly burst out in tears at his kitchen table with his work nook pictures orderly in the background and his weird tuft of hair perked up at the crown of his head – like an aerial connecting him with too much reality. He's clever, Talha, bright in the way that worries.

I would be very disappointed in 2020 by now, if I hadn't already known how years can be. It's hard not to take things personally, but maybe it's just our turn.

Anyway.

This isn't quite how I imagined I'd begin what I want to say here, but here we are together and being together is a help.

Here is our home – mine and Paul's. We live in our little household, a sealed island of home among other islands with more or less porous coastlines. In isolation, we're developing our prevailing emotional tones and various odds and ends that might become a culture, given time. When Paul next suggests we should build a wicker man out in the courtyard I might agree. I like to encourage the arts. I like barbecues. Why not both?

Basketry and roasted aubergines and possibly pagan songs. Maybe popcorn. Who could speak ill of that?

I'm planning to become eccentric.

'More eccentric?'

'Just eccentric.'

Part of our culture is back-and-forth patter. It deflects nervous tension.

'Mum, you're in flip-flops, knickers and your baking apron. You are at your destination. Eccentric. You have arrived.'

'It's hot. And don't you satnav me, young man. I will navigate as I wish.'

'Next stop, shaving squirrels in the park.'

'I resent that suggestion. Dyeing the squirrels, disguising them as dogs and training them to steal handbags… I do not deny, that could be a plan.'

We are ourselves. Thank goodness. We have that. And meanwhile the newly violent air flows and eddies out along Wicklow Street beyond our walls. It's the tide that wants to carry us away.

I always tell the kids to make a plan that will be your breadcrumb trail through the forest of distractions from what you really want to say. Once the trail's there, you just follow it.

Well, I live in this forest. It's my forest. My life. I imagine it has thickets of mad brambles, inconvenient streams and hollows, perhaps malign trees. But there is a trail. I made it. I have only to let myself remember how it goes. It's just that I generally prefer not to.

Still – I am the plan.

And forgive me if I now follow my plan and lay out our opening scene in the way a movie might. I am hoping – you have to hope – that this will ease me back into what happened, while keeping things slightly at bay. Plus, my story really is like any number of movies. I didn't ask to be in a spy scenario, or an action scenario, or a political thriller, but I recurringly have been. I am not an agent with violent skills, or a siren trained to be alluring for hidden blackmail cameras. I am not someone operating under a number of pseudonyms. Not really.

I am not a hero, heroine, anything like that – even though there is a villain. We'll get to him.

I am just a primary school teacher.

No. Forget about *just*.

I am a primary school teacher. I am the person who keeps your society working right from the very start and who tries to make sure it isn't full of broken people. Adding in a *just* is inappropriate.

I have only the usual number of names: Mrs McCormick for the kids and scam phone calls, Anna Louisa McCormick for forms and pretending to be an Edwardian duchess, Anna for most people, which became Na-na for Paul, although Na-na has now been turned into Mum. That's a perfectly reasonable alteration. I object to it, obviously, but keep my objections to myself, because time moves on and sometimes my emotions can be ignored. I can't force the poor guy to call for me in shops with *Na-na, Na-na*. People would think he was concussed.

To be honest, *Mum* has quite enough impact at the moment. It's like a soft punch in the stomach when he says it – that, or a bird catching light in my chest, something equivalent. This is true, always. Even on the days when I don't like him – incinerated skylarks, droves of them, each and every time Paul says it. He makes me wonder if my mother felt that, too, although I can't imagine that she did. Simple dislike aimed in my direction was an excellent day for me with Ma. Not her fault. She was built with a twist way before I was born. I'm all right about it now. And nature has revenged itself upon her and kicked all the marbles she had out of her reach. Or else there's no such thing as karma and randomly awful things do sometimes happen to randomly awful people.

By this point you can guess which option I'd say is true.

Poor Ma. Everything scared her and it made her savage. And now she is permanently terrified.

I think about her more than I used to now that it's impossible to see her.

That's the thing about lockdown – it has cleared away too much clutter and busyness. Reality is getting through. Suddenly I'm sad my dog is gone and that dog hasn't been around for decades. Apparently I never did stop being sad about it – I just successfully kept myself distracted.

Days are increasingly meaningless as individual lumps of time. They all last about twenty minutes, while simultaneously stretching for two or three months. Something about them provides too many opportunities for reflection. There are times when I find I despise everybody on Earth and also I want to forgive every single one of them. Certainly, I realise everyone needs it, the forgiveness. Quite a few of us even deserve it.

Even stupid, scared me could be absolved.

What else do you need to know?

Yes – long ago, I was known as the Amazing Annanka Ladystrong for a while. I liked being her. I grew up and into her aspirations. Into another name.

Also F.L. is attempting to rechristen me. He is testing pet names, but hasn't yet found one to fit. Quite possibly this is because I'm not a pet.

I do like F.L. There is nothing wrong with him. I'm pretty sure he loves me, very sure in fact.

I don't respond appropriately – that needs to be forgiven. And the trouble is, he does forgive me. He hasn't gone away. What does one do with a person like that? Love them back? Seems reckless.

Our current catastrophe has cut him off from our pretend island. He is stuck on what is an actual literal body of land surrounded by water with bays and a harbour and so forth – Colonsay. I miss him. I notice myself missing him. I regularly walk into the living room, expect him to be on the sofa and am once again baffled that he is not. He is absent in ways that are both small and fundamental – as if someone had removed all of my light switches overnight. I reach out just before I can remember there'll be nothing there.

I didn't anticipate such a thing. I didn't think I was capable of feeling this amputated about anyone other than Paul. This is positive emotional progress, isn't it?

Maybe.

In all the extra minutes we now have, F.L. and I – but mainly F.L. – are dealing with my disinclination to emerge from the forest underbrush in which I can remain a twitchy woodland creature, safely concealed from our relationship and its emotional consequences. Still, I sometimes baffle us.

Like all truly terrible situations, ours is also occasionally funny. F.L. did genuinely turn up one evening – back in the days of visiting and meeting and kissing and the rest – wearing two oven gloves and carrying a net. It was some kind of borrowed angling net – large but not quite big enough to catch a person.

'Why the gloves?'

'Against biting.'

'I don't bite.'

'Says you.'

'You won't get me into that net.'

'It's a symbol, Anna.'

'It smells weird. Symbols aren't supposed to smell of anything.'

'Multisensory.'

'You know I'm not a fan of prop comedy.'

'I know. I do know.' F.L. with his increasingly tired eyes. His net lowered a little and stopped looking jovial.

The thing smelled of septic ponds and small lives gasping.

I didn't say that.

F.L. makes me think of the word *foursquare*. Very straight back, tall man's torso, but short arms and legs. This is less obvious on Zoom, but he still has a very clear atmosphere of reliability.

All the worst people do, though.

It turns out the way to really progress our relationship has been for him to stay away entirely without intending to.

Missing him has been educational – if I miss him, I must want him near.

That net made me slightly furious.

But then not.

He's good with animals.

But some animals are, in the end, too unrewarding and feral. I catch myself thinking how sorry I am that he might be wasting so much time on me.

Paul. F.L. Me.

That's your whole cast, basically. That's all the people who count. That's all the people I currently want to think about.

Villains don't need introducing – they do that themselves, shove in where they shouldn't, and I don't feel I have to help.

We will get to him.

Our villain is in the other story: the one he wrote – the one that arrived overnight in an envelope with no postage – the one in which he speaks to me.

Spoke to me. I won't ever read him again. I won't ever listen to him again. He's done with.

By the end of this, he will be done with.

My trail through the forest is also an exorcism.

And his story will be included for educational purposes and will have its own font, which will look like this.

What he is, what he says, will look like this.

This isn't horrible enough, but nothing would be.

I will look like this.

Clear?

I do hope so.

Teachers – whatever hell we get stuck with, we'll make it an opportunity for learning.

Oh, and I will mention Sue Delara, our headmistress. Equally, I will try to avoid writing much about Mr Simms, who teaches Year Four and has an odd moustache that made me call him Mr Disease Face out loud at one Christmas staff party with too much advocaat on board.

Too much gin, in fact, but advocaat sounds more festive – it even resembles reindeer snot. And it brings on that warm kind of nausea all children of unruly homes experience when they consider the oncoming tinselly season.

Year Three teacher – Polly Larsson, who is good at graphics and can catch spiders in her bare hands. Year Two – Brian Scott, who cries at films. Year One – Mrs Parker, who talks to everyone as if they are four and, I mean, is she that wildly mistaken?

Year Six – Mrs Filmore. I try not to resent her because she takes my Year Fives away from me. She is supposed to. She's a really good teacher. Her *really goodness* alienates them from me. It's supposed to. They are meant to move on. And after the first few days of Winter Term, My New Year Five is just My Year Five. We do all move on as intended.

Year Seven – Mrs. Decker. She prepares everyone for the knocks and tumbles of possibly moving on to a more conventional type of school. This seems to make her a bit shouty. But she knows how to break into cars, which is occasionally useful. We don't ask her why she's so skilled with half tennis balls and bits of wire and so forth. It may be connected with all those conventional types of schooling.

But Paul and F.L. and me, we're what matter.

And this is the story that Na-na has not told Paul. She hasn't told F.L. either. She doesn't exactly know why.

Here it is now, though. They can read it when it's done.

Actually, Na-na does know exactly why she hasn't said all this before. That's part of the story, too. We'll get to it.

It'll be about shame. Of course. Isn't everything?

And now – because I'm really starting – let's pretend this is a film we're watching and it's very far away on a big and impersonal screen and can barely affect me. Or else, maybe I will peer at what I remember from inside a nice hedgerow and then curl up in my imagination afterwards, warm in some kind of soft nest, a fur-lined nest, a burrow, a warren, a drey, where nothing is a threat and I am unfindable and safe.

We begin with me being on Ludgate Hill, which isn't noticeably hilly, but that's London for you – false advertising all the way. Ludgate Hill is just a street – a road and a pavement pinned down flat by urban development.

This is November 2019, in the days before masks and tantrums about masks. Our last normalish year.

This is also a year during which any competent government might have kept on making sure we would be defended from new diseases and other predictable shocks and unhappinesses. But priorities lie elsewhere, weighing down the moral high ground in strange places. You can almost feel unprecedented forces tilting the paving stones.

And this is in the present tense because sometimes the past does seem to be – because of joy, because of PTSD. Feel free to guess which. They both bring things closer. Suddenly, here you are.

At least we're together.

And here I am, not exactly running through the mingling and re-mingling crowds that clutter up the street, but I am fast.

The pavements are only going to get busier because it's almost lunchtime. I am following a man and maybe the forthcoming bustle is in his mind, his plan for escape. He always has been good at making his plans for escape.

Ludgate Hill is not simply in London – it's deep inside the City itself, the special Square Mile where money dreams punitive dreams and marvellous dreams and grows large in its sleep, or else disappears abruptly because of miscalculations and maybe cocaine. If the money arrives dirty, this is where it will be washed, as if it is a well-loved baby, or a bedbound invalid. The poor here are immensely poor, but the money is well-tended and that's what counts. The people who come here to work all seem to walk with a vaguely grim purpose and mostly wear what I'd have to call sociopathic shirts – louche collars, sadomasochistic stripes – and the suits of maladjusted schoolboys. There's a general sense of braced elbows, shoving through the lowly multitude and outpacing the competition. Faces are aimed towards a destiny that includes excellent bets on Futures and subsequent helicopters, but also perhaps dead strippers and fatal heart attacks.

I am making myself mildly conspicuous by being female and not quite immaculately well-groomed. Also, I'm faster than average. My purpose really does have purpose.

The man up ahead of me has adopted the other local style, which is much smoother, a kind of slippy and entitled march. He has red hair in a close clip above the collar of a dark blue coat that isn't military but wants to be. An officer, maybe, or else a barrister, perhaps – that's what he intends to suggest. This is, after all, where England's highest law lives and he'll want to fit in. He seems a man of means and this somehow parts each press of bystanders as he approaches. There's enough learned deference and feudal instinct about the place to help him along and make his progress effortless. He is one of nature's prefects and doing well. Of course, he is – he's in London.

The man that I am remembering had no particular means and wasn't a redhead. Then again, I never knew him all that well. He had the knack of being almost anyone.

And I don't want to lose him. But it seems less than likely that I will, what with that very red hair.

He really never did have red hair.

Has he dyed it to catch my attention?

Or am I entirely mistaken? Did sitting in the Old Bailey and remembering our villain make me see him when he wasn't really there?

I might be wrong about this.

I might have misidentified the figure in the visitor's gallery, perched right next to the door. I hadn't noticed his arrival, but then again I'd glanced away from the proceedings after twenty minutes or so – away from Court 10 and its weary office furniture and green carpet mended with silver gaffer tape.

He sleeked off fast, with his executive-appropriate briefcase in his hand.

Court 10 is in the relatively modern section of the Old Bailey. You reach it by winding up stairs that feel like a prison, or a very grim B&B. The two are not dissimilar and both tend to be staffed by ex-military men. This morning I wound through over-curated passages, past notices explaining basic courtesy and how to dress, how to wash one's hands successfully. All visitors must keep quiet as Sunday and remove their hats.

Once I had been herded inside with the other interlopers, the proceedings oozed into action. The shabby courtroom alternated mumbles and pantomime boredom with occasional outbreaks of law among ring binders stuffed with papers and hackled with coloured tabs. A solicitor picked his nose with close attention and that's the sort of thing to summon outrage in any primary school teacher. The prosecution QC stood up every now and then to look more aquiline and blessed by nature. I began to expect he'd recite something from Shakespeare.

The accused were inside a Perspex box that prevented their wrongness leaking out.

The accused. I still can't think of them using their everyday names, the ones read out with the accusations, the scary list of crimes. Those names are far too small and bland to ever hold them. Back when I was Annanka Ladystrong they were Phil the Pill and Utility Bill, Dynamo, Magnificent Arthur and Percussion Karl. They were my friends and more than friends and more my family – like my particular, rare species.

Dynamo had lost his hair. Karl's muscle had turned to fat. Phil and Bill weren't next to each other, and they should have been, that should have been allowed, because they always were next to each other and a pair and brothers by choice. They leaned forward, leaned back, tried to smile across the distance at each other. It made them seem unreliable.

Court 10 was full of charges on top of charges. So many terrible-sounding things had been said out loud that it was difficult to see very clearly or to breathe. In 1999, it was alleged, a nuclear base and its sanctity had been breached. Sort of – there had definitely been the beginnings of a fire. This was not so much arson as a mistake involving symbolic paper lanterns and implausibly dry Scottish turf. Two MoD policemen had been crippled, although the crippling amounted to a black eye and bruises for one, a broken finger for the other – none of that being good, or legal, but was it crippling? I was biased, but also I did feel that if Phil had somehow acquired two cracked ribs and a smashed cheekbone, that might have been closer to crippling. His ribs and cheek were apparently inadmissible, though – as were any number of bruises and fractures among the accused. And the whole mess was being prosecuted after so many years. Why now? Why after so many years during which my more-than-friends could think they had made a mistake, had a fight, but then got away free.

It seemed unlikely they had got away free – feet kicking gloriously through heather in summer dawn, a dash to a camper van and off.

The mitigations and qualifications to every charge were muffled and lacked supporting evidence, while the acts were loud and terrible and suggested desperate intent. Nothing about the whole affair sounded like us, like the OrKestrA, like our merry little band of very harmless kazoo players.

What could be more harmless than kazoos?

None of it sounded like anything my dearer-than-family would plan. Indeed, it was emerging that someone else, someone I didn't know, had planned the action, someone sitting at the far end of the row inside the Perspex and staring at his hands as if they were a clue to something.

So my friends had been with someone else, with *Number Six*, the final one of those accused. And why would they have done anything with him and not the rest of us? Why would they feel quite comfortable or safe without the UnRule OrKestrA around them, the *Purveyors of Fresh Nonsense* and *Funmongers, Strollers and Wise Fools*. Why did they decide to be so horribly serious?

There's nothing bad about being a fool if you're honest about it. A fool is full of hiding places where truths grow and then sing out.

I hadn't known about the prosecution until Mrs Fire called me. She was organising – that's what she does. One of nature's schedulers and listers, she was making a rota of people to sit and support what she was calling The OrKestrA Five whenever we could. I had a personal development day I could take. There was no doubt that I would be there. Anyone could have guessed.

Our villainous villain could have guessed.

And beyond Court 10 and Mrs Fire's tiny propaganda operation, all the newspapers were staying oddly quiet. We barely rated a paragraph. It seemed thinking about the case made it hard for any journalists to see clearly or breathe and therefore they must have been suddenly like me, but for different reasons.

The whole situation felt at least out of kilter, if not suspect – like someone else's show we'd been shoved into, unrehearsed. And me?

I might easily have been behind the Perspex and one of the accused.

If any one of the Five had asked me to join them in something, I really might have. I might have trusted that we didn't need the whole OrKestrA with us, or maybe believed that we should leave them safely out of it. A suggestion along those lines might have won me over. And if their thinking really had become hard and dark and strange, I might not have noticed, because of their kind faces, familiar eyes.

That final member of the group – Number Six – I really couldn't place him, not from a demo, a concert, a committee, not from anything. And I didn't trust even the thought of him. He seemed like a type I had met before – hard and dark and strange – a hollow man you'd fill with anything required.

The man by the visitor's gallery door, the one with the red, red hair – after so many years, here he was – but only for a blink before his back turned and he was up and rushing, running out and away.

I could have been mistaken.

Yeah, but I wasn't, though.

Twenty years on and the accused were different but also much the same. In the OrKestrA we'd all tried to be demonstrably happy, actively happy, sharingly happy. I mean, we had genuinely aimed for that. And years of trying to live with those intentions had left the accused with soft expressions, fluid gestures, a gentleness inappropriate for Court 10. They looked like the kind of people who might want to cry here, or scream in the way any human person might have with coppers to either side and the law swimming all around their Perspex enclosure. Everything happening might take away the whole rest of their lives, but was carefully dull and blurry as it ground ahead. The tedium increased the terror. The lack of screaming kept on implying that nobody here was really a human person.

I looked away from the court, because of its endless, unbearable calm. The slow-motion torture theatre was beginning to make me feel sick.

I'm sure there were notices somewhere – firm regulations in place – about not vomiting in the presence of Her Dear Majesty's Own Justice.

I want to be clear about this – it was my will that made me glance towards the door, not some gesture, or manipulation that came from him. I wanted to look. And there he was, ready to be looked at – suddenly manifesting, like a goblin. He seemed to be newly rising from his seat, but could have been newly slipping into it.

The turn of my head sent him straight out and down the stairs.

And I followed. I chose to follow. His feet made this weird small disturbance, a sign of emotion inside a building where none should be expressed.

And it is him I'm following.

It is.

He's the stranger who first poisoned the OrKestrA.

I'm almost sure of it.

I spent years looking for him – we all did.

Now he appears, the familiar goblin, exactly when his doing so is going to disturb me most.

Here's your monster again.

I don't know if his hair is red now because that will make him easier to see. I don't know if it's bait.

I also don't know what I'll do if I ever catch him.

Five or six yards ahead of me, I see him get nudged a bit sideways and delayed by a slightly more strident master of the universe. He is given a *Die, you peasant* type of look. He doesn't seem to be someone who cares much about looks.

That would be right. The man I think he is always did thrive on the outrage of crowds: raising it, bathing in it.

I'm keeping him in sight but he's edging out more of a lead and the lunchtime rush is helping him and hampering me.

As I press forward, I have no awareness of how soon I'll be longing to fight through any press of bodies. Nobody on this pavement has any idea of who will die soon, who will be bereaved, who will spend months longing for human contact, looking forward to simply being annoyed by strangers.

There's no horror, yet, in facing a group of children in an unventilated room and knowing they're breathing in and breathing out, their livingness quietly threatening other lives.

Right now, in many ways I'm carefree. I'm just following a stranger, after all – how harmless. Relatively harmless.

Although I am fast, he's faster. He always made a habit of that. And as far as the City is concerned, I am plainly worth minimal respect. No one even considers clearing a path for me and I don't have time to bake a cake, or gestate a child, to prove I should get my fair share of the pavement as a thing of use and beauty.

And then the man suddenly fades left and disappears. I've been wondering if he really is trying to shake me off and now I'm certain. Something in the sideways dodge and slide of his whole body seems nothing like a master and commander of men.

And I think – *I'm not wrong. Redhead or not, I know you. I know you.*

I lift my pace into a run and hope he hasn't dipped in somewhere, shut a door and locked himself away. He didn't look smug enough for that. He looked like someone without an exit plan who was panicking. His gestures became more honest and more fearful.

I like him fearful.

I draw level with an archway that cuts clear under a building and accesses a narrow lane. This explains how he vanished. I dive in after him. I don't know what I'm running into, but I keep on through the shadow of the overhang, in pursuit.

Maybe he prepared this route, checked out his ground for dead ends and exits, the way you do before an action, or a demo. You never want to end up being trapped by geography, or authority – by the police.

Not that he would be worried by the police.

His footfalls are banging at the pavement somewhere, although all I can see are stragglers, waiting in line for snacks and lunches outside various little shops. Wherever he is going, he's in flight now, sprinting. There are fewer and fewer people to hide him as we progress, so this was a bad choice for him. Unless he is heading for refuge in a building.

And I am running at full tilt, too, and then more than that. I am not as fit as I once was, but today I am quite certain that I can keep on like this and go even faster, burn onwards forever if I need to. I can't feel my feet hit the flagstones. I'm just speed and direction. I'm Annanka Ladystrong again. I haven't been her in decades.

All my pasts are coming home – the PTSD and joy and PTSD.

I pass shopfronts with country house-coloured paintwork and signs about handmade this and that. It all blurs beside me as if I'm a train.

This is a warren and not the concealing and friendly kind. I am threading along bare and winding streets. Between high walls and tall windows, the sound of two people racing is bouncing about. I'm still not close enough to see him, but I can hear he's not far off. He has reached his limit.

And here's a small queue for something described as Bespoke Pasties by a little café that stands all by itself. I swing past it and this woman sitting in the window turns to look at me as if I am freak of nature and there's this moment when I look right back at her and make sure she knows that *Yes, I am*. Today I am. Possibly she flinches, but I'm already moving on.

There are doorways and doors and gated courts, but nothing seems ready to help him and take him in, because his flight is still crack-cracking shoe leather on stone up ahead. I take one last corner and spot his hair as he moves between three oblivious and startled pedestrians. And now I can see the whole man with his coat-tail linings showing blue as his legs work and lift the pale soles of his Oxfords. And here's the way a driven body can't help becoming true, showing what it is. Here he is.

Here's the man with too many names. I am making him run and I want to.

I want to make him terrified.

More than thirty years and it's only now I realise – I was waiting to make him terrified.

My throat hurts with hard breathing, or maybe I'm yelling and this is why heads flick and watch me. My heart's so loud that I think there are three of us for a while, slamming and slamming along.

I see him make a hard turn left and I follow him into the curve of another lane, which is a little wider and clearer now that so many heads are safe indoors and bowed over organic, or ethnic, or else traditional treats at prices that I wouldn't tolerate.

I don't know why he came here, what possible reason he had to be anywhere near the court. It would never occur to him that he should apologise to all of us, that he should kneel and beg and cry in front of me.

Whatever he said wouldn't be enough.

I'm running with both hands in fists, punching forward and forward through the air.

I want to hit him.

Of course.

When Primary Teachers Go Bad…

I want to hit him with something I'll draw up from my hips, from my spine, my memory, from more than thirty years ago.

He makes another left and slips a little and I want him to fully tumble and end up on his back, hurt and cornered. But then his arms swing out, wild and fast, for balance and he uses the weight of his case to keep him steady.

He still has his old skill set, then, still the funambulist.

I haven't kept in condition. I have been living a normal life, a middle-aged woman's gently inactive life. Still, any weakness I might have doesn't matter today, because I'm all mind over matter now and I'm gaining on him. The press of thin buildings on either side of us is somehow helping me to concentrate.

This is the day when I start being stronger again. Annanka is definitely back.

I suppose I should thank him for that.

Just as I'm almost in reaching distance, the lane ends up ahead and feeds straight into the maximum busyness of London. He's going to dive out and disappear into that.

And I realise I can smell him. The breeze is blowing back against my face now and it's bringing an aftershave scent that I don't want to recognise. There's the taste of his body in it, too, hiding underneath.

This washes a filthy sweat over me, but I don't stop.

He rushes across the final cobbles that lie between two restaurants and then keeps on, crosses the main road. Buses slide in and close my view of him, but I go headlong in among the traffic myself. I can't stop.

I warn Oakwood's Fiver Acorns against doing any such thing, ever. But here I am, feeling invulnerable in a stupid way.

I almost get hit by a cab. Or, to be more precise, a cab almost gets hit by me. I push at its bonnet and half expect the whole thing will reel back away from my hands, because it's nothing and I'm in the right.

Then I'm out again, clear of the traffic, and everything is very open and almost like a square, rather than a pavement. There's too much to see. On my left, here's the statue of Queen Anne we showed the children on a Spring Outing and here are all the little stones laid underfoot in careful patterns, because this is a nice place intended for visitors. And here come some tourists in a drift, with a guide lifting up an Italian flag at the top of a golf umbrella. And just to my right is the pale, broad mountain that is Saint Paul's Cathedral. It looks like an ugly white clock on god's mantel.

And here's our villain.

At a standstill.

He has halted by a pillar at the top of the grubby, but sanctified, white steps. He's apparently breathing so hard that his arms shake as they hold his high-end case close to his chest. I have made him be this stressed type of animal, this impersonation of how scared boys hold schoolbags. I have made him run away, made him hope for crowds, for strangers to be his chaperone, or his witnesses, or else his alibi.

He drops his head, but I have enough time to understand he's old now, isn't he? In his neck and his jaw and the sink of his cheeks he is old, and I have lasted better.

Good.

He is looking at his feet and apparently nervous, but not seeking sanctuary – unless the steps count.

It costs twenty quid to get inside for sanctuary.

I stay where I am and I make my voice carry, because I can do that. I always could do that. Strolling player to teacher – being heard is a transferable skill.

'Buster.'

I sound like someone else.

Also, I'm raging in my joints and fingers and in my stomach, in my chest. I have furious blood.

I begin to walk closer. My legs seem stiff – as if he has access to spells and is trying to make me stumble, but I am fighting it.

With one united mind, a cloud of pigeons flies up and away from me. Perhaps I seem predatory.

This isn't his name, 'Buster'. He doesn't have a name.

When he raises his face, he looks sad.

And that is a lie. He is no more than a series of lies, lie after lie. He is lying to me – in every glance, or word, or gesture, he's lying to me. That's all a lying liar ever does.

But if you were here, would you know what Buster is, know just by looking? Would you give him the benefit of your doubt? Would you trust me if I told you my opinion?

20

The narrator is part of the bargain when you let a story in. I tell the children this. I'm no danger, but not everyone is a friend. Not everyone's trying to help. Stories leave marks on your thinking: dirt and scuffs and footprints and areas with that shine you get when somebody drags something back and forth across a surface, over and over at just the same place.

I say to my class, which is Oakwood's sole Year Five, that it's important you don't have bad tenants in your head. You never quite know what some stories might be saying up there in your head. They could begin to play horrible music, or light fires.

Year Five is the best age. Nobody really notices at the time, but nine or ten, maybe eleven, is probably when we peak. Everything beyond that is just sex, bursts of anxiety and bodily decay.

That's an exaggeration, but I'm reliable, nonetheless. It's important to be reliable. For example, I will get back to St Paul's and the steps, I promise. Not now, though. I can't quite manage it at the moment. And many other things and people are more important than Buster.

Like Sue Delara, our headmistress and good witch guru leader. She's why we can all still see each other, although we're far apart. She trashed all the budgets and called our usual supporters – plus some extras – and duly accumulated a small hill of spare laptops and mendable laptops and dongles and routers and ancient cell phones.

So no one has gone without. No one should have to. We can teach online

Beyond us, the government is muttering and soundbiting about maybe possibly thinking of ways to help kids learn from home at a future date.

I'm guessing almost nothing will be done.

And somehow a very predictable range of people will already be making money out of not providing yet another thing we really need.

At least at Oakwood we have solutions and flexibility – and Sue. We've even been able to give some spare tech to a non-profit.

We're a private, but not independent, school and generally bounce along the bottom with funding. We're sort of bleeding to death right now, but at least we can still take some kids for free and teach as if we actually like and even respect all those concerned. Our plans for the future rely over-heavily on a nice old lady dying and remembering us in her will, which is slightly despicable of us, but it doesn't do to dwell.

And the Year Five Acorns meet online every day, and we can pretend we're cosy. We wave our Acorn waves and our Oak Tree waves and we dance our happy dance (only sitting down) and we open our eyes very wide to see our friends. I no longer tear up while any of this happens.

I can't say that being trapped on each other's screens is improving how we learn to add and subtract fractions and all that. Then again, who genuinely longs to pester fractions – except perhaps Kwakou and Talha? Still, we're doing well. Even Rosie, who's allergic to maths, is getting through.

And we leave painted stones on each other's doorsteps, because they're cheerful. I have sixteen happy stones outside my gate – one for each child in my year. Small class size is one of our selling points, although it's also why we have a small income.

Swings…

Roundabouts…

Literally and figuratively, we have both – but only at Oakwood, not at home.

And, anyway, how does one sterilise a roundabout? It seems that if we opened our doors again, we'd have to.

This all matters more than Buster.

Almost everything in the world matters more than Buster.

But the kids do need to be ready for challenges and hazards and people like him, people I call Stiltskins.

You know – the people like Rumpelstiltskin.

This is the month when I talk to the kids about *Rumpelstiltskin*. It's a very important story. And, every year, I make sure that my

Acorns know how to cope with Rumpelstiltskin, no matter what tricks he might try.

I'm sure you remember the plot: young woman is betrayed by her worse-than-pointless father and abducted by a horrifying king. Her father, for unexplained reasons, has led the king to believe she is capable of spinning straw into gold. The king is more than interested. At which point, we are unsurprised that the only person mentioned who has too much gold wants even more of it. So the king steals the unfortunate daughter and gives his order – *Gold, and plenty of it.*

Now, spinning straw into anything other than spun straw is not possible. The young woman is locked in a room with a spinning wheel and, most likely, heaps and heaps of straw. Her situation is dreadful. She may have allergies. She is certainly very sad and at a loss. Then an awful and magical person shows up suddenly when she is hopeless late at night. And she makes a bargain with him – it's an awful and magical bargain.

This reminds us that being hopeless late at night should be avoided and also that terrible people do frequently show up when you're vulnerable and distracted and in lamplight. Year Five knows that, in case of emergency, you ought to take a breath and keep an eye out for somebody helpful instead of just picking the first person that you see. They could be a monster.

The girl – whose name doesn't rate a mention – makes a deal with someone who turns out to be an evil and magical imp.

Year Five chose a name for the girl, because it's ridiculous that she doesn't have one.

Ranbir picked the most popular – Brenda.

Brenda… This makes us smile.

Brenda gives the imp her necklace. (We don't know what imps do with jewellery – maybe they trade them for fast cars, or use them to pay off gambling debts, we can't say…) He then produces gold for her, working furiously overnight, because magic and other weird things can often happen at night.

Year Five is brave, but cautious in the dark.

By morning, the king is delighted by his mounds of new gold, but naturally he wants yet more. This makes our Brenda distraught all over again, because the king may execute her if she doesn't achieve the impossible all over again. Royalty's like that – if it isn't killing deer and foxes and slow-moving birds, it's eyeing up execution hoods and axe blades.

As Brenda cries in the night, the imp reappears. This time, he takes the girl's ring – the only thing she still has that belonged to her saintly mother. All the Fiver Acorns disapprove strongly – Atticus suggests that Brenda's dad has actually locked her mum in the attic and – for some reason – sold all her shoes, but that would be another story.

The following morning, when Brenda awakes, she is surrounded by generous heaps and heaps of gold. Still, there's really no stopping this king and he wants enough gold to swim in, enough gold to line his castle with gold and have gold toilet paper and gold socks and the endless power that endless gold will bring him. He wants to marry Brenda, but only if she spins him even more gold. Otherwise there will be no marriage and also no Brenda. Of course, by now Brenda feels entirely hopeless and defeated – she has nothing left to give the imp.

She weeps and weeps, alone in the room that is now stuffed to the ceiling with expectant straw. When the imp appears this time, presumably demanding a sack of earrings and Swiss watches or suchlike, she simply cries even more. So the imp demands Brenda's firstborn child. Promising a baby to an imp is a dreadful thing to do, but Brenda wants to live, so she agrees. People often agree to awful things in the future, just to get by in their awful, impossible present. It's something upon which all Stiltskins rely.

The imp duly produces drifts of gold that could pave the whole city and make every one of the king's subjects rich – not that any sharing will take place. The king is overjoyed and finally satisfied – he probably moves on to more conventional aristocratic activities, like hunting pregnant dolphins with bejewelled forks from ceremonial boats. And he marries our exhausted spinster, making her Queen Brenda. This is a sort of victory, because it means she is much safer and gets to wear nicer clothes and not be locked up in a room full of straw every night. She also gets to wave out of carriage windows. Still, the king doesn't seem very nice, or as if he will be fun. At least he has stopped asking for gold, though.

In due course, Brenda has a baby – how and why that happens will be dealt with fully in Year Six – and then she's very busy with nappies and mashed pear and teaching him how to say things and walk. We decide that she calls him Ari.

Brenda forgets all about the imp.

Unlikely, but not impossible. Sometimes we can't bear to think about horrible, horrible Stiltskinny things and so we lock them up in little cupboards inside our minds.

There are other options, and the Acorns know how to use them. Their teacher understands the theory of this, but not the practice. She is chock-full of padlocks and cupboards.

Just when baby Ari has grown into a marvellous tiny boy with merry eyes and a useful number of clever fingers and toes, the imp reappears.

We might have expected that steps would have been taken, perhaps involving the installation of imp-proof locks. But we're sure Brenda did her best.

The imp laughs and rolls his eyes and is generally repulsive and gleeful and tells Brenda that in three days he will be back to take her son. He doesn't mention what he might do with a little boy and we allocate no time for speculation.

Some of us long to guess appalling guesses and some of us long to be freaked out by them and some of us are full of merciless certainties – so no guesses are taking place.

Brenda then cries as no one ever has and partially floods her queenly bedroom with salty unhappiness. The imp relents a bit – he is quite short and in danger of drowning – and he says that she can have three days to guess his name. If she guesses right, he will lose his power.

The Fivers are too old for fairy tales, we are aware of that. We sometimes still look at the stories, and other seemingly simple things, though. We take them apart and we see how they work. This term, due to insistent interest from Millie, Ignacy, Kwakou, Max, Talha – mainly Talha, he is an enthusiast – we have started Project Rumpelstiltskin. We have modelled Stiltskin heads – two of them genuinely disturbing – out of self-firing clay. We have invented Stiltskin dances. We have learned about straw. We have submitted ourselves to a Spinning Craft Demonstration from the utterly humourless Madeline Spears. There is not, apparently, a craft that Madeline does not practise with lumpy determination. She is always willing to demonstrate. And there are clearly complicated but innocent things wrong with her.

Having innocent things wrong with you will mean Sue will forgive you almost any transgression. When she is being *Mrs Delara, Head of School* she is the terminal threat uttered by staff and can certainly be forbidding and silence Big Room or a nastily riotous heart with one glance. But we all know she forgives us, too. That's in her eyes. She's mostly *Mrs D*. She's *Sue*.

And because Mrs Delara is also very keen that city children should know the country, I have found it weirdly easy to source and deliver small packets of raw wool to every Acorn household. This means we have all allowed our hands to be made soft by sheep grease, which is another name for lanolin. Then we have washed and washed to get rid of the dreadful sheepy smell.

For a while in that spinning lesson, everyone onscreen was feeling the same thing and smelling the same strong animal hotness and it seemed we were very together in all kinds of ways.

I don't think I'll forget that.

Atticus' mum was not happy about the wool, of course. She felt its allergy and hygiene and animal cruelty issues had been very insufficiently explored. (We truly had explored them – Oakwood loves nothing better than ethical exploration.)

Anyway, Atticus' mum called her son Atticus, so does she really have his best interests at heart?

As a class, we have written our own myths in the style of Rumpelstiltskin – all except me. And I have composed maths questions about weights of gold and spinning production and imps being separated into quarters of imps and fifths and so forth. We are not falling behind.

Still, we are not as happy as we might be. Tony seems worn out. Millie is looking haunted about something and I'd very much like to know what. It's hard to really have a Together Chat online.

A lot is hard – as if an imp had already called on us all and stolen our nice things. We can't go on an outing to Twickenham Green and eat vegan snacks and play non-competitive games. We can't visit York House and its squirrels and its statues of what we choose to call The Panicking Ladies Whose Clothes Have Blown Away. I am missing the lovely and Gothic and mad-all-over-churchiness of Strawberry Hill House and the garden that's for free. We can't do any of our close-together-and-holding-hands-cheerful things.

But we are *managing*. We live in a country where *managing* is presented as the height of indulged contentment. It isn't even the height of an evil midnight goblin offering bad deals. And that goblin was short.

I'm *managing*, too. I truly am. While children en masse can be wearing and demanding and tricky to herd, they are still extraordinary, still a constant source of contagious novelty and joy. Long-term primary teachers can turn childish and over-emphatic, but there are worse things to be. There's nothing wrong with a bit of wonder.

Oakwood ticks the Key Stage boxes, but nobody's forced into loathing the process. We don't teach anyone how to tolerate suffering. *Work hard. Work Fun. Work Better.* That's up in Big Room on an embroidered banner. If you've sewn something into a banner, you absolutely mean it.

Of course, Oakwood's always close to collapse. But we fundraise and we stagger on like a drunk man getting hit by seagulls at the edge of a quay. That's always the image I have when I think of us, anyway.

Still, we keep our footing – or we have thus far. Staff are on rolling six-month contracts, which is something one shouldn't ponder. In normal years, I get cluster headaches throughout month five.

But back to Brenda and her woes.

Last week the Fiver Acorns were thinking about the way Rumpelstiltskin stories might have started. Useless father, lovely Brenda, greedy king, tricky wicked goblin with a secret name – we tried to imagine which part came first. And we collected the names Stiltskin goes by in other places – all of those aliases that make him like a criminal, or a spy. We discussed. Acorns all long to discuss.

And I sit in the kitchen each morning and look at sixteen little faces being alive and keeping alive and saying the things they think with a bravery that may well fade once the world gets in at them.

When you're the teacher, you fake being brave. You're the example – that's what you're for. And a classroom is one place where you can keep reality harmless and reasonable and decently organised. That's because each classroom is partly a story we agree to be inside. Teachers believe the story more than anybody else, because we are inside it for much longer than anyone else. We're the ones who begin it. Beginning is scary and that means we have to go first.

When people with guns break into classrooms, it is so very often teachers who step between the bullets and the kids. I'm very unsure if I would, but I do know we have a tendency to act as if we're myths and legends and not people who will die. When you agree to be *in loco parentis* you enter a story about the future, one that has great power – one that might even mean you'll die for the future's people, which is to say, for children. That's not just an American thing. It happened in Dunblane. It happened in Dundee. It would happen at Oakwood.

I'd want to be brave, but think I might freeze.

Sue would be the very quickest to intervene, of that I'm certain.

Sue Delara – terrible shoes, odd clothes, wonderful leader.

She'd kick any available Rumpelstiltskin's arse.

This morning, I told Year Five that Rumpelstiltskin is a story with people behind it who meant well. It's old, maybe as old as the first proper writing, perhaps more ancient than that. For something like 4,000 years, there have been women and men and children who bothered to make up versions of this one story, who improved it and passed it along and therefore spread its good intentions. Imagine that – a story with no floods, no gods, no mighty heroes, just an ordinary person with a problem caused by lying and mis-used power.

And for centuries – at least centuries – people have told something like our current version. They have reminded us that some parents are unwise and that girls on their own should be wary. They have made it absolutely clear that everyone should really be clever as clever gets so that we will be able to deal with life.

Of course, Rumpelstiltskin's story ends in his defeat. Any story is a blend of hopes – for a reader, a listener, a purpose. And a happy ending is a little spell – sometimes wise, sometimes quite reckless – that tries to conjure hope.

For us, Queen Brenda ends up racking her brains and quizzing sages and sending out scouts and horsemen to uncover the wicked imp's name. Alone, back in the gold-filled castle, she spends the first night of her three promised nights running through all of the names she has ever heard anyone called. But when Rumpelstiltskin appears on the stroke of midnight not one of them is his. No luck.

The second night, Brenda faces the weird little brute with his mocking smile and she just makes up names like Carrotfeet and Wasptemper and Ugbug and Bovrilbreath. At least, that's what the Acorns came up with – among other things that were less suitable. Insulting the imp makes Brenda feel better, but she's still in terrible trouble and has only one night left.

Then the sun sets and heralds the final dark and, just in time – panting and dusty – her very last scout appears. He has gone the furthest and has done the best and possibly is secretly in love with Brenda. He tells her that he came to a strange house in a strange wood and looked in through its strange window and saw a strange and very terrible little man dancing in the light of a green fire and singing, 'Rumpelstiltskin is my name! She will never guess! I am Rumpelstiltskin!' He may also have said. 'Silly Brenda!' We strongly suspect it.

This news gives Brenda just enough time to change into her favourite pullover and comb her hair before – *Fooff* – up pops the imp with a sack just big enough to hold poor Ari. Brenda pretends to be frightened and baffled and then – just as the tiny nightmare has danced on its bony feet to the door of Ari's bedroom – Brenda yells, 'I know your name! You're Rumpelstiltskin! Rumpelstiltskin! Rumpelstiltskin! Rumpelstiltskin!'

And that defeats the imp and he disappears with a dreadful scream that nobody cares about, because he is done for and has no power any more. After that, everyone gets to be happy instead of bereaved and the trees blossom and the king becomes wiser and kinder and less greedy and the kingdom becomes pleasant and relaxed and that scout finds someone he loves, even more than Brenda, and everything you might think of that could be improved is improved.

And Ari and Brenda are sometimes so happy they can't even speak. They just dance. From wonderful room to wonderful room, they dance and they throw gold out of the windows.

For 4,000 years we have told each other what we think we'll need to know – that the way to defeat all monsters is by knowing who they really are.

In class we go gently whenever we talk about monsters. It never is wise to imagine them over-much.

Unlike our other sculptures, which are in the Art Display Zone of my kitchen, Alice's clay Stiltskin head sits with Tony's on a shelf inside my glass-fronted bookcase.

I've told everyone that the bookcase gives us a way to enjoy how very excellently wicked and artistic the heads are, without being scared of them. The books can distract and defeat any traces of Stiltskin power and the glass will keep everyone safe. This means that Anja no longer looks as if she's puzzling out ways to withstand immanent disasters.

So I did make up a new myth, after all.

On any given day, meaning well is helpful. Benevolence can often feel pathetic, but it gives you a little headspace in which to invent, to hunt out solutions. Otherwise, what would be the point? Reality would eat us up. We try and therefore become people who can try. It's best to understand – whatever we say, or think, or do with regularity, we become.

It's an everyday type of magic, but some people never notice it.

Irony can't save us from hearing our own meaning, the intention that stands by us, stands inside us, even when we want to run away. That's why I frequently yell bits of the Oakwood Primary Promise at my 3am ceiling with bad grace and probably my molars clenched.

I do keep hoping to improve my adult state.

And in Oakwood my name is a tiny song for Year Five voices – *Miss-iz MacCor-mick* – and I use it as an alias while I demonstrate functional adulthood of a type that can still insist on expecting a better world. This means that Oakwooders – our graduated Acorns – should move on elsewhere with at least enough positivity to get them through their twenties. Simon's dad, Anja's history, Bob's mum and Martha's mum, species depletion, climate extremes, climate collapse, the whims of unanticipated illness – we intend to stare them down and overcome.

And it's really not unusual for people to save each other. It's currently discouraged by our prevailing authorities, but that will pass. After all, when they're really in trouble, who will help them?

In case you were wondering, I'm writing this while everyone, as a nation, has a ludicrous, ludicrous day. In fact, the day drove me to this – back to writing, even though I'm tired. I am filling my yellow legal pad with my story about masks and names and helping and lies and drowning and credible monsters. I'm trying to make sure you'll have all my information, everything useful. Just in case.

Sometimes a happy ending is no longer unavailable. Sometimes you also lose the author.

And sometimes writing down distractions prevents me from stalking the streets and howling.

It's the 8th of May and suddenly we are celebrating VE Day. Front pages on the newspapers I don't buy are lurking in the corner snack shop to tell me we have always celebrated VE Day, but I beg to differ. I know we celebrated at the time – my grandparents lit a VE bonfire so massive it ruined the brand new, post-Blitz tarmac in their street and got them in trouble with the council. But there have been no bonfires since.

As it happens, Granny and Gamps and their bombed-out neighbourhood also lit a fire for VJ Day, which we will not be celebrating, for reasons that have never been explained. I would hate to think our national priorities include pretending we once celebrated victory *over* Europe, rather than victory for democracy in Europe. Yes, thinking that would give me a headache.

And across London – and elsewhere – various hearts are delighted that we're avoiding any mention of Allied Forces, or dark-skinned soldiers. They also refrain from remembering distasteful details about Nazis. After all, if one wanted to emulate them in any way, one wouldn't want to know how badly that would go. One never wants to get depressed before one has to. So we have conquered Europe, because this is a pain-free way that we can contemplate world history.

During my lifetime I have never at any point draped my house in bunting as if I am expecting brave Chalky White and cheeky Dusty Miller to march home, having liberated Belgium.

This isn't a celebration for Chalky and Dusty, though – they and their non-fictional comrades are busy dying before their time. Pensioners are a drain on public funds, wilfully insisting on yet more life when it will just be wasted on them. What are they going to do with it – buy more cardigans? More toffees? News segments show elderly faces crying at care home windows while relatives stand outside in gardens, restrained by bewilderment and sometimes nice herbaceous borders upon which they feel they shouldn't tread.

And what if the oldsters wanted to conquer authoritarianism again? Embarrassing.

It is much more sensible to duck out fast, not linger. For an everyday kind of person, what difference could an extra hour, or day, or year, ever manage to make?

I'm an everyday kind of person, though. And I want all of my possible years and days and hours. Some of them could be good. They might contain films I'd like, or nice pasta, or strawberries, or birdsong. They'd contain my son. I don't want to live in a country that thinks there's no clear point to me and I might as well jack it in now.

Setting aside any other considerations, even one suicide can gridlock a subway system, a motorway, a bridge, a railway. I'd prefer it if my obituary wasn't just eyerolls and bad jokes and ruined commutes.

And I'd prefer it if my poor, mad ma could stay for as long as she wants. She survives, survives, survives on chocolate and resentment and strange dark surges of maybe fear and maybe rage and maybe both. That's her right.

I wonder if the lounge in her care home has been decorated – red, white and blue nostalgia. I'd assume so.

And out here we're encouraged to view war as a series of singalongs – all of the victory, none of the fight and, somehow, no other countries were involved, just us. Not even all of us.

So I'm sitting in my courtyard, tension headache roiling, while the daylight throbs with heat. Somewhere in the distance they're playing a selection from what I can only assume is *Now That's What I Call Music from the 1940*s. I'm not close enough to be sure which tune is echoing about, but the swing and the tone seem just right for dancing in a basement while the sirens howl, but no bombs ever drop on you, or yours. We're all meant to be longing for bluebirds and ration cards and gas masks. They're the only protective masks we'll stand for.

Oh, and the bunting.

So much bunting.

Union flag bunting.

Some streets are nothing but swags and clumps and vast trailing lianas of twitching and flickering patriotism. It's like walking through a migraine. And every tiny piece of it tickles and slaps in the breeze and sounds like an escalating range of sex acts. Louder and louder and closer to my garden, faster and faster – the bunting is almost drowning out the music of Happy War.

And I'm hiding in the leaf shade – steadfastly being a boycott, but entirely out of sight. I'm under the trellis where the square of stinging blue above can't harm me. Every year, there's more heat and more heat and more heat. This summer is still aching with it, even though we're trapped in place and polluting less, because of an enemy too small to see.

I'd say we are being defeated by many things we don't see.

It's being a teacher; you're always explaining things to yourself in the hope you can then make them plain to others later on. I keep on with it, even though I know – nobody listens.

Still, someone has turned the music off and what I think is a wren is currently being triumphant among the flags. It sounds beautiful and true. Our neighbourhood has more birds every day – there's getting to be a dawn chorus. Paul and I can potter about and notice the world being gladdened by a lack of us.

The bunting, though – nobody can turn that off.

There's an upper flat, round in Britannia Street, so weighed down with bunting that I worry for the building's structural integrity. I somehow expect the living room is nothing but Winston Churchill piñatas being beaten into endless showers of shivering, tricolour, Empire-loving spikes. I want to shout up to them – *You know what bunting sounds like, don't you? You know what it means as a verb? It's very specifically – I promise I'm not lying – a term for having wild sex, dressed as a Corgi. Yes, a Royal Corgi. Sex dressed as a Royal Corgi that's wearing a Margaret Thatcher mask and a Vera Lynn wig. That's what you're celebrating, that's what the slappety, slappety, slappety noise represents.*

I don't even know how that would work.

And I'm a nice, quiet, orderly primary school teacher – I don't yell at my neighbours, however much they disappoint me.

I keep on being about sunshine and rationality and the future. I act as if responsibility flows upwards and outwards and we're all aiming for emotional growth. My vocation makes me endlessly expect that adults will be adult. I don't think that's too much to ask for. It's what I aim for every day with the lessons about verbs and poems and tadpoles and percentages and history from around the world and geography and facts.

And then, I leave Oakwood and the world of grown-ups is superstition, lazy assumptions, learned helplessness and self-loathing redirected into free-range hate. I end up being exhausted by the ways in which so many people let the side down, myself included.

But there are many excellent and adult adults. Paul and F.L. and Sue and the helping and smiling and chipping-in people who continue to act out of hope – they all slog on, no matter what. The care workers in Ma's home – I cannot imagine what makes them come in to work every shift. The van drivers and bus drivers and shelf-stackers and checkout assistants and hospital cleaners – really, all of the cleaners – and the warehouse workers and food-bank workers and all the poor bloody nurses… There are so many people we didn't quite understand that we needed so very much. They all became the grown-ups education hopes for.

I took a little break there – walked off for a minute and took two ibuprofen.

Bloody bunting.

I'm writing this longhand on a recycled paper pad. I am someone who is reducing their carbon footprint, even though we're doomed already. I am acting as if the future of *Homo sapiens* is not bound to be some kind of permacatastrophe and gladiatorial combats for drinking water.

I could despair, but it wouldn't help anything. There's no time for it. There's no point being nihilistic when it harms you much more than the people arranging your slide into oblivion. I try to enhance the present, crack a joke halfway up the scaffold so the people who make life miserable don't end up making me miserable, too. And maybe I can move on safe to the next moment and then maybe make it to the next. I put a lot of thought into adding enhancements whenever I can.

So – right here – I will give you the secret to making a great scone. You get it for reading this far. Enhancement. Reward. Information.

Leave it alone.

Honestly, leave the scone alone. Your ingredients are nothing. A scone is basically always made with the same old buttery, floury and sugary things – what matters is the touch. Just barely rub the butter, or butter-replacing product, into the flour or flour-replacing product and the sugar, or sugar-replacing product. Be delicate with every contact, minimal. As soon as the dough is unified, cradle it out of the bowl, set it down, roll it once kindly, cut it, sneak it across to the baking tray before it notices, straight into the oven and you're done. Treat every scone like a bruise, a recluse, a traumatised PTSD case. Be loving, but *leave it alone*. Then it will thank you by lifting and crisping and being exceptionally light. And you will be spoken well of and remembered.

A good scone, warm and just for you – it's a small thing. It operates at the level of a peck on the cheek, a smile in a bus queue, a nod. But it might be enough to save this moment, and this endless and tiny and infinite moment is all we've ever really got.

That's good information – the scone thing – useful. My mentioning Rumpelstiltskin and PTSD and a recluse will be useful later, too. You've already read a number of things that we'll get back to later. I'm not writing by accident here. This is going to be the story I intend.

So here's me – the recluse.

I'm sitting in the courtyard, as established, because of the grinding heat. We're going to have a boiled summer with no air and no sleep again. I'm setting out dishes of water for the new birds of newly peaceable London where planes no longer fly. People notice the ones still taking off and feel aggrieved by the strangeness of their noise and waste, the transgression in having freedom to travel and infect.

No longer overflown every few seconds, my courtyard is in King's Cross.

London encourages lying about most things, especially real estate, so I feel I'm obliged to insist this isn't much of a courtyard. There are no lemon trees in waist-high terracotta pots, no lavender beds. There is no Cotswold stone, no Romanesque cloister, no fountain. This is a leprous tarmac and cobble oblong in front of what once were stables and then a garage and then a refurbished residential rental opportunity owned by a Mr Charalambous. To the left and right of my hardly-a-courtyard are the blank masonry sides of later buildings. Its back is a high pre-Victorian brick wall. To the front is a barrier of wide old planks from the days of wide old trees. It stands two stories high between us and the street. You always want something between you and the street.

In my case, it's Wicklow Street. WC1X. Paul and I tell ourselves that X marks the spot.

Coming home, I step in over the sill of a human-sized door cut into the massive gates that make up most of our wooden wall. They were built to open up for seriously massive horses and carts. Once you're inside the yard, and have locked the door behind you, it's hard not to feel defended, even in 2020. That locking of the first door is always a moment I enjoy – unless it's raining. Then I'm immediately in a silent movie situation – I rush through a downpour towards a doorway, open up, dart through and then continue to be just as drowned as ever. I can't help but think of Buster Keaton every time – deadpan under his thin and flat deadpan hat – deadpan in the face of every weather.

Across the cobbles leading from the little door is the coach house that is our home. I rented it at first, then I bought it. Mr Charalambous is cautious in small matters – he wasn't keen to let me rent when I was so obviously broke. But in larger matters he's easily moved. And although I somehow thought I wouldn't be allowed to, buying was spookily easy. I'm not sure that Mr C. wanted to sell, it's just that he was rapidly persuaded by me crying a lot.

I'm a cryer.

I was a cryer.

I have moved from being in danger of weeping-related dehydration to something like average tearfulness.

I think Paul and F.L. would agree with me on that.

'Mum, look away – it's an ambient altruism advert.' Paul does still have to say that if we don't want an evening of tissues and hiccoughs and sobs.

TV compilations of dancing nurses in PPE, musical kindnesses in the street … the efforts of strangers to cheer strangers … this year has tended to leave me red-eyed and courting kidney failure. I suspect that I am no longer unusual – months of stress, uncertainty and trauma can keep almost anyone close to tears.

At least I'm used to it.

Mr Charalambous looks at me sometimes and I know he's still surprised by me and what I own. He's not as surprised as I am.

Of course, I don't own the ground on which my house is standing. Mr C. still owns that. Legally speaking, we're both forced to assume that he could and might somehow pull his fraction of an acre out from under my foundations like a dirty big tablecloth and just take it away. This means I have to pay him an annual fee to keep the land in position. If you want to do well in Britain, be a person who owns land.

We've been here for years, Paul and I, balanced above the earthworms of a relative stranger who is afflicted with riotous ear hair. The place is what you'd call *amazingly pleasant for London*. Running across the front of the first floor there's a wrought-iron gallery balcony thing on twiggy iron legs. It's probably safe to walk on, which is good because we have to in order to reach our front door, which is up on the first floor. So is the living room and kitchen and a weird little unroom, which is mostly for storage and damp at the back. In our waking hours, we look out from behind iron stems and fern heads like heavy-handed lace made by goblins. To access the gallery there's an iron spiral staircase with more goblin leaves and flowers all over it. We sleep downstairs, under the metal shadows. There was no way to get a mattress up that staircase. We did try. But we fitted three single mattresses in through the ground-floor windows just fine. One was intended for toddler Paul once he was grown and two were for me to make a double bed. That was because I like room, not because I expected company.

I like that my home gives me time to think while I climb up away from the world. The wobble of the metal steps would also give the household time to hear anything odd coming to find us.

I occasionally wonder if the Victorian coach-house owners picked their spiral stairs to foil over-ambitious horses. Freed from the cart, they might have yearned to wander up and nose about. With a nose that size, why wouldn't you?

But we are secure from all threats, including those posed by daring equines.

And I love this place. Find any group of women and one or two will always tell you about loving a home because it is the one they ran away to and where they learned they could feel confident and be safe. Wicklow Street is that for me. It gathered me in with my son – my son with the wide brown eyes that should never see anything bad again.

Paul and I both had nightmares. But they faded. Now we're endlessly hungry for sleep. And the plague means we are still together. He hasn't headed off on his planned international ramble, the one that was making me feel both proud and terrified for him.

Then again, he also isn't earning money. But we'll manage. That's what we do.

He isn't going to head off and be an Essential Worker, which is to say a Disposable Worker. He does volunteer in a community centre, wearing as much protective gear as we can cobble together. He has to be careful. Very, very careful. Please. We fight about carefulness levels. I cheat by crying.

I really mean the crying, but it feels like cheating nonetheless and he gets that patient look that I suspect he will wear more and more, should I live to be old and crazy and covered in soup stains I can't notice.

I regularly promise the universe that I won't be like Ma – no swearing at the carers, no unfiltered revelation of previously hidden hates. I don't think all of the loathings are even hers. They're just something to say while events drop out of the sun at her, guns blazing. I won't yell at Paul about fictional immigrants wanting to behead me while a factual immigrant holds a smartphone of whatever kind the future offers and shows him my odd little face with long white hair and occasionally wily eyes. I won't be that.

Poor Ma. She's keeping a series of worst-case scenarios at bay with 1930s racial slurs. That's all she's got.

And poor everyone else involved, of course.

It doesn't bear thinking about. When it's baking like this, not much does. I can feel my brain peeling away from my skull and shrinking – it will end up being just a grim sultana clenched round my past.

When the air indoors is too thick for breathing, I unlock the security grill – *London plus paranoia plus hypervigilance equals voluntary prison bars* – and I swing my bedroom window open, climb over the sill and that's me outside. I did once spend three or four months telling suddenly tall-enough Paul that normal humans don't leave buildings via windows and then it gradually became a sane and obvious option for us both.

But a clever boy who's worked out how to make things unlock has to lock them, too. In case of monsters.

Once I'm outside, I sit in my second-hand deck chair while the quiet sun sets and then look up at the burned-out khaki sky, which is our London version of the night. The stars are louder now, though. They are stooping close while we go through these days that are so silent we can hear the wards of ventilators running and running for human beings as they drift into dark oceans and sink away.

It can seem wrong to feel so peaceful here, in Wicklow Street, my first and kindest home.

And now I'm apparently going to sell up and move on – as and when the chaos will allow. This still surprises me. But I have already talked to three different estate agents – men in tight-cut suits who keep talking up *the courtyard* as if it truly does involve a koi pond under palm trees and Moroccan tiles. None of them was the right person to sell my home. And, after I'd shown them out and then never got back in touch, they've kept calling and calling my mobile. The agents all had greasy foreheads and a smell of sour coffee and sad, dirty cars about them. My home deserves better than that.

F.L. suggests no one need come inside, not until the very end. We can run virtual viewings.

If I can decide about leaving.

Only I can't.

F.L. is doggedly not rushing me. He knows t'ai chi and how to succeed in a conflict by using lack of pressure. I sometimes feel this is as unfair as crying.

He has plans for an island life on an actual island. There are many consecutive days when I have plans along with him. I imagine polytunnels and new-born potatoes and not ever waking to aircraft noise in the morning.

And I do realise, when the lockdown stillnesses have all withdrawn, that I will keep wanting this peace, this air, this birdsong.

We even have an island in mind. The plan is to rent on Colonsay and then buy. Or perhaps we could buy a piece of land and build a house – using money and expertise and methods that are entirely theoretical.

I picture us ruined and huddled on mud, sheltering from horizontal sleet among blighted potato stems and blueprints.

But on certain mornings I can feel that I want nothing more than to walk up the path from the harbour at Scalasaig and be in a clean new life and hear larks agreeing with me. I can picture myself being a person who could live in a hunchbacked, sinking caravan while making decisions about the ways windows should face, someone who stays calm during setbacks and delays. F.L. and I needn't scream at each other while damp runs down the walls and on to the Formica dinette table. We're better than that. He is, anyway.

And we could just rent.

We could house share and then rent.

We could just move to Oban and look out across the blue at a blue idea in a bluer distance where our dream still floats.

But I generally imagine the worse futures on the spectrum. Naturally, I do. Stress is a drug, a rush, a fix, a spell, a prophesy, a monster – it can lead to anything.

I perform qi gong exercises to calm myself.

Trouble is, I have to be quite calm before I can do them.

F.L. calms me. His tranquillising effect, even online, runs from *mild sedative* to *lots of valerian tea and a massage,* via *warm bath* and straight into *human equivalent of hot milk at bedtime and a tap on the head with a brick.* There's nothing alarming about him. This is, naturally, very suspicious and makes me expect secrets.

But all the things I've ever discovered about him have been kind. It's weird.

F.L. went to Colonsay without me just before lockdown.

I will nip up and scout around for us. I am not founding a cult to

welcome you, planning to give a big party at the end of which you end
up on an altar, or burying my other wives.

My 3am worries were much more down to earth. I suspected he
was picking a new setting for a brand new relationship. Who could
blame him? I am hard work… Any sudden urge to flee would be
more than natural.

But I'm basing what's natural on my endless desire to run for
the hills and I know – in my head, but not in my heart – that other
people seek out intimacy, as if it is not the emotional equivalent of
snakes on a crashing plane.

So F.L. left, stopped besieging me with his niceness, left me to
miss it, want it fastened in close. And then the pestilence arrived.
When F.L. had already landed on Colonsay.

He has now spent so long with his island hosts near Uragaig that
he says he feels resident already. He pans his phone round slowly to
show me the views – the green and blue and white flag of Hebridean
light. He sends me film clips of magnificent, sheeting rain. He says
we a lot and uses the future tense. He stands on sand dunes while
the signal stutters and choughs spiral about above Kiloran Bay as if
they are doing him a personal favour as a friend.

I have learned the place names of my future, our future, our
maybe future – Pigs Paradise, Machrins, Cable Bay, Kiloran. And
maybe *we* and *our* are referring to him and all the creatures, or to
him and the island. Maybe he's already thinking of himself as a unit.

Really, he means us, though – him and Paul and me – and me
and him.

This does appeal. It's not very suffocating, barely threatening. It
doesn't seem to have a catch.

So that means it's bound to summon happiness – and that tends
to bring on retribution.

I'm going to be superstitious when I'm older, aren't I?

At which point I can hear Paul already saying, 'Is that you touching
wood again?' I don't touch wood – I tap it my predetermined and
secret number of times, which has worked so far because we are all

currently alive. In a storm you don't rock the (wooden) boat.

My descent into magical thinking is going to be inconvenient. I suppose by the time we are actually relocating I'll just stumble off the ferry, garlanded with amulets, half blind with magic salves. One stumble and I'll end up in the water, weighed down by good-luck charms and a lesson to all.

I'm fairly sure my hesitancy about a cheerful and timely and healthy relocation is just Plague Stress pushing me towards self-harm. Self-harm is always a comfort when reality seems like a randomly merciless instrument of torture. Invent your own torment, own it, and you can feel that you're back in the captain's chair with your hands – *tap, tap, tap* – on the mahogany steering wheel. A change of pains is as good as a rest.

But a lack of pain – that would mean you don't need a rest.

And maybe I'm allowed to leave the lockdown London breezes that are still a bit haunted by drains and taxi rages and money turning in its sleep.

The island air will be good. I can believe that. And F.L. can work anywhere, unless the Wi-Fi suffers fainting spells. Paul is a grown man – a genuine adult – and will do adult things out in the world and doesn't need me to keep his room ready for him forever. Or it doesn't have to be this particular room.

Still, I'll miss Wicklow Street.

I want to tell the estate agents about the last time those big cart gates were opened. I was driving a hire van between them and arriving for the first time – a Ford Transit. I was born the same year the Transit appeared and that makes me fond of them. Everything I owned in 2002 only half-filled that van, mattresses included. Y2K hadn't ended civilisation, but it had been the end of what I could bear, or contemplate surviving in a place that was never my home with a man who never loved me.

I had made plans and followed through. I stayed awake all the last night, being sure not to make a mistake, not give a clue, not to die. And then I ran to my blue dream on the horizon.

The carpet in the Transit's cargo area was this deathly type of grey and smelled of asparagus urine, which I supposed was a step up from just urine. The whole van had looked much more likely to smell of serial murder sprees.

Strapped in his car seat up front was Paul, the world complete in Paul. He was so much of everything, so complete and extraordinary and so much himself that he weighed down the passenger side tyres.

That's obviously not true. It's a meaningful lie, though.

At that stage, I wasn't saving us both, I was saving only him. I didn't want what had been happening to seep in and change him. I didn't want anything cold touching his heart.

And if I was killed, then Paul would be left alone with his step-father. I wouldn't be able to stop what came next. Bad people distort your focus – mine was in pieces, but my body knew what it needed. It needed to leave, it needed to keep Paul alive and happy and to be alive itself. My mind followed, unconvinced.

By the time our first spring arrived here I had begun to experiment with relaxing. And Paul was such a very mellow baby that I stopped checking and checking and checking him for signs of damage. I could watch and see his dreams rush in, competing with each other to be sweet and nothing but.

And on a good March day we painted both sides of the wood wall and the gates light blue. Leastways, I painted them and Paul watched, hummed, slept, watched and held a blue corrugated plush rabbit that I secretly still have for his sake, although I've never liked her disappointed little mouth. Paul called her Hamdy for reasons they both kept to themselves. Sometimes he'd talk to her while he pottered on his blanket. While I painted I could hear as he ran out of words and made up more, which I took as a good sign.

I remember looking down from the top of the horrifying ladder and there Paul still was, waving his fingers at me and the clouds. And I couldn't fall after that, no accident of any kind would be possible.

Mr Charalambous had approved a slim range of acceptable paint shades. Paul picked one the colour of a winter morning sky – rather than a sour-faced rabbit – with one tap of a lordly finger against a plasticky graded chart. His choice was the best of the options, in my opinion, and I remember it giving me hopes that we would stay in sync, even when he got older.

There is a time when you'll wonder about your baby – are they going to be an intruder in your home, or a deeper and deeper friend, as they grow older. Then you smell their skin, though, meet their eyes with the big truths still showing in them, unforgotten. And you know things will probably be okay and you should concentrate your worry on accidents, toxins, rogue illnesses and unforeseeable threats.

We had escaped from Bad House and our small, domestic Stiltskin, who was still a monster, nonetheless. Anything that demonstrated the strength of our happily exercised will seemed overwhelming. Lord, there were tears. And certain words, or thoughts, or movements could illuminate everything, as if I wasn't in my life but had slipped sideways into a much better version of events – a novelisation, a movie, a play that would end with applause, not leave me being threatened in a brown-seeming little kitchen for being unsatisfactory. I had reached the end of the story and would no longer have to remember not to block the blows, because that's an act of defiance you have to pay for. After a while, even I stopped lying in bed and waiting to hear the midnight scratch and fumble of a raging key at the front door.

And, on our beautiful painting day, the blue went on, coat after coat, and was the big flag of our sovereign territory – earthworms, rocks and subsoil excepted.

What else…?

Moving in, I'd shared the couple of hours' lifting and shifting with a woman called Sam: blondeish, slightly overweight, just inter-fering enough to be useful for random assistance. I didn't like her and never really helped her back.

Knowing how to make scones doesn't mean you're a good person. I knew her because of working in a pub – putting my PGCE to emergency good use. I can deploy both amiable and stern crowd control, whenever it's necessary.

Sam brought a man called Greg with her. Greg, or something like Greg. He sat down a lot with his large, raw-looking hands curled on his knees and his head bent forward. Was his head very long? I've retained an impression that it was. I remember him looking like a pensive, cartoon horse.

Greg, the horse who made it up the spiral staircase. He wasn't much help.

Sam either ignored him, or rolled her eyes at me when he spoke, as if he were unbearable. Then she left with him for a drink in the brisk kind of way that meant he wouldn't get a drink, but would get sex. I remember being happy I could notice that kind of thing – the way human beings are with each other. I suddenly had enough headspace for that.

And hours and hours had already gone by without our being trapped or noticeably followed. It seemed I might actually be escaping, have escaped. I still felt sick, but not as if I would genuinely throw up.

The following morning I was very hungry and realised I'd moved in with no food for anyone older than twelve months. The corner shop where I bought assorted breakfast rubbish still has a kind of halo about it, even if their fruit has remained bruised and semi-terminal and their bread is still not made of bread. I plundered its riches and then dined on canned rice pudding and tinned ham between two grievous insults to the word *croissant*. I was so pleased with myself for packing a tin opener. The whole meal was completely magnificent.

I'm giving you these details because I want to be precise. Explaining everything I'll need to is going to be hard – that's why I'm practising now. No one improves without practice.

Paul called blue *poo* and this was hilarious.

Details.

There are van details, too.

By 2002, I'd already had a good deal of Transit van experience.

I still hate how familiar all vans feel. They refuse to believe I've moved on. That's a detail about me I don't think I can alter.

The fact that I can't swear any more is probably fixed, too. The Acorns should never hear swearing, at least not from me, and all of those words are luxurious and habit-forming, so I never say them, in or out of school. I shouldn't say *shit* either, but no one's perfect.

I suppose, if I go on with this, I'll discover if I can write down swear words. This is a trying time, after all, and expletives are supposed to help us withstand pain.

I'm trying to go on – and to write this as fast as I can. Then it will be ready, in case it's required.

Detail.

There ought to be something we leave – even if it's just a load of nonsense about blue paint – in case we're not around to answer questions later.

I aim to finish this by the time the final honeysuckles are making the dark sweet. They bloom for so long in our altered seasons.

Beyond that – I don't know. Who does?

Honeysuckle details. Tonight I have decided honeysuckle is the opposite of death.

I planted a common woodbine in a bathtub by the gates in our first, coolish spring of freedom. Temperatures were more predictable back then. I wanted their various scents to roll through the year and be around for times like this.

And here the scent is, with me now and sweet, sweet, sweet – something achieved.

I have a *Lonicera fragantissima* for early perfume, though the last of its flowers went in March. But I wanted many honeysuckles, many waves of flowering, and so I arranged that: *Lonicera periclymenum*, *Lonicera japonica*, *Lonicera henryi*. Back when we planted the first of them, Paul set his hands in the earth to wish it well. Then he licked dirt off his fingers for good luck.

I did not freak out.

Paul's initial months seem to have been stored somewhere indelible in my brain and I'm going to be toothless and dotty in my rocking chair – if there are still rocking chairs – rambling on about babygrows and eyelashes and small breathing in the night.

Paul didn't cry much. He was more likely to wake me up by singing these weird little tuneless tunes to himself. He still seems to contain inherent happiness. I have no idea where he got that. It's something I always want to guard, am poised to rescue, although I have noticed by now that his joy is not a fragile quality. He isn't happy about fantasies the way most people are and therefore isn't heading for a fall. Paul actually likes reality. I catch him looking at it, at pretty much anything, the way someone keeps an eye on a promising friend who is very drunk but may still be prevented from doing anything too fatal. And who know how great they might be tomorrow when they're sober…

Paul eating a bit of plant-pot earth was okay.

Yes, eat earth. I am paying attention, but that's fine. That's developmental.

I was already remarkably mellow and I had decided that it would be best if he found out that earth tastes bad all by himself, rather than having me snap at him about it. Snapping should be for emergencies.

Na-na snaps only when she is very tired and scared.

Frankly, 2020 is not helping.

So let's get back to talking about earth.

When you're broke and a single mother and stupid enough to be trying both in London, it takes a long time to organise enough earth to fill a bathtub.

But I managed.

Some of the soil was spooned out of parks on the sly. Green Park, Hyde Park, Richmond Park – I thought of it as exclusive earth containing tiny traces of cashmere and contempt. After the initial honeysuckle went into the old tub, I added pansies because they're cheap colour and who doesn't need a bit of that? Everything grew, which surprised me. Everything has always grown here.

When Paul was older he would tug off the honeysuckle petals, those thin redpurplecream trumpets, and drink the drop of sweetness from the base. He liked proving the plant's name was true. Fortunately, the plant snaked up much higher and faster than he did. There was always enough blossom left out of his reach. We let it do its thing and its thing was racing everywhere, winding around itself and then its relations. The courtyard has green walls this evening. The ironwork on our top floor is complicated by tendrils and blossoms and stems it never thought of. Another achievement.

Everything here is improvised, but it looks like a garden. There are plants in metal bins, metal buckets, three cracked Belfast sinks, some window boxes, tubs – the green closes over any ugliness and blesses it. Lush.

One slug and it would all be knackered. But I'm ready for them with beer traps and torchlight hunts.

I labour on behalf of life. King's Cross is a place where office furniture goes to die. The streets are lined with desk parts at shipwrecked angles and mutilated chairs. Beyond the odd waste bin, there isn't much that could hold a seedling, or a cutting, never mind a sapling. Everything alive in front of my house has taken effort, organisation, bargaining, finding, pleading, hauling, stealing. Roots here have fed on my eggshells. Stems and leaves and flowers and fruits have been made from my coffee grounds, my compost, Paul's nail pairings and mine – we're connected.

If I leave, I'd miss this.

I will take cuttings.

Turns out that writing this after sunset makes me feel better than scrolling Twitter and typing out *Sorry for your loss* so often that it now autocompletes. Political thinking at night is nothing for anyone sane and I am very, very sane. I'm so sane you would hardly believe it, and me neither.

I haven't forgotten St Paul's, don't worry. It's just that I need to tell you about Hunter Square, too. That's where the OrKestrA's Rumpelstiltskin – my Rumpelstiltskin – arrived.

Walk down the Royal Mile from the Castle and just as you reach the crossroads at Cockburn Street, Hunter Square opens out on your right. Of course, it might take you an hour to make the journey, maybe more. That's because this is August, which is when Edinburgh floats up and away, and the Festival lands down in its place. The town gets mediaeval and smells of sweat-impregnated clothing and breathed fire. Any main street is just a shove of pilgrims and mendicants. People display the old skills and magics: how to spin objects, how to juggle and disappear them, how to yell glorious lies that talk up a crowd, how to make bodies balance and tumble and drop.

Young people who need to be famous will hand you flyers for bad shows that nobody will see and magnificent shows that no one will see, either. Young men will walk about in monkey boots and desert boots and greenish-blackish oversized tweed suits that have never been on sale anywhere but second-hand shops. And there will be T-shirts worn with waistcoats and top hats.

Hunter Square is a Goldilocks space, just big enough, just small enough, and just a few steps away from the chaos and audience reservoir that is the Royal Mile. It's a prime pitch. You see it and ache to have it; the need of it itches in your teeth.

Really. I'm sure that's still true. And in 1984 the OrKestrA was newly itself and we couldn't resist the perfection of Hunter Square.

Back then, you could take a show to Edinburgh for a few hundred pounds. We were students being paid to get educated – imagine that. Not paid much, of course, but enough. Our second year was just done with and we were living on dried kidney beans we'd hope we had boiled for long enough to stop them killing us. We couldn't afford the tinned ones. Still, we weren't in debt. No one would have lent us anything, even if we'd asked. Loans with eternal interest, designed to enslave the poor, weren't a thing yet. I suppose we were in the fag-end of a golden age but didn't know it.

We had run our Edinburgh rehearsals in appropriated lecture rooms and studio spaces we had neither requested nor booked, but which eventually became available in the strange hours if we mooched around and located an unlocked door. We'd become midnight shoestring performers haunting a university that still wasn't quite just a teaching-for-profit hub and sponsorship opportunity.

Golden age – you see?

Although they weren't entirely carefree for me. Even breaking trivial regulations would hunch my shoulders and make my stomach wince. But I always did walk on grass if there was a sign that said I shouldn't. Troubling lawns was a very small debut in terms of civil disobedience, but I became bolder. We all did. But only with clowning, singing, the various kinds of more and less serious fun.

Nothing about us, nothing we ever did – I know this – should ever have swept a single one of us away into Court 10.

I never considered that others among us might have been nervous, too. They might have just gone along with our initial episodes of turf-squashing, room-stealing boldness in the same way that I did and let the idea of being inside a group make them feel defended. Mr Kink – he was genuinely brave. And Mrs Fire. The rest of us weren't. I think we were only daring ourselves to be bigger, stronger, louder, more useful, more alive. And we did it with love. I have no doubt at all that we did it with love.

When you're not stressed out of your mind trying to be adult, there's room for love.

It's one of the more wonderful and more terrible things to be – a person in a group and full of freedom and affections. Something in your wiring longs to cross savannahs with your troupe watchful around you, to gather foodstuffs and adventure, while never being far from a comforting touch… You're at the place where your love and your survival meet, a place of clever hominids and children and acrobats.

If everyone who's with you can be trusted, then you have everything – all the strengths and magics of our species. Most of them, anyway, and your blissful ignorance makes up for the rest.

In our stolen rehearsal rooms and silly group experiments, everyone really was trustworthy. We felt like being inside a contented home. I could almost smell that mix of coffee and good meals and clean washing and unstressed skin – the scents of functional households I'd sometimes visit as a kid. My house never smelled like that. And I didn't ask people to visit. The kids like me never do. We know better.

But I had this now – my odd type of family.

And to please my freshly adopted kin, I was spending hour after hour in my student bedsit learning to juggle. You start with three beanbags and they'll drop on the floor and on the floor and on the floor. Evening after evening after evening you seem stumble-fingered and pointless. But then you learn.

I was living in a room and a half at the top of a strangely tense family's late Victorian villa. I probably added to the tension – endless soft beanbag impacts gently annoying the ceilings below. Conversely, I did nothing to provoke the endless children's bedwetting, which was in situ before I arrived.

Often after dark the family's improvised urine alarm would go off on one or both of the kids' beds and push them further into trauma and wake everybody with bladder control, too. I would dream about fire engines and hoses filled with child pee. I'm guessing the whole of the household did.

Perhaps the kids never improved, perhaps they progressed to shoplifting and murder, even politics. I had no idea where I might progress to and kept any clues to myself.

And *drop, drop, drop* – but then *up, up, up*. The beanbags began that obedient cycle of flying, lowering, flying again. They'd kiss the sweet spot in my palm and spring back up every time. They made me a person who was different because of a strange and beautifully useless skill.

Several of our group had arrived already knowing how to juggle, while I knew only about Milton and Marlowe and Diderot and Racine – and ugly mood swings and keeping my head down. I could also name most of the female authors who've killed themselves – as if words were slowly toxic to them, like radiation with Marie Curie. As if women always have to pay more for whatever we discover, whatever we achieve.

Still, finding out the joy of juggling left me completely unscathed. And once my Paul was old enough, I added hand food to his brain and body food – *plump, plump, plump.*

The beanbags loved him almost at once. On his first humid afternoon they defied him, teased, resisted. But he kept at it. I couldn't watch and he didn't want me to. Fair enough. He kept on until dinner time, then went straight back outside after shovelling in what I recall as quite a good stew that deserved to be savoured. I remember him stalking off with a straight-mouth expression I'd expect to see before a Main Street gun fight, or the start of a polar exploration.

Then I heard a definite whoop. Then another.

I crept out to our top deck – not that he didn't notice me – and watched him inhabit an area of new magic. The honeysuckle scent was licking and rising and making the beanbags slow and hang in the slightly miraculous air.

And then we both went to sleep happy. It was after midnight. He was six.

Arguably an example of terrible mothering – but I'd say not.

Later, much later, he once came home from a party and told me that he'd stopped two random guys from hurting him by juggling beer mats at them and then empty glasses. I was so proud I cried slightly later.

I have come to believe that a person who cries a lot creates an access to happiness that others lack. When our circumstances change, we already know how to cry, but do so for different reasons. And it means that we properly know our happiness. It overtakes us.

And children can make you weep by being so much about *yes* and by racing towards life, eating it whole and by being just so pleasant. They surprise you by being better than you could imagine. That's worth a bit of a wet face in celebration.

By which I mean to say...

Paul has the sunshine in him.

The morning after his assault-avoidance-through-juggling triumph I asked him not to try any such thing again and to just scarper swiftly instead. But, then again, when you're cornered and can't run, you do need other possibilities. That's when the beautifully useless skills come in handy. We both understand this.

I was never that great a juggler with anything other than bean-bags. I got as far as the manoeuvre that is called Rubenstein's Revenge and that was it. But I was the English and French Literature source for our night-time band of lecture-room marauders. We had no name them, the raggedy straggle that we were – no one had realised yet that we had to be called the OrKestrA.

We are getting there, though – closing in on who we were. That's always a useful thing to do. Some people never manage it – they die in uniforms and marriages and nightmares that weren't even their own.

Commedia dell'arte helped us: Pantalone, Arlecchino, Pulcinella, Il Dottore – the traditional cast of comedy characters. Properly speaking they wore traditional masks, of which we had none. The traditional jokes, though, we could manage. I did the research on that.

And, yes, there are such things as traditional jokes, bits of business with plates and house flies and hearts in love and punches that are so perfect people save them and pass them on. They're a way of taking awful, irritating, foolish, maybe fatal things – like falling – and making them all of those things at once, but also golden, which is to say Funny.

Jokes are compressed and vital little stories about all of life's most terrible wonderful things. The good ones get handed along like heirlooms and religions and genetic calamities. They're passed across centuries because they're precious and they're useful. With words or without, they are a sensible human being's answer to reality and the ways that it hurts us and does not make sense. If we can't fight and we can't fly, we can be funny.

The plate-throwing lunatics, the Commedia fools, were so good at allowing their bodies to go wrong. They completely, balletically, horrifyingly mastered falling over – that universal misfortune that is funny and so shaming and which can atomise a hip bone and which lost Neil Kinnock an election. Commedia clowned and snapped slapsticks and pretended to eat flies and tickled inside minds from nation, to nation, to nation. They were High Art and Low.

Not that there is any High or Low. Entertainments with beautiful truth – enough beautiful truth – speak to everyone. They accumulate powers and then unleash them, light their audience. PhD theses and articles and god knows what, they invent terminologies – labels that choke off people's access to all the fun – but it's just to make the authors feel better about not being able to juggle.

The Commedia characters wore exquisite and difficult-to-craft, hand-tooled-by-artisans-from-Italian-leather masks. Our nameless group naturally could neither make nor source even one hand-tooled Italian leather anything. Also we did not want to be Pulcinella, or Arlecchino, or so forth. But we did want to be Someone New.

And we did sneak into a Film Studies lecture room and show each other what had emerged from a week's thinking about the masks we might like to use – about who we were really going to be.

We all have masks: Mother, Sergeant, Vicar, Boyfriend, President, Constable, Thug. We all use them as best we can, even if they were shoved at us by strangers and they don't fit. Picking one on purpose – one that is really yours and really you – that's when you begin to accumulate, to think about when you'll unleash them.

And this was when we really began – the OrKestrA. That one light-headed night we sat on the lecture-room floor and each one of us set out who we thought we might want to really be – spreading clothes and props out on the industrial-grade grey carpet that smelled of weed, old trainers and young daydreams.

And our new selves arrived, as if they'd been waiting for us to invite them. Both of the Apocalypse Sisters, Sissy and Hissy, appeared in an early form, with their claws and their terrifying smiles. Clumsy Mary appeared, with her glorious inability to stay on her six-inch heels or ever be a burlesque dancer instead of a giggling personification of erotic mishaps and narrow escapes. Cedric the Screaming Mime was self-explanatory. Phil the Pill and Utility Bill with their bowler hats and mirror acts were happier than I had ever seen them – every part of them made you smile. Dynamo was good at lifting people and already experimenting gently with his sparks. Mrs Fire wanted to fire-breathe but hadn't tried it yet. She threw cut-up bits of red and yellow paper and we got the idea. Mr Kink was fluid in all possible ways and suddenly unleashed a kindness, a benevolence, under his usual habit of smouldering.

Monkey Monk was a relatively recent arrival – he didn't say much. That night he was still silent but completely eloquent – all elbows and knees and climbing and springing and levers and cords of muscle and balancing and these brown and round and animal eyes. He came to rest, somehow, braced in a corner of the ceiling and hooted at us – Emperor of Monkeys.

His footprints were up there when we graduated two years later.

Some of us tried wigs, but they weren't what we wanted. Later, Monkey slowly grew out his muttonchop monkey whiskers and showed us the way – our own hair was best and we would use it to bring our proper selves into everyday life.

That night, we laid out our new personalities across the floor like multiple crime scenes waiting for chalk marks to run round them. We wanted to think about them, give them one last look, before we tried them on. Where our heads should be, we'd set white paper masks with the faces we wanted painted on them.

Mine was slightly horrifying because I can't paint.

Juggling was enough of a challenge.

The clock was sneaking past the back of midnight when everything was ready. Fog blooms were dreaming of the Ripper's Whitechapel and thickening around the streetlamps outside. That campus always did love fog.

And in our stolen room we'd doused the lights and there were candles set in saucers for our only illumination. I don't recall who added that touch, maybe Sissy Apocalypse. She's always good at details.

And ourselves were waiting for us in the flickerlight. No more hints and trials and whispers – we'd step in now, over our heads.

It's very odd to realise that the person you are in everyday life is so little of your own making. The carpety darkness was so still I could hear myself thinking, shouting – *God, I hate this thing I'm caught inside, I hate this series of lies and apologies and flinches.*

The candles really helped.

I stood there while Mr Kink intoned something about identity – he was our talker from the start. Something already mine was looking up at me from the floor. I had gathered the bits of her up as a series of jokes, but she seemed very serious now. I could be her. I could kick free.

I know, I know, people go to university and change, young people change, people hot-knifing far too much dope change, people being fed whole menus of fresh information and mild hope change. But this was different – this was our accidental ritual, the one that we would repeat with everyone but our very last member, who seemed to arrive as a fait accompli.

We stood and held hands without planning to. This was slightly scary, after all, now we came to it – so we needed to hold hands. Then we stepped forward, walked off a cliff above an ocean, then discovered we could float – no, we could fly.

Under other circumstances, I suppose we might have turned into a cult. Instead we devoted ourselves to being ridiculous in public. We hurt no one, not ever.

Overnight, over a handful of minutes that night, we became serious fools, as nature intended – there were ribbons, scarves, waistcoats, layers of cloth, Mr Kink's bare midriff, Clumsy Mary's paint-stained basque. Hissy and Sissy Apocalypse threw shapes and the whites of their eyes and teeth were like something you'd see beyond the reach of your happy campfire on a weird, weird night.

I threw shapes with them until I was running with sweat and the mask started sticking to my skin. I half imagined I wouldn't be able to take it off, would end up stuck with its big moonchild eye holes and its giant smile.

And I remember we danced a lot and shouted in new voices and didn't stop until the sun was risen. It really did seem like freedom. The dancing also made us realise that, whoever we were, we'd need music. This was unfortunate – only two of us could play anything – but, as of tonight, we were optimistic.

We were about to overcome.

And, when we were finally tired, we lay on our backs, side to side to side to side and onwards. And we laughed. We laughed the way people might waking up on the shore after a shipwreck.

Then we folded up our little revolution, gathered all the red and yellow paper scraps, the candles, the saucers, the old clothes of our old and irrelevant selves.

And then we walked out in our fresh skins and let them feel the pinkgrey mist of dawn. It was cold out there in the world. But we didn't mind it. That is – I didn't and that seemed to mean that no one did, because we had only one heart, unseparated.

From then on we were going to be more than just flirting and mucking about and planning for Edinburgh and instant fame. Of course, we did go to Edinburgh and did flirt and muck about, but we did it with definite traces of noble purpose. And there was no fame of any kind.

My new self? She was Annanka Ladystrong.

Imagine that.

Whatever else I pretended to be as an undergraduate, I was her inside. She was like keeping a brave grin beneath everything I said. It may be pathetic that she made such a big difference to me, but the 80s was a decade when women were still told to take groping and chasing and catcalls as part of life. We learned smiling and dodging, delaying and bargaining, running if all else failed. If we didn't, then we would be punished, one way or another. Marriage was still our best bet, pregnancy the reason we would never get that promotion. Even if we ran an office later, men would be puzzled when we didn't make the coffee and the lunches, too. Nothing was ever supposed to change or compromise but us.

Annanka Ladystrong was having none of that.

I remember swinging and jumping in time with Monkey across a muddy and forbidden lawn and then I was saying my name and saying my name and yelling my name.

Annanka Ladystrong.

Through all the years of old blokes copping a feel and the sniggers and sly fingers, all the cramped-in expectations and tutting frowns – she'd been waiting.

And she was absolutely furious.

Details.

That's the short version of how we got to Hunter Square.

That's why, marching up through Edinburgh, Annanka was there and ready for the world.

1984 was a year of manifest discontent that Orwell had somehow made vaguely embarrassing – as if everyone should have waited until 1985 to kick off. There were strikes and demonstrations galore. And where policemen saw hordes of unpatriotic freaks and politicians saw proto-terrorists, we saw captive audiences. If you're standing on a picket line, you can't exactly leave, even if you're being offered entertainment that is at first – to be kind – a bit rough.

Before Hunter Square we had inflicted ourselves on wildcat

strikes at Ferrybridge power station, at Lucas Aerospace, at Shirebrook and Wath-on-Dearne marshalling yards. We expressed our solidarity and conducted experiments with leotards and singing *a cappella* for which I can only apologise. At least we were young enough to learn fast and to meanwhile be treated kindly by men and women facing the end of every future security. Slowly, we grew to be more than just something people stared at.

Then Magnificent Arthur joined us and oversaw the running of kids' shows in union clubs for striking families. Cedric joined him and was a peculiar hit with the under-fives. And their mums. Something about being really little identifies with an adult who howls in bewilderment and fights with numberless overwhelming things that nobody can see. Something about seeing people in my own country without food – going without an absolute necessity – was staggering. Even now it's so familiar, how could it not cause adults to howl?

When we took Hunter Square we were already expert in singing to policemen, blowing kisses and slip-dancing sideways. We pantomimed our glorious leaders firing cops, because cops are just nationalised workers and must therefore be replaced. We worked out fairly quickly that jovial strolling players might suppress or delay a baton charge here or there. And we hoped we might destabilise the Thick Blue Line with songs and information before their violence was unleashed.

When anything kicked off we'd run away. We weren't built for chaos and cavalry charges, avoided bloodshed. Even so, Monkey Monk got abducted and kidney punched inside the back of an unmarked van. The guys who did it were in plain clothes, but laughed about being cops. He pissed blood for three days. Monkey Monk had the radical Christ kind of face that always attracts constabulary attention.

People were really getting hurt. The cops even hurt other cops. We would smile and almost sympathise when cop riders were unable to stop cop horses from trampling cop feet. It took them years to get hoof-proof boots, years to go fully paramilitary.

What was I doing? Annanka Ladystrong loved to breathe and whisper in police ears. Some of them liked it. Annanka liked it, too, took every opportunity to demonstrate her female magnificence – and her strength.

Back in my room and a half, I was lifting bags full of textbooks in the evenings, doing arm curls and squats. I was shaping a body appropriate for my new personality's needs.

Muscle development is tricky when you're broke. Annanka was hungry in urgent ways that I never had been. And she was always fearless.

That didn't stop me shivering every time I stepped out of our van in the early birdsong to the scent of barrel braziers and thermos coffee. I turned up anyway.

One dawn, as Mr Kink talked us up in front of the crowd and reeled through the legend we were becoming, our fanciful names and deeds, we heard him mention *the unruly orchestra* somewhere near the middle of his flow.

Cedric misheard this as *the Unrule Orchestra* – which sounded really excellent as a scream. And as we heard him bellow it throughout the day, we took to it more and more. So we took it, right out of the air, and added a special spelling. We had a name – the UnRule OrKestrA.

We were a troupe and strolling players and free-range funmongers and a family and such a thing as never was and we lived by the motto we'd shout at the start of every gig to help ourselves feel capable:

Move fast. Stick together.

Be Ridiculous and Impregnable Foolishness.

That generally kept us safe, although not forever. Court 10 was there already, I suppose, poised at the end of our line, the worst possible audience.

What defended us most at the time was the fact that we could leave. We weren't part of these communities. Nobody knew where we lived – not as far as we were aware.

We keep touring about in variously decrepit cars, buying petrol with whatever spare cash we could raise. We were the OrKestrA and we had our InstrUmentz. Clumsy Mary (Grade One trombonist) accompanied police manoeuvres with oompahs and plummeting out-of-tune slides. Percussion Karl made our snare drums morph from regimentally brisk to drunken Moulin Rouge and drag-stepped R&B. We did our best. We hammered dented saucepans. We had kazoos.

By August 1984 and Hunter Square, we were the UnRule OrKestrA: Hissy and Sissy, Mary, Mr Kink, Mrs Fire and Dynamo, Cedric, Phil and Bill, Arthur, Karl, Monkey and me. We thought we were battle-hardened and bullet-proof. In fact, we were the future accused, future character witnesses. We were the future dead from an overdose and the future mourners, were the future victims of this and that, our injury walking closer with every breath. We were the future betrayed.

Good thing we didn't know it – we would have been so sad.

I was oblivious as everyone else and rocking a Number 4 haircut – tight and natural brown at the sides with long and red spikes on top. I wore an adhesive Van Dyke beard, a basque, Doc Martens and tartan army surplus trousers against the cold. There was glitter on my shoulders. I've always had disproportionately wide shoulders. Ma called them 'mannish'. Suddenly they were useful.

Annanka, my shoulders and I were glad when Magnificent Arthur and Mrs Fire returned from scouting and announced our targets. We duly assembled the following morning in front of the Tolbooth Kirk with its mad, fierce, spiky roof that sends so many little needle hackles poking into heaven and keeping it up to scratch. Edinburgh is well aware of everything heaven's getting wrong. During the festival, it disapproves even more.

If I remember, we were rocking our kitchen percussion, two snare drums, the trombone, my quack-prone learner's clarinet – and the kazoos. Monkey Monk was practising on a fifth-hand accordion in every moment he did not sacrifice to romancing a sudden Australian girlfriend, but he wasn't performance-ready yet in either context.

Poor, shy Monkey.

The OrKestrA formed up and then promenaded and rattled and wailed all down the Lawnmarket's cobbled slope past shops for quaint Americans and bad gifts.

Ma would be pleased that Scotland has done better since. She sometimes remembers it as a mush of shame and folk songs and damp tenement walls. The home gives her tartan knee rugs. She swears at them in gibberish she claims is Gaelic.

The OrKestrA – loyal to every country and to none – hammered on down the Royal Mile between the surly pubs and frowning windows of pipe accessories and clan lapel badges. We gathered momentum and, when I glanced back, I could see we were being followed by swept-along pedestrians. By the time St Giles Cathedral was staring at us from under its dumpy, dirty crown, we were a definite thing, a snaking creature with a pulse.

We were off the cliff and we weren't just floating, we were truly flying – *up, up, up*. I could feel myself yip and howl between bursts of bad clarinetting. Even Annanka wasn't strong enough to hold so much joy.

That first time you step off the pavement and become part of a band, a parade, a demonstration, a kind of thrill shivers at your legs. It's like being shin-deep in cool water. If you find you're not immediately arrested, or instantly subdued in a hail of loosened teeth, then maybe everything is more allowed than you'd been assuming. Maybe you've reached out and taken additional power.

You're simply standing on a road, but you're also breaking the law. You're daring it to come and get you. It's intoxicating – saying *I will take this land* in the way that a landowner does. As are those times when you really catch and move and hold a crowd, turn a street full of pedestrians into an audience, an event. If I was a decent person I'd be handcuffing myself to metal stanchions, or lying across a road for the cause of peace and justice and sustaining life. That would be my best way to feel delight. I'm a performer, though. We were all performers. We did want to change the world, but we wanted to do it by being looked at. That is possible – teachers do it every day. First comes the showbiz and then the practicality, the audience participation and shared labour. Politicians mostly want the glamour and not the work. They cling to their weird little dignities and hate their audience, so they never have much of an act. *Forget about being the change you want to see – just come and look at the wonder of me.* That's why they hate teachers so much – and entertainers.

And how very easily people follow, want to lose themselves in one huge will. In mindless size.

Still, the OrKestrA didn't take anyone anywhere bad.

Pah-dubbah-dubbah-dum. Pah-dubbah-dubbah-dum. Pah-dah-dum. Pah-dah-dum.

We were out for stuff and nonsense and the death of our dignity.

Pah-dubbah-dubbah-dum. Pah-dubbah-dubbah-dum. Pah-dah-dum. Pah-dah-dum.

Utility Bill whistled out our signal for the start of an eight count and then we'd switch rhythms.

Dum-pah-dub. Dum-dub. Yak-a-ta. Dum-pah-dub. Dum-dub. Yak-a-ta.

In the Royal Mile we were a critical mass, had occult qualities and magics. The crowds up ahead backed out of our way. More followed in our wake. The vennels and tunnel-fronted closes were full of peering. Or this is how I recall it.

Then we began our right turn while Bill went mad on the whistle and we leaned a rock step back to make our followers giggle as they thumped into each other. Our drumbeats ricocheted up to the crow-stepped gables as we swung round the side of yet another soot-stained church.

Edinburgh fears it would rise and drift like a wicked paper lantern if it wasn't pinned down tight by churches.

And there it was – Hunter Square.

And there we were – the UnRule OrKestrA.

And we wanted our space.

Naturally, there was already someone in our rightful home, because it was too lovely to remain unoccupied. We halted and whispered our drums and faced a man in a grubby jerkin and hose who was ruining a perfectly nice morning with face-pulling and a diabolo. I mean, you can, but why would you?

He intended to be cute and quirky in a renaissance fair kind of way. He was just needy. In the world and in the classroom, any audience always notices your weakness and presumption. You can't be needy – no one likes it. In street theatre – as in possibly no other part of your life – you do get what you deserve.

We could taste that the baggy-kneed jester man smelled of paraffin as well as panic and burned hair. So he wasn't just a bad diabolo, he was bad at fire-breathing, too, and therefore a danger to himself. So we were going to save him, really. Or maybe not him – just his audience.

Among us, Mrs Fire and Dynamo had true sympathy with flames. They were snorting down their noses with contempt on behalf of all Fire People everywhere.

Of course, in theory, fire-breathing is not that hard. You take paraffin into your mouth and hold it there before spitting it out across a suitable source of ignition.

Always get proper training.

Never inhale.

And learn to suppress the bit of your reptile brain that hopes to keep flamey danger from your head and face. The craft attracts both geniuses and morons who don't know they're morons, but who can spit.

All Fire People swallow a trace of paraffin as they work and the oily tang of it permeates them and works out through their skin. Fire-breathers drink large quantities of milk to reassure their stomachs and clear their systems. Mrs Fire always said the secret was never to stop breathing fire. This meant she would never start to smell like an ordinary human being. She drank her milk and persevered.

And Mrs Fire was an artist, a pyromancer – she still is. She would light and relight and propagate fire in the usual way, but then she would really begin. A nice young woman who loved rice pudding and had Baptist parents, but there she would be in her street persona, rapidly and clearly insane, while in charge of a hellfire fountain. She would roam, exhaling successive demons in tall plumes. Mrs F. gave every indication of being thoroughly homicidal, as well as possessed. Her fireballs could also be seductions. She'd talk about burning your husband back down to his shoes while she stared at him until he shivered. Then she'd lick her lips. Skinny, fire-taming, sparky and blue-goggled Dynamo was all that could save the world from her sex vibe and her strangeness. If she let him.

When not a human bonfire, Mrs F. was one of the calmest women I've ever known – truly calm, not just in hiding. And she never hurt a soul. Never scorched an object. She did no harm. Court 10 should never have heard her name as any kind of incrimination, should never have dared to disturb her.

In Hunter Square she was scary, because she knew how to seem scary, I don't deny that. She crept up and laughed at the little jester man in a way that made him jump. He was all alone and we were us and we were going to take his stage away.

Not that he wasn't already throwing himself out. The holiday goodwill of August wasn't forgiving his unforgiveable fool's hat and his terrible bells. His crowd wasn't his crowd, it was just some strangers pausing and being dismayed by his misfortune before moving on. He needed us to be his exit strategy.

I remember looking round at us, at the way we were fit and nothing but ourselves and therefore had an animal thrum about us, a stillness with wild capacities shining underneath. And we were young. And the railway workers and power-station wives would smile at us with sad eyes – smile at the way we were unmarked and optimistic. We were like cut flowers to them – pretty in a way that could have no staying power.

Jester man was abandoned by his diabolo and moved on to fumbling his Indian clubs. He said something nervy that nobody could hear. Then the Apocalypse Sisters raised both hands high in their long red gloves. And high went all of our hands. This was our rollcall and location indicator, designed to work above yelling and confusion.

Mr Kink started his opening patter, rolling his hips and pushing out long, low and wily boasts of wonders in his rockstar huckster singsong, this beautiful flow of words. Not a word was credible, nor was it supposed to be. But he made you know you'd have a good time, you could believe that. He split the space clean in two, padding along in his pink high-heeled bedroom slippers and tan leather trousers with the lace-up fly, loose shirt in raddled orange silk. He gathered the civilians round him, got them watching the way he was all cheekbones and louche mouth and innocent eyes – and then he pushed them back to leave us a broad ring of performing space.

Jester man took the hint and started to gather up his props and clutter. He didn't believe he should be there enough to try and stay. Performance requires belief. I sometimes think Court 10 was intended to punish self-confidence among those deemed to be unworthy.

In Hunter Square, Monkey Monk was a certainty. He swarmed high up an impossible wall with his sticky rockface shoes: tight jeans, white T-shirt and a British Rail porter's jacket over that. His muttonchop whiskers made him Monkey, his atmosphere and Jesus hair made him Monk, and his jacket was about still owning the railways, owning all the things that mattered, about dignified labour, there to help in a dignified uniform.

He was never like cut flowers – he stayed beautiful almost to the end.

Once he'd made it to the highest available point, he unrolled his spine, stood up to his full height and stayed there like a natural feature, staring out across the space. He might have been manning the mast head of a land-hungry ship – he seemed that necessary.

And I could feel in my chest that we were about to be perfect, every one of us.

I wasn't wrong.

Next, the Apocalypse Sisters screeched in the way that Viking women might have as they tore up the shingle away from bright sails to kill you in horrible ways. They made you imagine wet fingernails and wounds, even as they dived into tumbles and grabbed magical objects out of nowhere – mainly very inoffensive knives. They also flirted horrifyingly. Then Clumsy Mary did apparently awful things with their knives and killed Magnificent Arthur, who came back from death all the same. Then he escaped from various other and lesser confinements before vanishing – or something like it – in a flurry of blood-stained handkerchiefs and flash paper flares. Cedric the Screaming Mime made the children far too excited – and then their parents. Phil the Pill and Utility Bill fought in slow motion with wooden spoons and made the adults laugh along with the kids. Then Dynamo and Mrs Fire brought back the proper terror. And all the while Monkey Monk leaped and sprang. And Percussion Karl percussed as necessary.

We were having a perfect gig.

And it was my turn next.

I walked in through the ring of watchers, which was deep and elbow to elbow, keen to see. Mr Kink shouted me up. I cartwheeled across the space. (Mrs McCormick no longer cartwheels – she's scared to find out she can no longer manage it.)

As soon as I landed, I braced myself and, all at once – *touch, touch, touch* – Monkey Monk frisked in and climbed up on my shoulders. Then he balanced on the point where his left foot met my forehead. (Imagine how Year Five would be amazed.)

There was a tiny piece of grit embedded in the sole of his shoe and it bit my skin. I didn't mind.

People cheered. It's always more impressive when a woman lifts a man, two men – Monkey Monk and Mr Kink, braced and angled out from me like the twin hooks of an anchor.

Being that strong made me walk into rooms quite differently. I'd see a smirk, hear assumptions being made as I walked past and I'd think – *Little man, I could pick you up and throw you.*

We had rehearsed the show to end after I'd picked up and, indeed, thrown, whichever male audience member I'd selected, clear into the arms of the Apocalypses and several audience helpers. I'd then dust off the volunteer, fold him and sway him into shapes, lift him up and let gravity worry him, set him down and grant him his applause before claiming my own.

After that, Mr K. would lead a nicely raucous reminder of each act with our assorted UnInstrUmental InstrUmentZ accompanying. We'd bow and march off playing into the figurative sunset after that. Gathering money as we went offended against our artistic integrity, but we did it, anyway – then squeezed into whichever pub had room for us.

There was a change of plans, though. Hunter Square was where our OrKestrA got its final member. He was slipped in at the end of the line-up so we didn't have to work out new transitions. I'd seen no one in the audience looking like our type, but then I had been focused on not dropping Monkey Monk, who was prone to making sudden gestures at strange moments. All I knew was that Magnificent Arthur had a friend who had a friend who had an act and Arthur had seen it and known it would suit and had to be ours at once.

Baron Sunday.

I was his warm-up.

Once I'd bowed and cartwheeled away, Mr Kink talked the Baron up – praised and magnified his name – and he duly appeared from between a pair of women in hen-night T-shirts. He paced slowly with a black lacquered cane, wore a mangled top hat and the kind of tailcoat you'd find hanging in any second-hand shop back then, like folded crows. He walked like an emperor in grubby white long johns, bare feet, torn white gloves and a scarlet handkerchief bleeding from his top pocket. All punctured dignity and maladjusted status, he circled about, bowing and doffing his murdered hat, especially to children. Some performers are fireworks and expansion – he was the other kind: stillness and concentration, outward resonance and a dead face.

He seemed older than us, but also like a strange, pre-teen boy. He might have been forty, or ninety, or ten.

The Baron did nothing exactly remarkable in that first performance, but he had an edge. From a still face, his eyes showed a bewilderment about his own abilities that was charming, infectious. Yes, the Baron was a charming infection.

And he was Proper Funny. Every part of him was funny.

Being funny is disarming.

He began with his hat, his gloves and his handkerchief – each followed the other up into the air with a beautiful ease while he looked on, deadpan, but wildly staring. Nothing he touched stayed in his hands – it all leaped up and away. His cane came apart in mid-flight and revealed a swordstick that he balanced on one forefinger's end before it apparently sheathed itself again without asking permission.

Some people don't mean to be watchable: they just are who they are and it makes you look. It's not glamour exactly, not charisma. Some people are just very simple and clear, like turning on a light. He was made to be that way. And all of the grace in his motion excused itself by being a little ridiculous. His agility hid behind his constant bafflement. A threat of incoming disaster cycled through his limbs and body. It never arrived, but made you feel compassion for him. The Baron was a man who could show you the way life comes at you and how you can be terrified but survive. It invited observers to be scared for him and protective.

That's disarming, too.

At the end of his smaller tricks he bounced about in a rush of applause as if it belonged to someone else.

Humility works well, too. It charms.

Then he summoned Mr Kink, whispered elaborately, arms

wheeling about, before suddenly falling still and waiting like a solemn child.

Details.

He made himself memorable.

I wish he hadn't.

Next Mr Kink announced, 'The World Famous, the Internationally Renowned, the Only, Original and Best Elastic Rabbit'.

This was the Baron's signature bit. He'd add elaborations as time passed – he always was good at improvising – but the essentials stayed the same.

First he would pick a child. The Baron had an instinct for coaxing out the quiet ones, the odd and the lonely. He would draw them to the centre of attention and gather cheers for them. Small objects would appear in his hands and in their pockets – weird little objects that weird little kids would like – and they'd be happy about the new presents and new attention and start to relax. The Baron encouraged the girl, or boy, to stand inside the sudden bursts of clapping as if they were a birth right. The praise of strangers, the generosity out of thin air – this might be a possible part of life.

Then Baron Sunday would headstand on one of our chairs. He'd gesture in ways that encouraged the child to do the same. Before they could panic too much, he'd lift the kid up on the chair and begin to turn them head over heels, as if their headstand was inevitable. But he would amiably change his mind as soon as they protested and set them the right way up, with their feet safely on the chair's seat, head higher than the crowd. After that, emerging slowly from one of the tailcoat's many pockets, we would see the Elastic Rabbit. The Baron would hand it to the child and then say – *Hold on tight. No, tighter than that. No, really, much tighter. AS IF YOUR LIFE DEPENDS UPON IT. HOLD VERY TIGHT.*

At this point, Baron Sunday would put on his blue-lensed little glasses and show everyone how a length of elastic was firmly attached under the rabbit's tail and leading away into one of his magical pockets. Sometimes the elastic even had small brown rabbit droppings hanging at intervals.

Often, they were sewn-on chocolate raisins and therefore usefully edible.

Baron Sunday twanged the elastic. He showed the audience how it could stretch and tighten and twanged it again so that everyone understood its nature. Then the Baron would begin to wind it out. Clearly he could stretch it and unroll it, but equally clearly there would be a limit to how far he could make it go. Everything does have a limit.

Then slowly, or quickly, or ornately, or simply, the Baron made sure that elastic was stretched way past any kind of sane expectation. He ran and lunged and stepped with it, pulling it tight and then tighter, in and out of the crowd, around waists, around couples, threading in and out of groups. The empty space where the child stood became a cat's cradle. Baron Sunday had to climb about inside it, or else navigate by trying to limbo underneath the strands. At certain points, little silk flags would appear and hang from the line that lengthened but also grew more and more taut, apparently harder and harder to pull, more clearly near its breaking point.

And it's good to be scared in a small way. It's good to feel a spring is winding somewhere and to know it will have to be released.

Baron Sunday would hesitate, here and there, as if he doubted he could risk another ounce of pressure, but then he'd swing his dead face and desperate eyes back and forth, scan the audience while they tried not to feel unsteady. Somehow this made it their fault when he pressed on. Finally, inevitably, the end of the elastic would be reached. The Baron would lift the last few inches up high for general inspection. But still he'd edge on just a little further. And the audience grew quieter and more tangled and tied together. There would be giggles and squeaks of fear.

So much elastic against so much skin – it was surely going to hurt when it snapped. It was bound to hurt.

While absolute silence settled in and thickened, the child would often stand above the chaos like royalty inspecting a possession.

After all, the Baron made sure to act as if he were obeying their orders, throwing quizzical glances and seeming to ask permission before tugging out even more insanity.

He understood how nervous children work.

Beyond anyone's guess at the elastic's tolerance, Baron Sunday had hopped and stepped and struggled, winding it back over the strands that were confining his audience. He was labouring now and could only ease gingerly a little closer and then a little closer still, towards the child who seemed so obviously far beyond his reach.

Everyone could see that some awful accident was racing in. The Baron's eyes burned with it. His grin burst out for an instant and then vanished, like a burglar's torch inside your house.

His finale involved stretching even the tiny remaining scrap of elastic in his hand – experimental – and then fumbling out from his pocket the blaring red handkerchief, before laboriously tying it to the elastic.

And then he turned, his attention making it clear that he needed the child to have the handkerchief. Of course he did.

For some reason, more men than women would find themselves calling out at this point, wanting him to stop. They seemed to feel the danger more.

The Baron would ignore their pleas, relentless but also apparently weak and tired and sweating. He'd fight those last steps forward until he could just about, nearly, almost – yes – extend a trembling arm and offer the child that very obvious handkerchief.

Red is always an excellent choice, if you want to be visible in a crowd.

I was never sure if the Baron let go of the elastic before the child could take it, or if – as they paused and breathed and met eye-to-eye – they made an agreement to be wickedpowerful and naughty and to send all those adults and other children into wails and screams and laughter, the wild red handkerchief snapping and flying and licking and rushing around and between and above and behind and among them like a righteous flame, or like a terrible, red idea.

And while no one was entirely looking, Baron Sunday would prepare his closing tableau. As the audience had caught their breath and turned back to face his performance area, they found him standing on the chair with the child on his shoulders and regal and triumphant and the air around both drifting and glinting with fine metal confetti.

In a way, nothing had happened, but it had also been so much, almost too much.

The first time I saw the Elastic Rabbit, I thought it was wonderful, generous, benevolent. The Baron picked a girl with dull hair and round shoulders to help him. By the time they took their farewell applause together, she was a queen. When the Baron jumped down from the chair, still holding her high, you could see she felt that cold swoop in the stomach of a sudden large drop. But she wasn't unhappy about it. She knew she was proof against more shocks than she'd thought.

Baron Sunday shook that first girl's hand with funereal care, gave a huge wink and then handed her back to her parents, her pockets and heart newly laden with small and mysterious things.

Every child that he chose seemed to realise their own magnificence.

And everyone survived, although it seemed that we might not. Somewhere behind the Baron was the idea that he might have the power to hurt us. But he decided not to.

I'm thinking this only in retrospect. At the time, I was just happy as Utility Bill blew his whistle and the drums and kazoos began our sign-off sequence and Mr Kink announced us in order of appearance for our final bows.

I took my cheers, the Baron next, and then we formed up in pairs to swing and stroll away. The Baron ended up beside me, because of our running order, although I now suspect that he'd have been there, no matter what, because he'd picked me in the same way that he'd picked the right little girl to help him with his act.

I glanced over and saw he was back to his resting deadpan face. It made him perfect for the kind of comedy where hideous things always threaten harmless people. Which is to say, he was perfect for reality. He'd shaped himself to fit.

Pah-dubbah-dubbah-dum. Pah-dubbah-dubbah-dum. Pah-dah-dum. Pah-dah-dum.

As we swung along, his elbow nudged me, innocent and kind and accidental, but also not. He inclined his head towards me and murmured out the story of himself, sneaked it to me from almost-still lips. He offered me Buster the English graduate, Buster the lost man who needed a little help, Buster who was taking a pause for breath to find his path in life. Buster who was so happy I was here in this so-new situation where he was going to need a special friend.

Pah-dubbah-dubbah-dum. Pah-dubbah-dubbah-dum. Pah-dah-dum. Pah-dah-dum.

He knew the story of yourself is what you wind and wind, tight in around anyone who listens.

Pah-dubbah-dubbah-dum. Pah-dubbah-dubbah-dum. Pah-dah-dum. Pah-dah-dum.

Phil and Bill and Mrs F., Dynamo and Mary, Mr Kink and Monkey Monk and the Apocalypses, Cedric, Arthur, Karl and me and then Buster – we waved and played and pushed through the crowds and the thin air and the future that couldn't stop us from eventually reaching Court 10. The OrKestrA marched away, that bit closer to the age of plague and flattered rages and simple stories and loud stupidity – our time that rejoices in chaos engineers and spivs.

The time finds you.

Everything finds you.

I don't remember when I christened our Baron, but it was soon after his arrival. His deadpan face required it. Everything about him asked to be named after the deadpan comedy king. I called him Buster.

And it's Buster who wrote the other story here. I don't know if it's any more true than the rest of his stories. I've read it once and never will again.

I'm putting him here, though – to be useful. For once in his life he can really be constructive. He can tell you what's inside the monsters that don't look like monsters, what's under the world that looks kind and normal.

I used to live in a kind and normal country, believed it was mostly that. I should have known better. I should have remembered Rumpelstiltskin.

I've given him a different typeface – it will look like this.

And I will keep on as I am.

2016, South Salem:

Outside the truck I notice the different air. I am not even a week in America this visit and still not used to breathing it. This time is the lastly time and then I am done with being specifically here.

The smell of New England wants to be always dry winds over granite and raw woods and rot in bark and sweet hearth smoke and conifer traces. Buildings and roads interfere with its needs, but not so much in my location.

I can taste that the easterly cold is the product of a continent. It feels hard-hearted confident and could easily overwhelm with force. Big winter is coming. I am not from a place of any size.

I do not like the trees today because they are in the way and too tall and too thin. They are an anxiety polygraph I think.

When I close the pickup door a blue jay drags its long tail up the sky and nags. The disturbance of me makes it leave and I regret this. I can hear cardinals which say teeo *teeo quipquipquip* and other diagnostic patterns. Verdins are identifiable as verdins because of singing *stayoutofhere*. A black-capped chickadee says its natural name which is *a-gony* and repeats that until I step too close and am sorry again.

I have lain out in places like this a high number of times and know the life here and the songs and species. Whatever I do I try to learn from and to not just exist while I am busy. I hope to enrich my time and engage.

This is the border land between Connecticut and New York and is forest grown over stolen farmland grown over indigenous farmland and fished rivers and hunted deer runs and that is how history makes things. Thieves win and so their thefts all disappear.

No.
You can't read him yet.

I don't want to leave you alone with him. He isn't a good man to have in your mind.

And he is convincing.

I'm a teacher, I try to teach. I want to be part of those 4,000 years we've spent telling one story, passing it on. And I know that the terrible people try to hide from us in our flinches. But we mustn't flinch. If we can't see the wrongs, we can't make them right. They're the very things we have to see.

I think that's true. But I live in a time and a place that's intent on staring at wrongs until everyone likes them.

I live in Buster's world and I don't want to.

I'm trusting that you might not want to either.

So.

Buster is Buster.

And Buster is a Stiltskin – a Stiltskin among Stiltskins – and you need to know him. In this time and place of Stiltskins you need to be able to recognise his type.

They always do well, of course. Stiltskins are so bright and strong and fascinating and they'll always feel so *necessary* and like a victory, a promised and blurry and nicely self-indulgent kind of victory that's just about to rise.

Now they are so bright, so thriving and so happy – so on trend and cinematic – so beguiling and televisual – so full of fine and uncertain excitements and thrills – so suitable for high office and grand rewards. They are winning. They may have won.

Their true names and natures are mentioned less and less often, so that even understanding them can simply make us feel alone.

But they are Stiltskins.

They're all Stiltskins.

If you read Buster, though, you can learn him.

And he left me his papers, his memoir, his confessions, his weird little fan fiction about himself. No news of him for years and then Court 10 and then he leaves an envelope full of his voice outside my home.

Inexcusable.

I'll tell you more about the envelope later – I can take only so much of him at any given time.

And I'll give just a chapter from him now and then – you need take only so much of him at any given time, too.

I apologise for his prose style. Sometimes he sounds like the man I knew – persuasive and eloquent and pushing your thinking about with the latest tale. Sometimes he sounds like a broken thing. That makes me glad. He should be broken and should sound it.

His words being here doesn't mean this story isn't mine. These are my papers, this is my page, my words, my notebook. This is like my classroom. I rule here, I reign. Nothing is here that I don't allow.

I am allowing Buster – Buster and all of the names he hides behind.

They always do have lots of names – just call them Stiltskin.

If you know him, know his taste, know his smell against your skin – meet the ghost of that – then you'll know every Stiltskin.

You will never be deceived.

You will know them all and that will be your power.

You will see them and name them and that will be your power.

You will find them and understand that you should run whenever you do, or else you should fight and you will choose the one that saves you.

Please understand.

I'm trying to give you everything that might help.

Know the Stiltskin and then run. Know the Stiltskin and then fight.

Those are your options.

Please.

There are no other choices to survive – there is only the one when you run, or the one when you fight.

Okay?

Okay then.

We'll read some of Buster now.

2016, South Salem:

Outside the truck I notice the different air. I am not even a week in America this visit and still not used to breathing it. This time is the lastly time and then I am done with being specifically here.

The smell of New England wants to be always dry winds over granite and raw woods and rot in bark and sweet hearth smoke and conifer traces. Buildings and roads interfere with its needs, but not so much in my location.

I can taste that the easterly cold is the product of a continent. It feels hard-hearted confident and could easily overwhelm with force. Big winter is coming. I am not from a place of any size.

I do not like the trees today because they are in the way and too tall and too thin. They are an anxiety polygraph I think.

When I close the pickup door a blue jay drags its long tail up the sky and nags. The disturbance of me makes it leave and I regret this. I can hear cardinals which say teeo *teeo quipquipquip* and other diagnostic patterns. Verdins are identifiable as verdins because of singing *stayoutofhere*. A black-capped chickadee says its natural name which is *a-gony* and repeats that until I step too close and am sorry again.

I have lain out in places like this a high number of times and know the life here and the songs and species. Whatever I do I try to learn from and to not just exist while I am busy. I hope to enrich my time and engage.

This is the border land between Connecticut and New York and is forest grown over stolen farmland grown over indigenous farm-land and fished rivers and hunted deer runs and that is how history makes things. Thieves win and so their thefts all disappear.

Underfoot is dry leaves with mud under and fallen branches and obstructing roots and lakes and reed beds. The terrain is mislead-ing and trouble at night although there is a big moon at this current point in the month. When I go navigating past sunset I cannot per-sonally show light and have relied on clear skies to help me.

It is day now.

I can see and be seen.

In between the narrow woodlands this place has true or also fake colonial homesteads and gambrel barns and saltbox roofs. People who are careful of their diets and fastidious in their reading material live here. They take newspapers and magazines of quality and do not cancel when the articles get worse. Being better crafted and more human than the news makes them happy. The decay of public discourse elevates them. They are happier every day. They imagine they limit their family's time online. They wear urban athletic ear warmers and walk pure-breed dogs and have access to important gossip. The pumpkins they bought to look perfect on verandas for Halloween are still here in November and ill under the rind and making carbon emissions.

A broad-winged hawk passes overhead and spreads predator silence beneath itself like something worse than a shadow.

After the farmers were gone this used to be mostly where housekeepers lived and other staff. It was an area acceptable for chauffeurs and eccentrics. I do not know where those types of resident have gone. The people here now are Manhattan retirees and commuters who live on lots with lake access or lots tucked in between the millionaires or lots at the edge of preserves. They don't know what they need to understand about the world and they won't learn. They have enough money to think in fantasies.

They have credibly country children who build woods shelters. Their dead fall branch and clumsiness structures have been left in clearings as if nobody here is afraid that vagrants and others will come to sleep inside them because everywhere is high-intensity curated. Under the child-improvised structures there is no usual mess of beer cans and pornography and cigarette butts. There is no litter. There are no empty syringes or paraphernalia.

Residents live here in calendar art and ideas of perfection. They are unready and rely on income-related hope. They preserve pollination highways and use kind pesticides and I know this because they put notices out to say so. Their wood shingles and sidings and picket fences and pioneer-style fences are all rotted by the same high water table and eaten up by the same insects that eat the forest. This is a place where people live in wooden houses and also a place that is about destroying wood.

As I drove in I passed workboots teams who may possibly not calibrate their diets for constant health and who do not drink imported bottled water and who may not read book reviews in order to have conversations. The bootsmen want to play radios while they hammer and drill and do other tasks but are not allowed to because of opinions about alleged sound ugliness. They are physical labour calorie burners. They are subject to the wishes of small house owners who insist on lordly sensitivities. The workboots men replace planking and window frames and porches with due reference to eighteenth-century skills. Maintenance. They seal driveways and clean gutters. Maintenance.

Leaf blowers call to each other across gardens. They are not a part of nature.

While proceeding at no more than 20 miles per hour I nodded to the bootsmen as a fellow bootsman would and I am certain they forgot me before my truck was out of sight. I have the facial expression of such as attend to unreasonable demands and fulfil honest duties nonetheless. My GMC Sierra has four-wheel drive which is suitable for the conditions. Each of my doors shows the decal of an established and genuine firm and nothing about me is too new and nothing about me is too old. I fit. Disappearing is not being unseen. Disappearing is being extremely the right fit.

Along streets where the houses are unfenced there are dogs willing to bark but not run. Flag lines along the borders of front yards mark the electric trigger points for collar shocks. The dogs have been taught their limits and so they are not really dogs any more and sit like people by their houses and become fat sad.

Corners and crossroads are fitted with hard yellow signs about school buses and children. This afternoon I passed one two three plastic boy shapes staked out on lawns. The running child figures have reflectors and red plastic caps and red flags. They are how adults prove they are careful about their sons and about their daughters although plainly less about their daughters. They are showing they are parents who deserve good fortune and not ever random mishaps.

I see the yard figures and I think they are sketchy and not convincing and I want them to indicate houses where families have cartoon children and I would like the red flag to mean the cartoons have dangerous violence. The boy shapes are modelled with only a curve as their one raised leg and only a straight line for the other. There is no sign of the proper bones or knee joints and so I can tell they would rush at adults with a strange gait and be fluid and frightening. They would have their reasons.

I am away from the cartoon neighbourhoods now. I have parked up above them near the valley ridge where wide-spaced seven-figure eight-figure houses are. Here all the hard yellow signs are for privacy instead of children.

I have learned my route. I never write down. I cultivate appropriate recall according to circumstance. I held this route in order to reach my location but will not utilise it again. I am therefore now unrecalling its details. I forget being prudent as a motorist and conforming to local styles on the 33 and then East Street along the reservoir side and down to the bridge.

I forget the circumstances around the sign there that says the road restricts at that point. There were many highly memorable elements at the location. The sign has been shot from 12 yards with buckshot in a loose spread. A shotgun slug has blown out a thumb-tip piece of it and additionally the metal post supporting. There are eight places where someone has tested .22 rounds. At the far side of the bridge there is a wide turn that becomes even wider and a passing place at the foot of a slope. The shooter would hypothetically drive down that hill and pull up and wind down his window and fire his shotgun and reload and fire again and replace that with his rifle and fire and then drive away. He could have done that. He could have done that without ever leaving his vehicle. There is a high probability that the shooter then continued driving in what would be the direction opposite to mine in order to inspect the sign and the work done which was not good work but all the same. There are people who are easily satisfied and people who are foolish and the sign is information about how those two groups contain the exact same people.

Multiple shooters was also a high possibility.

I need not discard my speculation, only where it took place.

I can remember deer-fenced vegetable patches but only in a general way.

Water stands in the valley bottoms and there is weak ice across it like fat on soup. That is not very specific.

I list what I no longer need and then the listed points and the listing go away like fog or like smoke or like hawk shadows passing above. I am unsaying the story. This is having control.

I forget Kitchawan Road which runs with a good deal of deep shade for cover and overlook outcrops. I forget taking Ferris Street and then Eskuyas Mill Road which is where I am standing currently.

I am breathing inside the predator silence at 155 Eskuyas Mill Road. Things taking place will soon cause deep recollection so I am making my scene feel loose and like seeing an old picture that is not relevant.

As a person I try to make sure I do not hold much. Whenever I see the white-tailed deer stepping as if they hardly touch I obtain identification. I am very light and this is comfortable.

My heart has room for efficient action because of my so much emptiness interior and it will hear me when I ask it to beat slow.

My pulse is intruding but is also controllable.

I think of being calm and what is needed for that to happen.

Pause. To pause is to prepare. Under some circumstances.

In my today circumstances there is time before I have to begin. That is my today luxury. I am my own schedule and will dominate events.

The breeze kicks sudden wicked. We are in a cold snap since two days past and the final autumn foliage rags are curled in on themselves and murdered with the new chill and dropping thick on the ground. I am cold but do not make this personal because then my skin will form memories and skin memories are hard to shift.

The leaf blowers will go to sleep in half an hour because the bootswork day begins and ends early.

I believe there will be snowfall just as soon as I am gone. This will bring cleanliness.

I have widely varied experience of weather and can discuss it with strangers. This is sometimes a skill.

I am still thinking of confident slowness.

And I stand here and like myself. I enjoy my breath every time it happens. I enjoy this being alive in a temperature that makes wide-awake minor pain in ears and fingers. It is refreshment. I enjoy tasting the distinctions of this place that is different from whatever the last place might have been.

I am preparing to be effective.

I am clean empty clean from my spine to my face. I am a boots-man with steel toecaps and the leather worn in. I am wearing my own mud-grey uniform. Shirt and trousers with maroon detailing and permanent sewn creases. Grey patrol cap with GSS logo and my not new but cared-for company bomber jacket. Maintenance.

I am just right.

I am not a state trooper. My colour palette means to suggest only that I am New York State Police adjacent and reliable steady. My image is marketing. I am a trusted employee of GSS which is Groundhog Security Systems which is Every Day Safe.

I am so much maintenance.

I am Albert Lockwood. This is an identity I have enjoyed and found very comfortable to inhabit. He has no passport because I decided he does not travel overseas, but his other documentation for identity is very high-level convincing. I am familiar tired. Underlying I am out of condition from too much sitting although my legs seem of good strength. My belly weight keeps me upset by shame in my background. This lends me softness and so I do not frighten people by being a nevertheless tall man and with hints of muscularity. I do not suggest power.

I suggest dedication to public safety and client safety above that.

I am Every Day Safe.

I am licensed to open carry a .38 but today I have only my baton and taser on display. I am non-confronting. I have a record of using the Leatherman tool in my duty belt for household repairs to help out as I am there anyway. No trouble.

The main house at this location is in five-acre grounds that are mainly lawns and rhododendrons. The estate is gated but the staff entry gate is only theory and I am inside it. I have parked my pickup in the space that is for Harald the outdoors man and his Nissan. The barn-style outbuilding to the south is where Harald keeps his mower and tools and leaf blower. He works Monday Thursday Friday. This is Tuesday. Serafina is the indoors person and would also park here in her Subaru but she does not ever work afternoons or at night because she knows better. Serafina cleans the rooms and installs fresh flowers and makes the beds and after she has served lunch she is free. She is every day fast out of the house before dark and not back until she has to start the breakfast.

The mail van looped back towards the highway ten minutes ago which is within normal timings. It will not return today.

The house is not large and can be run unchaperoned by one resident for days at a time without discomfort.

The hawk shadow must have lifted because birds begin singing again. The first note is always the biggest risk.

I am relaxed.

I move Albert forward because he is optimum now.

I take the red gravel path which is for people who do not admit they can walk because walking would be a demeaning activity. The golfcart rich can make themselves disabled in ways inaccessible to the poor. I let Albert smile at this. He is swinging along with docile strides towards the home and homeowner and will have no visible opinions from this point onwards.

The homeowner is not himself golfcart rich only most of his callers. He is another thing.

I am peaceful.

I reach an attractive but stagnant lake. Cypresses overhang and are part of its problem. Beside is a boathouse with a hand-split shingle roof and Adirondack chairs for bodies to sit in and be near their need for water that does not stink although this is unavailable.

No one is sitting. The homeowner is inside and alone.

Beyond and more visible by this point is his house. Two tall box shapes with the roof on each being a single slant. The whole structure is covered with black vertical siding to increase dominance. Inside are a number of bedrooms all with bathrooms and clever lights.

Twenty years ago the homeowner bought a forty-acre plot of wet nowhere and tore down the 1832 frame house near its edge. Then he built something of his own that is violent and a bad fit. Events of this kind happen everywhere.

In recent weeks the homeowner has undergone certain setbacks. He arrived at night without his driver and has been here for six days now without emerging.

In Manhattan his schedule and seclusion are complex. South Salem is undisturbed and what we both differently need.

From here I can see bunker-slit windows and the side of a balcony with wide views. It reaches always forward and expects grand gestures and parades. The rich have enough money to make their psychology pathetic obvious.

The homeowner has performed repeated patterns of activity indoors that have left visible hints behind his bullet-proof glass. He is a dark fish stirring phosphorescence and flicking in its tank. A three-storey drum of black siding holds a stairwell to the rear of the building. It wants to be a castle tower or else a furnace chimney. I have learned the interior floorplan. The house has open sweeps and sightlines of grandeur except for the uppermost floor which is full of segregation and mean proportions.

Red front door like a scream.

I think it is a joke by the homeowner that he made sure a terrible place looks terrible.

Even though I am close enough to be under its shade the building smells of nothing. It tastes like the air above a deep pit dug ready.

I am continuing to walk like Albert Lockwood who is a man with lower back pain and benevolence. I further embed his habits and information while moving and this makes me a feedback loop and is good. Albert takes Percocet daily with food for pain relief but not too much. He angles his head like someone regretful he will be causing inconvenience. Albert Lockwood is realistic and explanatory without intrusion. He is aware the homeowner is wealthy in the way that does not like to hear small people. That kind of wealth does not know when stories end or when to laugh or what is funny and this causes bewilderment irritation and subsequent discourtesy.

I smooth my beard which is a typical gesture. The bristles are salt and pepper and mean I look older than I am. My glove makes a strange noise against the hair. I cannot identify where I heard it before although I know I have. The sound is to do with dogs or horses.

The red door shines at the top of five granite steps and overlooks a blank tarmac circle.

I pause for a count of three before I climb. I have an orderly pulse and temperature.

I do not remove my cap when I ring the doorbell and look at the camera. I am not a servant and have expertise. I am clear about my status. If I narrow my eyes a little this indicates bashful awareness that my face seems broad flat unintelligent in pictures

The homeowner opens the slab of redness after my ringing and pausing for three cycles. He seems slow motion in a chemical-inflicted way. Baby blue cashmere sweater worn over bare skin and $500 jeans and bare feet. Very cut hair. Eternal tan of a travelling Caucasian. Against a white shirt he would look beach-front but also moisturised exfoliated. He is maintenance. He does not seem fifty-eight.

He is trying for poise but his body is disagreeing. A kind of unintentional grey rime has gathered at both corners of his mouth

My speed is operational on a good level and has good force and my natural real name is Albert Lockwood of GSS and I have appropriate eye contact. I hold out my real barcoded genuine ID badge for him to see. I sound just a hint Southern and give him sentences and patience he can lean on.

He looks at me as if I am a screen showing cartoons in a distant room.

I am very usual and apologise about how perhaps I have parked my real GSS truck in a wrong spot but I provide no pause for his response opinion because it is more important we both remember that I rang him earlier today. On the phone I was a reassurance balancing a moderate alarm and it is necessary for him to accept both and move on sequentially through our process. He is various kinds of slow and contains petulant resistance and keeps standing in his opened doorway which is no longer what I require.

Earlier today is very distant for him.

I smile with big dog ruefulness and run through the high vital nature of my call and the significance of other calls he has received during this calendar month prior from a Detective Martinez of the NYPD Criminal Enterprise Investigative Division. This was in relation to stolen art dating back to a theft-related situation of 1995. I am regretful but pressing. I say excellent words about Martinez and the ways in which he does not exist and has not ever. I am clear about the ongoing threat of a fraudster with already gathered knowledge and appetites for escalating additional frauds or thefts or financial or informational attacks.

I sound entirely human. I am being human.

I tell the homeowner that I am unable to vouch for his safety.

I lean into my gentleness of manner and think I am beginning to smell his skin. I state the necessity of my access to his computers and also his router and repeaters and VPN and also hard wiring and CCTV systems and also other places where electrical badness happens and where I can assist. I live to assist. Maintenance.

The homeowner seems relieved and concerned both simultaneous and in the wrong places. I note I have induced enough compliance to mean that he mentions where I will find necessary items.

I wait for a count of five.

He looks at me.

I smile.

And then he does and does and does step one foot back and then the other and swings round to lead me inside his home. He adds immediate impatience because his income means nothing should ever happen without his will inciting it. He has a nasal way of saying *Ifyoumust* which is a call that identifies his species. Because he is a bully I let him bully. This helps his mindset become more stupid with gladness at winning a contest between men.

I act like a subservient entity that has suddenly noted the quality of the engineered maple plank flooring as fitted throughout. I become tentative surprised and kneel to unlace my boots. He tells me *Ohthatisnotnecessary* in a voice people save for staff. I can feel he likes very much my bending at his feet and exposing the back of my naked neck to his ideas of violence.

I am laborious with my fingers and almost begin to remove my gloves. I tug at one finger for a while before I just continue as I am.

By the time I have finished my little struggles and am standing in my socks the homeowner is impatient to lead me along and inwards so that I can finish causing interruption and then disappear. He precedes my big harmless self at almost a trot and I follow and tell him *Whatafinehouse whatafinehouse*. This is not identifying. This is like a lyre bird singing the call of a chainsaw. I am the wrong thing.

Inhaling the corridor makes my mouth greasy with Italian soap and sex last night.

I stare ahead and study the homeowner and how soft his sweater must be and how his feet strike the floor as if they are surprised by it and how his nape hair is wet with sweat. He has made his body stupid as well as his mind.

I think how I could tell him that my truck is the right truck but has wrong plates. I do not think this would imply enough to make him run.

I am not the lyre bird. I am the chainsaw.

When the homeowner passes the head of his drum staircase I stocking feet silent run at him. I rushrush hard and brace my left arm across my body. For a moment I enjoy the feeling that I could be running strange like a green plastic child thing with black shark eyes.

My forearm shoves across his back. I hinge my fist out and forward to give him twist in how he falls.

Never push with hands. Hand marks are diagnostic.

This will be an innocent death. Hands were never involved and will leave no bruises.

I watch and then listen while he angle jumbles down inside the curl of his bare maple stairs. During this his voice makes a small noise that is like a wet cough. I follow him and am stepping at a mild pace. Rushing makes mistakes.

My cap is still in place. I am composed. I am Albert Lockwood who died in a sadly housefire and was prior to that a true staff member of GSS and real licensed security guard endowed with useful symbols. I enjoyed being Albert. He was like a holiday.

It is easy to have an identity. They can be shallow or deep. I go in and I go out as necessary. I make arrangements. I am maintenance. Other people who are only themselves and make no efforts are never as convincing.

Being Albert Lockwood lasted for almost a year. I grew him in place and became fully recognised and equipped. I used him twice for other purposes while he was alive. Then the fire. I do not think specifically about the arrangements involved with that.

This afternoon is farewell for Albert and his final celebration and finest hour.

Albert and I see the homeowner heaped at the stairfoot. Inside my gloves we are holding hands happy. The homeowner still has breath although it is thick. He is alive but with no purpose.

Chaos is hard for people. When you put them inside it they do not cope and have no solution for it that arrives in time to help them.

He is mostly on his face and knees but then struggle rolls to a kind of lying half on his back. There is something wrong with one of his arms and touching it starts him more alert. His blood is making his forehead like the red cap on a plastic child monster requesting traffic safety which is a very funny coincidence. He begins blinking and staring and sees me. I smile down at him and he expects that I will be human and assist.

At these times the people become whatever plaintive child they were and I have to watch.

More than one kind of trauma happens.

I see the homeowner remember I must have pushed him and he appears to feel very bad and piteous about this and he opens his mouth to say something which is when I lean in and catch him fast and use the intranasal syringe.

I press down the plunger and more than is needful of the substance is vapourised and goes quick and then quickly traceless into his blood. His brain and circulation fill and then both of them call to his heart and make it kick and kick too much and stop.

This is very strange for him. He has never died before.

As a result of this success I am almost finished with being here.

I train hard and fight easy which is Alexander Vasilyevich Suvorov telling anyone who cares to learn the path towards survival.

I am prepared for success.

The homeowner has become a credible body with natural signs

and circumstances. He is a man who was walking downstairs when he took an intoxicated tumble that caused his heart attack or else perhaps vice versa. Either order of events was most unlucky.

I can leave soon in the golden empty time between the bootsmen packing up and heading off and the other homeowners driving back in for their peace that is away from the city. The light will be dusk and confusing. The sunset glare will aid me.

I forget the necessary terrible task because it has been completed. I walk to the basement room that stores the camera information and make sure it is retrospectively glitched and will present a month of valueless fragments. I climb back up to the ground floor while being careful to step over the issue lying at the stairfoot. I avoid the fluid gathered now. When I can no longer see the issue it stops existing because my job was a good job well done.

I walk into what the homeowner used as an office and perform careful glove actions to make copies of his hard drives and also to open his phone and its interesting lists inside and its images which I do not need to see now.

There will be more lists and images. I erase nothing. His full culpability should be found when I am not here. This will overshadow the perfectly natural loss of a human being who fell downstairs while their habits and heart betrayed them. Rumour proliferation online regarding his demise will undermine all accurate hypotheses.

I do not think about the homeowner and his information because I cannot kill him again.

I am everything clean and finished.

Once I have driven Albert Lockwood out to Norwalk I will let him say goodbye.

I am almost back at my boots when I hear this small noise that is extremely identifiable happening upstairs. Someone has creep listened to events and stayed careful still and then been less careful.

I smooth my breath.

Any plan must have other plans inside that will rise to keep it safe.

I take the next plan. I take my not wonderful but small enough to conceal Ruger out of my pocket and start silent walking towards the stairwell.

Albert Lockwood didn't carry a gun today. I must be someone else already.

I soft cautious move into the drum again and this time head upwards. The stairs have a clockwise twist and so favour defenders according to mediaeval architectural tradition. Right-handed defence logic is against me.

My heartbeat is healthy and useful. I am at risk and am seeking to control that risk having identified its source.

I deploy my mirror in my palm to check options around blind spots and solutions for exit to the landing.

The situation becomes fast clear although with possible deception.

I ease my head round the angle to reassess. I live eyes see my problem crouching on the passageway floor. Her body posture and facial expression suggest I don't have to search further.

I will be abandoned solitary.

And I should have known.

Her presence was very possible to guess.

She was always here. She did not visibly leave or arrive during my surveillance because she is always here in the way that electricity and water are always here and ready for instant use.

She is huddled near the threshold of a room. That is as far as she has managed to retreat in response to my incursion. She is maximum alert animal awareness and my pause and transition into stockinged whisper foot noises on the stair were enough to alert her. Her situation is about being caught between two places where she does not want to be. She is fear rejecting both me and the room. She is ten maybe eleven apart from her eyes and her mouth.

I should have predicted her presence but did not in actuality anticipate that she or some other girl would be here. This was a failure.

I am still calculating impacts and solutions.

She watches me when she thinks I won't see and is deeply gaze alerted like a prey species. I am something sudden that she cannot understand but she is used to that.

I move smooth out from the staircase and very undemonstrative and placid and I notice that she takes my gun for granted as if it is only medium unusual and maybe inevitable.

I pace quietly as far from her as possible and quickly survey the other rooms which all have beds but are not quite bedrooms. Each unit is spartan but with disgusting elements that I give no further attention to because I still can only kill him once.

The girl maintains continuous observations of my search pattern and I know is tastingtasting who I am and what I will do. At some previous time the homeowner expressed his unlimited will by putting her in a Lolita anime sailor costume. This continues to mean she is his joke.

I still can only kill him once.

I have no other kill plans.

She has only seen Albert and not me. She could access continued survival on that basis.

But I have no way to solve her that would not undo my mission success newly completed. I am experiencing mental difficulty.

I can feel her puzzlingpuzzling what I will do to her. My doubt indicators are increasing her anxiety. She is experiencing non-immediate cruelty as stressful. She is weary baffled.

There is much less than an hour before I have to leave.

If she is still here in a living way after I go she will surely experience cruelties at the hands of implacable legal and youth care systems within minimal conceptions of what is victimhood. In any realistic scenario it will be very hard for her to thrive.

She will be my of coursely witness.

And at risk.

And I need a solution

And I do not know.

I do not know.

I trained hard to fight easy. I trained with Prav. I trained with the now old man Prav who was persistent clarity of mission and immoveable devotion to objectives.

I know his solution for this problem.

I am not him.

I am like him.

I am not him.

I am like him.

I step within her panic trigger distance and the girl slither darts into a far corner of what is no doubtly the room where she was kept. Bed with purple sheets and purple carpet and sex art on the wall and sex pictures and no window and a ceiling mirror.

The girl looks at me once as if the room is her fault. She is watching from under a panic wave and lost in distortions of depth and airless liquid.

I shake my head careful – *No this is his fault.*

This is his room and not hers. All these rooms are his room.

She is not responsible and the gaze of vengeance should be powerless to see her.

She is a thing with knees bent up in front of her and bound round by her arms and blonde hair over her eyes. Tight white and pink sailor suit that would not fit someone accustomed to eating food. There is glitter pink gel in her hair that is partly undisturbed. At first I think her bare feet are dirty but then I recognise that they are bruised.

I only did kill him once.

I can feel that Albert is looking at her in predictable dismay and I do not want him here because he is normal and will not stand it well.

She is thin. I see additional bruises and marks of binding and blood spots and the signals and signs of a man who was various bad absences collated into an absence of restraint.

I can only kill anyone once.

I am unsure if she understands me until I ask her if she has other clothes and a task-related resignation presses her hard down against the sex joke deep-pile carpet.

I am sweating. Albert is a burden because of his emotions and the tug of them under my skin.

I shake my head and tell her that I mean clothes she can wear that are comfortable and warm.

She stares.

This is taking too long.

Albert and I may not manage to form situation-appropriate aims and objectives. He is in my way.

Albert's face looks at her and gentle smiles.

And then she runs and I let her. Albert lets her.

She dives past me in the manner of a body used to avoiding the long and bad reach of arms and also accustomed to subsequent penalties.

I watch her go.

Albert watches her.

I note how she begins in a hunch on all-fours and then jolt runs in a way that shows how much her feet hurt.

Albert and I follow as she ricochets down the stairs. I hear when she stumbles and then I experience happiness when she saves herself and continues her flight. I am moving fast but am not exactly in pursuit. She has tripped over my boots and righted herself by the time I reach the ground floor. I watch her haul at the front door and then shine with the large instant of surprise at her world being unlocked.

Albert puts on my boots and I instinctive initiate my checklist so that I can be sure I am ready to definitively clear the location. I have several hours of grace before outside surveillance on the house glitches into spasmodic but increased usefulness.

The homeowner had no security coverage of his grounds. Stupid. Or another thrill. An edge to rub.

The sun is dropping and the dark is spilling sideways in strips across the landscape. I can appreciate this aesthetically while noting how far the girl has progressed in her flight. I pull the red door snug until it locks. The sound of doors closing is an established forgetfulness cue.

I keep my straight right arm low by my leg with the Ruger.

The girl is still trying to run on stones and thorns with bruised feet. Saving one thing hurts another. This is not a new discovery for either of us.

I feel the landscape tilt while Albert realises that the homeowner may have stood enjoying the view from his steps and watched her try to flee him in much the same way as us. That might have been part of his entertainment schedule.

We are down by the lake when I draw almost level with her. The reek of the water is repulsive and death reminiscent. Albert is sweating and bewildered. I am surprised when the girl halts what is left of her evasion by going inside the fantasy New England boat-house and leaving the door ajar.

She knew that the door would be unlocked. She has purpose.

Albert wants to hurry. I ignore him.

I ignore myself.

Within the thin boathouse walls there are sounds that are animal rummaging and as if the girl out of sight is an infestation.

I walk myself slowly closer but angled on a slant away from the dark of the swung-open doorway.

Then I stop because there are voices. There are two voices. I hear blurs of speech and gaps that contain small dins of move-ment and *pisztoly* and *őrült*. There are definitely two female voices speaking and saying fuss these two female and young voices *varjú*. Two whisper threads I can feel on my face.

So they are Hungarian.

The girl from the bedroom emerges with one arm leading and her head and shoulders next. Her expression is shattering into kinds of pain fear but also an attempt at blank control. She had some hiding place inside and is now wearing sweat pants to suit a larger body mass and trainers and a hoody beneath a cheap fleece jacket. The visual effect is overall random and has an atmosphere of poverty scavenging. The clothes are wrinkled as if they have been compressed in a small space for a long time but are clean.

She is followed by another girl who is another blonde. The homeowner had a great deal of choice in companions but consistent desire drives. The new girl is in another crumpled iteration of sweat pants hoody trainers fleece. Her face is mainly bone and skull topography. I do not think she intends to survive any more. She has jerk limbs like a dead thing animated.

The bedroom girl looks at me. She is holding a thin gym bag close with both arms. Real people have belongings. She is starting to hope about realness. I am not ever what anyone hopes.

I tell her *Jöjjön*!

They flinch. I am identifying as helpful communicative but they are reading me as part of some previous trafficking and blindfolding and beating and lying and abduction scenario.

I do nothing and let Albert be soft docile empathetic. I express peaceful non-dominance.

I repeat *Jöjjön* with a helpful degree of English speaker difficulty. I put the Ruger in my pocket. I slip my hands flat into my utility belt as if it is something to do with simple work and handicrafts.

Jöjjön! Albert might be close to tearful and tips back his hat as displacement. The emphasis is part of his rising panic and not aggression. He looks puzzled and then is very careful about pronouncing *Gyere velem*.

This releases words from both of them because if I can tell them to come with me and still not have harmed them I might be helpful. I might be from a kind place.

I am not from anywhere.

This may be a leaked signal overriding but I am anyway turning my back to them and walking on towards my car while the daylight ends itself.

I hear their whispers as if they are arguing and then two pairs of feet begin to follow me with one pair sounding like damage and the other like pointlessness.

I am already in my truck before they reach the parking lot and exhibit fear of my headlights. I peripheral vision see them sudden wary panicked. I don't turn to them or gesture. Albert maybe wants to but I press his thinking flatflat and uninfluential.

My lack of eagerness persuades them and they limp across to my passenger door. I think the bedroom girl is waiting to know if she will sit up front like a person or back on the truck bed under cover like a cargo. The boathouse girl is probably in her own death dream and wavers while she stands.

Ending them here is something I cannot do.

I reach over slowslow bored slow and pop open the passenger door.

The indoor girl pushes her companion up the high steps and into my cab. This is kind because it is assistance and not kind because it is using someone as a barrier for safety. It will be harder for me to touch the bedroom girl with the boathouse girl in the way.

The boathouse girl smells like a neglected dog. The scent of the other is more complicated and disturbing as she moves and fastens two safety belts and keeps on holding the gym bag hard tight obsessional. She closes the door softly and the cab fills with wrongness. I am swallowing sweet fear stink and mildew and animal dirt and other metal plastic makeup semen sweat combinations.

I begin to drive.

My route out is designed for one person.

I am unable to make consequential decisions at this time.

My motion towards the top glove box makes both girls shiver and their fearsweat stinks. The box holds two half-litre bottles of water and a power bar. I open it and hook out the bottle I'd already started. The water doesn't feel clean in my mouth any more because of the air being so coloured.

The truck has progressed out all innocent along Eskuyas Mill Road for some minutes when I cap the water again and hold it out to my side. The boathouse girl does not quite have the energy to withdraw fully from my arm. Recoiling is not among her remaining instinctive assets.

The bedroom girl takes the bottle and drinks angry with thirst. There is some but not much left for her companion who is not a friend and only the other thing which is a product of survival and combat intimacy and shame.

I reach for the power bar which is for fast energy high calories and protein, but I am not hungry because Albert has a tense stomach when faced with distress. I start to hold out the bar and the bedroom girl leans in to snatch it.

I hear the wrapper torn open with domestic and usual sounds that are inappropriate in our case and I thread the truck along the hairpins and away.

The sound of the indoor girl is like a racoon perhaps, something like a racoon biting and chewing nocturnally among refuse.

And this is when I should be already far and away on the uninvolved side of the hill and clearclearclear free. Instead I am still complicated while I loop north and deeper into New York before heading south for Connecticut. And my car is full of complication.

In the dimness to my right the bedroom girl is a soft shape. She repeats motions with her hands. I wonder if this is some stress superstition ritual and it takes me moments to realise she is now feeding the other girl bit by bit like cherishing a bird.

There is hardly another vehicle about until I reach the highway and slip in anonymous.

I do not decide what I will do. I let time flow.

I hear the boathouse girl refuse more scraps. The bedroom girl swallows everything left and is so anxious with needing that she coughs and then wretches. The other girl moans in reply. This seems a way of communicating between them as if both are familiar with retching and moaning and are making these noises here now for the usual reasons while also remembering multiple other nightmare occasions.

I lift out the unopened bottle and the bedroom girl grabs it with a saliva wet hand.

I am offering kindness which is a way to calm somebody. Making efforts towards the comfort of another person means that your harming them thereafter would be absurd.

No one is safe until they understand that human beings are very regularly absurd.

I am not clear which girl begins crying and then both are sobbing keening drowning and fighting to hold each other. I take care not to accelerate beyond the legal speed. I take care that I and Albert do not howl scream laugh or respond in other ways.

Slowly the girls tire themselves with stress reactions. Transition shocks and temperature changes and the sudden sugar spike make them eventually sleep for five then ten and then more minutes. They fill the dark with little breaths in the way alive people do. I am nevertheless able to drive as if they are not with me and to think about the time when that will be the actual case.

Miles happen underneath us and the time rubs like grease against my windows.

I make a decision.

Survival and effective action are reliant on decision making.

I must abhor both ambivalence and pathetic inaction.

The night moves on with me and I drive until the turn-off for Darien which I take.

The Darien railroad station has a park right opposite.

I slow and then pull up beside the park and the grass and low cover and all alone trees and thick darks that it offers.

Our stillness causes both girls to jerk full awake and I feel how they watch me with intensity. They are waiting for the terrible thing to happen although they do not know which terrible thing it will be.

I say to the bedroom girl *Beszélsz angolul? English. You speak English?*

This makes her nod. I assume that spoken English has been part of the inflictions undergone and has seeped in while no one intended that kind of education.

She begins crying again in a way that means she learned English before she came here and had a plan that was meant to be good. Albert is upset for her.

Afterwards I drive to South Norwalk which is the next charted point in my self-extraction. I park the truck in front of the auto wrecking yard as intended. I am still sweating. I walk away in the cold sting of the night and leave my keys in the ignition. Albert and I will never be here or use the truck again.

I walk carefree aimless along a preselected route that edges east towards the waterfront. I enter an area that is dark yards inside chain-link fences and rat bait and concrete block industrial units and dead spaces and dead cars and small houses with TV blue washing up against the windows.

I walk until I am very clean washed.

While I move I use adventitious shadow cover to take the pack-away duffel bag from my inside pocket and then take off my bomber jacket and roll fold it into the bag. My cap goes in with it.

I stand behind a tree clump to unbutton the shirt Albert wore and take it off. Beneath is my T-shirt with formed and wrapped and tacked with thread false stomach. When I tug and rip the threads I release a folded-up fleece sweatshirt and knitted hat. Inside the hat are flimsy running shoes. I put my shirt in the duffel bag and hold the other items.

I cut the fat from Albert and I am myself which seems odd funny and as if I am the outcome of a surgical procedure. As if I am the cure for his condition.

I walk with arms bare in the frost until I hurt. Then I have to dress again and preserve efficiency.

I step between a dumpster and a wall to slit the sides of my work trousers and pull them off and leave only the tight jogging pants I wore as underthings. I cut my laces, step out of my boots, slip into the running shoes that are good enough to suit a late-night jogger.

The boots and patrol belt which are all that remain of Albert go into the duffel bag. I no longer share his concerns. I can forget him.

I swing the duffel bag across my body and trot into the light like a man who just took a piss but who is running again now and covering ground well and normally.

Nearer the estuary the houses swell and draw back from the streets. They overlook seasonal leaf colour and are near golf opportunities.

One block from the water a blue Honda Civic is parked by a thick hedge and opposite a half-finished renovation.

I lean against it as if I have done my miles and can hop step in place for my cool-down with agile boxerly glory display and balanced protein but soft hands.

Then I unlock the Honda and get in.

I drive past the marina and day cruisers wrapped in covers in case they get wet. Next I slot into my preselected car park at the back of an office block and walk away from the street on to rough ground. I step careful over the dim terrain unsteadiness and reach an edge of the water before I throw the duffel bag and watch it fly in the blurred light. Then it lands and sinks beneath the surface.

I begin being the next man and my shoulders are looser and my driving style will be slick efficient discreet. I turn smart on my heel and get back to the car. It is obedient when I turn the ignition.

I forget the woods as I drive. I forget the hawk flight silence as I drive. I forget the wet hand brushing mine and the hunger sounds as I drive.

I forget opening my truck door so the cold leaps in. I forget the bedroom girl taking my cash roll because $1,025 will be something she needs and it will get both of them some way forward before they go wrong again and I have another roll much the same and no time to spend it.

I forget the two of them crossing the road to the railroad station where they can decide to go anywhere a train will take them for as much good as this will do in their circumstances.

As I drive it is all very easy to forget.

It might never have happened.

I won't have my normality be weaker than his obscenity.

I won't have what happens to him in my life, in my mind.

I will not stand for it.

Buster's manuscript arrived about a week into lockdown.

Just when we needed more fun…

We're still doing fine, nonetheless. Not that Paul knows it exists. Not that I have told F.L. about it.

Our days lunge past like animals in distress and are also somehow permanently stalled. Paul and I still don't have an actual TV set – no glowing anxiety aquarium insisting we stare at it while it squats in our personal space. But when I scroll past the broadcast telly online, all of the hosts and anchors are talking to us as if they're pals suddenly – solicitous and caring.

It makes me hate them. It makes me hate the adverts, too. Why wouldn't they clearly like us every day? Why would they bother only during this disaster? Somebody watching somewhere will always be having a disaster – why not always be kind?

And why wouldn't the news hosts manage to give me consistent information? That is their job. Why am I being expected to stay watchful for a micro-organism? How, exactly? And the plague is airborne, but also maybe not, and I should wash my hands, but also I shouldn't bother, and pets can get it, but no they don't, but yes they do. And wear a mask, although they might not work, only they obviously do because they're hardly new technology – we all know they work, why is that suddenly up for debate? Why do we have to doubt and – also believe – everything and nothing simultaneously, exactly when getting our information wrong might kill us?

And all kids are immune from pestilence, because…? Have the people saying this even met a child – they are delightful, but also a playpark for every infection you can imagine. And they stand too close and they touch things and chew things and are generally feral whenever they can get away with it. How could anyone believe that children won't catch and pass on yet another illness? And why doesn't anyone care? They're so delicate, the kids, we don't know what all this might end up doing to them.

But round and round the nonsense swirls – all the bad and babyish reasons for just not bothering to look after each other.

Teachers notice incoherence and fakery. In a sane world that wouldn't have to be a source of constant irritation, constant rage, constant fury.

Then again, maybe anyone who could imagine the world is sane quite possibly deserves headaches and fury.

My son and I, we're trapped here in our 500th day, or the 5,000th, 50,000th, I don't even know what day – time isn't just relative at the moment, it's hallucinatory. Nevertheless, we have not killed and devoured each other. We're okay. We're snug. We have put maximum effort into being snug, into triumphing over the Four Horsemen of the New Apocalypse – Idiocy, Cruelty, Learned-Helplessness and Fear. We disagree with any messaging that suggests pain might be what we deserve, that we should just give sugar lumps to each of the four eternally burning horses with their empty eyes and fatal riders.

I suppose the breath of any demon horse worth the name would simply braze the sugar into toffee. Double win.

Dear Lord – who are we now? What are we?

If I press my biro any harder into the legal pad, I'm going to make a hole in it...

Outrage is changing my handwriting, inventing a new font. It's making me look as dementia-besieged as old Ma.

Poor Ma. She has spent the past five years stuck in her recliner at Rosemary Lodge, facing the always-on telly. She occasionally yells and occasionally weeps and maybe sometimes knows why – and her TV has rarely said a gentle word. Too late now.

Why wouldn't broadcasters have a channel just for care homes? There could be show tunes and smiling and hits from the 60s and kind faces that suggest nothing is lost, only misplaced, only on the way back round to meet you in another form.

I label her clothes – as if she's at school – but they go missing anyway. The past, the plans for the future, the blouse with the Cluny lace collar – away they went. Her orange cardigan was a favourite and she properly mourned its passing as she didn't the passing of the lady in the room next door, the one across the corridor, the man three rooms along.

Every Sunday, I used to drive up and sit with her in the care home, which was gravy-smelling and not her home, or especially caring, but the best option I could find. The best option is still awful, is still not home and is only intermittently attentive. Its furniture and décor are coordinated according to a purplish-pink palette you would have to label Warm Testicle Selection.

I once said that and she laughed and those two facts may have been connected.

And perhaps it's the intimate pinky shades that have a power to calm us. I'd got used to being suddenly liked for a while because she'd forgotten who I was, had forgotten her only daughter. I'd got used to the constant need for pain relief, because Ma is drug-seeking now as well as demented… Her last hospital stay involved being doped to the hairline for ease of care and she's never got over it.

Tiny Ma – they made her a junkie.

It's all such a mess. And she sort of knows she's fading sometimes, but doesn't understand the ugliness of the new ways to die.

I hope that's true.

Little, tiny Ma.

You only let me touch your skin and hold your hand when I'm not your daughter. And even the air hurts you sometimes, and sometimes it's the rub of labels, the weight of your dress on your collarbone. Your body is barely keeping out the world.

There goes the biro again – straight through.

I'm going to end up stabbing myself in the thigh.

Ma with her white hair spread and fine and silvered against the cushion – I remember that. If they'd had time to wheel her along for the full wash and change and MOT, she'd rest in her reclining throne and look like a queen in Tolkien.

Sometimes I'd brush her hair for her and she'd smile.

And the TV presenters would ignore us, would talk about purchase prices and dole out the sacrament of anxiety: *eat, drink, for this is the concern of your betters and you should have it, too.*

I give it a week or so and they'll stop caring about us all over again. And that will enrage me all over again.

But I won't take it out on my child. Mothers are meant to love their kids.

Paul and I will stay all right. I am doing top-flight parenting and he is doing high-class son-ing. Either that, or we're bathing in each other's Stockholm Syndrome. But isn't that the key to any happy family?

He is very much better at this Plague Time than me. On some days he does take a few turns around the anxiety spiral, but the only outward sign of it is a slight frown and some tidying of cupboards. Every cupboard we have is far beyond tidy now: alphabetical socks, colour-graded shirts, bright shoes in ranks according to weight and usefulness. Across the world, people are realising that locked-in survivors of zombie apocalypses wouldn't be screaming and fighting – they'd be polishing surfaces, ranking tinned goods according to date and country of origin, dusting books. Our kitchen is fit for impromptu surgery.

I can feel myself tensing to withstand an outburst, but he doesn't do outbursts. My strange and peaceful son – he sometimes goes very quiet, but there's no doom in the silence, no threat.

When free-floating horror has me braced like a horrified spider in the top corner of a room he goes especially quiet and fills the teapot, gives me his *I'm here for you, you mad bitch* face. I'm paraphrasing.

His patience is almost never abrasive and I almost never poke it to make up for my inadequacies. Really – almost never. And he coaxes me down gently – should it be necessary – from whichever ceiling with all my arachnid limbs intact.

If he was thirteen or fourteen, life here would be much more volcanic – but even his hormone rushes back then were extremely unextreme. I try not to assume that's because he has watched me and seen how pointless and self-destructive catastrophising can be.

At least I don't swear, even though it's hard not to. Many things about being British are an invitation to swearing. I imagine if I ever did start howling out blasphemies and sex verbs and names of body parts, I would not ever stop. It would constitute another full-time job.

My beige vocabulary is a product of my vocation, but also I don't want to sound like Ma. I won't have big red words being screamed in my kitchen; I won't have anyone weathering the impacts of names and names and names. That won't happen with me and my son.

So I sit outside alone and write out my fury.

We've reached the umpteenth of April, although it could be March or December – months are just a theory now. And it's night. I'm writing this under the darkishness of London's sky equivalent. The heat keeps on, in the way that somehow March is keeping on – the shock of March and the regulations and instructions and the beginning of the deaths… Maybe it won't ever stop.

I've not had the time to write in a while. Or maybe I've not had the courage, or just the right weight of rage. I needed the Goldilocks weight of it, neither too little, nor too much. Too little and I potter about, watch movies, don't come near my notepad. Too much and the fury is like arthritis: I think of the dying and dying and dying, the unstoppable and unprevented dying, and it locks me in my chair.

And then there's Buster.

Buster's confession, his diary, his excuses for himself were left in a plain brown envelope, leaning outside my street door. He knows my address, then, and has made a point of letting me know and of infecting the pavement outside my home.

Like all very unclean and terrible things, the envelope didn't get harmed, or lost, or stolen. Nothing written on the package, not even my name, but I knew it was meant for me and guessed who had left it before I opened it.

Spells and curses are like that – they always reach you.

Ma used to say that in heaven and hell nobody has an address. She was, for a while, composing a kind of *Fodor's Guide to the Afterlife*. It was her way of preparing for the wrong disaster, the day on which her body died. She hadn't imagined her mind would leave first. So, like most of us, she wasted time fretting about risks that weren't too pressing, while the real problems walked right in, unobserved.

Hell never fails to be delivered.

Still, this is my story – it doesn't belong to terrible men, not even one. This is mine and is about me and is about all the people that I love.

The monsters have to be identified. We need to learn their natures, but no more than that. I never want him close enough to taste, not again.

That seemed like a very obvious thing to write and some Stiltskins can be obvious, revolting from the very start, someone to keep away from. Still, they stay dangerous – they're the type to gather power and violence, a following that can extend their reach, evaporate the distance between them and the normality they want to break.

But they do less harm than the Stiltskins who are so very good at presentation and so believable. They offer you hand-tailored attention, affection, love, the perfect fit. Only it's not perfection, it's just a methodology, a foot in the door. As soon as they're all the way inside with you, the door is locked and the Stiltskin has the key.

Eventually, you might get free. I did. But it's baffling how often you (by which I mean *me*) end up being fooled again by other Stiltskins. They damage your hope, other things, too. So the next Stiltskin finds you and the next. They know the trick of opening you up and walking in.

So you (by which I mean *me*) become solitary. Your other options (by which I mean *my* other options) seem only a series of possible betrayals. This is how they use your own love against you – and love is the strongest thing you have, you never want it to be against you. Your true story gets overtaken by the bad endings they prefer.

I think it's like the kinds of torture designed to make your body hurt itself.

I read about torture when I'm depressed. *See*, I tell myself, *things could be worse.*

But all of the books just remind me of Stiltskins.

I'd like my story to be the kind in which a mad king is toppled and the citizens rejoice and good-hearted people spend the first day of their victory lying in a forest on soft moss, inhaling the leaf scents and the honeysuckle and the peace.

But the Stiltskins make you wary of peace.

I'm away from the monster and the dungeon and the castle. I can relax. Only relaxing feels horrible, like waiting for the next disaster when you'd rather get it over with. The anticipation's hard to take. And at least your usual fight or flight panic is stimulating. Peace, it's dull. Isn't it dull, this relapse into civilised dignity that you've prayed for? And who's that over there? He seems to be a surly woodcutter with wolf ears and long teeth. Promising, promising. I must give him my house key and bank account details. Or what about this guy with the massive knife and the gore-stained shirt. He seems fascinating.

Stiltskins make you forget that disasters are not always necessary.

Comfort may not be the tension before your next, worse pain. In your home, in your job, in your government – every Stiltskin wants to make you scared of ease and liberty. They long for the chaos that helps them prosper and want you to long for it with them.

Living in Britain and the world in 2020 is – how shall I put this? – a little triggering for people like me.

I used to be able to summarise myself as follows:

Me (by which I mean me) = (absent father + unreachable mother + unpleasant incident + Buster + Bad Man) = Fortress of Solitude.

But then Paul happened and made my equation much more complicated.

Now I have the possibility of F.L. as well.

Me = Fortress of Solitude.

Me + Paul = Fortress of Hypervigilant Cosiness and Tomfoolery.

Me + F.L. = I don't know.

Me + Paul + F.L. = I don't know.

F.L. has opinions about my endless doomy watchfulness and resigned expectation of harm.

Who's laughing now, though, Mr Cheerful? Here we are in Plague

World with underlying species collapse and Climate Apocalypse? Who's looking sensible and proportionate?

But also, he is right – some disasters come whether we despair or not. We face them better when we carry hope. I understand the theory. He persists in his optimism.

And he is concerned for my well-being without many signs of overbearing micromanagement. He keeps sending me bath oils and scented diffuser thingies because they are lady-relaxing products. I try not to think of them as wasteful and say thank you and look at the camera on my computer and not the screen so that he gets eye contact, at least.

I try to imagine him sitting by the cairn at the top of Carnan Eoin. Although it's not so high, the world lays itself down beautifully below, wide and mostly blue. I've sat there beside him with my back against the stones and seen where the water fits the air. The mainland and the islands show like bodies and limbs caught in mid-turn under fawnish and brownish blankets.

I try to imagine there is still a Goldilocks space beside him, not too big and not too small and just the shape of me. He gives me that impression. He seems extremely trustworthy.

The dream of an island and starting again and having a life that's okay – it should make me excited. But expectations tend to disappoint.

And by then I'll be stuck on an island. I suspect islands make it hard to change your mind.

Oh, Lord, it's just exhausting – the back and forth of me. I do trust F.L., and trustworthy men can be trusted. But also the worst men in the world all make you trust them. I do, but I don't. I can, but I can't. My instincts are inside out and upside down. I know that.

It's just that I have worked very hard to have no Stiltskins in my life and I have succeeded and then all one had to do was walk through the thin and unresisting air along Wicklow Street and he could find me and maybe touch paintwork that makes me happy and certainly leave me his confession. I don't want it. I don't want him out in the world and breathing and blinking and moving about the way normal humans do. He is nothing human, not in any way.

But I'm ready now. I won't be the woman observant strangers pity, not again. I won't mind what I say. I won't tiptoe between episodes of someone else's outrage and try to believe they're rational. I won't meet someone's unreasonable demands and therefore make him feel inadequate and therefore make him react.

No more of that.

F.L. is not a Stiltskin and neither is Paul.

Details – I need some nice and kind and clean details.

Back to Paul.

And hello to Paul if you ever read this.

There was an evening, perhaps five years ago, when my son and I were hugging goodnight, and here was this over-six-foot creature in boxer shorts and a pyjama top, cradling me and talking in a rumble-talking in this new version of his voice. I could feel his sound resonate – my boy with the significant low notes. A fair portion of his upper body was inclining gently into the empty space above my shoulder. And I thought something like *Ah, so that's that, then. He's on his way.* He smelled of a soap that was paired with an aftershave. He needed aftershave, my tiny boy. He even had a favourite.

And then he'd shambled off, oblivious, on his slightly ginger-furry, bony legs, probably to read about hydroelectric dams, which were his thing of the time. *There goes Paul, who will very soon be expected to do man things. I hope he picks only the ones he'll like – they'll be the good ones.*

Tall Paul's all right. He has also been known as Small Paul during the times when his extreme elevation has seemed burdensome to him. Nobody wants to be always hard centre of the school photographs, head and shoulders above the rest like the spire of a bemused and harmless church.

In his teens he became more physically exuberant. I suppose he had more and more body to exube with. His arms and legs were growing at a rate he couldn't get used to and there were frequent breakages and bumps. He took to hanging by his hands from the balcony ironwork, higher and higher until he was one storey up.

As if his arms needed stretching.

As if I needed extra panic attacks at the languidly swaying sight of him.

I got him enrolled in a circus school – of course I did. Oakwood likes creative ways to solve its problems. The bouncing and trapezing did help.

He began going for runs along canal sides to get in better shape.

I began expecting he'd be murdered and left to the grey water and the ducks. But he was fine.

There were a short few months around puberty when his quiet spells alternated with crying jags. (For a while I worried he'd start taking after me.) But I think it was really some kind of knowledge of death. And the idea of ending and losing just walked in and tipped its inevitable hat.

Paul needed time to adjust.

Don't we all?

Thank goodness the crying did not coincide with my bright idea to get Brian Scott round one Sunday afternoon and let him deliver a *chat about manly concerns*. Brian deals with Year Two, but also Physical Development.

Manly concerns left Paul unfazed and the pair of them grilled burgers in the courtyard, because masculinity likes burned protein and greasy opportunities to be poisoned by whatever meat is left uncharred.

I ate peanut butter sandwiches and did yell *Please ask if anyone horrible has done bad things to him. I don't think that anyone has, I think I would know, but…*

I will always want to guard the gate.
And I realise I can't.
No one can.
Not all the time.

And this was around the time – I deny it all – that I started asking Paul if he thought he might be gay more than once too often.

We make a joke of it now.

Our household motto: *Best to Make a Joke of Everything.*

'Mum, I'm just buttering toast the way I like. I'm missing the edges, because I like dry edges, it's not a mistake. Also – not gay.'

'Not even a bit? Bi? Non-binary? Trans? Asexual? Asexual curious? I'm here for you.'

Sometimes my love is still expressed as overbearing micromanagement. I am aware this is very annoying, but it's not illogical – not if you're me. Love that is not recognisable as love will surely not invite any of love's troubles. That's my theory.

Paul and F.L. deal with it. They let me be. I think.

Hypervigilance can be tamed and put to use. It can make a smooth-running classroom – catch each spark before it flares, address each fear. Paul mostly laughs at my fussing and gaming survival strategies. He doesn't agree that zombie movies are the truest in the world because human beings are the monsters.

Still, I always can spot where the uninfected ought to hide. Improvised barricades and hiding places, that's me. Everywhere I feel naturally at ease would be reliably zombie-proof. I once did have a row about my *complete paranoia* during the final, perfectly reasonable, preparations for a school trip to, of all places, Göttingen. Paul did the adult thing about it afterwards, knocked on my door to give me a hug at 2am.

I am one of the generation that forced its children to be the grown-ups. They may save us yet.

And meanwhile, they are surprisingly, even shamingly tolerant.

Paul lives with the fact that some people see impending chaos in an unwashed mug. During certain periods of their lives they have been used to chaos appearing in mid-air from nothing and hurting them, so perhaps it is not unreasonable if they're twitchy control freaks. Yes, those people should just concentrate on relaxing because they are safe behind a sky-blue wall with honeysuckle all around. But then they get big brown envelopes from sad monsters.

And that makes it harder to be happy.

Even though people like that try to be happy in the ways that all sorts of people try to be happy, and good luck to them. Unless they're Stiltskins.

And we work on our patter, Paul and I, our double act – no audience needed or in sight.

'You have no other secrets to share, my one and only son? No troubling group accidental murders perpetrated somewhere in a bayou one summer with a ragtag selection of flawed acquaintances?'

'Nah-uh. Haven't run amok with a broadsword at an improvised donkey joust. Haven't battled super-intelligent squid in a flooded tube station and have not then accidentally released their resentful children into the local reservoir.'

'You do have to plan for the sequel.'

'Always. You have to plan so you can stick around for years and years. Then you come back as a hologram and then as an AI upload. Eternal.' I recall him saying that because he was too vehement. We both want to live a lot, these days – it's right under our skins like shrapnel. Every now and again, a sharp little piece of our need works its way up and out.

I didn't manage a comeback and so Paul moved on smoothly to telling me, 'All well.'

I have compacted a number of conversations here – the flavour of who we are – but I'm not being misleading. We like the talking, the fine-tuning of jokes – we like doing things our way.

All well is one of Paul's verbal ticks now. I don't remember when it started. At some point my clever boy realised he needed to chime out a night watchman's reassurance – *All well*. When I hear it, I believe it. I think he knows that. And I wish I hadn't made it necessary. He knows that, too.

'Anyway, we don't have a local reservoir.'

'We must, mustn't we? We have water.'

'Ah, my innocent, minute son. We are London. We have a concept we agree to call water, or a water-like substance enriched with additional treats such as lead and other people's hormones, and we pay for its leaky glories accordingly.'

When he leaves home – and only a world disaster has prevented him from being gone already – I wonder what will I do? With whom will I talk nonsense? F.L. is the obvious answer and wants to be the obvious answer. I think I want him to be that, too.

It's hard, though, moving from one double act to another. Wise without Morecambe – that never worked.

F.L. has his own style.

He has rhythms I don't expect, but they're not bad.

Or I'm simply a mother facing abandonment by her long-shanked offspring and willing to settle for anyone.

I mistrust myself.

That's only fair – I mistrust everyone.

Paul does not. My son has this way of continuing simple manual tasks while speaking that makes him seem both a happy amateur and tradesmanlike. He might be the hero in an old-school adventure, peacefully varnishing his dinghy, or snipping at a rose bush before spending the rest of the plot liaising with French partisans, or rescuing children marooned in hostile mountains, or deserts, or so forth. Paul just enjoys doing things – the nice things and the good things – he seems to avoid the rest. He's all there, all at once – entirely arrived – not split up into bits that worry forward into the future, or resurrect and flee bits of the past. He never seems to wonder who he is.

I'm like a bag full of broken kaleidoscopes, but I have produced a person with the knack of being unified.

I suspect, he was there in the womb already faintly humming to himself, pottering, building a spine, forming eyes and ears and fingers, checking that his heart valves worked – getting ready to set sail, to have adventures.

Details.

Odd that I'm noting details of my son.

I think I'm the most likely one to leave.

And then you could read this and see how I looked at you. Would that be possible? Would you understand the ways I love you? Would that help?

Will you want to remember the patter, the back and forth?

'When I was at school, nail varnish would mean you'd be banned from a career in the civil service. Or was it the RAF…?'

'Nail varnish is a human right, Mum. I am expressing myself, not my orientation. Girl things for girls and boy things for boys is so twentieth century… I'm still boring and straight.'

'First you won't be a doctor or a lawyer, now you won't be gay… How am I to bond over facials with all the other proud mothers, or tormented mothers, or maybe mothers offended in religious ways about human nature… Why can't you be a source of *drama*?'

'Facials make you claustrophobic.'

There are times when I undoubtedly irritate him.

He'll show me the white of his eyes and say, 'I want to be ostentatiously tolerant.'

'To make up for hating most of the neighbours – and all of the guys who hang around outside the pub?'

That's not fair of me – we both find it hard to like many of our neighbours. We think badly of the trust-fund stoners and the business suits and the business-casual Creatives who use adult scooters and apparently all have wildly piercing laughs. We especially do not treasure the meat-necked pub stragglers who used to blight our pre-lockdown small hours, leaving fag ends and dead glasses and dollops of vomit all the way down to the patch of pavement we think of as ours. They fought and grumbled like schoolgirls about love. They yelled in ways that were too angry and too sad.

And I loved Paul's nail varnish. He wore a trademark shade that he mixed up himself very carefully using a colour wheel to create much the same purple brown as his eyes. Red, yellow, blue and glimmer lilac.

I also wore it in solidarity. Not that decent nails survive even until lunchtime when you're teaching – and you'll keep them trimmed short if you have any sense. No fluid a child can produce should ever lodge under your nails.

Paul was an Oakwooder – reduced rates for staff – and so I think nobody much noticed that his fingers all ended in sparkles for a year or so. His generation is not obsessed about the boundaries between one kind of person and another, isn't utterly freaked out by blurred lines, or the smell of exotic food drifting down their high street. Even talking women don't seem to be a threat. They don't mind seeing love of various kinds. I mean, some of them are little bastards (look – I managed to write *bastard* – and again) but they do well.

In general, I want to believe that they do well.

I'm sure the mean and nasty little world we're all being encouraged to make will push in to change them.

Details.

I love that you eat recklessly under-buttered toast.

I love you, Paul.

I want to keep on.

Details.

Today's morning patter involved Paul's saying, 'I'm a trainspotter. And I like Northern Soul. That's as non-socialconforming as I can manage.' He looked at me with a characteristic quick twitch of grin that girls will – my guess – already like. 'And being gay isn't non-socialconforming. Being gay is super mainstream.' He then switched to his Quoting Mother Voice. '*Not in most countries.*'

'Well, it isn't in most countries...'

Teachers, we can't help telling people things of importance.

Details.

We aim to elevate. That's not a bad thing, not necessarily bad. Some grown-ups are not discernibly grown-up – they need work.

'I could really fancy Serge Williams, though. He's got eyelashes like an alpaca.'

'Who on earth is Serge Williams? See also: *Alpaca*?'

'He's that friend Benny used to have. You gave him curry once. West Country accent because he grew up in–'

'Street. Yes. I remember. *I grew up in Street. In the street? No, in Street.* Hours of fun. And, now you mention it, amazing eyelashes. Definitely an alpaca...'

'Which are known for eyelashes, mother mine. I have made an extreme and obsessive search history about them. Perhaps I am slipping towards alpaca-focused paraphilia.'

'I would understand. I would tell hairdressers.'

'I'm your hairdresser...'

'Just now you are…' I nibbled my own, lavishly buttered toast or, as Paul puts it, *heart attack with optional marmalade.* 'You know they save your searches… What's that going to make them think of you?'

'Who they?'

'Putin minions, GCHQ, harvesters of data points.'

'International Stiltskins? They can think I perve over alpacas. I am feeding them misinformation.'

We were having a synchronised good moment, but then the ambient hopelessness swept in and derailed me. Staying upbeat with Oakwood's Acorns can leave me wobbly in other moments – even ones in which I'm liking life. 'I don't know why I'd want you to be a lawyer or a doctor – they're less popular every day… This country, this…'

We were just singing our little happy morning song – knocka-bout jollity guaranteed – and I spoiled it.

Paul just said, 'Yes, Mrs McCormick.'

But then he turned round, holding his crumb-and-not-much-buttery knife with the vaguely goofy expression I, for some reason, like to think has to do with my dad. I'm not sure, of course. I only have one photograph of my father – he's looking terrified at his wedding. Well, who wouldn't?

Paul abandoned the toast-ruining area, 'Are you worried about something?' He sat himself back down at the kitchen table before starting on the last of the damson jam. 'Let's make this entirely about you? Shall we plumb the depths of chaos together and stare at the abyss…?' Then he winked.

Lockdown created our mutual support triangle – Paul, me, dogged F.L. – Paul is the best at keeping things mutual and not all about me, me. He is not seduced by the so many chances to fix old, battered and ugly inside me. Mellow Paul, whose damson jam was made by his mother and is therefore guaranteed free from stones. Fishbones, fruit stones, rogue fragments of gravel – nothing weird will ever be in food I cook you. Hypervigilance rules in my kitchen. Cleanliness, knife safety, emergency stockpiles – I've got it all covered.

Details.

Paul swears now. I suppose he's even swearing for two, given that I can't. He began it randomly, sort of charmingly, as he gained height – imagine Bambi falling on the ice and then having a lot to say about it. Now he curses languidly, often at the news, and I feel it would be hard for anyone to take offence.

Details.

This morning he steepled his fingers and peered at me, doctorly, 'You look worried. You definitely should be worried. There's so much to worry about. You should do it more often… Let's discuss some insoluble problems and human idiocy…'

Then he waited to see which one of us would break and smile first.

He'll be all right, won't he? Paul should be all right. It's good to be in a room with him. Other people say that, not just me.

He has brown hair towards the gingerish end of the scale. It's currently nearing blonde at the tips with all of this year's too much sun. Long limbs that are mostly not clumsy any more, overtly sexy signature dance moves that are also silly and therefore a mother may overlook them. He is currently trying to put on muscle and we are even doing mother and son weight routines. The very idea of that is sort of disturbing – like being dressed in matching sweaters – and, anyway, he isn't made to be anything but wiry.

He proceeded to gnaw at his drybones toast like a creature raised in a cave, just to provoke me. 'Doesn't this worry you? Infuriate? Should I do extra knee bends and chin-ups to make amends.'

My eyes blurred a touch, but I blinked and ignored them until they calmed down. 'You like doing knee bends and chin-ups. You're part gibbon.'

'As established.'

Something caught me under the ribs for just one breath.

Keep breathing. Keep taking breaths. The thing that is a risk is also essential. Slow and sure and out and in and on, keep on.

He went back to eating with one hand, while the other rubbed my back. Good at the right touches, is Paul. I assume – and then try to forget – that might be generally true.

Girls watch him pass and he is nicely oblivious. He's polite, he can hold a conversation, he can listen, he's gentle. These are good qualities but also they make me worry. Among my worries is the one that suggests Paul's too soft and some Terrible Stiltskin will hurt him and then I will have to break her Stiltskin legs and destroy her Stiltskin belongings and burn down her Stiltskin house and then I will get arrested because I am sure to be no good at crime and to end up in some smaller and even shabbier place than Court 10.

Paul never seems to let any girl in particular get near him.

I worry that my anxiety about relationships has spread into him.

I also realise I am a wonderful example of how toxic a waste of time worrying can be.

Hopefully, I cancel myself out – an incitement to worry but also a warning example.

I caught his free hand and brought it into both of mine – like a nice egg, or a little present. 'I'm not worried about anything.' Then I flashed him my *obvious and slightly cross-eyed lie* face.

'Fibber.'

'That's right.'

I hugged him where he sat and then kissed the top of his head.

'Dear me, Paul. I hate to mention...'

'I am not going bald.'

'Keep telling yourself that.'

'Nineteen-year-olds do not go bald.'

'They might.'

'Only if they suffer a massive shock.' I could feel his big bear-ish growl being amiable through his shoulders. 'Like hearing you're getting married...?' Paul shot me a not-that-joking glance. 'You can tell me... You can tell him...'

I began thinking of a snappy comeback about how conventional and patriarchal marriage is. Then I just felt bad about myself.

Again.

Poor F.L. He waits and waits while I cycle through relaxations of my vigilance and then sudden reinterpretations of his normality as camouflage for Something Terrible. It's not my mind that does this – it's my body. I'll smile all the way through a happily yelled Zoom call from the island, feel completely in synch and then my shoulders will ratchet high and higher and swallowing will get tight and there I'll go again – strangling myself with nameless fears.

With him stuck on Colonsay, our intimacy has been easier – all those stoney and wavey and mountainy and housey urban miles in between us reassure me.

We really do talk, though. I really am thawing. I really do like it when he draws me flip books, or we swing the laptop cameras round and show each other where we are – where we would be if we were together. It's cute.

No nudity, just cute. It's the same laptop I use for school, for goodness' sake.

F.L. proves over and over that he's patient – dropped connections and poor connections and bad weather and being waylaid and marooned by a death storm – death waiting in all of those stoney and wavey and mountainy and housey urban miles. He remains fundamentally steady.

It's only that 3am will wake me up some mornings and I'll find that he has already become theoretical again – not himself, but a series of dark theories that spin me out and down.

Curly-haired F.L. with his walking-all-over-the-place tan and his new habit of doing t'ai chi on the beach, even though the wind is supposed to somehow strip your chi away and probably you shouldn't risk it, even if it feels nice between your fingers.

He says dogs adore it. They sit on the sand and just watch as if he's entirely fascinating – this slow human dancing with no partner.

And sometimes he cries.

I hadn't entirely realised what it does to other people when you cry. Ma crying was different. I learned not to notice it. I didn't realise how much someone will probably want to hold you and kiss your hand and snuggle you onto a bed when you cry at them. When F.L. cries he's like a weird kind of hand grenade that blows strange, hot pieces of what I'll agree to call love into deep locations.

I can only assume I'm the same.

Sorry everyone.

We'll be chatting and then there he'll go – out-of-the-blue tears. I'm wearing him down in ways I can't help but shouldn't.

Paul – you have a stupid mother.

F.L. – you have a stupid girlfriend, partner, thing we haven't named yet because I want to keep it ill-defined in a manner that is low-level abusive.

F.L. – I do love you. If you ever do read this, you'll know.

And – while we're on the subject of people I'm treating poorly – I have absolutely no reason not to write out his name. Admitting that he's called something won't mean he has stormed my defences in any meaningful way.

Francis Lewis.

Easy as that.

Francis W. Lewis is him.

Which does feel as if my defences have been somewhat compromised.

Damn.

Only kidding – he's over the moat and possibly inside a bastion of my outermost ward. I await him in a machicolation of the next battlement in. We did loads of siege and castle architecture study last November. I find the terminology soothing.

Francis Lewis is a name with too many esses, but that doesn't imply moral failures or bad secrets – just that his parents were slightly unpoetic.

Suspecting him makes me as bad as our current newspapers – obsessively staring at innocence for signs of horror while ignoring the rampant horror that stalks, acting with impunity.

I am ashamed. Yet again.

And, walking through the forest of this story, Francis does deserve a proper introduction.

The path that led to Francis began – in a way that even I could notice – after the 2017 Sanfeng River T'ai Chi Group Christmas Party. That's the standard of dazzling social occasion I am missing while we're all lurking indoors and trying not to catch the Reaper's eye.

'We're avoiding it like the plague.'

'Like the what?'

'Like the plague, Anna.'

'Say that again.'

'We're avoiding the plague like the plague.'

That was a Francis joke early on. He shares my taste for repetition. Only young people like punchlines – this isn't true, but we are saying it anyway. We're all about matured tastes and ongoing refrains because we want to surf them into an ongoing future. One way or another, we have already caught the Reaper's eye. Passage of time and all that.

When the first rising wave of infections hit – and England duly hoped to ignore it until it went away – Paul and I (and Francis on Zoom) made silly repeating Black Death and Grim Reaper references to get us through our initial nerves. That was before the hospitals started posting that they were running short of oxygen, before the nightmare trod closer and closer, country by predictable country, before the photos of crying nurses slumped on floors – and crying relatives and crying patients. Then our jokes started being about everything else.

On some days our sense of humour went away. Funny isn't a cure for everything – more an analgesic.

Before all the new and unnecessary dying, I had rarely spent evenings doing much more than preparing for the following day's lessons. But I was trying to prise my horizons a little wider. I had settled on t'ai chi, hoping to dial back my tension and develop a non-Oakwood life.

It made me smile when I discovered the general t'ai chi consensus, which seems to be – *Apparently the softest and slowest martial art? The one for mellow, gentle people? Not so. We practise being soft and slow because we are the older and more twisted and more terrified and more furious kinds of people. If we learned taekwondo, or judo, or anything fast and full contact at this stage in our life, we would kill strangers.*

I'm paraphrasing.

Bear in mind this was back when killing strangers was frowned upon and not an interesting Kultur War option.

Killing anybody is wrong – still, I strongly suspect, if I said that aloud, the prevailing storm of wild opinion would knock it right back down my throat.

And to hell with the prevailing storm – back to hell – return to sender.

I am a teacher, I seek to elevate, even myself.

Getting back to t'ai chi – I loved it. Wobbly, clumsy, clenched little me nevertheless felt that I'd come to the right place as I began to learn the form of movements. Even I started sinking away from the stress of deciding where my limbs will be at any given time. Now it was decided beforehand, certain. I could feel the whole class was breathing together, the way that lovers are supposed to. We agreed to shape ourselves according to the precedent provided by centuries of people who were sensible and wanted to be brave and well. Over the weeks, a room full of variously shaky and tense and oddly shaped practitioners could open and close through postures in a way that was united, but not cultish, not military. As I turned and turned I could see myself reflected in the high church hall windows with dozens of other apparently normal people. I fitted. I was part of something harmonious, something that looked like a breeze combing fingers through a field of wheat. It gave me a safety valve, a warning klaxon other than Paul to keep me from the point where nervous tension clamps me into three-day migraines, or a rash. When I'm averagely content I can *kick with the right heel* and not fall over. Otherwise – not. Falling on my arse is the kind of very obvious sign that someone like me can notice.

I'm told that being incessantly braced for impact does not make for a joyous and comfy life.

Allegedly if I completely ignore my body and all of its notifications of distress it still won't admit defeat and shut up forever.

I do know this – I do know if I don't attend to its unhappy whispers it just shouts.

So I did something. I made a change.

T'ai chi stops the shouting. T'ai chi takes the dark and takes the light and makes them watermill around each other, usefully preoccupied, and pushing out life and life and life.

That's the theory. I mean, one can hope.

And it makes my fingers tickle.

Probably psychosomatic, but as long as it keeps on tickling, I don't care.

Although everyone in our class was technically part of the worldwide Gallant Fraternity, sociability beyond the lessons didn't happen much. Our festive Sanfeng River drinks in a knick-knack haunted pub were predictably stilted. Maybe Christmas was simply too Jesusy for t'ai chi ch'uan. Our attempts at bonhomie dwindled into pauses and fidgeting, unrehearsed and ungraceful motions that suggested leaving.

I left, too, but not alone. How bizarre.

I not only left the bar with Francis, I went back to his place. How even more bizarre.

I remember thinking to myself at the time – *Who are you and what have you done with me?* It made me smile.

We walked slowly, Francis beside me in the toffee-coloured corduroy jacket he thinks is good for special occasions and the faded blue work shirt and jeans that almost qualified as Double Denim, with a hint towards prison work detail. But it seemed to suit him. Shortish sides to the hair and a flop of curl on top. He had replaced his reading-and-looking-at-close-things glasses with his walking-about-and-far-away-things ones. Francis has three pairs of glasses for three different focal lengths, rather than varifocals. He refuses to find this inconvenient. He says he wants to see as much as he can of whatever is relevant at the time. He may even have said so that night – I do certainly remember it sounding like a mission statement. Either that, or like something a person would say if they had a suspiciously active appetite for life.

There are few things more threatening than people who have appetites for life – they're going to notice you and see your faults, eat them up. At Oakwood I can act like someone who approaches reality with enthusiasm, but that's for the kids, that's an aspiration. Standing, hunched and sepulchral, beside the real thing, day after day – how would I ever keep up?

Not that I intended to try – whatever we did, we weren't going to do it beyond tonight.

I'll let you in with ease, if I'm convinced that I never will see you again.

He was wearing light brown suede shoes with a noiseless sole. I imagined this might be intended to let him creep about and see even more of everything without causing a disturbance.

Then I tried to stop imagining because creeping about is inherently disturbing and anyone who did that would be a risk.

Quiet shoes aside, no individual detail about him was either upsetting or attractive, but all of his elements combined well – extraordinarily well.

And he has calm shoulders and a calm back. I had been watching their tranquillity for months as we span and stepped and pushed and turned.

I remember wondering if his hair would be soft, because it seemed very responsive to the air and as if it was quite fine. Something about it – this red and brown mass with a small life of its own – seemed to suggest jovial thinking.

Wanting to touch someone's hair – that's an expression of affection isn't it? Unless you're a hairdresser. Or weird.

131

I'm not a hairdresser.

His forearms and fingers seemed disproportionately long in a delicate way. They had always float floated through the required gestures of the form. I could imagine them mending robin's wings. Or maybe playing the harp. I could imagine them painting miniatures with a single-hair brush in the middle of a dustless Russian lake. The lake breeze would play games in his hair and maybe make him grin.

This and other similar scenarios occurred to me as we walked along beneath unChristmassy drizzle. In our elongating silences I wondered if we were pre-failing and there would be a doorstep handshake and parting of ways.

I didn't wonder if I was about to be murdered, cut up and put into bags. That's extremely relaxed for me.

Not that there weren't still occasional flickers of – *Are you out of your mind, though? Or did he slip something sedative into your drink? Did you trip and bang your head off the intended-to-be-charming high Victorian cistern when you went to the ladies, back in the pub, and are you now experiencing unwary waves of idiocy because blood clots are blossoming throughout your brain? Might you be dead within minutes?*

Do you have brain cancer?

But I kept on being perfectly healthy and feeling content.

Whatever we chatted about was inconsequential, but also content. *Content* – there's a rarity.

And, in fact, that whole Russian miniaturist thing wasn't too far wrong, Francis designs websites, makes illustrations pixel by careful pixel and potters about in all manner of virtual and pristine spaces making things that have never existed be there anyway. I suppose that's his version of being in the middle of a dustless lake.

Meanwhile, the street around us was oddly still. A fox trotted up to cross our path, paused and gave us an old-fashioned look, trotted on. The drizzle faded, but had left sparks in Francis' hair. Every now and then, he would give what I think of as his Secret Squirrel smile, very quiet in the streetlight.

It's a smile about sex, but not darkness, or murder. I do understand that. Sometimes you find a person you need and they need you back. So why not smile?

Then I went inside, stepped in beyond the front door of his mansion block – he lives off Elgin Avenue. The climb up his stairs made our breath confused and gave us an excuse to stop even trying for conversation.

After that, we were in his flat.

Easy as that.

Nothing in his hallway smelled of bleach and murder, or heroin squat dysfunction, or bad pot pourri, or cabbage, or was otherwise alarming.

I don't risk other people's homes without considerable logistical preparation and faux-casual enquiry. But there I was, anyway, flying blind.

This happened because Francis is doggedly, weirdly, clearly a man you could picture being bullied and punched in an alley and not ever punching back. You have to be a t'ai chi genius to actually use it as a martial art, but that isn't why he'd avoid retaliation. He's the type to get up again and bleed at his attackers, while fixing them with a defiant look. They'd break his glasses, but he'd ruin any fun they'd hope to have doing it. That's what you see – that he's non-violent: strong on his own behalf, but also soft. And you can tell he'd be something else in defence of other people. He's the soppy house dog that loves sofas and wouldn't remember its wolfish side unless you walked the wrong way towards anything it loved. Threaten what he cares for and he'd jump up and bite you in the eye.

Man Dies Defending Endlessly Evasive Woman – His Body Found in Alley with 'Impossible to Number' Stab Wounds.

Everything about him suggests that brand of headline. It does to me, anyway.

That evening I sat, surprised that I was on his sofa, and mildly buzzed by having drunk two Christmas gins with nasty pub tonic.

Teachers either drink a lot or barely at all. I am notoriously lightweight. I was also still glowing a little with the realisation that I had achieved quite good *beautiful lady's hands* in our evening's practice.

And no heavy ornaments were smeared with brains and there was no suspicious hook in the ceiling and there were no drag marks across the floor. This was a comfort. These were all comforting and contributing factors – still, I couldn't say why I decided that we definitely would have sex.

Although, being honest, Francis was the biggest contributing factor. But he had definitely decided not to have sex – he had decided to make love. Unforgiveable, really.

And I blathered away on his sofa about the primary school Christmas blight, which is glitter, glitter transfer and feral glitter.

The press and release and withdrawal and advance of our intentions were noticeably there against my skin before we even touched.

I possibly was hoping to move through the encounter by using his strength against him in a proper t'ai chi way, but he was doing much the same to me and with more success.

For a while we drank good coffee in what he said were his best mugs. I immediately anticipated that I'd break mine while realising that my shins were stubbly, my knickers were in no way performance ready, my bra didn't match them – who in hell actually wears matching sets – and my body was just going to be my body. And he's a man who wants to look at everything.

We chatted like people in a waiting room at a vet's – both trapped until we could find out if our sex animals were healthy, or would have to be put down. I briefly imagined mine as a kind of fur-covered aardvark with numerous genetic complications and an ill-designed beak.

The chat lasted so long I had settled into accepting that my aardvark's window of opportunity had passed. This relaxed me, but we'd drunk so much coffee by then that caffeine had simply replaced one stress with another. If I'd tried to *kick with right foot* at that point I'd have gone down like a head-shot moose.

I was effectively sober and surprised – extremely surprised – when I found myself getting undressed in Francis' rather sparse bedroom. His bed was rumpled but not disturbing and a far better option than standing still and being seen.

His pillow smelled of almost nothing, just a distant idea about clean skin.

Don't worry, I won't go into details. Nobody wants someone else's domestic sex details. On many occasions, I haven't much wanted my own.

That night, initially, there were no details. Oh, I might have gone through with something – a dutiful submission to intimacy, proof of life – being slightly dissociated but not actually having a horrifying time. Only with Francis my head got too noisy almost at once. Here was Ma yelling that I'd always be alone and always be a whore. Here was the Bad Man. Here were the Stiltskin men. Here was the First Stiltskin. Here was Buster.

He was clearest of all, under our sheets, and tainting my skin – reminding me of how convincing faked affection can be.

When I touched Francis I felt I was wearing some kind of awful, dead gloves.

But he did have extremely soft hair – warm silky animal kind of hair, little boy kind of hair. Neat ears. I could feel that everything was very pleasant, but also not really there and like a joke that somebody was playing.

And then I started crying.

And then Francis started crying, too – crying with me, or beside me, or something.

Ludicrous.

Nine times out of ten, if you are genuinely very unhappy, men will offer sex. They mean well, but have panicked and simply reach for the first fun thing they can think of to cheer you up.

Their first fun thing is always sex. Then maybe, I suppose, a cake, or a drink, or a car – according to income levels and inclination.

You can watch them – I have – being baffled in well-meaning ways:

Sadness. Damn, sadness. Oh, lots of sadness.

I have a penis. Will a penis help?

Or might I do something with your breasts?

Flowers?

I don't have any, but I could order some.

There should be a breast thing that would work.

Do you have a manual?

I'm generalising. Don't think I have not been grateful for the kindness of bewildered men. And then made sure to never, ever see them again.

Francis was proving himself unusual, or well-suited, or just soppy.

I was being surprised by him and surprised by this huge, huge grief – and yet also peeling away from myself and looking down at the mess I was and how I was inconsolable and strange.

The floating happens sometimes. A part of me will improvise some kind of full-strength opera of tears and the rest of me watches it from the stalls with a little notepad and prepares a bad review.

A habit of self-defence.

Then we reached a stage where Francis and I were just holding each other like sobbing survivors at the site of a building collapse. It was nice. It was intimate. And I was entirely there – every single bit of me, unified.

That's the thing about safe people – they make you feel at home. And home is where you fall apart, and home is where you may have to be put back together. More or less, several pieces missing – obviously.

As it turns out, perhaps nobody on Earth cries quite as much as me in bed and sober and not under threat. Or no one but Francis. He hiccoughed and wept – extremely upset because I was.

He is someone who likes to join in, but also he is empathetic – like a functional human being.

Maybe t'ai chi is a good bet if you want to meet functional people – not as louche and annoying as yoga, not as obviously stupid as the pub on the corner of my street, not as suicidal as a bus station, or most of the non-Paul-related rest of my life.

I made him weep. It could be depressing to find your normality on a better-than-average night is enough to make a nice person weep.

But before I could really slide sideways into that particular emotional digression, he told me, 'There's only me. There was only me. After fourteen. There was a big funeral and lots of hugs and then only me. If you're here, though, Anna… There was this accident, and I wasn't in it. I was at Scouts.'

Something like that.

'If you're here, Anna, I would be only me…'

Insane. You should never tell anyone something like that, never hand them so much power. And not on the first night – what was he thinking?

'Alpine butterfly knots. I was learning how to tie them. While they were having a car crash.'

I watched my hand holding his.

'You would be it. That would be lovely. It would be us and we'd be all right.'

There are people in the world who like to join in. There are people who are empathetic. There are people whose hearts are as ruined as mine, just for different reasons. But Francis is a singularity.

We lay in a sort of embrace after that until one of my arms went to sleep and one of his also – my left and his right.

Then Francis made us some more coffee while I got into his Sunday Best dressing gown, my reptile brain scampering up and down a checklist along the lines of:

Cries easily with apparently real emotion
Honest?
Does not minimise your existence
Honest?
Not frightened of grief
Honest?

Understands pain
Honest?
Puritan taste in home furnishing
Honest?
Cool lips
Honest?
Warm torso
Noticeable heartbeat – as if it's showing off in there
Caffeine problem
Lumpy artisan mugs
Honest? Honest? Honest?

How do you know? How do you ever know?

But you do, anyway.

What he is tells you. What he does tells you. Then the words don't matter, not so much. Lies like words, they can hide in them – they are much less at home in actions.

He and I sat looking at each other across the corner of his bleached-looking kitchen table and he wore his standard dressing gown – faded tartan – and I wore his shiny blue fake velvet one.

It's mine now.

Then we tried out doing silly things with each other on the sofa, as if we were a pair of teenagers waiting for our adult selves to catch us. Or as if we were a deformed and haunted aardvark and perhaps a hairless sea otter possessed of person arms and legs – and maybe gentle gibbon fingers.

Appalling to watch, no doubt – but no one was watching, not really. Although it is hard for me to entirely leave the thought of Year Five somehow observing and taking notes during any intimate occasion. The occasions have been rare and therefore not quite a part of my personality – much more an affront to my vocation. I can almost hear Talha beginning the avalanche of questions. We do welcome questions at Oakwood, after all – they are the start and heart of learning.

That's a funny noise, what is it for?

Why are you making that face, Mrs McCormick?

Is it a happy noise or a sad noise, Mrs McCormick?

I felt like a demonstration.

But this wasn't a problem – it made me smile. Then it made me giggle. Then, when asked a perfectly reasonable question, I laughed helplessly, cried a tiny bit and then actually explained myself, my thinking. And we both laughed.

We both laughed.

That's when it was all right.

So that's Francis the otter-gibbon-human hybrid who likes things that feel pleasant.

'I'm not sure who doesn't?'

'Francis, lots of people doesn't. Don't.'

He stroked my forearm to fill in a vaguely baffled pause.

'What do you do for a living again?'

'Teacher of tiny people. But I'm off duty. I am not thinking about them at all and not imagining them taking notes.'

This was our first proper aftermath. Lying back in the bed with – dearlordwhy – more coffee.

'I'm dyslexic.' That was his only defensive flicker all night.

'Really?'

'Yeah, why?'

'I love dyslexics. You're revolutionary by nature. You're…'

After which I got shy. Enthusiasms identify your soft spots. I wasn't prepared to map out all of mine yet.

'We get shouted at a lot. By teachers.'

'I promise I won't shout at you.' Which sounded like my mission statement and a very low bar. 'Francis. Frank? Frankie? Fran? You don't shorten well, do you?'

'Well, I try not to.'

'I'll think of something.'

So I had apparently decided there would be a future in which choices about names might be made and lack of shouting might occur. 'Unless you're about to walk under a bus. Then I promise I would shout. ' I had left the Christmas party with a plan of possibly getting through a necessary physical proof that I'm still female and then leaving as soon as Francis fell asleep. I had been prepared to feel resentful about having to find a new t'ai chi class for January, in order to never meet Francis again.

But neither of us even went to sleep – *so much coffee*. We just leaned against each other – *advance retreat, advance retreat, breath after breath*. Francis talked about Colonsay and the way the beach at Balnahard was the beach your mind has always made you dream for and how it makes something fit together in your head when you see it, as if you've had an open cupboard door swinging back and forth while you walk about and now it's comfortably closed and snug and nothing important will fall out, not ever again.

Safe people don't really understand safety – it just feels like normality to them. Injured people can choose to pass on the hurt, or to do no harm. Francis does no harm. This is not the same as being safe and not the same as being sly.

I may not be safe.

I have to say that here.

One of my problems is, I don't take myself seriously. That's supposed to be a good thing. But if you love me, I won't take that seriously, because loving me couldn't be real or important. I'll be pleased, of course. But your love will be insulted by all the ways in which I insult myself. That's not charming self-deprecation – that's how I may hurt you.

Which is a surprising problem. I'm always scanning for threats outside in the world, but when it comes to harming those I love, the terrible phone calls are coming from inside the house.

I have to take care.

In all the ways, I have to take care – of me, of Paul, of Francis.

I have poor judgement.

Which meant that – before we left the pub – I had sent a text of Francis' address to Paul so he'd know where to tell the police they should look for signs of struggle and DNA traces. I sent another text from the bathroom at something like 3am to say that I remained unmurdered, harbouring multiple reasons to feel ashamed.

Only terrible mothers involve their children in their sexual escapades.

In 2017, though, Paul was a young man.

This was all happening just before Christmas 2017.

We're already locked deep in 2020 and I still haven't got a grip and properly committed to somebody else's very obvious commitment. I have an excuse, of course – we're on different islands and can't meet. But I find it easy to forget how simple it was, our first night, for me to sleep, drop undefended into dreaming next to Francis, his hair reaching out to me across the pillow.

Never mind the coffee – it made no difference in the end; happiness was exploring my limbs like intravenous Valium.

I woke to the smell of toast. That didn't indicate – as I expected – that I was having a temporal lobe seizure as a punishment for pleasure. Francis was making toast.

I had slept in a strange room, strange bed, strange flat, with a strange man who was not strange. He had moved about and I had not woken. He had been quite able to do anything. I almost began to panic, but something of Annanka had woken up with me – not quite gone and not forgotten – so I climbed back into that dressing gown and tried to be myself but with an appetite for life.

Beginning with toast.

As I shuffled into the kitchen, eggs were boiling and, for a change, tea was on the brew in a swell-sided brown pot with a dribbly and brooding demeanour. Francis was a little nervy and that let me feel calm.

Halfway through the second egg I texted Paul to say:

STILL NOT DEAD.

He replied slightly too fast with something along the lines of:

WHAT TIME DO YOU CALL THIS ? I'VE BEEN WORRYING MYSELF SICK. DIDN'T YOU HEAR THE SEARCH DOGS AND HELICOPTERS?

Jokes can be a way to talk about anything: joy, concern, relief, jealousy or the end of a longstanding double act and subsequent tricky transition into a three-person team – more dynamic and more difficult to handle, but offering more complex rhythms, more extraordinary laughter.

Groucho, Chico, Harpo.

Never underestimate Harpo.

Paul ended his texting with:

IS HE NICE?

And a winking smiley face.

I blushed the blush of a renegade mother in mid-mischief, the blush of a teacher on a school morning who will therefore have to rush off very soon and pack away thinking about every fragment of this, keep it at bay and dodge home, hug her son, while remembering different hugs in a startling manner.

I kissed Francis goodbye and was beginning something, not smothering it at birth.

Then I had to go home, get undressed, then redressed, then head for a day of festive-themed learning and activities, centred around the Maccabees, King Wenceslas and celebrating the Bhagavad Gita's birthday. We had already made Hanukkah dreidels and modelled freezing peasants in the snow and kings and page boys and the gathering of *winter fee-yoohoo-ell*. We had written, this is still very clear to me, our own pieces about generosity, bravery, friendship and joy. (You had to pick one, plus joy.)

Our classroom walls were already thick with drawings of Krishna being extremely joyful, what with his flute and his being so glowingly blue for so many symbolic reasons. And a snub-nosed boy called Simon asked – someone usually does when we study Krishna – if we couldn't all colour ourselves blue to match?

No, of course not.

And what about glitter?

No. It's Satan's dandruff.

What we were doing was having fun. We were all of us – staff and Acorns – wandering about in all of these end-of-term layers of delight. We were all in the same delights. And I was in my own delights, too.

At one point after lunch, I just wanted to laugh so unstoppably that I had to step out for a bit.

And that's how joy arrives all over again – more and more – when you'd thought that your fair share had already showed up in the form of your gingery-kneed and goofy son.

Joy.

Lucky me.

I ended up weeping with laughter in the staff room at the thought of blue children staining everything they touched with Smurf prints and looking like the opposite of infinity and sanctity, but also being innocent and that would count for a lot.

And kids do also always have a bit of infinity and sanctity about them. Even the ones who leave you baffled – you'll catch sight of them and they'll have a brief shine of something – a hint of some deeper, remarkable child who might play a flute that sounds like love, might defeat demons, or hold the world behind a smile…

Details

I sat in the staff room with wide-awake December sun singing in through a nondescript window. It lay in a bright block across the bandy sofa and caught the side of the ominous old tea urn so that one particular little angle of the metal sparked.

Better than glitter.

The light warmed my hand right up to a straight line running from my index finger's knuckle to the outside edge of my wrist. It was all very fine.

It doesn't matter to the terrible people who are out there doing terrible things while I write this. Still, I can't shake these small kind details and the ways they happened to me, or seemed to, and how they all fitted together like that door shutting on a cupboard full of things that are secure now, that I don't need to search through any more.

I'm not sure how long I stayed in the staff room. I was discovered by Isla, our cleaner, who blinked at me and my whinnies of subsiding hysteria. That doesn't matter, either. It's unimportant in the world as we've decided to keep it. It's less than useless in this current version of our country. Here it's only the dreadful things that are meant to matter and be passed from mind to mind and headlined and scrolled through and allowed to put out every light that we have left.

I am tired of the dark. I am tired of life's thick brown envelopes arriving when I don't want them.

And I'm tired of being the way I am with Francis, of never quite getting it right. Online there are evenings when he seems less spontaneous and more sad. He combs his fingers through his hair a lot, as if he's trying to comfort it. But that stops after a while and I can see there's a new stillness in him and I'm not sure if that's a sign of depression and if the depression is my fault. Or maybe his island is less beautiful to him now that it's compulsory. Or maybe he has simply learned to be a tracker, hunter, wildlife photographer, and is sitting in his hide and waiting for me to emerge, adapting to my impossibility.

I don't want that on my conscience.

Once he's back home – not that any delighted homecoming seems credible in 2020 – he'll be in our Household Support Bubble, of course he will. That's when I'll have to stop keeping him in forever quarantine.

When he left for the island he still didn't have his own set of keys to my house.

But that's not what I'm scared of – Francis simply walking in unopposed. That's not under all my thinking, under my bed like a mutated childhood monster.

I'm scared of the dying, the comedy Reaper, the long-faced plague-masked horror that might take me away.

I can't tell the people who like me, love me, take me seriously as a human being how much of a coward I am. I don't want them to know that every time it's my rotation on Home Welfare Checks I can't sleep. I know that Anja will probably hug me. And neither of Millie's parents believes in masks. Bob and Martha's mum is spiralling and I need to go right through her house to help clean up a bit and all the rest and all the rest and all the rest.

Exposure, exposure, exposure.

I don't have a proper mask. I don't have a visor. No one seems to have a way to source them. Nurses and doctors can't, so I shouldn't even be trying. But I am trying. I'm scared selfish.

Sue keeps searching and asking everywhere for any protective supplies, but she's had no luck. We improvise with layers of old T-shirts sewn into bandanas and efforts at face coverings. It's laughable.

And every Monday, Sue's there on our screens and speaking to all the kids and all the staff and she's the same delighted, waving Sue with the purple streak in her hair and the bangle rattles and the scarves, but she's older and older. Her eyes have a hurt in them.

So really she's not the same at all.

No one is.

We all do our best and rely on hand washing and magical thinking, hoping for the best like kids who still believe in wishes.

And when I do sleep, I dream about infection, about respirators and sinking away.

I dream that I get it.

I dream about when I get it.

I dream that I pass the infection on to everyone I love.

But mostly I lie on my back in my bed and my jaw clenches and I can't swallow and I want to stay alive so much that it disgusts me. I disgust me. I'd do anything, just to live.

I love who I love and I really do want to be with them, to show them, let them see everything. And I want to keep on being me. It's ugly how much I want that – just to keep on.

I doze and then scroll through websites, looking for what may well be fake equipment, fictional equipment, equipment that costs too much and won't arrive for weeks, or maybe ever.

I'm pathetic.

I'm not who I thought. What I would do for the people I love would obliterate love.

Sometimes I sit down at my kitchen table in the dark and this knowledge will fall, will rush in against me and there'll be no hiding from it – I'll be certain of the ways I love Paul, love Francis, love Sue, love Year Five. No compromise.

Sometimes I go out and walk in the empty night hours – away from strangers and their closeness, the dangerous passing of passers-by. Up and down to King's Cross Station I'll look at the lighted windows. Inside all of those buildings are people who suddenly can't sleep and don't know if they'll survive. Maybe they know they might do anything to stay alive: not just stealing food, or picking pockets, working off the books – anything.

I love all the people I love, but maybe I love myself more than anyone else.

By the time all of this is over, I don't think we'll be civilised, not any more. We're in a machine now, one that makes monsters, and it didn't need to be this way.

And I'm writing silly nonsense things about how lovely Paul is – about lovely Francis – because then they can read it afterwards.

Once the Bad Thing happens, you will know who I was.

I still am who I was.

And I am trying to keep on being who I want to be.

And I do my job that I have to do and everyone else does theirs. On wards, in care homes, in warehouses, in shops, in delivery vans – we just keep on moving like tin toys, as if we can come to no harm. And people prop things up in their windows to comfort the kids walking past – teddy bears and drawings of rainbows. They're for the adults, too – for those of us who know we're just all-alone children set adrift in grown-up lives.

We act as if we're not frightened and hope to feel convinced.

And I can even think sometimes that at least I am not Buster, at least I am one real, relatively whole person and I love and am loved. I don't have to dump my confessions with one of my victims and hope that she won't just burn them.

I haven't burned them.

I'm putting them here. Measured doses. Limited exposure.

Perhaps 1990, La Grande Grève:

This is my wedding day for the only time. Also I find out my name.

A wedding and a christening then.

I am lying deep hidden in blackthorn and ivy and gorse. The headland here is steepsteep and semi impenetrable because of cover density with bushes grown thick to shoulder height and above. This prevents interruptions. Landowner decisions concerning territory use and access are also being of assistance to us here and this makes Prav smile because our principles oppose land ownership.

God or other powers have made the island end in hard slopes and drops on every side. There are shatters through the rock that are sometimes like stairs for a climber and sometimes unstable and a reason for drawn blood. The place has teeth.

To move across the cliffs south eastwards we would have to fly like the birds which are frequent and lazy or acrobatic in the semi constant updrafts. There are gulls of various sorts and predator raptors and there are the ones with dark feathers that turn silver when the sun catches their wings.

I am unfamiliar with birds yet. I am uneducated in all the ways.

If we could fly we would land eventual on horizontal ground where there is a Georgian cannon with cleared turf surrounding which is touristic. The site is retired and draws off possible visitors. It deters further exploration into the density of thorns by being easy and satisfying urges to see.

Islanders are curious and scramblers and fishers but they also have purposes and directions. They have no desire to be in impossible places or find needless exposure to risk. So they pass us and our hiding place and let us be.

Visitor walkers pass also and proceed quick to the photograph viewpoint beauty of La Coupée. This is a high narrow causeway built along the rock spine that joins Sark to Little Sark. It is prone to small and large collapses. Storms and other erosions will cut the link entirely in an undetermined time. For now there are mild and tiny possibilities of death falls down into the chasms that flank the route. Perils beyond the handrails excite those intent on visiting playtime versions of extinction. Then they will go home still unscathed and therefore more stupid incautious. Anyone can always die and this is needful information.

The island has a number of all-alone cannons laid out on its turf at less than strategic points. They lie restful embedded after sinking years. When Prav told me this he laughed in his type of noise punches which sound violent threatening. This is his genuine habit after years of adoption. He likes to be angry happy because this creates uncertainty in observers. By this time I think that I know most of his pleasures. I am wrong and only at the start of him and of myself.

At some point in this morning he murmurs to me You don't lie so long enough to sink. Then he does not bark laugh but only makes the silent shape of it because we are being quietquiet. And he keeps kneeling beside me and scanning the causeway and water and slopes in wide degrees for movement and observant threats.

He is furious smiling.

We have been overall very merry during this time together and go about our work with appetite. This will be my introduction to the actuality of the work. I have been trained over months but training is like shitting. Anyone can train.

Prav knows the island geography and the habits of its people and its weathers and sea and land risks. I could imagine that he is full of boyhood holiday connections or family root and birthplace renewals or otherwise regular trips. He presents details and layered facts like someone with real-life experience. He might have been here on repeated occasions.

He also might not. Effective research completion is having been everywhere already. Travel demands information. Arrive informed and appropriate local. It is best to project the scent and profile of a somehow translucent bystander or very normal visitor or quiet returning resident who blurs into no one much. Be whatever is suitable and useful.

Today we are being as usual invisible. Then we will be possible fishermen possible birders possible leisure wanderers although ideally we will be unnoticed and then gone.

Today we came here as usual across the water darkness from Guernsey. First we parked our appropriated car at La Tonnelle and set out from the beach there in the little Zodiac that we have temporary stolen from an empty and modern summer villa which is its big window ugly self towards the edge of Torteval. We are temporary stealing the villa also. We do not own things. We are better than that.

Prav finds what he needs always. As yet I have only known him in what is called the United Kingdom but I have realised that he has access to international resources and a taste for large and rapid relocations. I will come to share his tastes in this and other areas.

The Wall came down last year in Berlin. A small exhalation of hope followed thereafter and the East and West gangsters began to infect each other with their different violences. Commercial thinkers are suggesting the end of history and other stupidities while Russia turns into the money fuck bloodscape they require in predictable ways. You can smell the blowback coming.

I know Prav has worked for some government at some time. He has a post-institutional fury I recognise. I am not sure if he was East or West or both and perhaps he is not clear either. I think he was both.

I would already prefer not to be like him when I am fifty or sixty or whatever age he genuinely is. But you cannot do the things that someone else does without becoming like them. Actions are like a hypnotism or a blood transfusion or an organ transplant. They alter your meat and your thinking.

Prav speaks to me in occasional proverbs like Be a parasite of the parasites and you will never be a hungry man. This could operate as true predictive in Eastern or Western contexts.

My recollection of things he said is perhaps ninety-five per cent perfect. Words and phrases he repeated are accumulated within me absolute accurate. I have the memory habits of surveillance penetration. Also the particular musics of Prav are very clear and will remain so and I have borrowed them now and then. There are times when I resemble him on purpose.

On my first job which is this Sark job I do not know many things.

I am still full of the night water journey and the high thickness of stars and the sea dark that comes in and touches all over my skin as soon as we leave the shorefront and the gleam of St Peter Port. It makes me not a man and fearful and Prav knows it.

Our journey here hisses and smacks like bad mouths being hungry for a boy.

Prav knows the tide directions and strengths but I do not. When he makes me swim I do not know if I will die. I am tasks to complete and perhaps dying is a task.

Lost in cold water I panic urinate and am cold and dragged and kicked about whenever the sea laughs and flexes.

The sun is on me now however. It feels like love and I am dressed and this is our final day and the trials past and victory is promised.

I am lying in cover on my belly near Prav. My nest is part anchored on a thin patch of turf that sits on a little ridge between thorn bush cover and the rocks that dig their splinters loose venomous up into the air. My weight is supported mostly by layers of dying greenery concealed inside living branches.

Platform stability is complete because it is necessary. The situation is stable but frail. If I were to panic I could undoubted undermine my position. It would be most easy for me to slip down and be extremely damaged and then lost inside the salt and drowning.

I do not yet know that Prav will make himself my father in the small hours of our next morning. I cannot anticipate his scope and generosity.

I am not actively watching the water but am constant aware of it.

I try to reinterpret it as facts because this is a control mechanism.

Tides in the English Channel run metres deep and then withdraw to nothing. They race complex and muscular around and between each obstacle and are limitless information I do not understand. Guernsey and Sark are separated by speeds and routes I do not understand. I am a stupid land thing at this time. Prav is my ältester in all matters and at home in boats. He is made gleeful energetic by developing and interacting forces.

His intention is that I should trust him. My endurance strength is to be sufficient in any context he chooses for me. I am also to trust in all of this.

I will not be swept away.

Once I am broken loose from shore and in our little boat I have worksweated and fearsweated through our journeys. Every day this week I have sat folded low on the seat behind Prav and turned the tiller as instructed against the cave and cliff and death invitations in the sea. The depths have intelligence that tests and taps and bangs and presses at our craft and are subject to strange twists and withdrawals. Prav listens to the churn and flitter of waves against rocks out in the dim and blank as if it is a language and he keeps our route despite the swell and ebb of everything.

Our repeated crossings are part of the process that means my terrors are removed from me as they must be. Fear leaches from my skin and is sick sweet like a bad night of alcohol. The life of passages and currents in blind hours is slowly becoming normal metaphorical for me. Big water is lifelike godlike. The cold wet eternal soaks in and becomes certain resident.

I will go on in life with a reflexive false awareness of sea breezes during all pressured situations. I will feel it press my face and taste salt on my lips.

On the Sark job I row us into shore on our final approach because we are compulsory silence and can have no engine at that point. Doing this is ishachit which is donkey work. Prav makes sure my every day is filled with ishachit. It is a medicine for me and cures me of who I was.

I set Prav ashore at the feet of a narrow and deep notch that cuts the cliffs. He is cat steady and quiet. He will wait.

I strip and leave him my clothes as if I will want them again.

Then I must row round silentsilent inside the north arm of the target bay. I hear music on occasions from a boat anchored west and south of me. It shows its little riding lights and there is a spill of yellow jollity from cabin windows that smears over the waves.

Out in the bleak and huge there is nothing but sometimes ticks of white that signal places where sea deaths would be easy.

I pull the Zodiac ashore.

And every landing means the breakers push me forward pull me back and prove that I am very tiny small. I am silentsilent on the sand and on the rocks I keep time with the breakers as camouflage. I lay up our boat as if it is an innocent tender and of no importance.

The island has no streetlights and its houses are gone to bed. It is trust of neighbours and ghosts and traditions. It is low tax low infrastructure and millionaire discretion. It is ease of secrecy.

The horrible thickness of stars rushes up forever and is like a hiss of static and like magic happening when you are a child and hopeful.

Then I have to swim. Like god and angels Prav is still waiting and I must reach him through death.

But every dawn this week I am not the one who dies and have been strong afloat and efficient muscular and the day has opened slowly and found us dry landed already watching from our view-point where I lie but do not rest. I no longer rest because I no longer hear my body and because my body no longer speaks. I am becoming simple and not described by words. I get more and more clear different each hour. I think I can become another thing which is another man.

Already I am a man who knows each injury provides an education. Every swim helps me love the blindness and small hurts and colds and rushing ideas that come up from the lower fathoms.

This morning I almost overshot the bay. Some last-minute tug from it allowed orientation and was a mercy. Then Prav handed me back my layers and boots suitable for outdoor activities of various kinds.

The tides that suit us best run out today.

Now the morning is warm and from one direction smells of hot lichen on stone. Gorse and blackthorn high around me are spring thick with flowers and make me smell coconut and milk sweetshops and grandmother powder compacts. The blossom is overwhelming and like contagions or easy ideas.

And this our last day and now we will finish and be task complete because I have been task effective. Or else today is the day when I fail and prove myself not useful which is a dangerous fault. Today the ground is swinging and pitching beneath me in hallucination waves. This is maybe god bark laughing at me.

Four hours ago I made the scramble here. Quietquiet. I descended and then ascended with his pack and then did the same with mine. I am our equipment packhorse stupid animal. I am subject to irrational and rational repeated tasks because this is necessary and we both know it.

Prav climbs only after my last trip which is when we occupy the far side of the headland and our viewpoint.

As always I broke the way to our resting place through the brush. My hands bleed repeated when I do this because of thorns and there is tearing of my clothes that are ideal for birdwatching and nature appreciation and very reasonable for my situation. The tears go to my skin but my skin does not communicate.

There is no established path to our nest. We make a new route each day to avoid informative trace generation. We operate safely which is to move light and slip into nowheres.

I am already like Prav in my going naturally to not existent places.

While we work up the incline dawn is a blue and grey thought of itself in a line behind Guernsey. We are still in shadows when we duck below the far edge of the headland and make no silhouettes. Our site is made for us because it is natural solitary and it overlooks

La Coupée and the steep amphitheatre bay that is unfurled down from it and is called La Grande Grève. Deep anchor opportunities are here. This is perfect for our needs and proves we and our actions have predestination.

When you position yourself correctly you become predestined.

I can see our Zodiac sleeping and being harmless in the high gravel. No one will steal it because of maritime honour and such reasons.

A lone boat rollsways at anchor in the bay and has done so all week. The boat dreams and plays music in the night and keeps inadequate watch. Prav says it has intentions to rest here for a month or more. We need it to be solitary and it is obliging. This is predestination for us and even an invitation from chance and all other forces concerned.

Day on day we have learned the regular shapes of onboard life.

To be regular is to make yourself frail.

The sweet and warm nest we watch from is homely invisible. I do not permit myself consideration of the so many branches and concealments for tiny things and the recently disturbed habitat areas. I am historically afraid of spiders and insects and their crawling and biting and stings. Prav knows this. In his opinion fear can no longer exist. I am agreeing with this truth.

Imagined and petty fears are like corrosive substances or thin fissures that fill with weakness and burst in the first frost. They must be removed for safety.

Prav sees the panics in people immediate and feeds on the manipulation energy this gives him.

Prav is fixed beside me and crouching low immobile like a landscape feature. Unless I look directly at him he no longer reads as present. And I do not look anywhere near him because my attention is as it should be and leaning out over the light sparks and colour gradations of sea water. I name and recite each shade in my head as my stillness progresses – *duck eggs and milk green and indigo green and Prussian blue and midnight shapes of reefs and monsters.* I side eye see the outcrops underwater like sleeping creatures of violent capacity and great extent.

Prav uses Carl Zeiss Jena binoculars that he wears constant during the time we are on the island. They represent the only weight he carries. He is invisible slow with them now to keep eyes on the causeway. He passes his time also with reciting obscenity whispers. He switches between languages and tempos. At this current moment he is German. *Friss meinen Kolben. Probier doch mal. Friss Arschloch.* I recognise the phrases because they are among his versions of my name. Whatever he calls me while I train I take as my name. I am always in some way training and have many names. This is agreed between us.

My inbreaths sink me closer to my support surface which is bracken over small branches and ivy mats. There is also a rolled coat here for equipment support. The deeper I sink the less I am here and in the end I will be integrated countryside and will give no life clues.

We do not wear ghillie suits. Prav expects me to become only an object like him without the aid of fancy dress. Then no eye will ever find us while we work and afterwards we will be instantaneous very normal as we walk away.

We have rehearsed normality and walking as much as swimming and climbing and rowing. I had found both normality and walking difficult for some time.

My concentration is drawn out like a mooring line and fastened to the boat in the bay. The prayermurmur Prav makes is also fastened there. *Deine Hurenmutter ficke ich. Ficke. Hörst du?* His hatred is a firm thing for me and a comfort.

Later I know that his German insults are mostly 1930s Berlin sex scene. I think this is unextinguished trace information about adults screaming at a boy with skin that was half apparent Volksdeutsche mother and half Namibian transgression.

I believe he intended me to discover him a little by inference through his curses. A person's curses are useful deep diagnostic.

Prav never gave anything away without intending.

Prav is half occupier and half occupied and his energy charge accumulates between the two. Prav is the little Berlin boy with no father and then no mother. Prav is a visible sin to be destroyed and the defiance and survival of destruction. Prav is a child in rat basements under bombed-out buildings with emptied window eyes. Prav is a biding of time while the Berlin Trümmerfrauen knock the mortar off dead bricks and wash themselves virtuous with labour and are alivealivealive although maybe bereaved and maybe raped by their 1945 liberators, their April conquerors. He is a catalogue of observable scars and ticks left by trauma and by the usual pretence and loathing that fascism imposes. Prav is the specialist in living beyond death scenarios.

But at this time I had seen only a small percentage of his detail.

Deine Rennpferde Mutter.

Berlin before Hitler was rich ecological with specialist whores. Prav knows the names of every type.

Deine Steinhure Mutter. Ficke ich.

On Sunday which was our opening day I cut the branches and cleared for our operational functions and cover retention. Prav liked that my task was blasphemous sabbath labour and made me sin. I was the stated Christian. I was the only one labouring silentlike with loppers and then using the dying brush for added conceal-ment. I transgressed and accepted the freedom in transgression. I was constant learning.

Prav watched. Prav waited.

I see Prav growing up among bullet holes and polyglot graffiti. His name and his self shattered and became many with higher efficiency than my own. I think parts of him are perpetual sur-rounded by women and cripples and other freak children and that he is filled with echoes and instincts and obsessive eating of bread. He watches like that kind of man. He waits and is attentive in the manner of prey as well as predators and the one impulse seems more embedded than the other. His name is Prav or Ve or Fow or

Croasseur. He favours Prav which is the short form of Pravednyy which is to say that his name is Righteous. It is whatever he chooses or accepts because that was the beginning of his strength even inside his initial smallness.

In future times I will use my guesses about his life as family background for identities. Stories referring to his multiple types of scar will forgive my useful eccentricities while I present myself as his son.

Prav the grown man is perhaps nearer sixty than fifty at this time but has a squared-off hard-muscle body that walks low centre of gravity and tranquil and dangerous in a manner that is youthful permanent. Our Guernsey training hikes and exercises beneath the sun have turned his skin to its darkest and what might be a luxury Med seafaring brown. He climbs the violent tilts of St Peter Port streets as if they are nothing and presents as a fresh-berthed high-end leisure sailor with a new season pilot jacket and tan slacks and yacht loafers that are Italian handmade. He might be visiting his money or indulging a whim to eat lobsters on the way to Normandy.

In our Guernsey versions I am dressed as his crew or perhaps failing adoptee or perhaps sex mistake. The majority of my skin remains close to addict pale because of past things and any casual observation will see cracks in me. I cannot present as ordinary. The twist in the black of my eyes is visible obvious although I have not drunk or used in thirteen months. We lean into louche assumptions and make sure our interactions allow multiple narratives to propagate.

Prav is expert in the necessary wealth arrogances and gestures but is also not quite ordinary. His hair is African diaspora frizz when Guernsey prefers Caucasians. Prav earns eye flicks and unease.

When I wear hat is less confusing for atmoroskyi fucks. When I cover the schwartz they love me.

On combative days his chosen Zegna T-shirt is high contrast white when he orders his crab bisque and lobster in the booked by phone exclusive finance gossip restaurant. On days when fury does not entertain him he wears fawns and ocean-appropriate faded blue and morphs unremarkable into a person of generalised investment capacities and beliefs who likes his sports outdoors. In this mood he does not softly soft tell waiters *Thank you delicious yayichka well done yayichka koronovanya* as if this is not insulting but only compliments from some drifted aristo eccentric.

Prav has a gift for voices and can deliver English as a perfect melodious Wykehamist or as a tearing at syllables Odessa Vory. His German is Kreuzberg sharp original. I believe these parts of him although they cannot all be true.

He is showing and teaching me how to be anyone and I am happy learning because whichever anyone I pick it will not ever be me. No substance could destroy me as effectively as Prav.

The way to God and Paradise is death.

He keeps our passports in an inside pocket or otherwise secure in various elsewheres. I have never had access to mine. I know my current name and that I am Maltese and this is enough.

My re-education involves repeated rising pressures. This is to be expected. In our first weeks I would be teary grateful when he decided I could sleep again after keeping weights aloft and maintaining positions and endurances and running equipment drills suitable for naked darkness. I became shamed pathetic. I indulged useless rage. Then I passed beyond the burden of thinking. I changed into being active present one hundred per cent.

By now I can lie in our nest and believe I am at peace and near the start of power. I think I am clean simple. I believe that weakness lies in complication.

Prav was initial untiring readiness and observation while we worked. He projected bored revulsion as incentive and fact. More recently he has instructed me to work without him. This is because I have shown that I know when I will vomit and when I will tremble and when I will start to black out and have made it plain that am able to ignore such indications of my weakness.

By the time we reach Guernsey I assume I am continuous strong effective. The shape and bearing of me says this. Other men keep a step back in the street. Soon I should read as impregnable and complete.

Yesterday after dinner Prav found me asleep in the garage that is my place. He woke me in the standard way to field strip the Dragunov with instant readiness. My perfection was insufficient in perfections because life is unjust and this must be remembered and because my hand eye body totality is being consolidated to absolute depth. Therefore I have been awake since then continuous for punishment repetitions of *ishachit* sweat tasks and more reassembly disassembly cycles of the Dragunov. Then we set out from the villa to the boat and the journey across the will and intentions of water to Sark.

I feel lightheaded alert in a way that reminds me of amphetamine. I am my own chemicals now.

Prav is very skilled in disassembly reassembly of body and mind systems. I am subject to his alterations and there is no leaving this because we are both certain that my original form was worthless. We are in an inevitable destruction with two possible outcomes both of which I accept.

A sudden seaweed breeze is lively and kind and my lungs enjoy it. The target boat rocks and Prav narrates the journey of a couple as they distantly cross the causeway from north to south. He gives his opinion of their sexual urges and misshapen genitals and then fades to quiet as they disappear beyond the far rise.

A small bird sings close but hidden. I do not know it is a wheatear and cannot quite hear what it says because I am not skilled yet in anything that matters. The melody sounds like a tiny perhaps brass pulley winding upwards into a kind heaven. I picture the sound as gold in flutter drifts above my head and while I listen I keep looking through the scope on the Dragunov and the boat is all solitary tender under my gaze and close intimate magnified exposure entirely for me and trapped there in the reticle. Prav has told me the vessel is a motor cruiser from 1933 and a rich person toy ever since it was built. I have stared for days at the honey glimmer teak deck and the snap shine of bright work and the clean cream hull with indigo at the water line showing and hiding and showing and hiding as the waves lap placid. Her current name is in tall gilt letters *YUDINA* across her stern.

The inhabitants have showed themselves at intervals. I have seen their lips move pointless silent and their faces have made trivial expressions. Unnaturally intruding observation always feels like power and godliness although it is made from lenses and mechanisms and nothing to do with my body or myself. Prav and I have pressed our insight judgements down upon each of the three men aboard. To us they are tiny and shrinking.

The boat is crewed by two *kachi* bodybuilder enforcement types. They like to be in shorts and skin to let their Vory prison tattoos speak. One kachi man has dirty blond curls and a dagger inked horizonal along his collarbones from hilt to point but disappearing at his throat as if the blade has stabbed him through the neck. Prav calls him *Maurice. Doris* is the larger-muscle narcissist with a shaved head and belt-level tattoos that show a pair of eyes. This is his version of a joke in English.

Prav explained in his best public school voice. *The eyes make a face you know. His dick is the nose already and his ball hairs are the beard. Such a terribly funny joke in a Russian prison.* Prav knows whole catalogues of things that are funny only in various prisons.

Doris carries a sixteen-point big-man criminal star on each shoulder and Prav says they were earned.

For now Maurice and Doris are still below deck because their onboard days start hungover slowly.

At present my view is of the after deck. A paperback edition of *Le Loup-Garou* is still resting on the seat of the solitary canvas chair. Most days it ends up there. It may be meant to indicate intellectual intentions. The chair is placed for the boss captain who is paying for the charter with an account at BCCI in the name of Ezra Crovetto which is as nice a name as any. A breeze is flipping the cover of the book half open and then losing its grip and beginning again. This is also what always happens. At this time *Le Loup-Garou* is not familiar to me and I do not know French yet.

Prav calls the boss man on the cruiser *Labyrinth* for reasons he does not explain. Labyrinth suck smokes fat Havanas and has backswept demigod hair restrained with some kind of heavy oil that keeps it wet dark even though he never swims. His taste is for Hawaiian shirts and Fila tracksuits and silk blouses and Speedo briefs. He has a range of attack postures and looming that relate to some hypothetical or true time before his flesh softened and dropped and before his gut began to hang low over his tight-packed dick and balls. He makes phone calls while standing and pacing or stares at the sea as if it hates him or throws the book down on the deck and sits in the nice canvas chair that is only for him and drinks Vedett beer and eats fine dining meals that Doris brings and sets down proud on a butler's tray table.

Prav knows the true provenance of everyone aboard *YUDINA* but only I know what I see which is three men being melancholy lazy as a family with frayed authority structures and sudden bursts of shipshaping. Doris and Maurice lie private on the saloon roof occasional and talk at reflective length with bonding attitudes. I think they are not lovers.

By the time Labyrinth comes up on deck the *kachi* are usually thus at rest. Maurice is at once alert and dashing obedient. Doris is slow and uncanny to make a point about having no need to rush. Sometimes Doris will simply keep resting in the sun with arms crossed behind his head and then close his eyes for sleep or similar activity.

No one ever seems to read the book. They move it from here to there and I wonder if it came with the boat.

Prav tells me *Eleven* which is the time and something I need to know.

I breathe active regular and keep my hands loose. Today can be exactly like yesterday and the other days before. There will be only one material alteration which will seem in several ways slight. It will relate to a single motion of my hand.

This will be the first time for my hand and the proof and saving of me in my new calling.

Although I have other motivations I want very much to please Prav.

Prav begins growling gentle repetitive. *Eben khui. Pena. Putana.* He has made the switch to Russian. *Khui.* I don't know which of the men on the boat he is calling a prick. He could simply be talking to me.

I inhale gently and exhale and inhale gently and exhale and after the third inhalation I release only half my breath. Then I begin again.

This cycle is like a meditation and is also a red thing. I think of it as red and all red things are spiritual. I am about to perform a spiritual act.

The sun on my back is like a large hand touching in possible admonishment or else comfort.

According to the pattern established Maurice emerges aft at ten past the hour and wearing this time red yacht shorts and nothing else but glamour sunglasses and deck shoes. He pulls at the line that tethers their inflatable dingy and brings it alongside the swim platform with unnecessarily dramatic hand over hand pleasure. I can see him thinking of his flex and power shape and how much it requires an audience. He is familiar with the motions and equipment necessary in this context but is not a sailor.

Doris is out of sight but already nearby and observant indoors. He indicates this by throwing the habitual pair of empty watertight bags at Maurice's back. These will hold party supplies and food when they return. The ship has appetites and likes fresh produce and live lobsters and bottles of sweet wine. I watch the bags arc from the doorway and gently hit Maurice. I have seen this happen every day but from differing angles according to currents and wind shifts acting on the boat.

Doris then appears from the wheelhouse doorway shadow

with a teeth smile because he is in dominance. This morning he has picked out blue shorts and a tight polo shirt in saffron. He is barefoot but carrying leather loafers. He wants to keep his shoes presentable and salt-free on the journey over to the bay sand. His motions are quicker than Maurice can manage and deft luxurious. He understands that your bulk is fatal to you if you do not have mobility and speed.

Maurice is a little genuine annoyed in his eyes but also soft dog smiling and gathering up the bags. Then he steps over the stern and on to the swim platform and then down into the boat. He throws the bags between the two bench seats. Retrieving the stowed oars always defeats him a little and he is clumsy silly with them while Doris laughs and spits over the side to save having to clean the teak underfoot. He makes a shout I can see and then hear and this is some kind of goodbye called back to Labyrinth and is therefore moving in the current context.

Then Doris is neat dangerous fast and suddenly sitting in the boat and settled with the line cast off and looped quietly in his hands. Maurice is flapping the oars out of the water and missing the rowlocks and then finding them and then wheeling around to bumble and pull towards shore.

While this happens I keep up my red breathing which is in out in out in half out.

My heartbeat is rising and I could believe it is pushing my body up off the bracken and making my back twitch and I have to stop this.

Prav will see.

Prav has already seen.

Prav is the eyes of god.

Prav is the bird above that watches.

Prav is Righteous and Righteousness.

I am ashamed and then have no time to be ashamed.

I keep on with inoutinoutinhalfout and I think clearly that I am not in any hurry.

And I think that my hands are relaxed.

And I think that in a while I will draw a line with only one finger and that will be everything and easy.

I imagine the little dingy slopping and fighting and pitching in the surf and carrying the men towards the shore. And when Doris steps out into the shin-deep waves he will squeal and stamp at the cold because it is only May and the water is unkind and because he does this every time and likes it. Then he will pull the dingy safe to land with Maurice still sitting onboard. This is a demonstration of strength. They will leave the dingy close under the cliffside and then take the oars and bags with them and then climb the zigzag steps back and forth across the uneven terracotta rock face. Prav will be able to see Doris complaining about the effort or the heat although climbing the 300 feet or so leaves neither man troubled.

His words will drift and shred in the wind before they reach me.

And I am watching the cruiser and not them. I am what is next.

I think of my face and my skin touching the cheek rest. I think of the way I am settled and easy. I think of 10 miles per hour windage in irregular gusts. I think of Prav.

I breathe inoutinoutinhalfout.

Labyrinth emerges from the dark of the saloon doorway.

He is moving slow tender cautious because yesterday was too much beer and sun.

He is an alive man and going about the business of that with all the customary functions.

I hear myself swallow which is not normal. My throat is too loud.

I am made of looking. I see him walk himself behind the swooping fine black line of the stadiametric rangefinder. He moves himself behind the graded markings for 10 then 8 then 6 then 4 then 2. The lenticle makes him indicate that he is 250 metres from me.

This is one of the numbers I need.

I hate the maths of guns. I hate the trigonometry of firing at an angle.

When I can decide what I use it will not be guns.

In these Guernsey nights I have lifted and lowered and held jerry cans of water and told Prav that the cosine by the distance to the target is the angle range. Aim for 250 meters and I will aim too high and be stupid ineffective and prove that I am shit.

I have sworn to call him Prav when this is correct and Fow when this is correct and to know by seeing his expression when he wants the Russian and when he wants the German.

I am wrong repetitive and bound to pay for it until I know and see what a face truly intends. And I am most grateful for this opportunity to learn.

And when Prav was not there I told these things to myself because I have to learn and because he would know if I did not.

Labyrinth is wearing a pink and yellow Aloha shirt. Yellow shorts and bare feet. He has the slightly thick ankles of an older man. A breeze flurries gently within the expected parameters and presses his clothes against his body which will feel nice for him.

I am unable to guess if he would think his outfit is appropriate for the occasion.

Prav murmurs *Ya pomochus' na tvoyu mamu porosenok.* I can tell this is for Labyrinth and not aimed at me. Prav has told me that Labyrinth is a terrible terrible man and has done terrible terrible things. I have believed this.

Believing is important because it lifts us above the way we are being paid money to do this thing. We are not prostitutes. We are the operation of morality.

Labyrinth picks the book up off his chair and stares at it. My observation is close enough to see a tired surprise in his expression. Perhaps he has never quite noticed that he has a book before. He sits and starts to flick the pages with his thumb as if he is counting money but he lets his head lift and then just shuts his eyes. He is mainly sad this morning. His thumb keeps counting pages.

Prav says *The dumbfucks are at the top of the steps. They are on the causeway. Doris standing talking. Doris still standing. Now they are moving. Now they are moving. Now they are behind the hill.*

They are gone. Clear. No eyes. Clear. All clear.

He sounds odd. *Clear.* He sounds gentle parental.

He will keep telling me *Clear* until conditions change or until I fulfil my obligation. *Clear.* I can hear that he wants me to be quick. *Clear.*

As the sun set on Wednesday Labyrinth came up on deck and Doris followed and the light was too dim for detail but Doris was shouting and his arms wheeled until Labyrinth caught his hand. This made Doris instant quiet and then I watched them kiss just like two people with a past and thoughts and feelings in the present and a future still to come.

Clear.

When they embraced I could see that Labyrinth was weeping while his chin rested on the shoulder of his employee and maybe lover or maybe something else. Then Labyrinth lifted his hand and rubbed the tears away to nothing that Doris would notice in the dark. Labyrinth and I were the only ones who knew about his sadness.

Clear.

I breathe inoutinoutinhalfout.

Clear.

And I am the one who sees him now. There is no one else.

Prav tells me *Velika Rossiya a otstupat nekuda. Pozadi Moskva.* I know this is some motto from Soviet resistance to Nazism days and about never retreating because Moscow is behind. And this is supposed to be about your love of Moscow but is also about your fear that Moscow is liable to do Christ knows what there in hiding behind your back.

Prav has no more patience to give me.

Clear.

I breathe inoutinoutinhalfout and I hold the breath.

The Dragunov is a good gun. I can recall it in great detail.

I draw a line. I imagine a line and I draw that line. I imagine a line and I pull the top joint of my right forefinger as if I am drawing that line in the air.

The trigger has a three-pound pull and something crisp about it.

Three pounds is not very much and drawing a line against resistance and then past the point when it gives is not very hard. It takes close to no time. The whole series of events is small-time domestic.

The Dragunov has a bolt like an AK which is a Russian reliable and therefore favoured thing I suppose. I do not have the sex dick gun love problem and do not obsess over attributes. I know the gun because I need to. I am aware that the Drag has semi free-floating spring-loaded hand guards around the barrel that move and give when you fire and are strange alive. There is also the liveliness of wood in the carved stock and a satisfaction in the way you reach through the key-hole cut into it and take a snug pistol grip.

There is nothing wrong in a useful object.

I used it.

I have an idea that I pulled the trigger just when he had risen to his feet. Perhaps I was afraid that he was leaving to go below.

I am not sure.

I cannot recall the moment when the bullet hit.

I think there was a noise like a hard door shutting that changed at once into the sound of ripping. Like ripping a tall curtain between me and something else. All that in an instant. That was the sound.

Afterwards came a flock of echoes fading.

Single shots happen on the island in a farmer way. Our single shot did not seem too remarkable. No one came running.

It was a single shot because I am good at my job. I did well. Prav rested his hand on the back of my neck as perhaps a tenderness gesture.

I do not recall the mist around Labyrinth and his head or the pieces of his head or his fall to the deck.

I am fairly sure I saw him lying and almost intact in many ways but with blood on the fine teak planking and on the silly shirt he never should have picked for this occasion.

Done in one shot.

When I fired it did not feel like the other times and it was as if the gun understood my purposes.

One shot.

The police never let me even try for the Firearms Unit. Prav laughed when I told him.

Where that book went puzzled me. It seemed to disappear.

And then Prav patted my shoulder but said nothing and we were still for a long while probably a long while. Probably a long while. And I was peaceful in my heart and breathing.

I lay on my back and watched the sky be its ordinary colour and a pair of wide-winged darkness birds drifted and slow flapped over us mirroring each other in their tilt and climb and dip. They talked as they came with small contendedness apparent in their passing back and forth. These were the only birds that Prav had not yet named to me and explained.

He smiled at them and said *Moy brat. Moya sestra.* This means *My brother. My sister. They are mishpocha. They are family.* Then he Eton drawled. *So you are a lucky chap and get to meet our people from the first. They know death and are frightfully fond. They've taken the trouble to see you and perhaps think well of you because you are a hunter. Not crows. More than crows old man. These are ravens. These are the real bird. These are the play and voice of the underworld. These are what we deserve.*

Prav had a great and superstitious fondness for ravens and would always call them *my brother my sister* whenever he saw one. The are the friend of hunters and killers of lives.

I watched them wheeling in the depth and height and being skilled and joyful. I had nothing else left to do. It seemed we shared delights.

And they seemed to me like gaps in reality. They passed over the blue and then the mist and fine cloudy air and aboveabove fast above the sea but they were also unchangeable somewhere else.

They are highly obvious but not and therefore a lesson. A shadow can hide anywhere when it wants to.

I supposed the birds might want to feed. I had made food for them.

But they played and flipped heels in the air and tucked themselves tight into fists only so they could fall and cry their pleasure in falling. Then they would spring their wings out flat again and stop.

They need to know the air and so they know the air. They need to know themselves and so they know themselves. Hamavin yavin. And now I know your name. I think I do. You will need a name.

He smiled at me and there was no fury in his eyes.

We should go back first. Come on. The abracadabra says that we have to pack up so we can catch the tide. A chap always has to abide by the abracadabra.

His speech is thick with public school slang along with the other various clues men give each other to gain access where they need it.

He is occasional Talmudic.

Hamavin yavin. Whoever understands will understand.

We had three hours on average before the two *kachi* men would return with their groceries for a meal that would not take place as intended.

We removed our traces from the site and began to extract. Everything went easily and mildly. Prav carried his own pack and walked ahead of me to break a new way towards fields and touristic access to normal things.

The blackthorn flowers came apart and flew as we emerged and ceased to be other selves and were only strollers. White petals in the air and underfoot across the deep bowled grassy paths. White petals like confetti on our shoulders. Prav grinned at the drifts as if he could be the usual type of happy *See this? Voo zett mareeay. Verheiratet. You are a married fellow now. You have married it.*

We took a long loop round to La Coupée again and the path that leads open and conventional down to the bay and our innocent but stolen boat. We passed other singular and grouped amblers with smiles and nods and weather remarks and landscape beauty admirations as would be expected. We were conforming conventional. By the time we looked out at the bay again the tender for the leisure cruiser had gone and so had the leisure cruiser and there was only a memory space in the water watching us.

We took the steps that cut back and forth across the slope and downdown to the water.

As we descended the ravens skimmed back up to our left and raced fast to altitude. Then they became fists and fell back down again and bark laughed while they dropped *roik roik roik roik* and were clear joy.

Prav nodded as if he had planned the scene. *Verheiratet für immer. Like the Catholic Maryfuckers. Like ravens.*

I pushed him out through the waves in our Zodiac and then climbed aboard. I think we crossed over the death shadow of the cruiser and of Labyrinth as we motored out for Guernsey.

I remember the water sparks and gulls and guillemots and the cliff sharpnesses slow revolving back into the distance were all fine and holidaylike as we proceeded. I thought I saw the ravens celebrating up high once more and gleaming like mirrors and also being silhouettes and then dots and then gone together.

Afterwards that evening in the villa was our last and we stayed at home for a dinner Prav made from one of the freezers with lamb chops and carrots and broccoli. We had bought bread in St Peter Port. No meal could happen for Prav without bread.

There had been no *ishachit* since we had landed and set the stolen Zodiac on its stolen trailer back in the stolen garage. We washed away the salt and cleaned it and then arranged a little dust until the boat might have been there and resting for months. I had been allowed to sit at the table with Prav and to eat like a human being and share bread.

Dessert was ice cream from tubs of vanilla and strawberry and chocolate. Ice cream is for clean children for good children for sinless children. I cried while I ate. Prav watched.

Then we sat in the rose and beige lounge on matching leather armchairs. Prav drank whisky quiet and I drank water and decided this might be in the end a strength for me.

I thought that only my pointless emotions made me truly different from Prav.

And then our peace ended because peace always ends.

Now we will finish. Raskolotsia. The Russians call the process raskolotsia. You are not quite finished yet.

So I was not yet a human after all. I was not perfected.

And we walked outside to the paved courtyard at one side of the house that I had not ever visited before. The air was countryside sweet and cool after the kitchen table. The courtyard itself had a military punitive atmosphere. That would be why he chose it.

I removed my clothes as instructed and felt myself walking out into my sea and standing beneath my surface. I stayed upright and hands at my sides for the process as long as I could. This was not hitting with fists because Prav had explained that his fists were for equals. Prav used the belt that he took from his pocket. All the while he called me *Kerosinshchik* and *Narkoman* and various other names for addicts and drunks and useless filth.

There is filth in every country.

All the while he yelled. All the while he would ask me his name and know I was thinking the wrong name and punish me.

I made no sounds because I knew the rules for this from long ago. *Hamavin yavin.*

The rule is silence and to be something that withstands.

But kneeling and curling tight and hands around head is how it always ends. You always fail.

When you are a child they never stop until they want to. Stopping your pain has nothing to do with you. *Hamavin yavin.*

But this was to do with me. This was to do with making me gone and beginning again. I was falling for the joy of falling and I would rise. I was the creation of purpose. *Hamavin yavin.*

When our procedure was done Prav kissed my head and put the belt into my hand. East German army enlisted belt with the standard buckle crest that is hammer and sickle and compass in a hoop of rye sheaves.

I could have guessed the hoop from looking at my skin.

I kept the belt with me a long while. Cheap leather and pressed

172

steel. It made me clean new innocent in fresh boyhood.

Then I threw it away because I need nothing and that is power.

I had stayed quiet and withstood Prav in the same way I had my father.

And Prav was my better father and Prav was my priest. He christened me.

So you will be Elijah. Under the other names that is who you are. True name. The ravens nourished him in his wilderness and let him live. Now you come and be Elijah.

I loved him I think.

Now I make you Elijah because I have Vav at my heart. I am Pravednyy and I am Vav. I am the letter at the heart of the right name of god. I destroy and I create and I can name what I create.

Because you are strong you are Elijah.

Next morning over breakfast I knew the love feeling and I thanked Prav and I was at peace.

He told me much later how I would have been a propeller-mutilated body found washed in from the sea if I had failed any one of his tests.

I knew this. I felt it. *Hamavin yavin.*

For a number of years we were together and merry and at peace. We earned and shared our only moderate fees from a range of sources. Death is rarely as costly as people think. Prav took the larger share.

We were early adopter Bitcoin users and therefore became sudden inexorable wealthy. Capitalism loves an unknown that can be traded to irrational high values.

I became an extremely rich man. I have always found this very funny.

I stopped being an apprentice later.

I began to operate as solo later.

I learned French later.

I never read *Le Loup-Garoux.* It seemed unlucky.

Buster.

He didn't look like murder.

I suppose no murderer lasts long in civilised company if they do.

When he arrived that Edinburgh day he was – now I think of it – an overly perfect fit for the OrKestrA. Buster was precisely and exactly what we'd said we needed when we'd put the word out in whatever you might describe as Radical Improv/Musical Street and Demo Comedy circles.

Those circles aren't exactly enormous and it was a little odd that we had never come across him, not even heard of him, but Buster had his explanation ready. He'd been working on paratheatre projects in Haiti and Rome and the South of France. Plausible. We all knew about paratheatre and Poor Theatre and Jerzy Grotowski with the crazy hair and Ginsberg beard. I wasn't the only one of the OrKestrA who longed to be inside the 60s instead of the 80s – setting the Paris barricades alight with performances strong enough to reset the world. We wanted to suggest the shapes of hope and better futures. We thought dreams could create new realities.

We weren't wrong. I have always found it odd that people who work in the arts can be so hesitant about their powers. The populists and fascists – the thugs – hardly pause for breath. They're like artists, but their medium of choice is pain.

I'm not sure I ever took our hopes and potential all that seriously. We weren't anything to change a world – but we could make a few dozen people really happy and that's not nothing. But I was following my usual habit of never taking anything good seriously.

I know that Václav Havel, the Civic Forum – the so many activists of the Velvet Revolution – really did clown and reimagine reality and act as if a whole authoritarian country was something else until it became something else. Their time was ready for them and they were truly remarkable, but they could have proved to us that any holy fool can slowly overwhelm any secret policeman.

Sometimes.

Just sometimes.

While I write this, I'm aware that my government is happily watching a virus eat up so many, many good things – our arts among them. Enough of us agreed, decades ago, that maybe fools were pointless and joy was unnecessary, maybe all the arty nonsense that kept us sane in those first lockdown weeks wasn't really sturdy or practical. The ballet dancers twirling in living rooms, the video feeds of piano concerts in the street – they were expressions of love when we had so few other loves available. They always were expressions of love and without love I don't know what we become.

But apparently we're going to find out. That's the official position.

It sneaked in over the decades. And, over those same decades, I did what too many of us did – agreed that I ought to forget time-wasting fripperies like having a voice and amplifying joy. In a primary classroom, such things are excusable, but not in life.

Now it's too late, I can see – in among all those self-indulgent artists and twee fools there was a direct threat to people who hate people and want most of them gone. The voice and the joys belong to death. I wake up and feel my safety being tugged about by sadists, snipped away to let in chaos, because chaos is profitable and worshipped in myths about genetic supremacy.

Sometimes I think of the waste of it all and it gives me this kind of vertigo. I have to throw up.

My nation's ultimate authority is grinding forward over us. It's still sending spy cops out to splinter lives. Decades ago it peered at a handful of semi-professional strollers and players, at fools with a taste for flash powder and hairspray, paraffin, kazoos … and it set out to ruin us. How weak must my country be when jugglers are an existential threat?

Spy cops versus the kazoos.

I wasn't expecting I'd be furious until later in this section, but here I am – raging in spite of myself.

The bite and scrape of it never leaves – like rats in my walls.

Buster was a very credible part of our RidiKulus RevOluTion. He was clever about it. He didn't say he'd met Grotowski, naturally, but he definitely suggested that he had met other, stranger, semi-religious theatre practitioners. No volunteering information: just a glancing reference here or there. On evenings when he was very drunk, or apparently very drunk, he would drop every trace of his deadpan mask, get passionate and talk about attending non-tourist Vodou ceremonies. He mostly went for the French pronunciation: *Vaudou*. I believed him when he described being overcome and shaken by the real identities of real gods, who dipped in and wore him, then let him drop.

And was that just some weird, racist fantasy of his – *natives won over by white man who shows them how to do their own culture properly*? Was he confessing a truth? He was, after all, inhabited by strange life for all the time we knew him. For all the time I knew him.

Each of us swallowed his backstory in a way that suited us – and poisoned us. We ignored any problems about his provenance.

And Buster was just so very useful. In our world, if you could lift and carry all day for a couple of pints and some of the Apocalypse Sisters' dhal then we let you hang around. He started with that.

And he was Proper Funny, don't forget.

He had that strange fault line, running down through himself – the one that makes you funny. It's an asset with the likes of us – and it makes us forgive hints of darkness, bleak eccentricities.

Being funny is an asset among most people. Funny is the drug that takes away our pain and we all love our dealers.

Our current leader needed to appear only a little clownish and we handed him the power of life and death.

Buster was Funny and good at heavy lifting – a double win for us. And he could make pizza from scratch. And he knew a real, live poacher who could get us game and fish. And he could play the guitar…

I think these things were true.

He told us his job involved freelance delivery of cars for dealers.

He was a remarkably, even inexplicably, good driver and quite rapidly acquired a battered Transit van. Vans are gold – how else do you transport all your nonsense and foolishness and stuff?

Vans are a filthy spy's way of becoming indispensable by inches and then becoming well-informed. Van drivers learn plans for equipment, for events, storage spaces, meeting spaces… Finally, the spy has asked so many, very reasonable questions that the easiest way is very clear – we invite you inside every planning session.

But our planning wasn't secret, anyway. The OrKestrA was just there to make picket lines smile, or entertain children. We made cops seem foolish – occasionally even made them smile. We weren't the revolution, we were just clowns.

And we had kazoos.

Sometimes ocarinas.

We didn't matter.

But we were still infiltrated. Serious people sat in offices, had meetings with paperwork and charts and enjoyably flexible budgets and went to the trouble of sending a spy to us.

And Buster the spy embedded himself so deep that he transgressed every possible decent regulation, every check and balance, as if his life depended on it and we were some desperate terror cell. He was like shooting a teddy bear in its silly, funny, soft little head.

Odd that Buster did once try out a comedy bit with a squint-eared teddy and a gun. The way he threatened it was sort of funny – a twitchy authoritarian being freaked out by nostalgia, plush fabric and lost love. But really it all looked like a broken heart. We told him it was too dark.

We never asked ourselves why someone would see a small tenderness gathered in one place and want to blow it apart?

Why would he have that thought?

Why do all of the everything he did?

OrKestrA spent months, years, trying to work out the whys of Buster.

The ways groups find out about espionage seem pretty standard.

Your Ridiculously Useful Person starts to be depressed, gets more and more drunk, more and more stoned, makes slightly mysterious trips away even more than usual. Perhaps they arrange some big event, like a birthday party, or a fundraiser, or a concert. That's really their secret goodbye gesture, their honey-tinted final set of memories to keep. They want to pretend their real self was the one being loved and that they have something clean and real that they can miss.

The morning after their last hurrah, they cease to exist.

I've talked to members of a few proper activist groups who were more wary and sharper than us. They tell stories about group meetings being called and exits being sealed behind suspected infiltrators. They describe lying, lying, lying men – almost always men – who cried a lot when confronted, as if they were the ones who'd been violated, as if they were baffled by the sudden withdrawal of fellowship and affection.

I did hear of one female spy. She apparently tried to escape from her inquisition by launching herself through a pub toilet window. Halfway out was all she could manage. She just stuck there – legs and backside wedged above one of the bogs, showing off her clichéd, tie-dye festival harem pants. No one shouted at her, or harmed her, but no one helped her, either. They simply sat in what I picture as an orange and brown function suite and voted to revoke her membership. Then they held a vote to inform affiliated groups. They were immaculately democratic. And then everybody went home. Perhaps some women used the toilets before they left, ignoring noises of distress from the one locked cubicle where legs were wagging sadly above a cistern.

Eventually, two of the bar staff – one pushed and one pulled – got her out at closing time.

Her nickname had always been Sheila the Nark and she'd lasted a matter of weeks. People hadn't cared about her. No one had listened to her childhood being replayed late at night. No one had hoped that her pain might break and blow away like a vanquished spell and be forgotten. No one held her tight through what seemed to be genuine panic attacks. Sheila hadn't been family in a family of choice. Sheila hadn't been funny. Sheila had never been able to betray that.

Sometimes informers simply drive off into nowhere and disappear. Maybe they suspect they're about to be unmasked, maybe they've simply completed whatever grubby little task they've been assigned, maybe they have been subject to budget reallocation. Maybe they turn off whoever they were as if it's outdated software they'll never run again.

Is that possible?

Buster just vanished in mid-sentence, stepped out to check on some thought he'd seemed to have, one he didn't quite name. Then nothing. Gone.

After a few months, Monkey Monk got a postcard from Buster. Sweet Monkey with his nerves that crept out and ambushed him too often – someone else Buster destroyed. He didn't want to show me the thing, not at first. In case it hurt me.

Monkey really loved Buster, maybe more than I did.

I remember the OrKestrA's van-haunted dawns. Off we'd drive for this or that picket, this or that performance. On some weekends we'd just appear among playschemes, or shopping trolleys, or the dust in community halls. We worked on the principle that *good surprises should occur in every life*. We swung around twists in village lanes and threaded between lavender mounds and clotted cream stone walls – down past the church and the post office, stop at the pub and here's the show. But most often we'd be drumming and letting rip past betting shops, pawn shops, takeaway shops, forces recruiting centres – all the blights that feed on blighted neighbourhoods – and then we'd set up in some half-shuttered mall full of hollow-eyed mums and the kids who take after them.

We'd be out on the road before the birdsong, giddy with earliness. Monkey would sit beside Buster, riding shotgun in the cab. He'd gently and regularly pass Buster pre-opened bags of Minstrels and thermos caps of carefully poured tea, half full to prevent spillages during possible bumps and swerves. There was a tenderness between them. It was the light, odd, distanced kind you get from prickly cats who decide to like you and then show it with gifts: mice on your doorstep, damp moths.

Monkey's hand shivered while he showed me that postcard, holding it carefully by the edges so I could read it without touching it.

I am so sorry about the situation. Tell everyone I am so sorry.

I was included in *everyone*. How nice.

Spanish stamp and postmark. On the front, a colour picture of the Pont Neuf over the Seine. We'd busked along there one autumn. The silverbluc light in the far perspectives made us think we could be like this indefinitely, just wander and gig and wander. The experienced lean of the buildings pleased us – all those angles being the right kind of beautiful. They were slapdash elegant and surviving. They winked down at us and apparently suggested that walking through body heat evenings in Paris and learning new skills and sleeping on floors and making do could last until we became old and very happy and quietly admired for artistic integrity.

We didn't have Sheila the Nark to overhear our dreams. We threw them into the deep dark nothing that was Buster.

I wouldn't find a silverblue distance, not in Paris. He'd always be squatting in a corner of it somewhere, contaminating.

When Buster disappeared, I was the one who checked his bedsit, who called the hospitals. I was the idiot scanning the local papers and calling the police.

Finally, I caught a train out from Victoria to East Grinstead and Lister Avenue and the house where he'd said his troll monster Stiltskin father lived. Buster had driven me there once – just to look – when I got overly curious about his past. He had needed to show me something as convincing as an actual house with a bit of a lawn out front and bins and a lockup garage and peeling paintwork round the windows. I think he just walked us around until he saw something right that caught his eye – those windows.

I'd made sure to memorise the address. I'd thought, I suppose, about arriving on the doorstep and battering at the troll's door until it came out. Then I could vanquish him with news of all the ways in which his son was wonderful but haunted, by the memory of paternal cruelties, still squatting in a corner of every possible clear and silverblue distance.

That was going to be like a post-marriage banishment of ghosts.

I was stupid enough to believe and plan for all the parts of that sentence.

But there was no marriage, just as there was no Stiltskin in East Grinstead.

Full marks to him for picking a comedy place name.

A woman lived at the address – tucked in with her middle-aged daughter. They'd been there since the 60s.

When the reality of them hit me, I threw up on their bit of lawn and they were really nice about it. The mother then held my hand while I sat on her very pink sofa and her relatively pink daughter brought me tea that was syrupy with sugar. Good for a shock.

We all steadfastly discussed how the heat must have been too much for me on the walk from the station. It wasn't even noticeably warm, and I was shaking as if I'd come in from a snow drift. The rim of my cup kept tapping at my teeth and I wished it were only half full because bumps and swerves were obviously all there would be for me from now on.

I can recall looking past their heads and saying, 'You painted your windows.'

They looked at me as if I must be very ill in some devious way. I distracted them by asking if I could go and wash my face and they let me. Then I thanked them both and walked back to the railway station.

I might have been mistaken about the address, of course.

But also I knew I wasn't.

Neither woman had heard of anyone with the troll's name living in their patch of street.

I told the OrKestrA.

They'd already guessed.

My son and I live in a time when caring enough to organise food for the hungry, or to advocate for breathing, or clean water, or similar luxuries will mean you automatically anticipate surveillance and malign interventions. Back then, even with so much sabotage of the miners and their supporters, the OrKestrA never considered counter-espionage, or why they'd need it. We didn't feel the dogged shift of elaborate growth under our feet, this pale spread of hunger for spies and bad information and torture chambers, this need for wishful thinking and self-fulfilling prophesies. We knew about the baton charges against unarmed crowds, the new laws suppressing dissent, the redefinition of useful words – and we thought those were our only problems. It took us – took me – what I'd call a stupidly long while to see the spies and spies and spies, the mass of them springing up like fungus in the dark to make it darker and let the death in.

Collective noun: an overkill of spies, a rape of spies.

The countermeasures deployed against freedom remain consistent: mislead, dishearten, confuse, rob, divide, smear, splinter, violate. That kind of power always aims to violate – it's insecure and knows it's petty, fragile. What could make you feel more transcendent than to break all possible restraint?

I sit here in my courtyard and the heat is full of camera feeds and mobile phone feeds and rumours and counter rumours. I can feel pilfered information constantly passing close over my skin, flexing between me and the muffled stars. Real people are unconvincing and fake people climb into minds like burglar gods. We're all in the espionage business now, all passing on useless noise from device to device, all fighting the narrative, trying to shape it. And the more spies there are, the less truth matters, the less consequence matters.

That sounds cynical.

Oakwood wouldn't approve.

Nor the OrKestrA.

Nor would I.

The OrKestrA didn't really exist by the time we were kicked along into the next stage of our grief. This involved a trip to St Catherine's House, where they keep – among other things – the names of the dead.

We were looking for the names of dead babies – the name of one particular dead baby. We weren't the first.

There's a dirty seam along which coppers and fraudsters and influencers and spies and politicians meet – like lice on a prison uniform. It's the place where shadow people are made to inhabit the stranger fantasies of uneasy governments. In the kind of movies I avoid, dashing and resourceful spies on the side of Right are given cover stories and identities by soft-spoken clerks and eccentric master forgers in well-intentioned offices. Then flawed, but courageous, and weary, agents do necessary battle with fanatics and horribly well-equipped conspiracies.

In reality, agents infiltrate grieving families who need justice, or troublesome MPs, or trade unions, or an OrKestrA of clowns. That's not very Red White and Blue of them. Nor is having a police force that steals the names of other people's babies.

In a merciful country, no authority would send its creatures off into the General Register Office for an inquisitive day or two. In St Catherine's House – and in Somerset House before that – the creatures wouldn't search through death certificates, looking for those issued during and close to their own years of birth, those with ages at death recorded as 0 years.

That's how they used to do it – create clean identities for themselves. All they had to do was pick a dead infant and then appropriate its potential. I don't know how they do it now. But there are still spies and they still have fake names, fake habits, fake personalities.

I suppose the Stiltskin creatures look for identities they feel might suit them. They favour retaining their own initials, or maybe their own first name, a birthplace to suit an accent. Maybe they sniff out names suitable for people who will be happy to use sex and apparent love to help their workplace identity seem convincing. Surely we'd need a special name for the kind of human being who could talk and hold and touch and kiss without ever really being there at all.

Buster used sex as a comedy bit, a hobby. He wore love as a costume because he could, and his country thanked him for it. He didn't care. He isn't someone who can care.

My betrayal wasn't necessary, wasn't personal. It was simply an expression of intimate violation as Standard Operating Procedure.

Some of the spy cops fathered children.

But a nod and a wink and all's forgiven among the boys.

Somewhere, I suppose, Buster has been forgiven.

He went to St Catherine's House, got a real birth certificate, a real name created by real parents. He picked one out, noted its real birth date, which those same real parents commemorate in god knows what lacerating ways. Then he set to work using his first theft to create every other document he needed. All of the Stiltskins steal from parents, from families, from love, from the future, and build an unclean life on vile foundations.

Find the real name and then generate real documents. There was no such thing as a digital footprint then. It was easy to exist convincingly with very few early traces. If your face was missing from a relevant school picture then you just said you were off that day with mumps.

And I spent one long Thursday afternoon in an especially Albert Speer-looking section of Aldwych – all monumental white stone facing and bronze Art Deco details. It was half term, so I could make the trip. I'd planned the whole thing with the Apocalypse Sisters. Hissy was a speech therapist by this time, and Sissy an elderly care worker. God help her now.

They were wearing the same screaming purple lipstick they always had – nail varnish to match – because however they earn their living they are still the Apocalypses at heart.

The OrKestrA members have generally scattered across the

spectrum of jobs that involve looking after people. I think that's for much the same reasons that we strolled and tumbled and kazooed – trying to ease the human problem of being so very short-lived and breakable.

People laugh at slapstick because we all fall over and know how it feels. People also laugh because falling is terror and the end of us, so we mock it to make it seem small. At least, that's what I think. And we strollers and tumblers had all decided that our lives would be about rising after our falls.

Over the decades we did try to revive the OrKestrA now and then, but it was hard to find the joy in it. We had been built round a wonderful idea – that anyone could choose to be anybody and then do anything. Then the Stiltskins had shown us too many versions of how terrible that could be.

Our reunions were soured with memories of Buster. He'd infected what made us lovely and broken our timing. Slapstick, tumbling, joking, music, living, flying – they can all be manifestations of the joy in perfect timing. Get cautious, self-conscious, injured, scared and nothing works. Half a second too late might as well be a year too late – each one of your efforts ends up on the floor. Buster was the end of easy laughter.

We answered him in the end – we cared and we keep on caring and try to grow and save things, save people. That's a solution to creatures like Buster. But caring and mending is slow work when one Stiltskin can ruin so much in a moment, a thought.

Poor Monkey, of course – we didn't save him.

And the anger and the memories blew through me and made me unsteady there in Aldwych. I stayed outside, wasn't setting foot in St Catherine's House. The records were sleeping there, I imagined, dusted with contagious guilts. The Apocalypses went in without me. They always were the bravest of us.

I kept on remembering Buster's smell, the scent of his skin, his hair in the mornings. I was unable to believe the St Catherine's corridors wouldn't reek of him.

He must have spent hours there, carefully fumbling through other people's grief, turning it into his impunity. He must have touched light switches, door handles, left behind traces the way that polonium would, or anthrax. I wanted no part of that.

So I lingered in the street while Hissy and Sissy made the necessary search. I don't believe it really took them all that long. It was only an illusion that weeks went by, swirling up and down between the high façades, time arching its back against the window glass. A couple of times it pushed me close to falling. Not a pratfall, not a merry tumble – the kind of fall that means you're nearer dying than you'd thought. I anticipated being unable to really explain why I'd hit the pavement – just a silly primary school teacher looking up at a gathered crowd of staring pedestrians.

Then again, I was in Westminster – maybe nobody would have gathered and I'd just have lain there while nice shoes stepped over my body and away.

Eventually the sisters both emerged, smiling in ways you might to calm a stammering kid, or to cheer up a residents' lounge full of people with swollen feet and medications. They were good at both those smiles.

Vertigo slapped at my head while I tried to smile back. I wasn't at Oakwood yet, was still feeling my way as a teacher, so I didn't have a repertoire of smiles that might suggest inviting futures.

Then the sisters walked on either side of me until we reached the nearest café and could talk. We weren't shocked by what they'd learned, not exactly shocked. By then it was really pretty much what we'd expected.

Phillip Stirratt had barely existed. He'd slipped into life and then died the same week he was born in 1956.

1956 was a credible birth year for Buster because he was just that bit older than us. He'd spent a few years becoming a cop before they sent him off like a poison pen letter – still young enough to be credible among people in their twenties.

We settled at a corner table and Hissy made me drink over-expensive hot chocolate for the sugar. I was cold again. I was feeling all the places he had touched me. I was feeling as if I was trapped in a dead person's skin.

We'd had a plan to make the day more about reunion than dis-interment, to have an early dinner somewhere nice. I tried to back out and just go home, but they wouldn't let me. You always can trust the Apocalypses to create rousing finales. They knew I was living alone – as it turned out, in a very ramshackle version of impregna-ble solitude. I was weeks away from giving a Terrible Man the keys to my everything.

Hissy liked this Thai place in Soho, so we walked up north towards it, took things gently. As we promenaded, Sissy and then Hissy started to whistle the OrKestrA's marching tune.

Too-Rah, Loo-Rah.
Too-Rah, Loo-Rah.
The UnRule OrKestrA.

That made me cry a bit. A moderate amount for me. They wouldn't let the mood drop, though.

Too-Rah, Loo-Rah.
Too-Rah, Loo-Rah.
The UnRule OrKestrA.

We always used to whisper that, tiptoe marching along in the silences between musical onslaughts. Whisper and then escalate towards shouting – that was our way, *to be like a happy and irresist-ible idea.*

Too-Rah, Loo-Rah.
Too-Rah, Loo-Rah.
The UnRule OrKestrA.

Joining in, being part of the OrKestrA – it was like running home and shutting a sky-blue door behind you and laughing because you can, because there is joy in the air around you, sparks in your lungs.

Too-Rah, Loo-Rah.
Too-Rah, Loo-Rah.
The UnRule OrKestrA.

We began to muck about in OrKestrA kind of ways. At one point – the Apocalypses were still in extremely good shape – they lifted me under my elbows and swayed me, bent-kneed, back and forth between them like a big kid on a swing set. And we kept on advancing, cleared the pinched little pavement ahead of us.

One discomfited man glowered at Sissy as he stalked across to the opposite side of the street. I could feel her fingers tense as she switched to one of our signature ditties for demos. It was sung to the tune of 'The Battle Hymn of the Republic' and we used it whenever we spotted pre-enraged types, the models of masculine dominance who always looked more impotent and paunchy than Aryan supermen should.

Sissy skipped straight to the chorus in an undertone that wasn't very under.

Glory what a tiny penis,
He has got a tiny penis,
What a very tiny penis,
That's why he's fur-i-ous. Yuss, yuss…

And then we giggled and ran and ran and didn't look back because no good comes from looking back.

But Buster followed us.

The man with a name he stole, a birth date he stole.

Not tiny, dead Phillip Stirratt, not born in 1956.

The dinner with Hissy and Sissy was okay. Subdued. They were very kind, and I hated the way that unsteadied me while I loved them, loved them, loved them for it.

And I drank tom yum soup for the first time. It was spicy enough to numb my mouth, burn it clean. Almost clean.

And that wasn't a story about Buster – that was a story about people who kept on going in the space beyond him, who built things he could not imagine.

Normal people live one life and try their best to make it their own and beautiful and useful. The Stiltskins who are too weak to be anything more than lies can only keep running and leaving behind each mistake they've tried to be. They run and hide, then run some more.

They're nothing. I try to believe that.

The world will eventually heal over the wounds they cause. I try to believe that.

No one can love the Stiltskins and this makes them feel inadequate. They end up alone with their trophies and fictions, their sad little gaslighting autobiographies. I try to believe that.

Buster and his big brown envelope of pages – that's all he's got.

November 2019, Camden:

This pub is not called The Happy Bargeman but something similar. It is in a standard wasteland section of a Camden street. Running almost exactly east-west from here are stepping down rooflines and Victorian shitbrick and modern shitbrick. Street level is daytime cut-price hardware jumble stores and shopfront bowls of bruising fruit and betting shop window hopes. The street residents have no doubtly intentions for sleep but we do not. We are flush hot and luxury successful with lock-in excitement. We are 3am privileged and loud.

I am in pubworld which is no longer my home.

I am in England which is also not my home although it is England that has left and not me. This means I am in the country that presents under the alias England. The identity relies on repetition because it is otherwise thin research and paranoia with outbursts of dark sentiment. It reads inconsistent unconvincing and causes unhelpful dissonance among those who remember other Englands. The presentation is unprofessional.

I am standing at the bar. A constant nudge of crowded men is jostling each other in a way that will be fighting before dawn. The air is loud expressed joy pretences and ambient perfidies and the workday sweat of strangers passing and repassing. In a far corner someone with sad hair is attempting local character status. He is trying on eccentricities he has seen in films and swallowing pints of alternative happiness with enough force to wet his chins. He does not concern me.

I am here with Nigel.

I am here for Nigel.

Nigel is not his name.

You will eventual guess him. He was always a destiny that would end in bad tall headlines. I assume that you perhaps still read papers or have anyway ambient awareness of their promoted narratives.

Not Nigel is masking his persistent contempt expressions with half smiles and gestures that lift his hand over his mouth. He suffers from tiny repeats of snarling that begins in his upper lip. This is beyond diagnostic and more an advertisement of dysfunction.

Nigel presents himself as dominant excellence in all contexts. Nigel is belief in genetic blessings and the inherent sins of effort. Nigel is wrong in his self-assessment. His remaining unavoidable self-awareness episodes eat him in his spine and he produces cruelties as compensation. He is a boring example of a boring type.

The outside world is still living and waiting beyond the pub and the street and neighbourhood and the flags although the preferred national psychosis would rather it did not exist. In the outside world there is minor visibility news from Inner Mongolia where pneumonic plague is spreading mildly. A new influenza is being low-key reported in China. Intelligence operatives are considering harm potentials. They remain consistent lamenting from their silos of pointlessness and watch this England being voluntary naked stupid and in cruel hands. The whole island is an addict myth of longing to drift alone and glorious in punitive seas.

I am watching Nigel show me his main deception tell and imagining that cold and godly waters are rubbing and laughing around my shins. One sudden push of current and anyone might fall and slide beneath the surface. London rests in a dish of smog and this is useful to mask the other kinds of immersion and fighting for breath already in place.

Even after this job I am planning not to leave and this is a large mistake. I am nevertheless a mechanism that adapts after each mistake. I will soon make a large course correction.

Pub voices are agreeing and disagreeing about referees and transfers in traditional ways. This is one of the things they have instead of conversation. Clientele here are eighty per cent police from the local station. They repeat headline phrases gathered by osmosis in canteens and patrol cars. They mention liking teams players sex acts children dogs women. On my right a man who is wearing a desperate tie expresses desires about hooking marlin in Cuba. His voice is Essex washed over Midlands. He is postures of Hemingway with underlying Thermos tea and trying to kill hatchery-bred trout in little ponds.

The room leans back on an agreed myth background that is royal stability and London as White Mayfair deterring the hordes of Black Chaos and also Pimm's being served forever in county gardens with old lawns.

Nigel is blurred assurance with ignorance as appropriate relaxation. His constituency sees these as his defining and admirable traits. He walks above any perception of threat and is the officer delighted to kill men because this will confirm him as the hand of god removing the vexatious weak to aid the strong. The army would of coursely spit him out immediate and he has never tried it but he indicates martial ability in the cut of his jacket waists.

Nigel has background suspicions that he is successful because of fashion and wealth and contacts and not individual genius and believes this is his worst and most truthful burden. He is thriving nonetheless because emotional abuse fun has been made the encompassing culture and policy and ritual and income generation. In this England torture is pre-eminent and he is good at creating torture scenarios. Somewhere the bad father belt is always slicing down in soft places. I could taste leather as soon as I left the airport. The cab drove me in citywards with a soundtrack of radio phone calls from the glad deceived and the performative rage indulgence that answers them. Everywhere is slippy underfoot and smells of gaslight.

A man with unironic facial hair is murmuring to a bland companion further along the bar. They are loving their little boy secrecy and have fingers already curling at the thought of invisible envelopes packets cashrolls treasures unnameable. Pubworld is loving itself as careless England made small and hugged indoors. And in among the cops are thrill seekers like Nigel and men intent on shadows and hard business. There are also a few fakes and absences concealing themselves in human skin.

There is also me. I am being very true and present and Tom. I am high definition and also blurs deployed where appropriate. I am total awareness and mood engineering and narrative control and information gathering and indispensability and apparent goodgoodgood gooddog charity case who wants to be a friend. The environmental emphasis is on bonding and shared sins which is a happiness for me.

Nigel loves his monologues. He is talkingtalking all this time and I am intently and affectionately not listening. Hearing him creates substantive impulse suppression exhaustion. Whenever I pay him adequate attention I want to inflict great havocs and harms upon him. I am emphasising calm and situational awareness to compensate.

Beyond his shoulder four regulation haircuts and two failed types of neat are being huddled jolly at a table. One of the non-regulation men is a cruising sharky shark and huntsman pretender like me. His cover is average good when he concentrates but he leaks anomalous glee fascination in each energy dip from his companions. They are loose loud and will be looser and louder. They are thirsty for faster boundary collapses. Only one of the regulation haircuts would be troublesome in a physical confrontation. He would damage the little sharky shark at the first clue of perfidy. Sharky shark is anticipating meat chunks and blood feeding. The others men are swimming defenceless in a chum bait stream and he is sniffing close closer. I recognise his face but would know he is a journo anyway from his flavour. That particular appetite is in the mood around him like a heat haze. He collects useful kompromat items for other interests. His preference is to avoid all publication and therefore maintain the tensions in each target. Information is leverage and income and not righteous rebuke.

I am righteous rebuke.

Sharky shark has body movements that focus around his awareness of his very clever recording device and very clever cleverness. His torso bias and avoidant gestures little finger reaches are ridiculous neon indicators and the table deserves him and is bringing him on itself.

I am watching from high places.

I am a higher place.

Nigel is meanwhile laughing in self-joy admiration. I have made this a response trigger which means I create an automatic admiration smile with a soft tail of shyness and awe. I maintain sympathy body mirroring between us and he is standard anxious for it. I am what he needs which is hangdog love obsession. I present as craving for his insults and display pleasure after every punch. When certain comments hit I let my face fall. I offer him a deeptrue childhood disappointment reaction that overloads his sadism junkie delight. I am regular damage evidence and occasional tearfulness. Nigel is a small selection of obvious pressure points and my identity as a person called Tom pinball lights them in rotation. It entertains me to imagine that I am racking up high scores.

I am also entertained by my deepquiet inside and under. This is because I can adore his oratory delusions and also remain pure noble. The gantry mirror shows me as most likely a slack muscle poor diet beta fanboy. This is as I should be. I am a stumbler. I spill drinks. I am small indications of self-harm and limp aloneness. I am a perfected personality and also clean effective within my truth in a place where I rest and play.

This is why the abuse survival is training for the best deceivers. If we stay alive we are already always hiding and in a place of truth and safety far away.

I could say that I am currently enjoying a total body lie trip and exhilaration opportunity. My physicality is obedient and leashed for appropriate camouflage and appropriate display. If asked I would state that partitioned existence becomes easy and that Prav helped and trained me towards optimum completion. I wake up non-committal by established practice. I am dull humdrum when at rest and any observing eye cannot help sliding onwards. I am whoever I want. I am also whoever you want which is better and a fluid solution to any challenge.

My body was once a sum of habits and genuine intentions and therefore a betrayer. The first thing removed in my process was my policeman identity. The policebody has pseudo-soldierly posture and learned constabulary gestures. Stress injuries distort it. Personal guilt and personal outrage produce patterns of muscular tension. Police off-duty dress is a cheap shade of military casual with determined lack of taste in lower ranks and a fondness for thug indicators. Policebodies long to fill rooms with power projection as problem solving and are inappropriate for domestic settings. Police brotherly love prefers to categorise and fragment and favours street gang aesthetics. Police life despises non-conformers while encouraging animal pack hierarchies. Police minds hold the public to be a devious and fractious and deliberate provoking invitation and moronic and demanding enemy. Also the public are community members and family members and especially wives which is unfortunate and a continual irritant.

Policemen do not understand policewomen but do want to see them naked.

I can scan the room and see where higher-ranking policebodies are acting expansive and happyflaunting better jackets and finer skin while their gathered subordinates rock and touch shoulders in boyish solidarity displays. They do not in particular feel that they need to look at me.

But I see them.

Policebodies have a rage for order and ache for affections. Hates are nurtured in obsessive compliance with station assumptions. Police dignity is fragile and then violent. Policebodies have evolving laxity towards tattoos. Policebodies smell of blue serge regardless of factual uniform composition. Policebodies are grown in stuffy cars and stuffy rooms and stuffy gyms. They are made of high-calorie snack foods and potatoes and brutalised emotion. Policebodies thrill to jokes about black bodies and camel jockey bodies and dyke bodies and poof nonce perv bodies. Policebodies tell stories that linger on fantasy sex and domestic sex and rapes and autoerotically dead and otherwise bizarre cadavers. Policebodies wax sentimental about kids while also ignoring all signs of dark proclivities or strangeness in Blue brothers. Policebodies fix like gun dogs on tales of personal bravery and of resisted provocations and of natural and excusable boot and fist and imposed asphyxia responses. Policebodies feel their voices shiver when mentioning boys who are good little soldiers and sending flowers and helping heroes and acknowledging mother love.

Police are good and not good in Aldis lamp signal flickers.

I am enjoying my privacy of thinking continuous while I buy and pass Nigel a tumbler of high-expense Scotch with a suitable wince.

I can sip my own drink like an empty pocketed and sad-sacked animal.

This does not prevent me from remembering my police home that was once upon a time. On arrival with the force I aimed to be only goodgoodgood police. This marked me as immediate outcast and suspected homosexual smalldick commie freak. I aspired to the proper execution of my regulation duties and believed my Hendon training. My unending and inevitable failures were daily and hourly applauded. I was shelved as a thing untouchable and alone in sick buildings with shitwork paperwork to keep my head down. I was nonetheless sustained by dreams of future purity and righteous action. These caused me to fail harder.

I was the boy with the big sheriff badge still pulling at the stitches in my sweater and saving no one.

Blue thinking required that I become my father who was all policebody and all savage Blue instincts. I aspired to be his opposite. I aspired to be the implacable force that picks up the wifebeater childbeater monster and throws him down and hurts him and stops him and keeps him stopped with painfears and cowed apprehension of fatal weakness.

I can taste the wifebeater reek tonight. I can see the gleam and grease of it on the man leaning by the far window and fiddle fiddling with a beer mat. He is treasuring his frustration for later use.

Locker rooms were the worst while I was police. I would be tranquil and donning my authority and then the stink of domestic chastisements administered the previous night would stride in and would be like a low blow or a coward slap against me.

On a number of levels I began to conceal and dissemble while going about my work.

I began also to drink. Alcohol abuse is an acceptable Blue hobby. I dissembled more.

I pondered abandoning my hoped and longed for Blue home but was unable. My internal structure was still afflicted with tricycle adventure memories and queen and country shivers of bold nobility and vengeance promises. Being police was my salve and access to precious worth.

My dissembling was imperfect and noted as a semi skill by my Blue overlords.

I was encouraged to fold up and slide away from conventional uniformed matters like the useless and unpalatable object I was held to be. At this time covert operations were a novel and mistrusted playground made for misfit animals and castoffs. I put in my application for transfer and my superiors found the desire that I should stop existing in my current form was very mutual. I was duly reassigned and blessed.

Undercover was my boyhood home monetised and my childhood weaponised and my tolerance for painfear and compartmentalised existence made triumphant.

So I perfected the junkie shamble and carefully pleaded for fixes in piss and vomit streets. I dived down in the sea of it and thinned my limbs and presented the twitchsweat evidence of need. I lived in localities unbearable without fast and slow anaesthetic. I started to inject distilled water and thereby cultivated bruise punched veins. I stopped brushing my teeth. I stopped washing.

I became extremely congruent with my persona.

I documented purchases and small bad deeds and became topflight deceptive with vertigo accompanying. I had an eye for exploitable friend equivalents. I made dealers pitylike me.

I explored degradation as a sex alternative. Bear in mind that I sought sex alternatives from my first step and outset.

I did feel that sex as conducted while in disguise would be ignoble.

I explored blackout drinking as a sleep alternative because it seemed like vulnerability avoidance. I had a high and almost justified certainty that I would leak less information if my days were alcohol waking dreams. I explored my cover persona as various life permissions reinterpreted. I did need permission to sin because I was a good boy with a sheriff badge still shiny in a locked-up childhood drawer. I told myself I would pursue perfection and reasonable stress release by becoming absolute and a perfect picture of this or that perfect thing.

I swam in the midnight waters and began to use. There is a strong public assumption that no policebody would really and visibly and recklessly use drugs and so I embraced addiction as professional development. My using was impregnable concealment.

A junkie gives the most successful presentation of a junkie.

Pubworld was my friend and home and base of operations for many months before my perfection took a solid hold and made me leprous unwanted. I then adopted a preference for the street. I became distasteful unremarkable and a thing to walk past. I liked my mind in splinters. I was a success.

I forgot which were the things I should forget.

I was damp wall housing and iron shutter neighbourhoods. I was transactional encounters and tears and begging. I was hiding and wounds and running bad errands as the small fry people do and I was also betrayal for the genuine small fry people although they were my only family.

I was fear of excessive speed and spiders.

I was reporting late at night in darkened cars because daylight would reveal too many points for criticism. My reports remained good effective. Boiled down to my bones I am mostly a memory and catalogue of things. I am ideal for my vocation. This was to become uninspiring as self-knowledge.

The police minds who read my reports had no patience for structural damage to the drug aristocracy or for community redemptions. The command level appetite was for little people crying and being damaged in swing-punching arrests while the streets they left behind remained subdued by appropriate chemicals and their lowlier versions of landed gentry squire. The aim was to punish presumptuous crime and also ambient resilience and ambition and organisation among the weak unworthy.

I had not saved neighbourhoods or children. I had followed the secret police religion which is idol worship of ruin added unto ruin and treading down of the downtrodden.

Back in the Blue fold and waiting for my next assignment I would enjoy that my skill set usefulness provoked hate admiration. I would wait out sudden sweats in the office toilets and afterwards make the required jokes about food that was not English and therefore poisonous. My decline was smiled upon as promising by brother officers.

I would be taken as native guide on operations to suppress illegal raves. This was a time when music and youth and dancing were held to be the only pressing and media monetised threats. I would watch domesticated coppers waste their time panting over nighttime fields of cow shit to exorcise the fear of youth. Policebodies grabbed up fretful students into vans and mocked their strange vocabularies and threatened them with jail time and corroded drug futures.

And I would return in my policebody disguise and watch my Blue brethren kick in the often kicked-in doors of people who had been my almost friends. Once my superiors had fumbled the hope out of every single high-level prosecution I would return to pubworld and be angry with reality and pick fights. I would stand in 2am car parks and scream in the thick of darkness.

This helped me construct a masculine reputation and I was

increasingly seen to harbour large promise. I am a born deep diver and this was noticed. I am a born surveillance and penetration asset. And a golden age of deep divers hiding in among the peddlers of dissent was unfurling into 360 degrees of unrestraint.

And then an invitation to join the Squad was offered like a carpet sliding in silky under my feet. A place of dark waters wanted me and I wanted to plumb depths. The Squad was the ultimate library of concealments. The Squad was careless rich. The Squad was glorious whims and impunity and government hatreds expressed in all maximum forms and methods.

This was known.

I lived in a free democratic country where resistance and criticism and agitation were consistently organised as part of our free democratic restraints upon established powers. I was not disturbed to know that our free democratic dissent was consistently infiltrated by our free democratic police. I would be wearing my shiny badge and would seek out only terroristic and other high-grade threats. Unregulated thinking and enquiry were not my targets. I would be a seeker after terrible dreams and only deep pretenders like myself would ever get close enough to find them. I was about to be a hero cloaked in the secrecy I would need to keep me humble.

I did not agree to classify dissent as Class A drug equivalent and therefore destroyer of communities and pure youth. I hoped to hunt for swastika thuggery and bombers. I hoped to be brave in the face of loathings and insurrection. I would listen to the wife beaters and their secret theories of why they were righteous and their hate excuses and then I would put them away.

I did hope that.

I began by hoping the Squad was absolved in advance and forever because it was a swift and irresistible good.

The Squad was sanctified. Surveillance and penetration capacity had been swelling out like tangible expressions of governmental thinking.

When I joined the Squad I would be sanctified myself and drink its wine eat its host. I would maintain the true meanings of good order and peace.

Blue thinking holds that radical opinions are naïveté made manifest. Its own corruptions and naïvetés are coddled like brave little soldier kids.

I think I remember my first day and walking towards the Squad in its special building with its midnighty purpose tangible immanent. That day I accepted my inevitable my future. The Squad and I happened to each other.

I recall that I had high breath punching up under my shoulders and a pattering chest and also wet hands and other indications of fear and smallness and delight. I was entirely sober with my night prior being early to bed and virgin clean. I was trying to achieve consistent poise and heterosexual certainty. My walk seemed nevertheless inadvertent dysfunctional and my self-dismay forced me to stumble on the threshold.

I was not yet myself.

In pubworld with Nigel I can remember this past awkwardness because it is useful for Tom. I have given him physical unease and seafaring metaphors and bashful half smiles to follow because he is a freely confessed poor swimmer. The mentions of salt waters entertain me while I look out of his eyes and steer him about.

On the day of my induction into the Squad and the deep Blue kinds of lying, I must surely have made my way across the foyer and stated my business to some reception person with authority to maybe deny entry and maybe give directions as a welcome. The words and names I let out were large and burning in my mouth like a first boyhood whisky or a sacramental wine. Then I took the stairs and not the lift to prove hardness and regretted it in sweat and minor disarray when I arrived at the stated floor for my induction.

I think that I straightened my tie on the landing and then went in search of the door without asking directions because asking would be weak. My way in led between commonplace police desks and police chairs and low-grade police clutter and domestic police eyes observing and unimportant police chat. I tried to proceed as if I were already transformed transcendent. I believe that I was following the tease trails of manly laughter with a special collegiate flavour. They did lead me towards the Squad door that was half open careless and waiting up ahead. I think the Squad always laughs when the door is open. They aim to maintain debonair mythology and force mystique.

Crossing under the lintel was nothing and also a deep tumble feeling and glory. The room smelled of power and ashtrays and playground and classroom setbacks now made good and paranoia and dirty teeth. I went to report myself as ready and able and functional. And in return all my skin and self were gathered inside the special laughter and the special jokes and the special methods.

They let me in.

I joined the Squad and was preforgiven and no sin could any more be a sin. I jumped from the cliff they provided.

I picked a new name and stepped in to continue the life of a dead son with all paperwork in agreement.

This was an easy thing to do and had justifications.

Permanent lying is a speed rush and I was permanent. I pitied my brother deceivers who ferried themselves between activist total commitment and brief returns to the wife and kiddies and loud dreams.

I withdrew from targets to an empty house full of set dressing for someone who was dead. My persona tastes and interests dominated as more interesting and worthwhile than my own. Often I returned to operations ahead of schedule.

I built in a habit of tiptoe standing and rocking back and then once more before standing. I used this to shield my passing joys and my hunter gathering of information.

I am watching Nigel and thinking that almost no one knows the sunlight of being fresh born and a wonderful pretender. Infants are too young to appreciate their birth. I am frequent gratitude and swells of happiness. Nigel sees me but does not know that I am the twenty-fifth hour between the days. I am the wingtip in the shadow between the trees. I am a dead boy made alive again and remarkable in the manner of all dead boys who walk about and have passports.

The hurt of parents somewhere did touch the Squad as we searched the death certificates for entry points. I believe I remember that. I am certain an uncanny moment happens when you find the name that suits. There is regret. I am certain that to mention I felt only my elation would be diagnostic monstrous.

There have been occasions when I have stood at the quiet fringe of this and that cemetery in the corner where they keep the little graves. Visitors leave indoor toys out in the weather as company or sacrifice or demonstration of specific loss. Colours fade from birthday to birthday. I have not been unmoved.

I smile at Nigel as if I am yearning sadly which perhaps I am and make a small cough in sipping my drink that is a difficult clumsiness to perfect. I present myself as suppressing the desire to choke and feel Tom flush from his collar upwards. Nigel licks his lips and continues with information about finance. He uses the word *dot* when referring to numbers with a decimal in order to mark himself as one of the wise and stock-trading classes.

Tonight my tie is cheap and a light shade of fawn the better to show soiling and here is a new stain as my glass sways too hard and spills a little. My shirt is grey white and an incapacity indication and made of bad synthetic threads. My suit is a wrong brown and stay-press drip-dry shit. I am designed to be Sun Tzu at war.

Feign disorder.

Pretend inferiority.

Encourage arrogance.

Nigel is listing brand names in order to impress and bewilder. He is blurring consonants. His thinking slip staggers and he loses words.

No one should be impaired among strangers. But Nigel thinks that he is among friends.

His suit is predictable dark blue English wool and made by Dege

& Skinner. He has an account. Soon I will have to be bewildered again and impressed again when he tells me about his account with Dege & Skinner again.

He is pleased by sad small things.

The ambient music has jumped up louder and Amadou & Mariam are singing about Senegal Fast Food and Paradise. Some of the Met boys are dancing and laughing ironic while they let Black French syllables touch and run on them like rain.

Nigel is quite unable to think why he is less audible now. He flickers irritation and cocaine. He starts telling a joke with a punchline about genitals because he wants revenge sex violence to happen and his punchline is as close as he can get at present. He is narrow and has damaging capacities like those of a nail. This is to say that he would do not very much without expert operation. Because of money and commercial influence power he suffers from delusions of freedom, but he has never been somebody else and never been able to do much of anything and anything and anything. He knows how to break things which is not a skill. As his one and solitary self he is the pretence his softness and failure hides behind in the manner of other public school broken child things.

My coughing is done with and I increase the smile I offer him by thinking of his confidence in bloodlines and genetic explanation for success. Nigel is obvious failure and multiple disqualifications as quality breeding stock. He is fantasy eugenics and suppressed awareness of septic roots.

I have provable superiority. I can be true but also fathoms deep in darknesses and hollows where the strange life flourishes. I have awareness powers to be whatever is required and still on duty. I might be watching and also convivial or kissing or fall down drunk or raging. My surface does not communicate true meaning.

I watch Nigel rub his nose because he needs uplift again. His tongue clicks every time it adheres to the roof of his mouth and then pulls free. The addict mindset is in dominance throughout this version of England and he has therefore been swift elevated to Member of Parliament status. He is ideal as representative of the perceived majority. Junkie nihilism is low-effort charming and has washed Nigel into a low-level ministry position. The low-effort charming media help him and he can be generous appealing with joy bursts. He synchs with prevailing headlines by chemical instinct and repeats their threat excitements. This has brought him already close to his public life catastrophe phase without my intervention. I enjoy his ignorance of this.

I nod and chuckle in the ways he finds reassuring.

But I am a clean man with solidity and mental permanence. I have years of bloodstream freedom. Prav made me better effective and I have improved on his improvements. The current climate leans in repetitive against me and advocates oblivions and failure despairs but I am impervious. I grin at my environment. I grin at Nigel. He pauses and frowns for a beat. I have twitched his instinct because he is at the sensitive animal stage of his intoxication.

I adjust my demeanour soft but fast. I head tilt sloping downwards and fold my hands to guard my crotch and then look gently fondly at him. He sways back on his heels and licks his lips with tongue out through a half smile. Nigel is not a wolf but has stolen wolf valour signals. I let him.

I am non-dependant powerful.

I am well.

I do not fail.

I am in pubworld but the opposite. I am the opposite of this lounge bar that is humid narrow and held between smallpoxed real Victorian anaglypta and reproduction Victorian tiles. I am original fake. I am a non-detectable former policebody. With every trip to the gents or turn to the bar I am a wink and smile confederate for all comical glances and a beg your pardon amenable traveller between clots of policebodies. I cycle through personalities out of boredom wherever Nigel cannot see. At one table I am a neat joke insertion at the proper moment and the chance to step away under the laugh. When I pass another I am the obvious good and sound man that somebody must have met somewhere because I am so familiar and such a good fit. I can be the brief satisfactory chat and then farewell because I always am circling back towards my mark. Nigel should never be left unattended for long.

Nigel is ineffective deception and little bursts of childfear and helpless disclosures that all leave contrails and heat hazes round his head.

I want a gun.

I despise them and yet I want to see one now in my hand.

I want to see his blood brain bone spring lightly in the air.

I am using hatedream energy to give me a shine of credible delight through these hours and hours of being among people who are shit and smearing themselves in more shit. I am covert laughing at them in my spinal column. This is keeping me upright functional. This is keeping me close to Nigel and in pubworld.

Pubworld is laughter reconfigured into howling. Pubworld is wet emancipation from thought. Pubworld is glorious public nuisance and disorder thuggery. Pubworld is after-hours locked in with the Blue and Met tastes of assumer necessity and noble impunity assumptions. Pubworld is Nigel flirt slumming and imagining this will lend him credibility. I have no residual longings for the chaos energy on offer. I have my passports to better chaos. I am warm at heart with contempt.

Contempt facial expressions are unmistakable and draw the eye and trip multiple alarms. Therefore I do not allow them.

I can do what Nigel cannot. I can be malleable intelligent within my own will and desires. I have purpose. My personality is effective separated and I am being Tom Stott with no errors or fluctuations in his behaviours and physical manifestation. Tom is jolly in the rancid beer stink. When he moves he steps gingerly and is needy convivial while picking a path between foot patrol boots with moisture-wicking laces and presentable CID Oxfords. Tom offers respect smiles. Tom is underlying excited by cocaine-dusted toilet cisterns and generalised glee. Tom conveys obvious yearnings towards privilege friendships and strength proximity. He pines for secrets.

Ten months of careful cultivation and slanders of my not existent wife mean the barman serves Tom glasses of tonic and tonic or
Red Bull and Red Bull or soda water and soda water. Meanwhile I
am Tom projecting astonishment delight at every time Nigel offers
attention as punishment or as treat. I also hint at an exploitable
fury underlying and a shamed and shameful knowledge of inadequate class status and infected background. I am evasive about
past violent transgression. Hints of bloodshed mayhems hook Nigel
in strong every time.

My own self is quiet and under and lets Tom be dog faithful.
I catch my own eye in the gantry mirror and am content to be a
private joke. I turn my head back and imagine future spilled blood
scenarios. This generates smiles with Duchenne real eye expression
for Nigel. I am bonhomie and cramps in my forearms from unex-
pressed desires.

My work is high-grade demanding in external and internal detail.

My work insisted I be Tom in pubworld who is peering at blue-
bottles dead among the dust on low windowsills that are lost
behind the backs of the sticky green banquettes. There are Britain
First stickers on the inside of the toilet doors as an ambient maso-
chism indication.

Nigel likes it rough.

Nigel has no understanding of rough.

Nigel who is not called Nigel but might as well be. Nigel is an
adequate descriptor.

Tom and Nigel are very together and our togetherness has taken
two years and will be worth it but not yet. Tom has a habit of leaning in and low and forward and almost as if he will lick or kiss the
hand that feeds. I find it hard to stop him literally whining for the
affections that men give to lower forms.

Nigel is thriving on my servant energy and is unable to notice
that Tom is factually taller than him and leaner and more powerful.
I have packed my fast hard graceful self away but it is still with me.

Nigel currently is using me to reconfigure every one of his Stonyhurst shames and social exclusions. His inability to conjugate the subjunctive mood of *Sum* is nothing and not worth mentioning although he does keep mentioning it while his eyes flare. He no longer knows what he will say next. He is repeating his favourite stories of boyhood promise and praised intelligence and almost believes they happened. We both know that he was an obvious freak and has always been recognised and shunned as such.

Each morning his glamour fades under ignorant use and he blames this failing on whoever he thinks of first. He prepares to appear normal in the ways that other people might prepare to play King Lear.

But good old Tom relieves all burdens and always slightly mispronounces the most entertaining words. Tom is a vast and shining ballroom full of small and large humiliations where only Nigel ever gets to dance.

Christmas is approaching. This means that Nigel will soon attend the annual Jesus concert of what he enjoys calling his alma mater and what I shall call Stonyhurst College. The warm candles and nostalgia event will take place in a nice Victorian Westminster church. Nigel will try to play the head up and shoulders back game and mumble his way through the later and therefore unknowable verses of Christmas carols. It would hurt his pride to ever be seen reading from the stylish commemorative programme and he must keep his face to the gold of the altar because then it will surely bathe him in a messianic light. He aims to demonstrate that what he does not already know must not possibly be worth knowing. He will sit at the end of a pew near the Martyr's Chapel and wonder why anyone would ever be martyred. The tedium of the service will overcome his tiny disciplines after eight minutes and he will become the sighing and glowering shoe swinger boy he always has been.

After the pantomime is over and the benediction has been dusted socialistically across all shoulders without favour, Nigel will march to the current headmaster with a handshake. It will be a limp gift offered badly. Nigel will radiate his version of vehement sanctity and run gameplay postures of already having joined the saints and bishops among the Old Boys. There will be experiments with the gestures of a man who embodies moral value. He will oscillate between this and a sense of uncleanliness that makes him brush and wipe at his hands clothes face hair. He will leak the flicker smirks of someone feeling the warm rush of fraudulence pleasure.

He is an amateur.

At times he will be unable to disguise his layered furies against all those early Jesuit attempts to garden in his soul.

Before and after god is formally noticed and sung to with compliments nobody will talk to Nigel for very long. He is unpalatable even as a nostalgia object or as a means to advancement. The headmaster will be fast polite with him and then away.

Men like Nigel are accidents to stare at. He mistakes fascination horror reactions in others for having charisma. But alone between the pews after his botched singing there will be the moment when he knows he is still repellent. He will feel the nakedness of that.

I will watch him mainly from the shadow stillness of the Calvary Chapel and be a still and quiet outsider but context congruent and therefore unnoticeable. My hair will be in good order and my face calm dominance at rest with festival warmth overtones.

I will see him failsweat. I will be happy.

When the church is almost empty I will leave. I will be wearing the knee-length midnight cashmere coat and black leather gloves and blue with white polka dot silk scarf that is inevitable for the scenario. I will cross myself and bow and holy water dip in the customary way as I leave because I am undoubtedly Catholic at that moment and my Crockett & Jones black calf leather brogues will make a nice sound on the parquet floor. He won't even glance my way at the terribleterrible threat I am.

While I stand in the din at the bar I am already looking forward to Nigel and his Christmas service and hoping to see his wounds and count them. A track by Whizkid is playing and I truthfully like it.

I frown bewildered at a Nigel comment and this allows him to explain the obvious and be delighted emphatic. He has moved on to using most of the words he put into a two days ago op ed about whiny maleness or white terror or Christian precepts under threat or the loss of carefree humour or suchlike. He never stays on topic. He has a high tolerance for his own absurdity.

I am breathing dead beer and sweat and piss and carpet filth and trace basement damp and a high floral content aftershave from Nigel. In the dark he would smell like a dying posy in an old woman's bedroom.

Nausea cigarette stink is wreathing and hanging in sheets at throat height while devilwillmakecare men smoke tobacco indoors. The lock-in illegality enables every other large and small transgression. Toilet cocaine is becoming table cocaine in plain sight. The company is one of gentlemen and rented companions only and so the ladies WC is reserved for screwing. Pauline and Star and Natalia are already here along with the tweaking underage one who is both Candy and Ann but also sometimes Crystal because she forgets things. If tonight is like the other nights more girls will arrive and the screwing will spread like dry rot into the corners of the lounge bar and the snug. The men here long for heterosexuality as a demonstration sport.

Soon I will take Crystal into the car park at the back and I will listen to her talk about her daughter who was taken into care. We will be there for as long as she needs to smoke her cigarettes. I will not touch her even when I hand her money over.

I think of myself as an uncle who is Dickensian benevolent although this is inaccurate.

Nigel and his pleasures are tedious predictable and offer so many pressure points that he is ninety per cent self-harm. He likes a hot room full of wrongness and likes the habits of ill health and likes the company of furious men from lower classes and lower incomes and likes uniforms and likes name-drop celebrity slanders and likes thick-fingered intrusions and bruises on female skin and likes his drink and likes his weed and likes his charlie. He is currently a wide black button-eyed boy and is joy squealing and dabbing at a nose bleed with an Aspinal silk pocket square. He is dapdapdap patting me with his other hot and damp hand.

I would like to cut it off.

That would be a disruption and a provocation and he speaks well of them both. It would also be a personal challenge to excel which is something he also says he likes.

I could see if he enjoys the challenge of being amputated.

Nigel is shames and secrets he only enjoys when he tellstellstells. Confession does not affect his soul other than badly. It is his demonstration of inherent rights. Playing him as a mark is not a triumph. Playing him is sitting down at a naked piano with time to spare. I listen to him and never mention details later. I am blotting paper and emptiness for screaming into and what he wants. I am a working-class born-to-fail trophy pet. I have been with him to witness his swings between indiscretion and remorse and forced forgetting because I do not matter at any level.

But he gives me headaches and migraine visual distortions.

I decide I will leave for another moment and make appropriate apologies and promises and small fanboy requests for favourites in his repertoire when I return. I make a pussy joke and he tries not to laugh so that I can be punished a little. I oblige with displayed sadness and little boy motions of having a too full bladder.

When I make it to the gents I do piss because I did have a mild need to. Then I wait in the stall for another arrival. I unbolt the door and walk out as I pop tablets with a fast hand and no explanation to confirm my fallen status for the audience of two drunk coppers. They give automatic approval grins although all that I have taken is ibuprofen

I wash out a sink and fill it with cold water and then bury my face under the surface. The cold is good.

I have to go back and be Tom again. But the cold is good.

I will remember this moment as very beautiful although I will erase the where and when.

I am almost done. The project is almost done. Only a few months more.

The bluebodies break wind at each other from one stall to the other. One of them begins to tell a joke about a Jew and gay sex and Jew sex and a prostitute. He loses his thread.

The sink is not deep enough to let the water fill my ears.

The cold is good.

Tom likes it also. Tom is happy with everything.

Tom lifts his head and shakes it and lets it seem sweat wet and tugged-back careless. Then he pushes the swing door open to let in the pub noise.

I steer him out through the press of happy raging policebodies. I smile momentarily aggressive.

I know that on a Saturday in mid-December Stonyhurst will hold the customary hare and hounds race across Wimbledon Common. Nigel will attend.

I also know already that next year he will be extremely unavailable to join the Old Boy runners. I know that he will be unable to jolt through his version of unself-conscious hearty man efforts. He won't jog shake mud-spattered thighs past the usual handful of cameras at the finish line.

Nigel will not be available for anything as planned. This absence will not be pandemic related.

It is relative easy to show someone affection when they will not live long.

After a while in lockdown you realise the air in London always had this faint burned rubber taste and now that's gone. Still, we're no cooler.

But something about the quiet version of the city, the quiet version of the world, means that we look up more. Last month – which was April – was all about Venus and how it was blue bright and especially clear, nailed up for us to see beside a storybook wink of moon.

Year Five picked sky names they'd be called for the month: Deneb, Cygnus, Draco, Ophiuchus, Raselhague. We thought about all of the people in the past who spoke Latin, or Ancient Greek, or Arabic, and who peered up like us at how huge the night was and how like an absence so vast it becomes a presence, or like a cave full of eyes, or all kinds of other worries. They filled their sky with legends so that heaven would feel cosy and make sense. Or maybe the legends and the star names made it all stay where it was and not seem to be considering how it might draw them skywards into the nothingness and eat them. (I didn't say that last bit, obviously. I always find outer space terrifying and therefore take extra, extra care to ensure that doesn't show and make the Acorns tense.)

Anja had been sort of fading in isolation, looking more and more numb on screen. When I turned up for Welfare Checks she would be a distant movement in the shadows beyond her doorway. When her mother brought her forward she had to be almost dragged along by the arm like a captive – or like someone now afraid of invisible death swimming past in the outside air.

For some reason, she chose Raselhague to be her name. It's a binary star: one of a pair that are somewhat smaller than our sun, but more than twice its mass. Something about the name pleased her, caught her interest. She seemed to like the idea of being two things dancing round each other, both at once. And then it could be revealed that Raselhague means *head of the serpent collector*.

This was somehow an instant, perfect fit. During the rest of our morning Anja rarely lost a broad, incautious, birthday surprise kind of grin. Our personal project time involved everyone drawing and writing about Raselhague. We did this with each of our harmless new names and it was her turn. When she worked, though, I could see this time a sort of fire and secrecy was lighting her. Lots of pens were deployed while she threw up occasional glances at me, of the kind that would usually indicate illicit fun.

But Anja had always avoided any type of fun. Back in our non-virtual days, she would generally spend her breaks out in the playground looking like a baffled and elderly tourist She seemed to be worried she'd lose her passport and not be allowed to go home.

That day, when we read out our stories, Raselhague was a winner. All of the drawings seemed to be tributes heading Anja's way. Year Five had decided to be spontaneously lovely in directions I had not anticipated. Atticus, gentlemanly as ever, dialled up his courtesy into being actively gallant. Simon was quiet but definitely admiring. Millie the haunted aristocrat was happy to grant Raselhague significant status. Millie operates according to a personal and internalised little version of Debrett's and she was suddenly and definitely in favour of both Raselhague and Anja.

And that morning our new, small heroine went last, top billing. I did wonder how Anja would handle the attention.

I had no need to fret. Anja took to the spotlight like a clean and sober, mid-career Judy Garland. She was gracious, she was audible, she was smiling, she had suddenly worked out how to lock eyes with the laptop camera and hold us like a much-loved veteran news anchor, or maybe a mellow sports star delivering well-tailored anecdotes. We nodded, we smiled, we applauded.

She had decided to occupy all of the space reality offered her. No more hiding in corners, no more voluntary retreats. Anja was going to occupy all of the space that her presence deserved.

Even miles apart, just a little grid of faces and glitchy sound, we all got a contact high from Anja and her definite arrival inside her own life.

Her drawing of Raselhague was remarkable, too – it showed a

girl in boots and sort of red and purple robes, apparently dancing through a field of perky snakes, all of whom had raised their heads to watch her, like sentient grasses with bright tongues.

I told our headmistress Sue about it that evening. She came round and stood in the courtyard, wearing her cartoon dog face mask. If you only glanced at her, the effect was goofy, charming, cheering. Here was a slightly dumpy woman, past middle age, wreathed in coloured patchwork cheesecloth and sporting a black and white animal's nose in the shadow of her yellow sun hat.

Things are bad, but not so very bad.

She'd lost weight, though. And when she looked at me, she was also looking through me at something dreadful. I could see her shoulders rounding, the famously brave posture fading whenever she lost her thread and couldn't concentrate.

Still, she was delighted by my news in a Sue kind of way. 'Anja, little Anja. I knew you'd do it. I knew she'd do it.' And she clapped her hands the way she might in Big Room and then started to dance.

Sue Delara's dancing is a mishmash, mostly bandari, but with some bhangra – lots of lifting and seed-planting motions – thrown in. Sometimes, when we used to be very delighted about something in Big Room, she would lead us in twirling and little silly wiggles and hops in place. Even the smallest acorns could manage that.

I don't think I'll ever enjoy any one of those dances now without calling out her pet names for moves, 'Happy Hands, Happy Hands, Snakes, More Snakes, Happy Hands low, Happy Hands high, Push the Boat, Push the Boat, Baby Bird Dances, Baby Bird Dances and whirl, whirl, clap and whirl, whirl, clap.'

Back when we were all in school – apparently both moments and years ago – she used to do more kicks and low dips. It's hard work, seeming that joyful.

I join in.

Tell no one – I do like a bit of a dance.

Two middle-aged women in a London courtyard – *Baby Bird, Happy Hands, Snakes, More Snakes.*

I didn't make her lose her dignity by asking if she was okay.

She looked at me, bright and fierce, breathless, 'I do this in the kitchen, you know, most evenings. Practising. Morale.'

That evening she really was close to the Sue I'd first met, this giggling blur of shades from orange into reds and browns. 'My mother never really showed me any of this, but then her mother didn't want her to learn and that's how not knowing starts, isn't it? But we have to know and remember. Sustainable, self-propagating knowledge – it's so easy and its opposite is so hard, but we still get it so wrong, so often. Not that my mother didn't know other wonderful things. People prioritise.'

Her arms slid and slinked up away and above her head. She has a fluidity that always surprises me in someone so solid and definitely there. 'We become what we prioritise.' She smiled and span and closed her eyes.

And maybe anyone could be themselves, entirely themselves, given enough of a pause. Nobody wants a lockdown, only a pleasant pause with space enough to find your best-fitting life. Then everything would be fine.

Maybe our current state of emergency and three-word slogans could even provide that pause. There has to be something positive we can find in it.

What's the point of nightmares if they teach you nothing?

Sue stumbled, coming out of a twirl, and nearly fell. I ran in and caught her before I could wonder if hugs were okay yet, in all the intentional jumble of hints and winks and rules and lies and contradictions that we have instead of a pandemic strategy.

There we were, our arms around each other and still alive and trying to be, if not triumphant then functional. We try to be functional. And reassuring.

We need reassurance and sometimes there's no one else who can provide it.

2020 is so very strange, but so very familiar. Anyone who grew up with a Stiltskin in charge of their household, anyone who's ever lived with a Stiltskin, tried to love a Stiltskin, run from a Stiltskin, anyone still dealing with a Stiltskin – we've all been here before. We know the playbook: lies, evasions, snap changes of direction, bullying, breaking, escalating risks. Every day tenses our spines and gives us vertigo. We flinch.

And, holding Sue, I noticed that she seemed just a little too shocked by a simple stumble. And there was much less of her than it might seem underneath her layered plumage.

I am a very jolly bird and, look, this is my plumage.

Eventually, we stood apart.

And I should have said. 'The cobbles can be slippy.' I should have said. 'I'm tired. You're tired. The whole planet is so tired.'

Instead, for a few moments we just faced each other – two people in a clown tornado that roils about and picks up whoever it likes and disappears them.

So tired.

Stiltskins exhaust you with their obvious absurdities. Even if you never dare to say a word, they know your bewilderment is eating you. They don't always need to hit your body, not if they can keep on punching you in your mind.

Sue told me the inevitably reckless news, 'They're talking about going back to physical classes in June.'

'That's too fast.'

Sue was staring across at my oldest honeysuckle, which is glossy and dense and healthier than ever. Our plants, at least, are thriving.

Sue nodded, 'I know it's too early to go back and I will delay. But some of the parents are going to want it. Some aren't coping alone, some are already home-schooling older children, there's not enough help … it's a mess.'

I don't say a word about how suddenly so many people who took us for granted are finding out that teaching is hard, a bit of a grind. Sue doesn't like bearing grudges, bitterness. I suppose I don't either.

I tell her, 'I know.'

Sue grins for a wicked little moment. 'No one will remember we actually matter. Afterwards. It'll slip their minds.' Then she brings in her hands and rubs her palms together. Whenever she does this it suggests that reality has been rolled out on to a lightly floured surface and cut to size and really she's done all she can. 'I am so pleased about Anja. And good news deserves a dance.'

'Any time.'

'I'll come again and get my feet used to the cobbles.'

'Yes. Of course.'

I think we were glad to be wearing our masks for more than just medical reasons. They do cover a good deal of what you might otherwise end up expressing. If we'd started crying – well, you know me… Not that the various sadnesses aren't still obvious, but indulging them does no good. Nobody needs more weeping, not now.

'Really, Sue. You just come round whenever you want. The courtyard is nice and safe and airy.'

We hugged goodbye.

Are hugs safe? I'm still not sure. Masked hugs?

I watched her shoulders hunch as she dipped out through the wooden doorway and into the way things are beyond my garden.

Still… *Celebrate victories while we can, even the smallest. From what is small as an acorn, a celebration as tall as an oak may grow.*

Oakwood has many mottoes and that one's a bit clumsy , but I don't think it's wrong.

And there is still joy available. Anja now comes online every morning and waves her arms and announces, 'Head of the Serpent Collector!' and we all cheer.

That's victory. That's pure.

You never know what will work for a child. There's always something somewhere – a hobby, or a hat, or a sport, or a musical instrument, a trip somewhere, an animal, a job they'd like, a person – there's always something for a kid that will make them want to live. The job is to find it. A school is supposed to be the place that supplies and supplies and supplies so many options you find one that works.

Head of the Serpent Collector.

To Anja this has a density of meaning that religions manage to gather only over centuries. As far as I can work it out, she's both head of all serpent collectors and the Serpent Collector who controls serpents' heads and so it goes on. Quite possibly her power is still expanding in extraordinary, startling rings.

There she was again today – it's Thursday, 7th of May – sitting the way that a confident child sits. I never quite understand how someone who seems irrevocably hurt will suddenly reach out and pick up that one perfect addition they can use to mend themselves. Somewhere, they've always known it should be there and had this longing that tugs in the way that a little compass tugs at the whole direction of a ship. This is how the unmendable mends itself.

I think the sadness in some kids – perhaps all kids, all adults – isn't exactly whichever trauma ambushed them, whichever acts of unforgivable vandalism, whichever bad luck, whichever types of poverty; it's also this constant knowledge of an absence that could be our cure.

And the sadness can turn to darkness. Some kids get lost. I do believe almost all of them could have found something light to fall in love with, given any chance. If I didn't believe that, what would be the point of teaching? What would be the point of most things: democracy, courtesy, normality and so forth?

Tonight, Year Five promised we'd all look at the supermoon. It's this month's wonder, or one among our available, suitable wonders. We must always look for wonders – they sustain.

My son and I went out and walked in the dark and the moon watched us, definitely curious and huge, leaning in close. I could feel it staring down. The whole disk was goldish pinkish, like a strange metal in some story – an element used to make magical objects, one that can't help attracting heroes and terrible crimes.

And that's enough delaying.

I have to say it now, don't I?

I have to write down what happens with Buster the gone-wrong boy when I corner him up on those steps at Saint Paul's.

So we're back on that day, then.

And I don't stop and wonder if the whole chase thus far has been some kind of Buster-style dark joke, Buster manipulation, Buster trick. I don't question why he's stopped and turned to face me, once he's outside a cathedral named after my only child.

Yes, I realise the saint and the cathedral came before my son, but I like to think of them as being named after him. What would be more important to me, after all – a misogynist former tentmaker who wrote Jesusy letters, a big building stuffed with monuments to empire, or my son? My Paul's what matters to me. And when he was tiny I did, indeed, tell him we'd eventually visit the whole cathedral that he had to himself. This came very close to making him irreligiously confused. He thought everybody got their own cathedral.

Another maternal misstep.

But I believe I'm on solid ground here, righteous. Buster, breathless and halted outside St Paul's, seems both tired and cornered. He's, at the very least, allowing me to feel I have the upper hand.

I've been running so hard that I want to just keep on and push right through him, push into him as if he's water and make him feel what I've been feeling for so many years.

Also I want to be nowhere near him. He repels, seems infectious in an unknown way. I do want to punch him, but I'd rather keep him long, safe miles away, because he does things human beings shouldn't ever manage to. I don't currently know how many things, but it's already unsurprising to me that he won't enter somewhere blessed.

He gets no sanctuary, won't even try for it.

There he is in his neat-fitting and how-can-he-afford-it suit and coat and his maybe-club-member's tie and the shiny leather shoes – just an average Westminster sociopath. Only he's not: that's just the wrapper.

Inside himself, I can see that he's still Buster. And he really is older by that quarter-century or so. He seems healthy in the over-stretched way some middle-aged men get: too thin, too tanned, too much sinew in his neck. His haircut might be military, but I'm guessing that he's not a soldier, that it's just part of another costume.

All this is happening long before he sneaks in under cover of the plague and hand delivers his filthy envelope full of his filthy excuses, but I can see that he hasn't just gone back to being some type of policeman.

Policemen are out in the air a lot, but never do seem to get a tan. There is a hint of the subterranean about them.

I possibly wonder – as I have before – if he was, or still is, some-thing in military intelligence. I possibly wonder all kinds of things, but they smear round my head like a dirty rag before disappearing and I don't want to touch them anyway.

A little breeze rises, hits my face, and I inhale that old-man barber shop smell of Brut: like lavender and Christmas and wet leather. Whoever he is currently has kept on wearing that, then. He does hold on to some things. Underneath the perfume, there's an acrid chemical tang that makes me think of undertakers.

Also my heart kicks up a gear, because this is him climbing inside again, making me inhale him.

I recite various scripts provided by various therapists and sup-port groups. They remind me that he doesn't get to touch me any more, not in any way, because that is a privilege and I will never grant it. He is not part of my universe.

Still, he's in my lungs. Buster the disease, the one-man pandemic.

I'm not furious. I am some other emotion that hasn't a name, or not one that I know. I am nothing like Buster – no one decent is – but already I think he would know the way I'm feeling. I think that it's with him all the time and tastes of murder.

Meanwhile, he's acting at me – showing me run-to-ground breathlessness and soap opera tragedy eyes. There's a flicker of weird colour in them, or an unnatural intention. I see it just for a moment, as if a shutter opens for one blink and light hits a mechanism in there, hard and operational.

'Buster.' I sound weak and querulous, which annoys me, so I try again. 'Buster.' There are times when you want to shout blood, though – meat, teeth, poison, anything more solid than words.

He shakes his head, as if he means *I don't know*, rather than *no*. Then he rubs his forehead, gives me his tired little boy act and there's a shine of tears that may be on the way.

Good at emotions, is Buster. If you didn't know better you'd trust every one of them.

'You're not going to say anything, Buster?'

I don't think I want him to say anything.

'Not anything? Why did you even turn up? You knew I'd be there. The OrKestrA's family. You knew at least one of us would always be there.' I'm apparently not weak and quizzical any more. I sound like the women in London streets who clearly have lives in freefall and who hold plastic carrier bags with the logos worn off – women who are hectoring and close to screaming at things that may not be visible. 'Buster? Is this your fault? Is the prosecution your fault? Did you do this to us? Can't you leave us alone?' Yelling women attract worried stares and then policemen. I have already crossed the threshold to gather stares.

And I am so tired of policemen. I am so tired of watching their hands on their machine guns at tube stations, or the way they try hard to not quite see you as your massive demo marches past. You won't exist for them until you're scattered, until nightfall, until they kettle you into a crush. Then the cameras and credible witnesses are gone and the boots rush in.

I've had years to find out about policemen – about burglaries of troublesome households, political households, questioning households – burglaries than were cop intrusions and feral surveillance squad intrusions and messing with your head intrusions for cop fun.

Sometimes I lie in bed and think of cops and cops and more cops prying into papers and underwear drawers.

And there's Buster on the steps – cop surveillance that crawled into my bed.

Police are supposed to be who you call when you really need help. But they're just Buster, under the smiles and promises to do better, they keep on repelling the decent people and being only Buster, the small and dirty brokenness of Busters.

He opens his mouth and I'm sure he's going to try some version of, 'I'm sorry.' If he does, I think I'm going to start howling and the howl will last for twenty-five years and make up for twenty-five years of my silence. The Endlessly Howling Woman – tour guides can add me to their routes.

In fact, here I go, anyway – deep breath in and ready to start.

He flinches. I made him flinch.

I haven't done anything yet, but he's scared of me – is what I think.

Good.

Very good.

Is what he lets me think.

But also I'm being ridiculous. I'm being the batty woman in the street. I am not using my words and I am supposed to be better than that, so I fumble for something less animal. The first thing I can manage is.

'*We are friendly and helpful, we're kind and polite,*
We mend and don't break things, we do what is right.'

Stupid of me, but on I go.

'*We grow every day in our beauty and light,*
We learn and we're brave and we sleep well at night.
We sleep well at night. We sleep well at night.'

I yell it. Then I yell it again.

I think I may not be able to stop repeating it.

'*We sleep well at night.*'

I'm howling happiness and sunshine and trying to feel joyful and proud as an oak with my shoulders back and lifted chin, like a child with a good future.

But my voice is thick with crying and everything is getting distorted and cut up into sobs.

'*We sleep well at night.*'

He's watching me the way a beaten farm dog watches strangers. And maybe it's the look on my face – even though I'm quiet now – that makes him change his mind about offering any type of answer.

His hands drop straight down to his sides, hang there.

I wonder if I have been too threatening and if he finds me frightening. I regret it. I feel uncivilised

How stupid stupid stupid is that?

Once I've read what's inside Buster's envelope, my guilt will seem hilarious.

He was standing there, deadpan but laughing at me inside.

And meanwhile, I'm breathless and my throat is raw and the mountainous side of St Paul's remains unimpressed.

I hear myself yelping, 'What?' My nose is running and I swipe it along my wrist. I would never let the kids do anything so feral and a rush of shame dials my volume back up high. 'WHAT?'

Of course, I don't mean *what*. I want to ask him *why?*

And his body, his physical balance, is changing. There's only a glimmer showing, but it says that everything about him will snap-shift very soon.

I don't want to be a person who can spot this. I don't want to recall the ways in which it was exhilarating to understand someone else's body in so much detail, to love it so tightly that you seem to share it with them and to be doubled and extraordinary.

'Shit. You're such a little shit. There's shit grained in me. I still find these seams of shit. Of just shit – and that's because of you, Buster. That's because of you.'

He keeps on watching me.

'You're making me think of shit and I don't even think of words like that because I am this clean, clean person now. I follow a clean vocation.'

I will eventually believe that today he anticipated me the way he anticipated everybody. He put me inside another of his plans. I was never special and am not now. He made me feel special – like a sad kid standing on a chair and watching elastic tighten. Once he had me, I was an access point, a component inside machinery that only he could see. There was no intimacy.

Buster pays constant attention and that feels personal, but he's only making sure that he will fit. He can't experience normal human ways to feel and think, so he has to stay intent, intense – intense about his choice of shirt this morning, intense about breaking Monkey's heart, intense about anything. It's what he has instead of love.

Outside Saint Paul's, I'm still almost assuming he's damaged only in ways that can turn into slapstick. I'm thinking that he could be part of the good joy and skills that are expressed as slapstick.

Right now he is still pretending – looking like a man who was broken into fragments and who became Proper Funny in response. That would be a response. I think he might have lied about how he was broken, about all the cracks, but I'm still assuming he's a person, a man and not only the cracks.

But everything, everything, everything was a lie. Even his way of being funny was a lie. Buster could even poison comedy – Buster's an absence of life.

But I look at the breeze searching his hair, patting his coat, and I miss what we were in the OrKestrA. I miss that more than what we were together in our bed, in the trap that was our bed, the trap he made into our bed. I miss being in a ring of happy humans who are looking on in types of admiration, being a double act, being alert and alive and unified. I miss being physically certain.

We were funny, Buster and I. We were The Indelibles, The Twosome, The Whosome Twosome, Baron Buster and Annanka

Ladystrong. We stood apart from the everyday and its people by being more committed to each moment. We were glorious in motion in the way that delighted animals seem to be.

I think that was true.

And you made me like it, Buster.

You made me like the sunshine of it.

But you weren't delighted and you weren't even animal. You were something with no names.

Buster keeps on watch, watch, watching. He's at high readiness. I can see his arms are deeply peaceful but concentrating, too – as if something might come flying at him, any time now.

There have been nights when I dreamed the knives I threw at him were real.

In our act we often did a lot with knives. This seemed innocent, ridiculous.

I would fling them – apparently randomly, apparently in a rage – and Buster would catch them every time, a deadpan man coping with life. It was funny. The blades swam clean and fast through the jolly air and – clean and fast – he'd have them by the handle.

The women always laughed at the knife act more than the men, let out long, contented screams about female exasperation as pantomime.

They didn't know the half of it, did they, Buster?

As a double act we were all about back-and-forth anticipation. Buster must have found it commonplace, but I was amazed to find myself being one half of a single intention. I'd feel his hands grip each dummy kitchen knife as clearly as I could feel myself send it spinning towards his eye.

I believed we were the opposite of danger. I believed he and I were fooling the audience. But I was just another mug punter – someone else he played and baffled to achieve a predetermined result.

Buster licks his lips and the action seems feral and therefore true – a reptile need to taste the air.

I have many reasons to hate him, but I'm surprised by the one that seems to hurt me most. By betraying the OrKestrA – me most of all, but the OrKestrA, too – he ruined the ways in which we were magnificent. He took the happiness from our chosen family, took the Funny, or certainly hurt it and made it timid. Funny can't be timid, that doesn't work. Exactly when we most needed to be all we could, he pushed us inwards and made us small.

I remember a moment, remember flinging up an arc of dinner plates and knowing that he was catching them behind my back, whisper soft, and stacking them up neat.

How could that be so beautiful when Buster is Buster?

All that apparently effortless beauty – and I was an idiot and loved it.

But love is the correct response to beauty.

I wasn't wrong.

He was wrong.

I make myself study him, pay attention to the costume, the mask. The OrKestrA version of Buster would never have worn that coat, those shoes, that tie. They'd have burned his skin. But maybe when he went back wherever home was, he was this thing, dressed this way. I stand there and wonder if he's looking wealthy because he is – if he turned us all inside out for cash and prizes.

And I want to burn something. Everything.

I want to burn his neatness, his gloss of success, his coat with its nice, sharp cut and hand-stitched lapels.

The Buster I knew liked cardigans.

Our whole act, in its final form, was based around matching cardigans and a street theatre representation of the bland domesticity. We'd reduce our fake marriage's prop furnishings to ash and splinters and eight minutes flat. Every object became magical and flew: lamps, chairs, our comedy baby, which is all the child we ever made.

Our dream home became a cascade of disasters, an exorcism of every worry in the crowd. Nothing that happened to them could be worse than us.

Annanka Ladystrong would lift Buster up, bend him, fold him, throw him so the crowd would have to surf him back to me. It seemed a nice proof of my power. I would balance him high and laugh.

He'd be lighter now, easier to lift.

Buster, I couldn't throw you far enough.

Throw and catch and throw and catch – but in the end everything fell.

Newspapers burned, so did the telly.

We'd accidentally lose more and more clothing as the mayhem rolled on, until eventually we were performing in bizarre underwear and spangles. And suburbia proved to be both fragile and perverse – as suspected.

When the carnage was done, I'd reclaim our fake baby from a fake godparent in the audience. Then Buster would reclaim the crowd's attention, pop balloons stuffed with paper rose petals to make a burst of instant romance. We'd stand under the drifting crimson, still and together at last. We'd finally see and be seen. We'd kiss.

It worked well in dry weather, or indoors.

There's no trace of that in his face today.

Deadpan man – that's why I called you Buster. After Buster Keaton.

I gave him the beautiful name of the kind and generous deadpan king, the master of bone-breaking grace.

And now any silly and sweet moment with a man makes me see cheap paper petals getting dirty as they're blown along a street. Even F.L. doesn't quite take that away.

Thanks, Buster. Thanks so much.

You took why I laugh. You took what let me smile.

I can feel my jaw locking, my neck locking.

'Do you know how long it took? Do you know how long?' I'm trying to talk about how many years I spent rebuilding, but I don't make sense.

A place with Buster in it can't make sense.

The lunch crowds are everywhere now. They ought to realise that our performance space should always have been left clear for us alone.

And Buster's not showing me deadpan, he's showing me *psychopath at rest*. He is a kind of nowhere.

'You're just going to stand there? You're just going to stoneface and stand there?'

The Whosome Twosome made apparently dear things collide, destroyed all of our heirlooms and treasures. We were a conversation conducted in the languages of harm.

The Bad Man that Paul and I fled from knew all about that kind of chat. He didn't play it for laughs.

Buster didn't either – he was making me act out the damage he would do, exploding a home I thought I'd have, a family, making it trash.

'Was it easy? Did you have to rehearse that, too? All the lying? Were we all easy? Was the OrKestrA just stupid for you?'

And I can count *one Mississippi, two Mississippi* – just the way we used to – between the moment when I'm sure he's about to run and the one when I see him turn and start away.

There he goes.

I think all of the blasphemies I never say aloud.

I think phrases unsuitable for my vocation.

I think words that are poison.

You little fucking fucker you fucking shit.

I see his back disappearing into the drifts of normality shifting around the cathedral, human people being inside their lives. I can't recall how he got down the steps to pavement level. His descent somehow happened faster than I could see. He seems to have this weird push of reversed gravity around him. He repels. It gets him fast through the clutter of human beings.

And then he's out of sight.

There's a pause while I discover that I apparently can't breathe or move, or think.

If anyone should have died it should have been Buster, not Monkey Monk. If anyone should have needed to blank out his own thinking with chemical help, it shouldn't have been Monkey with his boy's soul and his body that got more innocent the more it undressed.

And I stumble forward then, like someone who's just been shoved through a curtain and back onstage without a script.

No rehearsal necessary. I run after Buster. Full tilt, hard, pelting, I just run.

I do that because I am unaware that he isn't just despicable. He is a trapdoor into nothingness.

I round the flank of the cathedral through what seems thickened air, as if he's leaving a vapour trail of altered atoms to resist me. In the shade of the wall he has snap changed into a brisk, professional walk. He's being what matches his costume: someone who never runs, who makes other people rush for deadlines and fight with public transport, who makes them sweat. Buster's even putting on a swagger, while he heads east along the gargantuan side of the allegedly blessed building that is doing him no harm. He's still going fast, but not so fast that I can't keep up.

I follow him between the leafless trees and bundled-up couples of the churchyard and then on across the broad complications of traffic along Cheapside and New Change.

The architecture is abrupt and very modern here, in spite of the old street names. It's the usual story – those with the power to make our decisions think we won't notice the damage they do, the knock-off tat they leave us with – as long as they preserve the labels.

Buster doesn't look back. Not once.

That's how little I mean to him.

And now we can be back in my courtyard again, safe behind our big blue wooden wall. I had no time to write these past weeks. Or maybe Buster made it hard to come back to my pages.

But they are my pages, this is my story.

And we're all safe, for the moment.

But two days a week I'm back in the classroom with Year Five.

I'm not in the army. My going to work is not supposed to mean that I might die.

If I could express a preference, no one in the army should die, either. They could just build things and guard people and escort the desperate to safety. Constructive risk taking – it makes them happy. I've checked.

But right now it would be quicker to number the jobs here that haven't suddenly mutated to involve maybe horribly drowning on dry land and alone.

And soldiers get shot at, but they also do get to shoot back. That's mostly their point.

We just die. Picked off, with a cripple here and corpse there – when will there ever be a cease fire?

On my first day back with the kids we were joyful to see each other. There they were, a simple and lovely thing: waving and bouncing children in a room. We had made it this far and we were still able to wave and bounce.

And crying was not a possibility because how would I deal with that safely in a mask and how would they understand it?

We talked about which people make our hearts shine – and our eyes shine. That's important. We then changed the subject rapidly. Also important.

And I was looking at them through air that might murder us. And Ignacy has asthma. And how would we even know who might be killing who?

We can at least all wear our masks because no Health Minister can bully us at Oakwood. He picks on council kids. So they have to be in classrooms with no mitigations and therefore withstand the test of infection. And therefore the relatives of council kids and the co-workers of the relatives and the people who stand too close to the relatives of council kids – and so on and so on... We all have to be tested to destruction.

I try not to wonder why. Buster has made me more and more incurious – sometimes there's no why and only this big, dark *Why not?*

At least headmistress Sue has set a fragile truce in place and only those willing to protect themselves and others can be here. Masks welcome, naked faces please stay at home, and we'll see you onscreen.

Like a Venetian costume party.

Except obviously not.

Like 'The Masque of the Red Death', but with no style.

And we're all together – Acorns and Oaks – and doing our best with big eyes and newly patterned and variably coloured faces. We look like what would happen if soft toys tried to re-enact a medical drama.

But everyone has to eat and drink in Big Room. And every staff member takes a turn overseeing on the lunch rota. The jammed-open windows and doors bring in the taste of the A316. We can't afford many air filters on top of the laptop expense, but we have some. We try to stay well. We are free to try. We don't have to choose between resigning and something we don't name because it's standing so close beside us and could reach out at any time.

Millie's mum is locked into vehement reality denial and sending round strange YouTube videos on the Parents' Forum. Millie doesn't join us in classes as she doesn't wear a mask because of deeply held religious reasons she can't explain and neither can her mother.

Maybe Jesus doesn't like cloth. His crucifixion statues are always underdressed.

I do like Millie.

But I don't want her here.

Millie's mum is litigiously Correct – if not Right – while the rest of us are Wrong and possibly in league with dark forces. You'd think all her newfound surges of belief and moral certainty might at least make her happy, but in fact she looks awful, haunted. Online with us, Millie says the woman barely sleeps. Keeping track of mythical conspiracies and endlessly shifted deadlines for the apocalypse is more than a full-time job.

So many bad ideas are conjured up now at beyond the speed of thought. No one is really keeping up.

I can't start to get angry about it. I have no more room.

There is always a bright side, we just need to find it.

That could be misleading information, even if it's up on Big Room's wall with the other Oakwood sayings.

I still do my share of the Welfare Checks. I still go round to Millie's house. Welfare Checks, lunch duty, accidents, hugs, the strangers we pass in the streets: I live in the age of fury and Russian Roulette.

Take joy wherever you find it and smiles will travel with you.

Well, I mean… I do give it a go…

I determinedly gladden myself by watching the wren who lives with us at Wicklow Street. There are two, in fact. They ought to be enough to keep me permanently elated.

Sometimes we are the bright side. We can shine.

Three days a week, we're still online, cosy again. More than cosy – the cobbles get hot enough in the sun to hurt my bare feet.

Three days a week – online and defended.

When I came home from the first school day, I stripped off in the courtyard and then threw everything I was wearing straight into the washing machine. Then I came in and soaped myself in the shower, scrubbed and scrubbed.

I concentrate on being glad that Oakwood can take care of us.

We can be more careful than other places. We take precautions. In this we suddenly resemble the better public schools where all the pandemic rules are not about enforcing death.

I keep my full-strength masks in paper bags and use them in rotation. I don't have enough to throw them away after one use.

The cloth ones I can wash, but how much good they'll do me seems intentionally vague.

Having to stand up and be the example of happiness and good futures in a totally unprotected classroom – I can't imagine.

Everyone inside the hospitals, wearing bin bags and making do – I can't imagine.

Hissy in her hospital and Sissy in the care homes – I can't imagine.

They phone me sometimes – the one or the other – and can't make whole sentences, they're so stressed out. Nothing has ever defeated them, but the time that has caught us all is making them different.

They're not going to resign. They're staying. All over the country, people are staying in situations where no one should have to be.

That's not being the bright side, that's shining until you burn up and nothing's left.

I mainly get by on denial and distraction.

In the evenings I watch our two little wren-shaped dabs of bird being still alive. They seem to enjoy existing just at the corner of the eye, tick-tailing around the nest box Paul and I didn't think would even attract blue tits. They keep on trusting us with their tiny futures. And they keep eating, or carrying off every scrap we offer them on Paul's swinging, rat-proof bird table.

They're a great distraction.

The bird feeder isn't really rat-proof. Nothing is. London is a rat amusement park with adjacent pleasure grounds for bed bugs and TB.

The rats are simply finding our bird table unamusing for rat reasons inexplicable to us and, no doubt, keeping watch from the lapis lazuli Jacuzzis in their local crime boss lairs. (Paul used to be scared of rats, so we recast them as Bond villains with ornate plans for domination of multiple fast-food chains.)

According to Paul, the non-fictional rats are waging civil wars over food resources since the restaurants folded and the leftovers dried up. How very evolved of them. Cougars in shopping centres, goats conquering Llandudno, nature generally kicking back and playing in our absence – it seems the other species are bounding forward while we lurch back towards the caves.

We have just been told we've ended our *national hibernation*, whatever that is. Everything is just the same and just as fatal, but our leaders are bored by pretending to care now. They assume we share their lack of self-control.

Or something like that. My Stiltskinny PTSD is very active. If anyone asked me whether I felt as if I was trapped in a national Bad Relationship I would say yes. But no one ever does ask – do they? My headache is up at around eight out of ten most days and pain-killers are in short supply, so Paul massages my shoulders. I pretend that he's making a difference.

Restaurants are sort of operational again, but far fewer people than anticipated want to sit in rooms with potentially plague-bear-ing strangers. Our government declares itself puzzled.

It's puzzled in the way the Bad Man I ran away from was puzzled when I disliked having my arm burned against the grill. I recognise that appetite for harm. I suspect the Stiltskins of cosplaying every possible darkness to see what they can get away with. They kill us for not being them and to make themselves feel special, but they dress it all up in the pseudo-science of mass infection and dreams of genetic superiority.

I'm sure that I'm wrong.

I'm equally sure that nobody will stop them.

What kind of low thing might you be, if you stand up tall only when you're on a hill of corpses?

Sometimes I am the bright side. I can shine.

We have all these extra new graves, but we don't talk about them.

One imaginary death in a Cotswolds village, or an otherwise gorgeous location – that would be on telly. It would be investigated by amateur sleuths with upper-class names, or loveable policemen with charming quirks. We'd want to know everything about it. If only all the healthcare workers had died in a country house in 1936 – then we'd be entirely fascinated by each and every one.

But they're blowing away in drifts like leaves. And there are always more leaves.

I could wonder what sort of country would feel Sunday evening programming with a cuppa and some biscuits could be improved only by an hour of murder, neatly resolved in the last five minutes. I could ask how a place like that might eventually turn out.

Or I might try not to.

I put my efforts into loving the wrens.

And I love Paul.

And I love F.L. – who is Francis, who is here, right here. The end of precautions meant he could leave the island.

Francis offline and In Real Life.

It was a bit of a shock. It's all right, though.

No. Genuinely. I am enjoying it.

I am.

And I love him more when he is in person with his redbrown farmery tan from so much walking and odd jobs undertaken outdoors. His hair is almost blond in places and I suspect it misses dancing about in sea breezes. He has let it grow out into this fine cloud of potential wildness, potential something. He looks like a person who belongs somewhere – somewhere that is not here.

And I love him anyway.

Only a few months of practice and it's easy to write that I love almost anyone. I mean, why not? There might be limited time and I might contain a great deal of love.

Talha and Rosie and Max, Tony, Atticus, Alice, Simon, Anja, Bob and Martha, Millie, Ignacy, Kwakou, Hassan, Ranbir and late-addition-but-catching-up Sam – I love them in the way that teachers love their pupils. I don't always like them, but I do have a baseline, practical love for every single one.

I'll remember them – each Year Five, each kid – and think it would be nice to meet them when I'm a hundred years old and they have become successful polar explorers, or brain surgeons, or sculptor-slash-activists who meet me in the street and are kind and say they owe it all to me. Or some of it to me, a bit of it.

I also love Sue, dancing Sue, very noticeably weary Sue.

She turned up here on Sunday afternoon. I knew she'd be round as soon as she knew that Francis was back on the mainland and in the house.

Yes, he is living in my house. He got past the moat, the keep, every one of my defences – I think it happened while he was sitting at the kitchen table and I was filling the kettle. When I stood up to make us a cuppa he was just visiting and then when I sat back down again, everything seemed settled.

I couldn't recall that I'd mentioned this to Sue, or really anything much about him.

Apparently, though, he has come up in conversation.

Lockdown has changed all of us.

Sue seemed her joyful self. She always says a weekend lie-in does wonders. And her arms were hugging a biscuit tin full of pistachio cakes – and a courgette cake and also a lemon drizzle alternative option wrapped in foil.

'You're expecting us to burn a lot of calories for some reason.' Francis taking the tin while Paul aimed his Son with a Shameful Mother grin at me and took the two foil cake parcels.

I guessed that she was actually making the round of all her staff in case they were nervous about the In-Person Days. I guessed she would just happen to be passing each member of staff at some point in the weekend. Oakwood is as deep-cleaned and aired and prepared as it can be to prepare for each Monday, but I knew she'd go back and check it again herself.

We have all developed obsessive-compulsive lockdown quirks.

Sue hooted one of her full-strength laughs and rubbed and banged elbows with Francis in some kind of huge Morse communication. 'You were right!' She winked at me. Being masked always brings out the pantomime in her. 'Definitely!'

'I have no idea what she's talking about,' I told Francis.

And does letting Francis inside mean that everyone – not only

Sue – will now assume they can gallop up and have a good rummage through my privacy? Are all my fortifications just rubble now and bouncy castles? I don't think that's fair.

I played for time in the face of Sue's enthusiasm and tried to act like a person who finds unexpected social situations fun, 'I have no idea what you're talking about, crazy lady. Who are you, even?'

Paul naturally broke in with, 'Please ignore my mother. She is experiencing hormones. Change of life. We don't know what to do with her.'

Francis was slightly uncomfortable, too, but leaning into it. 'Would anyone like a drink? There's ice. Or just ice. Would you like to hold some ice? Where I've come from it's not… It isn't this hot.'

Paul, Francis and I agree that *slightly uncomfortable but leaning into it* is the best we can hope for on most days.

Francis stroked at his hair and it reacted by expanding visibly, joining in with the absurdity, 'I would normally offer coffee. I normally do offer coffee. At this temperature I can offer only iced coffee – so you'll all feel more hysterical than usual but with cooler teeth… Iced coffee?'

And if Sue was aware that we were trying to cheer her up while she was trying to cheer us up, then we were ignoring it.

Best to ignore almost everything…

Sue waggled her arms in the air experimentally. 'I always regret my general solidity. I am unable to be as sinuous as I should, as liquid. I am a solid. It has its own advantages…' And she met my eyes and I tried not to understand why. Then she winked and turned to Francis. 'Yes, you're Scottish. So we must be cousins. I am Persian, but a little Irish. And British.' Sue took the hand Francis offered her.

And then they danced.

They all danced. Paul and Francis followed Sue as she span and gestured and glanced over to me often as if I were something happening that was slightly odd but not yet an emergency.

They're not careless people, they are only unguarded and at ease with themselves in a way that I am not.

I did want to join them.

I wasn't suffering the usual spasm of commitment phobia – I was just watching something beautiful. All of the brightness I know was there and dancing in my courtyard.

I wanted to see everything, every bit of it.

This morning I went in and said good morning to Year Five wearing a latex animal mask over my depressing and medical-looking one. I was aiming for safety and fun.

I have gathered a selection of full head masks based on creatures with noticeably roomy noses – an ostrich, a duck, some kind of a camelish thing and a slightly tyrannosaurus-flavoured dinosaur.

This was intended to ensure that my ears and hair and neck don't feel so infested by the time I've made it back home.

But it makes the kids happy to see my eyes and the top of my head and I like them to be happy – it's not just a good thing, it's useful. They learn better when they're happy. Everyone does.

But I thought I might get away with being a jolly yellow duck.

More accurately, I knew the duck would be very much hated, but I thought they might get used to it.

The class went very quiet when I first appeared. Anja looked properly alarmed.

They didn't, of course, believe I had been replaced by a sentient duck. They're Year Five – they're not, in that sense, little children. They just knew I was hiding from them and that my hiding meant I was afraid – of them, or of Something. Being afraid of them hurt their feelings and my being generally afraid when it's my job to be courageous – well, that couldn't happen.

So I carefully peeled off the duck – made sure to keep my other mask in place as I lifted it off. Duckie sat in the corner like a reproach until Goodbye Time. Then I did pop it back on and we had fun a bit. We wiggled and arm-flapped and I set some homework about being a person with an animal's head and what would that be like. I hoped for narratives that were non-threatening and contained no hints that a person can be suddenly altered overnight in anything other than fascinating and enjoyable ways.

I could see Sam looking on throughout the day like a small anthropology professor studying a ritual from far away. That's a legitimate approach to life. It's not very rewarding, but it's definitely a position. For years it was the only one I had.

Tony hugged me for too long and too hard at Goodbye Time. He's the one who's panicking most. If his grandfather could suddenly vanish forever, maybe anybody can – you can watch that scroll through his thinking, over and over. Sometimes his anxiety almost completely fades and his mouth relaxes, sometimes he needs to touch my arm, or ask me a non-sequitur question just to feel involved. His panic seeps into me from his fingers. But he's doing what he needs to and no one should argue with that.

For my part, I may not ever have prepared and presented lessons with such high engagement and such attention to detail, just to keep us rooted in the classroom and in the moment and not thinking of anything damaging and in wait.

It's disappointing that I didn't uncover this better, deeper type of teaching before now. I'd always imagined that I was quite good at my job.

This year insists on showing me all the places where I disappoint.

But it's Tuesday night – almost Wednesday morning – so we're through both of this week's In-Person Days. Tomorrow and 8am will come round for our singing and waving online. I can relax.

Only I can't relax.

Next Monday is up ahead and waiting.

It will all keep on.

If I don't keep writing this, I will just endlessly scroll Twitter, because the stress that will surely generate tends to dampen down the stresses I've already got. On the good nights, they cancel each other out – on the bad nights they combine and amplify. It's a fifty-fifty bet which one will happen.

Twitter is people, only more so. Twitter after dark is abandoned children running wild to get attention. Twitter is the id, if it could type.

Twitter is also multiple errors of multiple varieties that any teacher might long to correct – any person might. That's how it tricks you to engage – by being mistaken in all of the possible directions. De-educate and infuriate. I assume this is the future of entertainment: not craft and skills and art – only enticing mistakes that will eventually drown out everything that's true.

My own Twitter account is very quiet and anonymous. If I write anything at all I don't mention Oakwood, or my profession. I aim only to keep things happy. I look for threads in which dogs recover from neglect and end up snuggling on sofas, wearing bandanas and rakish hats. Gazelles triumph over lions, mongooses bond with hyenas, all manner of animals show every sign of out-evolving us and thriving. Pleasant families stuck at home create composite orchestras, or else they build Fairy Gardens at the foot of trees in suburban streets. I watch complex mechanisms being triggered by tumbling marbles.

I stare at dominoes.

They domino.

It's satisfying.

In among the amplified loathing and violent algorithms, real people are trying to please each other across the huge and worried world where triggers trip and everything tumbles and each effect cascades forward in only the worst ways.

'I can hear your teeth again.'

Teachers promote factual information, social skills, generally agreed morality. The internet is no place for us. Paul can tell when I've sunk too deep. He has learned to check on me if I'm alone for too long with the laptop.

'Think of your molars.'

He does this meerkat head pop round doorways, or out through windows, or peers between the various bits of lattice in our external ironwork. Then I get the dental comment, or similar.

He can't hear my teeth – at least, I don't think so. But we are both aware that I now have upper and lower mouthguards to stop me cracking more molars while I sleep. Romantic, eh? Hinting at bedtime sex is all about pulling out my mouthguard now – as if I'm a middleweight in the interval between rounds. I jaw clench as I dream. I grind my teeth more than anxious herbivores, out at the edge of the herd. I wake up tired.

Paul cuts sage from our bushes and goes off to make tea with it for me.

I'm meant to be his mother and look after him.

He has taken to raising his eyebrows and giving me manically cheerful grins of encouragement whenever I glance at him. It's a lovely gesture that is also humiliating

Last week, he borrowed my lizard head and served tea wearing that, while acting exactly as normal. This would have been entertaining if I hadn't completely freaked out because one day I might have been using it in a classroom and what if he borrowed it straight after and I hadn't cleaned it yet.

Not that I'm aware of a solid protocol for fiction lizard decontamination.

I shouldn't have yelled at him.

He was just being both practical and kind. Francis did not scold me about it, but he looked sad.

And how did they learn to be so civilised? Paul didn't inherit it from me.

The only things that currently punch me in my heart more than getting Paul's help are those moments when he really does need me. Then I'm the one who notices how silent our silence has got and how long it's been since one of us called to the other about a cup of something, or a meal, or a snack. Or else maybe it's time for qi gong, or t'ai chi, or why not do some kick boxing outside in the courtyard air, which we hope will be all right as we rush it down into our lungs… But then I look for him and where is he?

In structureless days, you need a timetable. Perfect. Let me at it. I have scheduled the ears and whiskers out of our weeks – including the schedule for unscheduled space. Francis was timetabled on arrival. So I always know where everyone should be.

It's that unscheduled space that's risky.

I do worry for Francis, too, but at least he's a grown-up. At least we can agree to accept his apparent resilience as factual. Apart from on the days when it's really not.

I have a private schedule of checks on them both. Wicklow Street's normality reminds me of juggling practice – check on Paul, check on Francis, check on myself – make sure it all stays airborne, remember to smile.

But on some evenings, there's my boy on his bed and holding a book but not reading it, my boy with his lamp not lit, or my boy in the early-morning kitchen and picking up broken shards of some crockery something he has dropped and his eyes are wet with a boy's tears for having spoiled something.

Last week he accidentally smashed the only mug left of the pair we made together for his sixth birthday.

Horrible idea for a birthday outing, but the mugs slowly became our favourites.

Never have favourite things – they're the ones you will use most and therefore the ones you end up breaking.

Whenever Paul's sad, I do exactly what he does whenever I'm gloomy. I gather him and we lie on my bed and don't mention the sadness especially. We just lean side to side and watch comedy, comedy, comedy on my laptop. We keep on going until we start to laugh. That can sometimes take hours – but, after all, part of comedy is the waiting.

At the moment, things being what they are, any kind of prolonged laughter lets me do what I do most naturally – cry. But that's a remedy. I don't mind all those toxins running down and dripping off my chin, the sinuses clearing, the lungs getting a workout to prove they're still sound.

In this household we know our medicine and we take it.

The night when Francis joined us for our dose of Funny – that was a little tense. The three of us tucked ourselves together on the bed, like pups trying to stay warm. Not that we weren't already close to heat exhaustion.

And then I waited to know what Francis was going to laugh at. There's no remedy if a couple don't crease up at the same things.

We were all right, though.

When I heard, when I felt, his first little snort of amusement, then the first big punch of Funny rushing through him – that was a moment. That was more important than when I gave him his own set of keys.

And here I would point out that when our current leaders are called *clowns* it does offend me. Actual clowns throw themselves under the bus, every time. Themselves. Not other people. They only ever stand on their dignity if they're using it to wipe their feet. Our present government – and any foreseeable other government – are clowns only in the ways that John Wayne Gacy was a clown. They love having the power to be bizarre without consequences. And they love to scare kids.

They're not Proper Funny and wouldn't know where to start.

And thank whoever god is for every human person who has ever been Proper Funny – all of them, bar one.

Snug on the bed and watching the Proper Funny People, I come as close to time travel as I can. I go back to when my boy was a boy. I feel my long, tall Paul breathe and shift in precisely the ways that only he does, or ever has. The years have magnified him, but he's the Paul who was there on the bed beside me when this was our safe house and new and I was trying to be sure he didn't guess how much I felt besieged. We'd be triumphant in the half dark.

At first, he was too small to laugh for much reason beyond the fact that I was laughing and he liked the sound, the taste, of it. I was so intent on very clearly having fun for him that I really did have more for myself. And no fear, or shame, or darkness soaked through me into him.

Now he is a connoisseur of laughter, chuckles, giggles, hoots, snorts, sniggers and the rest. He is pleased by sudden exhalations of delight.

You can't say we're not a good audience.

I raised him on Proper Funny because it was the only thing that I still trusted. Even Buster hadn't been completely able to ruin it. No one had. Initially, I was showing Paul video tapes in the rattly player that lurked beneath – and was also somehow part of – the smallest, yet heaviest TV in the world. The tape player died first and then the telly went a couple of days later – as if they were a doting married couple.

Paul would eventually greet the strange combination of sliding and clicks that accompanied tape insertion by yelling, 'Funny!' *Good lad, make your mother proud.* Then I'd climb back on the bed and Paul would be Paul's temperature, with his skin smelling of his skin. I would slowly stop thinking of how many loans my previous partner/jailor had taken out in my name, using my details, or when he might eventually turn up and prove that everything good was as paper thin as always. I wouldn't wonder how long Sue would let me keep teaching in her school when loud noises made me flinch and schools are basically built out of bad smells and loud noises. I clearly still spent more time crying in the staff toilets than might be considered normal. I also spent far too many years dropping and breaking objects that people needed. (Dropping and breaking under stress is a family trait.) I am particularly drawn to commemorative ornaments, crockery and wing mirrors.

But Sue never said a word. She makes everyone a project, makes everyone succeed. I kept on being employed and loving the kids and loving Paul while he bounced and giggled his way from Year One upwards as an Acorn that grew to an Oakwooder who was tall and then taller and then really surprisingly tall and therefore a little abashed. He did well. In spite all of the times that Bad Man told me I would ruin the bastard boy and never manage on my own – we both did well.

So there.

And some evenings we'd pretend that we could actually snatch glimpses of Paul's limbs growing out and out. It seemed likely we might see his hands or feet edging visible millimetres further from his torso.

Our collection of VHS tapes started to be inescapably out of date, not long after I'd bought a brand new player for them. Eventually, we changed the format, but not the content. We remained ourselves, my funny boy and I, watching DVDs where Proper Funny happened to Groucho and Chico and Harpo – but never poor Zeppo. Eric and Ernie and Katharine Hepburn and Cary Grant and, yes, Buster – Joseph Frank Keaton, the one true Buster – they stayed themselves, too. We'd scrutinise Steve Martin's pratfalls for varying applications of technique. We were cheered when Leslie Howard was not yet an anti-fascist matinee idol – with high-minded monologues you tolerate because he has beautiful ears – and just threw his much younger and carefree self face down and tumbled over and about. Joyful indignity is also anti-fascist – it couldn't be anything else. Chaplin, beautiful Chaplin, knew that. He made me realise that all of the Proper Funny People, they're beautiful, too. They just make sure to move so fast that you don't notice. They pick humility, go for laughs. And, in doing so, some of them become much more than pretty, more than serious, more than sonorous. Even Leslie Howard could do far more than play stuffed shirts who fall in love, stuck being Ashley Whatsit in *Gone with the Wind* – he didn't deserve that.

Laughter is also cheap, of course, and almost as filling as food. But Proper Funny does ask for a kind of payment, eventually. Enjoying it makes you too happy and too tender for normal life. It dials up your awareness so that you notice the absurdity, the cruelty, the dying – the things your fools and strollers notice. That's why authority never likes Proper Funny – and the feeling's mutual.

If you're someone who makes Proper Funny, you pay in broken spines and hearts and a kind of progressive surgery to expose your imagination. Proper Funny will expect you to notice everything all the time.

Paul seems unscathed as a comedy consumer. But then he is very good at either being with kind people, or by himself. He isn't impolite in the face of boredom and thuggishness and all the jolts and jars of life – he just has the knack of disappearing, slipping away from the damages they might do. My boy knows about pre-emptive self-defence.

We both know where he got that from.

These days, we watch online comedy content. But Stan and Ollie are still shiny with weird lightness and painstaking joy – they still dance for us. They can still reach and pull down the shadow of a blind against a wall. Stan knew the places where Proper Funny and Proper Magic meet and let each one do magnificent things to the other. That lasts forever.

I'm hoping that lasting forever might be contagious while I watch.

I'm hoping to last.

And Paul is Paul and I'm his mum and we're still here. We still get to watch all available decades of beautiful, funny people, see wild ideas leap along tangents, or spiral into dreams and jolly nightmares. And so much of laughing is about changes – of status, substance, meaning, heart. So we get to remember that everything can change, and therefore we can change everything.

Happy changes only.

There's no dying here.

There's no dying close by.

Except it is close, I know it is. Maureen around the corner in Swinton Place spent the winter in two sleeping bags and a tent for warmth because the DWP cut all her money – said she hadn't replied to a letter she never received. She hasn't been well since. She was hoping to go back and work in the museum again, but she no longer mentions that. Last year's pneumonia gave her scarring on her lungs. The pain bothers her less than knowing she doesn't matter.

The Department for Work and Pensions is a Bad Man organisation. It promises to give her time to recover and rebuild – but it's all just the usual cruelty and gaslight.

They cut her off from all support and it took eighteen months to go through the layers of appeals and get some of her benefit money back. Then they cut her off again.

I leave her bags of shopping hooked onto her doorknob, but we can't have a cuppa inside the way we used to, or pretend that I didn't bring the tea and the posh biscuits, that they were already there. The last thing her lungs need is me maybe bringing her something that kills healthy lungs in healthy people.

On the phone, she sounds like someone very far away, like dying.

And I don't like calling her.

I do it less than I should and that means I'm a failure as a person. And I know I'm not really helping – I'm too small to fix what's hurting her.

Sometimes I am not the bright side. I do not shine.

And so much of life now is choiceless choices: shoes for the kids, or birthday presents; food for yourself, or food for them; fight and be beaten, or give up and fade. And most of us shine in the way that stars do – showing dead light from a past and a place where something is already gone.

I have to insulate myself against ever thinking stuff like that by frequent applications of nonsense.

Never let anyone tell you that nonsense is unimportant.

And:

Never despair – the morning is closest in the dark.

It's a nice thought.

Now we're back in the Oakwood building I go and stand in Big Room when it's empty and read every one of the slogans. I can currently manage to believe in at least two of them.

And Paul and I listen to nonsense and talk nonsense and watch nonsense and hug, hug, hug. And Francis and I make up nonsense about human seals and seal humans and gull humans and cutting the UK up into manageable islands with lots of kayaking in between and eventual happiness.

None of this changes all of the dying outside, beyond Wicklow Street. But it changes me. And I often do hold my boy too long and too hard, the way a kid does with someone they're sure is going to vanish soon.

I make a point of remembering indestructibly good things.

Scones.

Ginger Rogers being funny, not just dancing.

The way Cary Grant will perpetually be in *Notorious* and leaning against a doorway and looking at Ingrid Bergman as if he's already in love.

Francis' hair.

Or Paul being fluidly contented, up on the trapeze at those circus workshops. Something about being so far overhead stopped him fretting about his height. The bars and straps and silks and flights were his right thing at that moment – they met him and mended him, made him the opposite of falling. He'd swing and climb and tumble and balance and catch, as if he was designed for it. Like a monkey.

Like Monkey Monk. Like the gold heart of Monkey Monk.

One night, one strange, gold night, we made a shining child, Monkey and I.

On most days I thank him for it.

And Paul's circusy arms began to be corded, muscled in the Monkey way that leads to holding and not ever letting go. What more could a mother want? His torso became corrugated – like something sculptural, or an art school pencil drawing. That continues to be the case. He is this elongated whipcord, elven person, a demonstration that my genes weren't as much of a blight as I'd suspected.

And sometimes I breathe in the honeysuckle and I'm just glad that Paul is Funny.

I would have loved him anyway, but he is Funny.

I had suspected he might be. I had hoped. Then I watched him demonstrate his fresh new aerial skills and I saw – everyone saw. The poise he maintained and the motions were correct, they were effective, but they just couldn't help being funny, too.

He's Proper Funny.

But I don't want him to have poor Monkey's too-much-awareness burning away.

Let him notice just enough, please – just enough to be humane.

Please may Paul stay far from the tar-stained tinfoil and chemical dreams. Save him from a day when it all stops working.

Out of his bedroom window, Monkey just stepped and dropped. He never lost his balance – he threw it away.

And please may Paul be careful with himself.

Please keep him from the falling.

I didn't notice.

The clever teacher, know-it-all show-off me, who gives other people lectures – I didn't notice. There the whole time, but it took me this long to see – Francis isn't attractive, he's truly beautiful. He's like Paul. He's the beautiful kind of Proper Funny, too.

His style of playing the fool is so successful, such an impregnable defence, that I never realised he was hiding. I never recognised who he really is.

And then I did.

Last night, we were all scrunched on the bed – it's too hot for scrunching, but watching movies without scrunching would be sad. Gene Wilder and Marty Feldman were being glorious and Frankenstein's dancing monster was being extremely alive against all the odds and I glanced across at Francis and he was finally, fully at rest.

Just the same man, but entirely different.

Here was I imagining I was the expert in self-defence – building my walls and ramparts out of panic and bits of the past. But it was Francis who was bunkered down and locked away, his camouflage perfectly achieved.

I was so amazed by my own surrender that I didn't bother trying to know if he was still unsteady, if that last page of the treaty with reality was still unsigned.

He felt me looking and turned, looked back.

I am very lucky.

Imagine that.

Our government of Stiltskins changed its mind.

First they said it was completely essential that we should go back into schools and a tragedy if we didn't and tough luck if teachers – like so many others – burn out or get sick. Also, never mind the days of work you'll put into preparing as best you can for this situation for which no adequate preparation is possible.

But now we should forget all that.

Going back to school is the worst idea that anyone could have and so we never did. We must all stay at home until the autumn and why would we contemplate doing something else?

This is what Stiltskins do – kick things about and keep you guessing. They give you whiplash, bump all your plans and bits of safety about like mice in a concrete mixer. All that matters is the constant demonstration of absolute power. Stiltskins feel small if they can't convince themselves they're transcending reality. They want to be the worry in every morning, the rat that gnaws in every head.

If people are hurt, so much the better. It's a social thing, being able to hurt with impunity. Producing death with impunity … well, that's a Stiltskin Christmas Miracle.

I'm betting they'll have to cancel Christmas – and leave it until the last minute.

But I'm relieved that my risks will dial down until September.

But now I know that in September there they'll be again.

But a Stiltskin decision has saved me.

But the previous Stiltskin decision put me at risk.

And they will go on and on and on and on, doing the same again…

This is my life, but not my own. This is my life, but it doesn't matter. This is my country, but viewed in gaslight and with lots of flags.

My superpower, though – I've already lived that way with other Stiltskins for too many years and I no longer give it my consent. And millions of other people are out here with me and have also survived the kind of harried and shattered existences Stiltskins make.

We see the Stiltskins and know them and know their true name.

The knowledge doesn't defeat them, but it does mean that we can resist.

Other Stiltskins have already taught us the ways to wage asymmetric war.

We laugh as much as possible and we hug and we yell the Oakwood promise. And we bide our time.

Maybe 2000, Glasgow Hillhead:

This is Glasgow. I breathe in and find the usual undertaste of malt and of the sea although any salt water is far away.

I think of school mornings here and how the dawn was always sea filled for reasons I never knew. Glasgow always wakes from a dream of being somewhere else. The island and hill coast people settle here and perhaps affect it with their homesickness and their need to hear waves breaking close at hand.

When I stepped off the sleeper train there was talking. Even early-morning Glasgow is talking and strangers telling the stories of themselves out to each other. Glasgow talk is interpreted as aggression by those unfamiliar. The volume is louder or quieter but not ever gone. It may be a kind of hard and inquisitive affection.

I walk to a breakfast café and pass time with fat and starch meals presented as good value and masculine profusion.

Then I walk out to the west where there are rivers out of sight and underfoot. At various times I can feel the shake from the underground trains passing out of sight. They round their little loop in the cool earth between subsidence foundations and Victorian tree roots. The trees make everything sweet with having lived so long successfully. Where I am heading now has soft air and leaf mould between cobbles with honeysuckle feral in thin back lanes.

I was there this morning to make my necessary preparations.

Glasgow West End is studentland and upgrade kitchen conversions. Victorian villas formerly smashed apart into hostel rooms and bedsits have been bought up and reunited by the strength of new wealth. They serve their original purpose again which is to demonstrate money joy. There are new roofs and damp-prevention measures. There are luxury penthouse availabilities.

Glasgow West End is also junkieland and burglars slipping small children through small windows like bad post through your letterbox. They rob the poorest of their nothing because the poorest are the least defended.

This is not a Glasgow fault and happens everywhere.

I can hear money washing back into the city. It is like a resurrection of the old Tobacco Lords and other royalties made by cotton income and steel income and steel chains. I was taught the historical figures of power for this location. I know the streets named after slavery places and resource exploitation.

Luxury demand is turning city centre shops upscale impractical.

Glasgow is the magpie city and is sharp eyes and instincts and winks. Glasgow is meat market stories and crane-driving stories and merchant navy stories and a pub open somewhere round the clock. Glasgow is singing drunk and gold sovereign rings on tattooed hands. Glasgow is born-again abstinence and laser ink removal. Glasgow is jokes instead of punches instead of jokes. Glasgow is thin limb people who are psychological crisis as street theatre.

This is perhaps 2000 but perhaps 1998 and I no longer know. I am not sure.

Face disfigurement using box-cutter blades fixed in pairs has passed out of fashion. There are fashions in all things. Swords are no longer worn concealed in the legs of trousers. Violence power families rise and fall. Machetes remain useful in the ways machetes are.

I walk and plan and walk. I prepare. I drink coffee in constructed bohemian and genuine bohemian surroundings. I read the cheap gang tags in black marker on walls. They are not the same as I remember but not so different.

National Service veterans are buying port and brandy in dark pubs. They fiddle compensation money for being gunshot deafened. They join union social clubs and pilfer funds. They hit their wives on Saturday nights and whenever the Old Firm plays. There are many traditions to feel as I pass.

The daylight is short because I am in winter.

When I am back at Kelvinbridge I look down and the river is in strands like a muscle and the hippy shops will soon be closing and seem closed now. The day fades as I make my second loop west.

Down in Thornwood, mothers will be screaming at their

going-home-time children to do them good. They will beetle climb together up the steep of the streets. Hillhead Library will be dreaming of self-education and revolution and letting homeless strangers warm their feet. Govan will be philosophy and suicide and insurrection. The clever kids in every district will already know which car locks are the easiest to beat. The high flats will keep being suicide made manifest.

I know this is true because it is always true.

I am not anyone but I am from somewhere.

Glasgow is objective lovely and subject to regular blessings of sky light. This is also true because it is always true.

Nevertheless I do not often come back. This is for reasons.

Along my long way from Central Station I have climbed and descended landscape that is unsubdued by buildings.

Now I am locked in my final route.

I turn left at Queen Margaret Drive lights because I want to be blinded with looking at sunset eating the far foot of Byres Road. I turn my head and see it there and being generous predictable for me.

Home turf is good and also an encouragement to complacency risks.

The blood sky and the red sandstone make a match I appreciate. I am currently no one but myself and therefore can appreciate. I have sensibilities and can be pleased.

Here Glasgow is hill brows and hill drops and honey masonry between the red. Here Glasgow is tall thin windows and stained glass in the front doors and fingerplates making declarations in brass that are muffled because of tarnish. Here is intentional design aesthetics and grace remaining unaltered in certain areas because of the city being left to rot and therefore sleeping on unscathed by thug developer greed projects. Indulged Celtic poverty saved the tumble wall gardens and big trees and sections of the past.

The more the West End is improved the more it is cleared of original inhabitants because it has become too good for them.

My childhood makes no difference to my affection. Glasgow never hurt me.

But Glasgow is still fatherland. The old man is still down in Partick and still the troll under the bridge. He moves between tenement flats burning his welcome. He is the consistent drunk neighbour problem. He turns his stereo to maximum and passes out. He screams for arcane reasons repeated. He exists on a downward gradient of habitability.

Perhaps the stereo is sold since I last checked. He is endstage. He is leaving his front door open to the communal close because he has lost his last key and anyway cannot manage to make keys fit in locks. He is plumbers who no longer come when he reports hallucinated leaks. He is no motor control and reported crying. He is the absence of his escaped and then deceased wife. He is pubs strung out along Great Western Road with preference for where the Orange flute bands drink.

I do not need to make him dead. His living allows the world to enact righteous vengeance and justice applied upon a perpetrator. This is kind exceptional to all customary circumstance. He should suffer and does suffer. This delights me.

The rain comes and is like a privacy falling round to guard my path. Garden and tree leaves on all sides are twitching under water touches and look like applied electricity or pain expressed in spasms.

Winter dark rushes in hungry.

I climb towards Dowanside Road again. Room lights are showing comfort and windowsill bottle collections of blue glass. A black cat with white bib and paws runs to me along a wall top and is apparent certainty that we are friends from long acquaintance. He softhits under my chin with the crown of his head and sets front paws on me and loud purrs while he rubs my overcoat with the left side and then the right side of his jaws repeating.

There is no possible reason for him to believe we have met.

I delay with the animal and this is a gentle time and quite moving.

It feels like an approval of my immanent recklessness.

A woman in a grey trench coat and paisley headscarf and brown suede boots and maroon handbag passes me and smiles at my being kidnapped by a cat. I am also smiling which is appropriate and useful. We nod almost simultaneous as she goes on towards the corner with Crown Road South and I remain behind and am an innocent waylaid and perhaps about to blush.

The cat takes several minutes before he is satisfied.

I left-hand tickle and pet him in a way that someone reasonable might.

My hand is warmed by him through my glove.

Tuxedo cat. They call them tuxedo cats in America which I do not know at this time. I am uninformed at this time. I have enough training with not enough experience and so I am young confident stupid. I am a danger to myself. I am burning with the fee I was paid to come here.

The tuxedo cat has settled again on a wall across the street but then hops down and follows me when I set off towards the corner. Beyond that point it breaks away on its own affairs and I go about mine.

I take the curve of Crown Road South and continue until reaching a small car park at the back of a known landmark pub. This is a suitable location because it is plainly there and yet the greenery surrounding makes it also seem to merge with the park alongside and behind. It almost disappears.

Grey trench coat woman is standing beneath one of the high-high trees that border the car park. She is therefore saved a little from the rain.

I wonder why she has no umbrella although I also do not have one. The woman has picked a spot in the shadows of a far corner. She is between the tree and a Saab 900 which seems black but is factually blue and only distorted into lying about itself by the sodium light.

She sees me and smiles because here I am again the man who is tolerant of animals and merry at heart.

The woman is called Veronica M. and works in the Glasgow Passport Office. She has a boyfriend who is moderate good at judo. Her mother died last year and her father while she was attending senior school. She is above average intelligent. Her flat is not far from here. It contains house plants and objects from Tibet although she has never left Scotland.

I enter the car park and then pause with calm demeanour. Her face is smiling and then confusion and then not. She has categorised me as happy stranger and then as possible threat and then as business appointment.

There is no one else here and only two cars which are the Saab and a Vauxhall Astra with a dented front passenger door. They are gathering weather in droplets that break and track down downward.

We are in the gap of peace between weekday late afternoon drinking and weekday evening drinking which will not last long.

I step careful forward while reaching inside my coat and one-handed slowly begin to lift out a fat envelope as agreed. My gesture is amateur and obvious and she finds it reassuring that I am foolish about exposure and have no craft.

She shakes her head once which is a reproach and makes me project regret and fumble the envelope back out of sight.

I say the name that is not her name.

Miss Black.

She says the name that is not my name.

Mr Parker

I have meanwhile closed our distance and passed the Vauxhall and rounded the Saab.

I am more concealed now and her shoulders relax consequent on this.

We swap sentences that are courteous meaningless and I stare about in the manner of perhaps a person assessing a possible new home. I gaze along the stretches of fence and also at the tarmac underfoot and the leaves above and the deeps and shapes of leaf boughs arising from the slope between us and the pub. I am wide eyes and fascination.

Miss Black is a minor and cautious source of quite good finished passports and passports to be finished elsewhere. This is an income stream that she balances against risks including prosecution and imprisonment and unemployability upon release.

Also she risks offending or alarming figures and families of swift power. So they have sent me to her. I am their strength and fist. I would prefer to be my own.

Threats she has left unconsidered tumble round her as leaves might flurry.

She is an unsuitable person for her situation and cannot quite harden her mouth at present and cannot perhaps forget the cat and how pleased it was with me.

Her hands shake. Her headscarf is in planned coordination with the maroon of her bag and she has thought about these things and her shade of nail varnish is natural neutral but with a faint tint of red. She gives some attention to details but not the right ones. She is expressions of innocent hope to transcend a staid ensemble and low heels that are appropriate for workplace conditions. The trench coat leaches the colour from her face and is not a good choice.

She passes me her envelope with what she thinks is exemplary caution.

I open it with average clumsiness and give cursory examination to the contents in order to amplify her stress.

Miss Black is tangible fretful that I should now hand her my envelope.

I have no reason to enjoy making her wait.

Then I relent. I am nervous apologetic.

She edges out and naked eye estimates the money. She wants me to believe this is genuine informative for her. I am apparent oblivious and searching my coat pocket and come up with keys that I drop immediate and almost catch but then lose completely with a foolish grab that sends the whole bunch flying.

I am forced to rush over by the fence to retrieve them.

Miss Black watches and is almost amused.

I would prefer her to be something else and someone else.

But I am doing my best.

There is a rattling and strange noise behind her that is perhaps an animal. It moves fast.

She turns her head to see what it could be.

It is the distraction.

I set it up ready and under tension earlier today. The elastic was anchored to the fence and then passed around a tree trunk and then threaded back through the fence slats and then woven through them until it could be anchored again. I prepared my scenario this morning. It took me some time to knot little lengths of thick metal wire into the elastic strand at irregular intervals. They were there to aid the noise and strangeness.

She was not guaranteed to look round when I set it all in motion.

Her doing so was only instinctive likely.

As I gathered my dropped keys I untethered one end of the elastic. I used the thin and black kind that is hard to see even in daylight. Also it is always hard to see what you have no cause to look for and what has no reasonable reason to exist.

I picked up the strand and held it ready.

I added a little stretch. That is old habit and nothing to do with necessity.

The elastic rabbit was always better if I waited to the last and added a little stretch.

This is all of the best I could do.

Nobody normal wants to see their death arriving and so I arrange a distraction.

The dragging wire pieces make a scuttle of disturbance as the tension is sudden released and therefore a long and narrow illusion of life contracts.

She looks to see what is behind her. People do.

This would be a reason for our laughing together a moment later when we are reassured that nothing is very wrong.

Perhaps it was a bird that startled or else a cat.

I hit her once with force on the side of her head near the temple while she is still glancing away.

There is no moment later.

The hammer has been sleeping inside my right sleeve and the handle drop slides easy into my hand.

Hitting twice makes a mess. Blood pools in the first wound and will splash. Once is best.

She offered me the side of her head which is what I wanted.

The pterion is a good place to hit.

Afterwards I am a solicitous stranger bending over a poor unfortunate although it continues to be the case that no one is looking.

All of the chances I am taking are refusing to come undone. They are absolving me.

She dies very fast as if she was only half-hearted about ever being here.

When I check I can see a little of what was inside her head and where she kept her thinking and what she remembered and what she liked.

I reach and take back my envelope from her hand which feels not alive but also not dead yet.

Then I see there is blood in a large amount.

Probably the middle meningeal artery is severed.

I hate that. The mess. Even the last heartbeats are enough to make this mess.

I am confused because I should have noticed the blood at once. Blood hands and blood in the dark blue of my coat and blood on my navy chino trousers.

I hate when there is mess. This is the result of distaste and also practicality.

But I am dark with rain already. The tarmac is dark with pools already.

I stand and breathe in the green quiet and I taste salt and the water falls hard over me and I am safe.

No one is here to see me or sweep me from my course. No one calls out or interrupts.

I fast lift her body over the fence and set it down into the wood and shrub area between us and the pub.

Between me and the pub.

I am lucky. I am many times blessed. The positioning of the Saab and the Vauxhall were fortuitous.

I do not like killing women.

I did my best to do it kindly.

I did my best to be caught.

The world indulged me and wants to keep me free.

I cannot argue with the world.

I walk back the way I came and look for the cat. I liked the cat.

I am unhappy when I cannot find it.

I walk back east under the rain and am clean enough by the time I sit down to eat dinner and then reach Central Station and the luggage lockers. Later I take the sleeper further north.

Blood on clothes is not something that general people expect. It is always hard to see what you have no cause to look for and what has no reasonable reason to exist.

The sleeper train takes me in and I clean myself in my cabin and change my clothes.

I lie on the thin mattress and smell the ghosts of coal and outside there will be places where ravens sleep and they will know that I am passing in their dreams. When I wake it will be Inverness and I will drive a hire car further to the next place and I will see the black wings of my family flying and the sun making them silver.

One bird will dip a wing because that is the signal and salute to every fellow hunter.

I am sure I will see that and I will feel well thereafter.

I am the proper working of the world. It therefore shows me signs and wonders.

Sometimes it overwhelms, the way Stiltskins thrive.

Every opportunity an opportunity to draw blood. No cruelty is ever unappealing, no kindness is ever contemplated, or ever left unscathed. Every morning more graves and a clear and clearer longing for higher balconies from which to wave as all that we are shambles past: the bereaved, the tired, the wounded, the battalions of terrified rage addicts, the ghosts and the lost. It's like being inside an apocalyptic folk tale about the ways in which a very stupid land ended stupidly.

I know I'm being didactic – but, then again, what did you expect? I'm a teacher. And just imagine if there had been even a little more explaining before we followed the Stiltskins down their Stiltskin path. I occasionally wonder what would happen if somebody stood in every available square today, explaining, 'Our current circumstances are mostly shit.'

Just that.

Wouldn't numberless shoulders drop, wouldn't there be millions of sighs from people thinking, 'Oh, it's not just me then. This really is shit, isn't it?'

One might hope.

There I go again – hoping, even in the midst of discontent.

Even my cupboards are a mess.

One of lockdown's few benefits was that we all had neat cupboards – all of that time and so much to tidy. But every part of my beautiful well-ordered storage space is now just unmanageable, because of the stockpiled cans and dry goods, rammed in at every angle. It's a physical manifestation of fear. How else can I cope with the trade failure shortages and the global warming shortages lining up beyond the pandemic shortages. I assume there will be more shortages to come.

And more need to buy tinned tomatoes.

I've been over-ordering a little since 2016, although my stores won't defend me enough and I have no power to predict what I'll actually need. I do see that. Catering-size sacks of lentils will do only so much to stop the whole island sinking away from beneath us.

I look at my ranks of tins and feel guilty. Then I take some to the food bank and then buy more. The food bank is sinking much faster than me, but anxiety has made me selfish. I'm not giving all I could. I'm lying awake beside Francis imagining the jolly abundance of East German high streets circa 1965. I'm lying awake and remembering that the heat makes tinned tomatoes turn explosively rancid. I'm lying awake in the dark and the darknesses

I don't like to think of the darknesses that hide and thrive behind race hate, the bigot whispering, the fantasies about rigged individualism and time travel back to the age of theft and Empire.

Our current circumstances ... and so forth...

And I don't like to think of it.

Except I do.

And I am furious.

Why not lean towards communal improvement and humanity? Why would that be so terrible? Wasn't that gentle togetherness we all clung to in the first weeks of lockdown something wonderful that got us through?

Apart from the fury, I feel stupid.

Not that I believed the lying liars who lied in order to steal my country. I can spot a Stiltskin yards away and they were just doing what Stiltskins do. But I underestimated how much harm they'd cause. I cultivated hope and that wasn't what I needed.

I was stupid.

Reading Buster's pages, I know I was stupid with him – hopeful and stupid.

After you get your pocket picked, after you're scammed, after part of your identity is stolen – you feel stupid. You shouldn't. Deceivers do nothing but practise their ways to deceive. They're good at it. You didn't volunteer for them, invite them. Nevertheless, they make you feel as if you did. It's one more con.

And it protects them, because if you fell for a trickster and you believed them, anyone disabusing you isn't bringing you good news

– just a demonstration of your shame.

Thinking of him, thinking of what he did, shouldn't have the power to make me feel so very clearly that I'm this little, ugly idiot, that I'm stupid.

He shouldn't have that power.

But he does.

I took a break there to walk over and kiss Francis on the top of his head. His hair somehow still smells of Colonsay, of bonfires and coal smoke and a soft outdoors with peaty water – the atmosphere it prefers.

My Francis. Can I say that? It doesn't seem wholly inappropriate.

I wouldn't mind being his Anna, his Annanka.

We stay up all night and talk like people who have forgotten how to have normal conversations, like released inmates, like lunatics, like animals who can speak. And maybe we'll never have to learn about practising modesty and restraint – maybe we'll talk nonsense until the day we die.

Keep that day far off, though. Please.

Francis padded away with a little bow after the kiss and told me, 'I shall ask cook to make madam a cup of cocoa, should that be agreeable.' He has fallen into using a posh butler voice and talking about the management endeavouring to ensure my satisfaction. That leaves an easy joke, just lying there, but he always sidesteps round it, because we appreciate subtlety. It's a lost art, but we're bringing it back.

The butler began as a part of his camouflage, I think, a part to play while settling in. It's something else now – a dream we have together. In our heads we inhabit this vast old-time hotel with hundreds of staff who appear one at a time and all look exactly like Francis. Paul and myself are regularly cast as the only guests.

'The management advises, Madam, that care should be taken when leaving the garden and exploring the wider grounds. Vortexes of pain and disfigurement have been seen in the area. Also take care when approaching the Ultimate Abyss – its outer edges are unstable and may not necessarily remain beyond the orangery.' He brushes his left hand over his hair, which he probably knows will not calm it, but raise up a gleeful cloud of static and wilfulness.

It's nice, writing him down while he happens – makes him seem very *here*.

In case of emergency, or the risk of disappearance, the management advises you take notes.

He lifts his face to the balcony, 'Young Master Paul, the Billiard Room has dropped into the sinkhole again, this time along with the portion of our library covering S to W. We regret these are circumstances beyond our control.'

Paul sometimes pretends he's an Eton Old Boy vampire, but we often feel we see enough of them everywhere else. He spent the whole of yesterday as a burned-out rock star hiding from the press. But he prefers being staff, really – it facilitates his kind of double act with Francis. His favourite roles are Toby the Put-Upon Grocer's Delivery Boy and The Unnamed Entertainer who performs feats.

I don't resent the fact that Francis as an addition has meant that Paul may well be having much more fun – or certainly larger fun – than he did with me.

When we're losing ourselves in our scenarios, I can manage to imagine that Wicklow Street would lead us into a merciful country I'm very happy then.

Really. In the gaps between everything, we're happy.

And now the butler has brought my cocoa. (Which turns out to be pineapple juice over ice, served in a mug.)

And I have drunk it.

Lord, it's so hot – so world-endingly hot.

And I have hugged the butler in passing and almost taken it for granted. I suspect that most functional families grow up with a lot of hugs in passing. I wouldn't know, but I'd hope so. I mean, what on earth would stop you, if you could arrange that?

My poor little ma never was a hugger. Today's Zoom with her was pleasant at first, because she mistook me for a long-ago former neighbour. Then she remembered that I am her daughter, while also catching sight of Francis. There was an amount of screaming after that and bad names. Eventually, there was an intervention from some kind of agency carer who got everybody's name wrong.

If the staff can't remember names, what hope have the inmates got?

We needed a number of purposeful hugs after that. We held on with intention, like people dropping down a well.

But we're at peace again, I think.

And Paul is up in the kitchen practising ukulele chords.

And Francis is settled back into the deck chair by the oldest honeysuckle. I think of her as the grandmother, the original and best.

So I suppose I am safe to remember when I was at my most completely stupid.

Buster cried and it made me stupid.

He sobbed his way in.

When everything else has failed, a good weep is generally effective – you'll get what you want.

Don't think I don't know it – weepy Anna McCormick, her tears another superpower.

Buster and I were close already by this time, but when we happened to be alone and he started weeping and shaking – that's when he took everything valuable that I had, when he stole me the way he had stolen that dead child's name.

I do believe that he suffered from panic attacks. He said they were about his childhood and the episodes seemed genuine. Over time the whole OrKestrA saw them, fretted about them. But this one night, the others were already tucked away sleeping on improvised beds in the damp community hall where the OrKestrA was camping out for a week of action and kids' activities. Buster and I were alone among the wonky cupboards of the little kitchen.

He suddenly went pale. Can you fake that? Then he dropped his mug – institutional enamel – which only bounced on the lino and splashed out the last of his tea. He darted away from the table as if something had burned him or hit him. Within moments he was huddled in a corner, back against the cold stove door and trembling, sobbing.

A normal person goes towards that sort of thing and offers help. So I hugged him.

I sat next to him on the lino and I waited.

I suppose he waited, too. Half of the effect of any act is in the timing.

Eventually, he blubbered out that he felt very guilty about some terrible thing. Then he cried some more.

I'm sure that his suffering was nothing to do with conscience. He was deceiving every one of us. He was about to deceive me the most. I'm sure that didn't trouble him. I'm sure that he simply enjoyed playing the clown, playing at being a part of our OrKestrA family and then playing at love. I'm sure he enjoyed being loved – even if the man being loved wasn't him. Living a life that's only filthy and unreal must have its drawbacks, outbreaks of symptoms. I'd like to think that's true. His doubt and unhappiness were convincing, maybe genuine. I didn't understand what caused them and maybe he didn't – but they were also useful.

Buster grew more peaceful after a while and, being a normal person, I did what I could – I told him a story. That's what the normal people do: bind the wound, make the cocoa, bring the dinner, mend the broken, make a joke, be distracting, hug the weeping, hold the hand, tell a story.

I told Buster my favourite story.

It's the same story I have told to class after class of kids, to Paul, to Sue. Eventually I'll tell it to Francis – Francis who brought back Colonsay driftwood for my bedroom mantlepiece and tiny oblong fragments of sea urchin shell, each piece like a counter for some unknown game that only happy people play.

The story isn't mine, but just borrowed, passed along in the manner of any useful story. It's a *hadith*, one of the sayings of Mohammed. Year Five knows about *hadiths*, about faiths, about parables, about prophets, including Mohammed.

This is the hadith of the murderer, as collected by Imam Muhammad al-*Bukhari* many centuries ago. The form of words is my own, but all of the mercy they hold belongs to the story.

There once was a murderer.

The murderer had killed ninety-nine people.

One day, he goes to a wise person and asks, 'I have killed ninety-nine people. Is it possible that when I die I can be forgiven and reach heaven?'

The wise man, who is maybe not so wise, says, 'No. Of course you can't be forgiven and can't reach heaven.'

This makes the murderer unhappy and so – in the manner of unhappy men – he kills the wise person.

And now he has killed one hundred people.

The murderer is all alone again and getting older and still searching for answers and for paradise. This troubles his heart and means he goes to find another wise person and speaks with him. He says, 'I have killed one hundred people. Is it possible that when I die I can be forgiven and reach heaven?'

We might say the second wise person really is wise. He replies, 'If you die in this country it will not be possible that you will be forgiven and you will not reach paradise. There is, however, a merciful country. If you can reach that land before you die, there you will be forgiven and you may enter paradise.'

The murderer thanks the wise person and duly sets off on the long and perilous journey to the merciful country.

In due course it is time for the murderer to die. He has only just reached the border of the merciful country when he falls and his soul lifts away from his body.

And the angels contend with each other over his fate. Some think he has crossed the border and lies inside the merciful country. *Paradise will be his.* Some think he never quite reached his longed-for destination and will therefore be denied access to heaven and, anyway, he's a murderer. He's a terrible, terrible man.

But then god moves the whole, large world beneath the murderer and makes sure that his body is inside the border, is safe in the merciful country.

God will move the world to ensure mercy.

Even a man who has killed one hundred people can be forgiven and be at peace.

I told Buster that story. That one.

How much more stupid could anyone get?

And we made what I thought was love that night – there on the kitchen floor. Volunteers kept it very clean. I recall it as a reddish colour that was buffed away in places from over-emphatic cleaning. And I wonder if he was trying to emphasise his passion, or spontaneity. Perhaps he was building in degradation from the very start of us.

In the morning of our afterglow – the OrKestrA noticed it, naturally – we all climbed into the van and Buster drove us to give a show for the Easington Women's Support Group.

The women in Easington were running a strike for their men's jobs in the pits, for their community – doing everything: food parcels, fundraising, bringing in poets, keeping up spirits. They were on fire. And an army of cops with no numbers were occupying their town, waving ten-pound notes at mothers who couldn't feed their kids, calling them names…

It was terrible, what was happening to them, but they were so bright with resisting that you could have read the paper by their light. We went over to cheer them up – this was right at the end of August in 1984 – and all they did was make us happier and look after us.

And that morning I thought they could fight on forever if they only had a love like mine.

Stupid, stupid, stupid – patronising and stupid.

They had too many loves to count. They had the best love – they loved people.

And I believed I was in Easington with a man who was an ideal fit. He was beautiful, so was the OrKestrA, so was I – everything was beautiful. That sort of adolescent trash.

I thought all of the possible loves were with us, together in one place. Really, they were, but Buster had no place in that.

And maybe there is a god and maybe He – or She, or They – has access to world-shifting mercy.

I don't.

There does have to be mercy. The terrible people need it and so does everyone. The Stiltskins must get mercy, because the acting out of mercy cleans and saves us all. Without it, normal people are either eaten away by griefs or become the new Stiltskins.

But I don't forgive, I can't. And, yes, there has to be mercy, but there has to be justice, too.

And meanwhile it seems that more of us wake up each day with a free-falling pitch in their stomach. We dream of failing parachutes and tightropes that snap. And some of us tell our kids the stories that let them learn how to be themselves in ways that do no harm.

I think that's the best preparation, but maybe I'm wrong.

Certainly, I'm a hypocrite, because I still want to kill Buster.

I have wanted to kill him for years. Not one hundred murders – only one.

But the thing is – I won't do it.

I never will.

Even if I could do it somehow, to kill him would be just one more way of letting him steal me from myself.

I have my rage. It's always close to howling. But I try to do better than indulge it. And rage is just a way of hiding. It was acting as a distraction to stop me ever feeling grief. I have become happier and less furious – *Thank you Paul , thank you Sue, thank you Mr Charalambous, thank you all the Acorns and thank you Francis.*

That is a good thing, but I know the grief is coming for me, coming closer the more I relax. I tried to solve that problem by getting busy, then busier still. But you can't really be that busy in a lockdown.

So here I am, left alone with what's true.

I never did stop mourning for Monkey Monk. I never stopped being sad for the kid that I was and the ways I was lost and too scared for the big world. I never stopped grieving for my mum and the ways in which she was lost, is still being lost. I miss my perfectly motherly mum – the one that I invented to get me through, but never met. And I never stopped missing the real, live and silky-furred dog that we had for a while until my mother handed it to strangers, because it was too much trouble and because I loved it.

I never stopped missing the OrKestrA after it broke up and faded.

None of my sadness ever went away. It wasn't dead and won't lie still no matter how deep I bury it.

And I know that I live in a furious country that's full of busyness. We must all be so very, very sad.

That last section was a bit too glum. I'd never tell the children anything like that. And adults are only tall children, myself included, so I really should do better.

Reality's hardly my fault, but I should do my best to improve it. That's probably a human duty, isn't it?

So I'm going to add in some nice things here – *pleasant details*. These will be more than averagely necessary because then I'm going to tell you more of what happened when I followed Buster – as much as I can stand.

So – *pleasant details*.

I've told you about how to make a good scone. There's no other baking secret I can offer. I did attempt to establish relations with sourdough bread, but all sourdough does is brood in the back of your fridge and insist that you feed it flour and then more flour. It's even more petulant and sensitive than normal bread. Have one bad mood in its vicinity and the thing will turn itself into vinegar and Cthulhu snot.

Unpleasant detail.

But it did occasionally like me and turn into bread that wouldn't cause tongue ulcers.

Pleasant detail.

And who the hell ever invented bread, meringues, cooking your woolly mammoth meat instead of just eating it raw?

Sorry.

I'm delaying the next bit of Buster, but I am so sick of him taking up space in my life. I don't want him here, too.

Could you bear with me? Could we just think of something nice? At the moment, it's August 2020 and our Chancellor of the Exchequer is presenting himself in photo opportunities where he holds up plates of Common People Food in a way that he feels is inviting. I'm guessing his intention, but it seems that he hopes we'll forget that we're being offered discount dinners inside an exciting experiment in mass viral infection. Ten quid off a burger to test if your genes will entitle you to survive.

Something like that.

If you're waiting on tables, I suspect you can anticipate wearing black a lot more often outside of work hours.

That'll need several *pleasant details* to balance it out.

Francis' hair is still happy – the rest of him, too.

Pleasant.

The wrens are doing well.

Pleasant.

The multigenerational blackbird babies are also thriving. And staring. They stand on one leg and ponder us, philosophical.

That may be *unnerving* more than *pleasant.*

And last week Francis and I repainted the big wooden gates between us and the street. Same colour, just fresh. When we were out on the Wicklow Street side, passers-by would stop and comment, would be maskless and overly close. And every time, in the same cheery voice, with the same delighted hair, Francis would just say, 'Are you six feet away? I'm not sure you are, you know. Try and picture a coffin – the length of a coffin. That will help.' You would hear the smile in his voice, even if you couldn't see it, because he was wearing a mask – the one that reads *We're all mad here.*

And who could argue with that?

Francis' jovial tolerance almost irritates me and then I remember that joviality and tolerance are handy if you have to deal with me.

After a while, the passers-by of Wicklow Street left us more and more alone.

And, after another while, once we were finished with the ladder, we interlaced fingers and both painted as we stood. This meant that Francis was having to work left-handed.

'Don't you mind?'

'No. I try and use both hands to do things.'

'For when you have a stroke?'

'For when I have a stroke and am paralysed down my right side. It's practice.'

He isn't less apprehensive than I am. He just takes his fears less

276

seriously and plans for their solutions.

And our brushes rose and fell in unison and it was like dancing. We were a double act, trying out a brand new bit.

Pleasant.

And this is the part where I'll get out the big guns and tell you about Colonsay.

Highly pleasant – lots of detail.

I managed to make a trip there with Francis. This was in May 2019, back before I strongly suspect the world ended and everyone just kept going, anyway. We all ran off the highest cliff there is and our feet are pounding gamely, trying to catch the thin air and somehow stay in place. We're all *Looney Tunes* characters now.

May is a good month in the West of Scotland, full of early cuckoos and kayakers making their paddle blades glimmer at the back of people's holiday photographs.

And Francis has persuaded me to catch the ferry out from Oban, pass the red and white striped lighthouse on Kerrera Spit and roll into the nitrogen-blue distance.

Everything is just the right colours.

Mull glides alongside and is steps and ramparts. Argyll looks like grand knees under velvet bedclothes.

So many pleasant details.

We went up on the top deck to be near more and watched the wake thickening behind us, felt the breeze pounce. I remember thinking it was pushing everything terrible far away, taking us into this diesel-flavoured peace that stung the ears and numbed the forehead and span on a strange slow axis as we progressed.

Defensive people love islands – they help us to see the threats coming a mile away.

And the light falls constantly at the angle of miracles.

Pleasant detail.

I do love the water, love its wild blue eye – all poor Mother's fault. When she was morning sick with me she hit on the idea of cancelling out my nauseating influence over her by taking boat trips. My earliest times were faintly affected by rented pedaloes and skiffs and trips out to Brownsea Island and thereabouts from Poole. We lived near the water in Poole until I was two. Living in Poole only until you're two is another *pleasant detail* – it means you can't remember Poole at all.

I sometimes think of Ma stepping off from quayside after quayside while I gave most of my attention to forming a spine, growing kidneys.

Thank you, Ma.

And I am so sorry that you are so tiny now inside your latest new cardie, Ma. I am so sorry that it looks so big and like a blanket when you stand in the lounge window and wave like the queen of Rectory Hill Lodge.

I'm not sorry that you're waving – as far as you know – at just three friendly and slightly interesting strangers: a gangly lad with delicate fingers, a flamboyant-headed man and a woman with your undiluted Roman nose. You like them, these strangers – they seem to cheer you.

Pleasant detail.

She hasn't lost me, she has gained someone she likes.

And god we need things that we like, just little pleasant things, details we can cling to – it's not much to ask.

The Colonsay boat trip delivered a lot, as boat trips should. I run them between my fingers like worry beads. The memories differentiate – a pleasant detail like sipping tea while you lean on a deck rail and look out over the wild blue mind of the sea and there is what you are told are the ramparts and tawny greeny lionskin curves of Mull. And here is Francis reciting place names – Scoor and Ardalanish and Knockvologan. And it seems that you barely know him and already he's someone else, staring into the breeze with his chin braced high like a sea dog explorer. He has no other choice – his hair would blind him otherwise. You mention his adventuresome expression and he gets shy. But he doesn't get angry. There's no violence fumbling its key at the late-night door of somewhere bleak.

And we're wearing our second-hand tweeds and a Fair Isle sweater, a Guernsey – have more clothes packed for the journey, clothes that are all also the costumes we would like to wear in our future. We want to be like a black and white movie, with all of the anti-fascist values, but none of the wartime pain. We want to sit in rooms with Bakelite telephones that hardly ever ring, surrounded by naturally, actively happy people, easily happy couples and solved mysteries and laughter.

It's too silly for one person to attempt, but with both of us – *why not try?* When we fail we might at least have a good future, here and now, a wealth of *pleasant detail.*

We're not in a sad little craft, fleeing war. We're not foundering. We're not holding children and belongings while the sea starts to eat us up. We are among the fortunate.

Guilty detail.

And we looked like a costume party breaking out in the midst of multi-pocket hiking trousers and sensibly weatherproof layers, but we didn't care, and Francis leaned in close beside my ear and pre-empted my paranoid rushes, by singing them to that *Sound of Music* tune about favourite things:

Black balaclava to wear while you're sleeping,
Soft shoes and gloves to be safe while I'm creeping,
Clothes line and bin bags and shovel I'll take,
Also twelve knives for variety's sake…

He was warming my ear and I was keeping my arm around him while the wide sea pressed us together and then rocked us not too far apart. And that was precisely when I discovered that pleasure is pleasant and has no inherent penalties I'll have to pay.

And then Jura drew close and showed off its austerity and its twin mountains and, apparently, every man on board tells every woman on board, 'Those are the Paps.' In response, we decide that we will always call them the Balls of Jura. The Big Pointy Balls of Jura.

Pleasant detail.

And Colonsay crouched down low to hug us in, and the white of a lighthouse showed like the single tooth in a lopsided smile. And pale gable ends caught the sun and I could feel I might be turning into this other happy woman who took kind things for granted.

Pleasant detail.

No border control, no guns, no malign assumptions – only buttercups and larks climbing with their songs until they vanished, were only music.

I had two weeks with him there, with the land and sea and sky butterflying away from each other in white, green and turquoise echoes. I felt drunk with seeing double. I felt if I saw such things every day, I would be permanently happy, would be delighted in the rain.

A holiday isn't a life. I know that, but it can be the start of one. And there's something about small islands that can so easily suggest they have a childhood for you – a new and better one they'll slip under your feet.

Over and over through lockdown I'd look at Francis on my screen and smell warm turf and coal smoke, seaweed and gorse and the damp life of the machair. I'd remember the pair of us walking together up the warm flank of a hill, carrying our bags, which were going to get heavy, but Annanka wouldn't mind.

And Francis sang, half murmuring, while we both rose away from the sea:

Murder and mayhem and strange alterations,
Posting your fingers to different nations,
All these atrocities making me grin,
These are a few of the horrors within.

That's another *pleasant detail* – the way I loved him for it.

So we've had a break and thought of being Elsewhere. My third favourite hobby.

There does have to be hope as well as mercy.

And, as I was coming indoors, I went and kissed the top of my son's head. He is reading something called *Language, Truth and Logic* in my deckchair. It seems both promising and unlikely that such a book would still exist here and not have been burned at once.

Then I kissed the top of Francis' head and he told me, 'Thank you, Madam. The staff appreciates all expressions of gratitude for our services…' He was scrolling through Highland property online. He says prices are rising – too many dreams are aiming North.

Now I'm in my bedroom. The dark is darker here and I need that, even though it's also hot enough to sting my skin. I'm propped on the bed between two cold water bottles and waiting to acclimatise.

I'm not built for this. I'm a Celt. I think of my ancestors leaving Africa at a sweaty run. I imagine them dreaming northward dreams of frost and drizzle, glaciers, snow – all the things we're losing now.

I spent so long worrying if Small Paul would have any kids, or maybe get too busy because of being a ground-breaking lawyer for oppressed orangutans – something magnificent. I wondered if he'd be restricted by inheriting my nerves. Or if calling him Paul was a mistake and I should have tried Mike, Steve, Bernie? Which unforeseen, terrible thing would be my fault?

I didn't even suspect that his later life might be spent mostly underwater and yet also somehow on fire. Plus fascism. Who knew we'd try that again?

Unpleasant details.

But those wrens – still doing well.

We feed them mealworms, which smell delicious, and we probably should get used to eating insects before they're the only option. The wrens will probably let us share.

And that's enough.

Enough babble.

Enough distraction.

I can start.

I'm not ready, but here I go in any case.

So let's be back in that November day again, November 2019 – the one with Buster.

And suddenly we're present tense and Technicolor, IMAX, Sensurround – my heart's rabbitting in my chest – because PTSD is nothing if not emphatic.

Screw virtual reality – what you need is embedded trauma.

And I'm in London and I believe that I'm being very clever as Buster runs away from the cathedral – flees from me with his attaché case and his City-smooth haircut. I think I have driven him into retreat by expressing my dignity and power.

The lunchtime interval of calm while the lowly people rush-eat is deteriorating fast, but no crowd on Earth will slow me.

In the City you can gauge the importance of strangers by noting the speed with which they head back to their work. Those clinging to low rungs on the ladder are jolt-walking all around me, too tired to keep their pace up, but doing their best, already sure of arriving late, humid and unsuccessful.

Buster's pressing on with exactly the correct amount of savagery – he looks like management and is deferred to, not impeded.

I'm trying to think that I'm a free agent and have made good choices. I'll never have to labour or triumph in the City. But, as far as it's concerned, I surely look like a failure in cheap clothes, someone bizarrely unconcerned by the needs of money, by the turning of it in its great big bed to save it from pressure sores.

I feel humiliated. Buster is always about humiliation.

The streets beyond New Change are darkening with the flutter of more and less expressive linings at the hems of nice overcoats. Shoulders and foreheads are set at London angles. Sue would be making everyone *stop right where you are* to do a bit of instant stretching and relaxation. She'd talk to them about what spines are and why we have them. There'd be dancing.

Quite possibly no one but me would like it – too high a chance of emotions waking, consciences even.

Buster has the momentum of someone stalking back towards an office in order to make heads roll. He is money's righteous fury.

I don't hate him. I'm doing whatever is beyond that.

But I'm not whatever he is. I'm not entirely dark inside.

Still, there's a moment when I scare myself – rushing between mismatched glass tower blocks, both with a blue psycho sunglass sheen on their windows. I am so very angry.

And I could just go back to Court 10 and be safe with Hissy Apocalypse. She's down on the rota as this afternoon's guaranteed supportive face. Her colours would shake up Court 10. They'd be brave enough.

I am free until the evening. Sue has granted me a Mrs Delara Day, which means that my current Year Five is probably in Big Room with her and writing a group poem. Or they may all be outside in our minute school garden, weeding things and inventing autobiographies for insects. Whatever else happens, there will be hopping and twirling and snake arms at Home Time – our Goodbye Dance.

What business wouldn't thrive so much more if it had a Goodbye Dance? Its heart would pump clear and clean.

Because of Oakwood, I'm a person who is clean. Buster hasn't made me twisted. I really believe that. I am a clean thing that he fears and not a stupid creature dumbly following a trail of bait. I am not so very easy to fool.

The sky has settled into a flat and dirty grey, but it won't rain. My class can be safely outside and curious without sad consequences. They will enjoy the change while I chase down my past and wonder what I'll do if I catch it.

That red hair of his is glimmering in the crowds. Whenever I think I've lost him, there is this blink of colour in a shop window, or a twist of his body that is unmistakable.

I'm feeling sick again.

There's a moment when I seem to see the inside of his wrist, flaring pale like something subterranean.

He is threading north and east, choosing the littler streets and lanes as if he has a vermin instinct that wants to be quick against walls and then out of sight.

I want him to trip and fall and break his nose, scuff his shoes, have his briefcase snatched by some underclass marauder. Then he'd find me standing over him and laughing like a wolf. That would be enough to satisfy.

No. It wouldn't.

The cold river wind is being channelled between buildings that seem intent on leaning and swelling overhead and stealing the airspace until they close up tight together and there's no daylight at all, only brutalist sheet glass and marble slabs the colour of dried blood.

I keep up the pace. I endure.

I pass little pockets of buildings constructed on a human scale, Victorian holdouts. Mostly they've been saved because they're something to do with Jesus – churches like tiny old women who've forgotten their way home.

Then I'm suddenly in a thin street with Buster and nobody else.

And I know I will remember this – every detail – more than blowing out Paul's birthday candles, more than everything blessed.

I can hear Buster breathing. There's more marble in this weird and oddly popular shade of old blood. Underfoot is a weird, smooth surface reflecting dully. It's very hard to make any stone this ugly and yet someone has.

Buster slows, begins to walk. I can't see his face, but I understand this is his way of laughing at me.

Because I don't know him, I'm unaware that I am in great danger. But my instincts are unnerved enough to tilt the weird stone underfoot, make it seem to wince.

I slow down and I keep my distance. My breath hurts my throat.

His head starts grinding round as if he might look at me. Before I can find this horrifying, I'm running again. I'm running because I want to hurt him.

How stupid is that?

But then he lunges forward again, sprints round a corner that's tucked away up ahead. I discover that I'm yelling, 'What do you want? What did you ever want?' Things like that.

This does no good. I simply emerge from a side entrance for Liverpool Street Station, screaming like any one of London's strange and desperate. I feel the tangible chill of being ignored by a city that's used to ignoring.

I see Buster darting fast inside an almost empty tunnel lined with shopping opportunities. We are nowhere near the rush hour and I let myself feel certain he'd hoped for a crowd to hide him, made a mistake.

Inside the station, he is perfectly revealed, a shadow under the glare of the glass roof while he rushes across the wide concourse. I see his head tick up for a moment and check the indicator board.

I don't have a ticket for anywhere and he probably does. Men like him always do have escape routes.

Yes, he lurches towards a rank of barrier gates on his left, conjures a ticket from somewhere in his coat, gets through.

I head for the same gate he used.

It feels infected.

I watch him climb aboard a train heading out for Clacton in five minutes. And I tap myself through with a card that will take me only to the end of Zone 6.

Primary teachers don't dodge paying rail fares.

But I no longer seem to be me. Or perhaps I'm an earlier version of me, one who improvised more. Perhaps I'm close to being Annanka again. I do hope so.

On the Clacton platform, I wait beside the train. I'm sighting down the long curve of the carriages to spot him, if he tries to slip away.

And then I'm onboard and the carriage is pushing through an artificial night of burrowed points and junctions and tracks upon tracks. I can see myself in multiple window reflections. They all look like somebody failing badly and in the sort of trouble that won't get help.

I drop on to a seat and catch my breath, smooth my hair. I try to seem only an averagely harried commuter, nothing special, not an Oakwooder gone astray with no right to travel past Stratford and no plan.

I can't call anybody, can't text Paul to say I'm going to be late. No phones are allowed in court, and I had no intention of depositing mine in her majesty's care – so I left it at home.

This part is all blurred, mixed up in the speed howling past against the train's skin and all the kinds of death that come with it. I think that I inhale, exhale, air rushing in deep and hoarse and hard, not calming me, making my mouth taste of coppery risk.

I just have to do the next logical thing, though. Then I will be logical, reason in action, dignified.

I can smell Brut, just a trace. Brut and his skin.

I stand, happy the train's motion would make anyone seem unsteady – not just me. The next logical thing is to search Buster out.

Only one carriage is even close to busy. Buster isn't in it. Nor the next.

Every time I step through a new pair of gangway doors, the hangover fug of a different fast food greets me. One carriage is thick with a sweetish teenage kind of cologne. No Buster. In another a solitary studentish man reads a Kindle. No Buster.

I'm paying attention so hard I could draw everybody I see: a foursome of women peel the lids off their single-serve plastic glasses of Prosecco and immediately break out in shrieks of laughter. A man bellows Important Things to another two men who are clearly impatient to bellow Important Things of their own. They have to transcend the fact of their being on a train – and not even in First Class.

I stumble and sway through carriage after carriage.

Irrational.

I could be with Year Five now, I could be with Hissy, I could be somewhere kind.

And there is no Buster, not anywhere.

And I have run out of train.

But he is still somewhere. He isn't supernatural, can't vanish.

I'm sure of that. Almost.

The stink of him – faint, unmistakable, faint, unforgettable – trails through the carriages, through the reek of stir fries and vinegar chips.

I wonder if I've learned the scent of Francis' pillow as indelibly, if Paul's baby skin, his first hair, have been stored so perfectly and so deep.

This makes me furious.

But the next logical action is to check which toilets are occupied and which claim they're out of order.

I have, at least, made him scurry through the length of a train and then hide.

Crouching in a toilet – I imagine him crouching – how very, very appropriate.

Stratford swoops past, its shopping opportunities jutting tall above the station. Brand new apartment buildings make ugly statements at each other over our heads. Shenfield slows alongside – I'm illegal now – and still no trace of Buster. I linger in doorways, check for fugitives, study uninformative toilet doors, am an inconvenience to others. Year Five would be scandalised.

I am halted roughly halfway down the train – my lookout post for every station, so that I can see if he makes a move before the rails take all of us away.

At Chelmsford, most passengers leave: the wine ladies, the bellowing men, some shoppers, two clumps of boys, a pram and its parents. Those left behind are somehow softer, quieter, less curated – they look like the kind of people that a mugger would select. Buster would enjoy himself among so many easy targets.

I am still – up and down – scouring the carriages, the stressed person who causes more stress. A woman in pink dungarees half stands to ask me, 'Have you lost something?'

The way I tell her 'No' makes her stop preparing the expression those who are helpful offer the helpless.

I want to cry.

I just want to cry.

I want to be at home and crying.

Also I want to never cry again.

I want to be unaware that even in children's stories not everyone gets what they want.

And this isn't a story that ever touched a child.

When we reach Hythe, the train stills and ticks and gapes its doors again. I spring up to surveille the platform and the dungaree woman sighs loud enough for me to hear.

I don't care.

I stand in the doorway and see nothing of use to me until a student shambles past, in among a few others much the same. Only he's older: paint-smeared black overalls, brown hair with a little grey in a Number Four cut, red plimsolls and a shapeless jacket in army green. Something stooping about his walk is clearly a lie.

He's carrying not very much in one of those big tartan nylon laundry bags.

That's a lie, too.

He is all a lie.

Buster hid in a toilet and altered his costume, but not enough. I'm very used to seeing him in character. That's how we started, after all.

Still, I'm barely in time to hit the platform and watch him stroll towards the level-crossing gate.

Buster is Buster – he can't change that.

I wait behind an ugly bit of hoarding – my turn to hide – as the gate lifts and he lopes away, calm and easy. He seems like a man heading home. I suspect I am watching him be whoever he is in that home.

I never enjoy crossing railway lines, not in a car and not on foot – it always feels slightly like suicide, no matter how steady I am at the time. I wonder if that tiny prickle of extinction calls him, too. Maybe he likes it.

Over the tracks, I follow him past a Victorian bridge that spans a green-backed canal. This is the kind of wasteland limbo he would favour. He's threading himself along between brick walls and razor wire and businesses to do with cars. Here and there are brave little touches of public art like monuments to failure.

He doesn't look round.

I am confident that he's off guard and hasn't seen me. I don't know why I choose to be so innocent in an area so clearly full of bad possibilities. The daylight is still functional, but dimming and this is nowhere to be after dark.

I pass a pub that looks as if it never opens and never should.

This has been such a long day, and I am so tired that I get baffled by a roundabout, another roundabout, pedestrian crossings apparently designed to cull the hesitant.

I wish I was here with Hissy and Sissy. We'd be unstoppable then.

I want to be here with Monkey and hold his long, fine hand. Only this is such an unloved place that it would hurt him.

Sweet Monkey Monk – Buster killed him. We all know that. Buster's betrayal and the end to optimism, to the OrKestrA – they stopped Monkey's heart. The heroin was incidental, just the emergency exit he happened to choose.

His funeral was the last time we reunited before Court 10.

We gave Monkey a proper send-off. Mrs Fire stormed the whiny little crematorium keyboard and deviated savagely from the grey little repertoire of permissible hymns. We wore what finery we'd kept and could still fit into. We played drums.

We brought kazoos, but didn't play them – they're not a funeral instrument.

Mine went on top of the coffin and then behind the curtain. I hope it burned with him and rose with him, ready to help him build nonsense.

If there aren't kazoos in heaven, why would you bother?

And the funeral had no trace of Buster, no filth intruding to ruin everything.

I suppose that's because his damage was done already and he could move on.

I realise that missing Monkey, missing everyone, has made me cry.

And Buster dips down a curving slope of road beyond another bridge. Its turn makes him almost double back and he glances up, already smiling, meets my eyes. Smiling. He looks right at me and is smiling and then skips into a jog trot.

He knew I was here then. He was unwary because he doesn't care – I'm not a threat.

I wipe my face with my sleeve, which is something that sets a poor example for young habits.

The next logical thing I should do is go home.

There is always time to make a better choice.

Only I don't want to make a better choice. I want to stop Buster's heart.

I don't know how, but I want that very much.

I sink down after him and reach the riverside, where this strange succession of raddled vessels looms up from a haze on the water.

There's a big, red lightship, I think – it looks like a monstrous toy. Masts and funnels loom tall over the quay. A strange, feral smell is rising up from the dwindled water and the furrows of glimmering mud. That same smell was there at St Paul's, was mixed with the aftershave, the reality of skin. He's an animal thing that's found an animal place to hold him.

Far ahead, Buster turns and then drops at an odd speed over the high concrete side of the quay. I half expect to see him wallow or slither and swim away, a water creature suddenly.

This is Buster the man who'd bounce children on his shoulders and Buster the man with cool lips who could kiss like a human being and Buster who knew about shadow puppets and Buster the hole kicked through everybody's hope.

And I run the way I used to when I was eleven or ten and alone in the park with my silk-furred dog. I could do nothing about my mother or anything else, but I could run.

Like this, like this, I'd run.

My dog would be delirious with the race of it.

Like this, like this I'd run, and it would be a way of screaming.

Like this.

And I would be nearly fast enough to manage to escape myself.

Like this, like this. I am so fast.

I run with my eyes shut. That's a stupid thing to do.

Then I'm standing still above a tiny grey metal ladder and I'm remembering how, in the end, I would come to rest and my dog would come to sit beside me and her happiness would spread right into me.

I know we really loved each other.

I know I'm alone.

I know there's the ladder that leads down to wherever Buster is.

And I know that I'm not someone who can stop a heart.

When I lean my head towards the water, I'm scared that I might see Buster staring, smiling, might get lost in a vertigo ripple of mud and water. His smiling – I'm surprised the river doesn't thrash about with it.

I blink and I breathe.

I'm fairly sure I breathe.

Something rattles in the chain-link fence behind me, but I keep on leaning forward until I can see.

At the ladder's foot there's a barge with a wide, long, filthy roof: moss and rot and bubbled black paint over something like tar paper. Objects abandoned across it have stopped being anything more than rust and weather damage. A person might guess this had rotted here for years and is uninhabitable. There's something inside, though, pretending to be rats. Two feet are trying to sound like more.

It's only because I remember myself as Annanka that I turn my back to the wrecked barge and begin climbing down the ladder to step on board.

As I drop into the cool and cooler I remember, I remember that Annanka was lucky and strong. I keep moving and keep thinking that I am me and I have Paul and I have Francis and so I am also lucky and must be strong.

Still, when I reach the barge's roof, neither one of my hands can let go of the ladder.

Buster used to talk about when we would start living on a boat. We were going to fix up a big Dutch barge and have kids and put flowers in jugs and keep a little terrier to follow us around and look pert on the roof as we slipped by the ordinary people on the towpath.

You'll commit to a great deal of detail when you're being fed regular promises of happiness and love.

I don't want to let go of the ladder and touch his boat.

I don't want to remember how much of my strength I put into picturing barge life: Buster with a beard and water safety lessons for kids who'd all swim as blithe and sure as otters. Washing would jig on a line strung from stem to stern, white as innocence. And we'd maybe join in a little fleet of barges with the OrKestrA. And maybe and maybe and maybe.

The barge roof looks like a sickness and gives unevenly when I put my weight on it.

He made all our future's love and promise into this.

27th/28th March 2020, Nanjizal Bay:

This, Anna, is from the proximate past and after you saw me and after you were on my boat which has since been moved to another location. The boat was a good one and I used it for many years and regret the loss of it. Or I am using it still.

You will have noticed that it was called *The Sunday*. And that is the new name I gave it because it is mine and a part of me and so was Sunday the Baron. I was able to enjoy being the Baron and a source of smiling children.

That is a part of me.

You noticed me in the Old Bailey.

I have decided my discovery was due to poor tradecraft practices that were influenced by emotion. Emotion is sometimes involved. Also subconscious reasons. Also I am more accustomed to hiding in country. Cities are not my place. In moorland or forest or any natural terrain no one will ever find me unless I wish.

Or sometimes I am easy to follow because I want somebody near to me for reasons. Sometimes I am waiting for them and am the end of the route they chose to follow which they thought was very clever although it was not.

I perhaps wanted revelation and perhaps to confess. I am confessing now. I think that I want to.

To be a person no one else can know is occasional unpleasant. My life is very light careful and also solitary supermax confinement.

I am in a position that might require sympathy although I understand it conversely might not.

On my boat you were my visitor which is what prisoners in civilised places are allowed. This idea of England is not civilised but I received a visit all the same.

Prav would despair of my multiple absence of tactical solutions.

I am very tired.

I am considering courses of action. These will affect no one beyond myself. Your receipt of this does not imply that you should or will read it. The reading would be your choice.

I will solve my tiredness soon.

This document constitutes risk outside my effective parameters. It also initiates a process that I will not control. I will not control you. I did not consciously control you. I was at work and acting in accordance with aims and objectives that were flawed and which I have left behind.

I think I disappoint myself.

I have tight sensations in my head.

This document is incomplete but enough. If you have this you have everything.

The best evidence of me would likely derive from my most recent activity which was Nigel. It was a source of satisfaction. I am therefore completing my record of him. He was a pressing need although I would not say my last.

Nigel was ripe and soft open by January 2020. He had learned to be consistent impressed by my perhaps criminal weeks of never explained absence. You will recognise the pattern of absences and know this is a double life indicator that is reliable although doubled lives are intentional hard to see. Doubled people exist in the twenty-fifth hour which is outside reality and is where magicians keep their mechanisms and where targets and other civilians cannot enter.

No one reasonable with suspicions would anyway guess my relevant other life.

Absence that is properly prepared for gives the target an appropriate empty space to fill with just what they want. Nigel provided his own best cover narrative for me. This is how to make a benefit out of a necessity because it is necessary for things like myself to go away from time to time.

To remain sustained effective everyone submerged must come up slow for air now and again. When I had a policebody and was with the Squad I would leave my established context for the purpose of debriefing. I was also intended to rest for certain numbers of days although I did not like to. There was additionally the need to submit plans for approval and set up resources for future exploitation.

I would make regular early returns to each operation because being inside it was objectively a better and more rational life.

We policebodies had a safe house that was south of the canal in Leamington Spa studentland. Our comings and goings and noise were unremarked. We were cigarette smoke and dope smoke and instant coffee from a catering tin with the contents clumped and ruined by wet teaspoons. And we were skinhead identities and radical vegan identities and non-violent geopolitical identities and football terrace kidney punch identities and swastika identities. We exhibited high and repeated emphasis on Left-leaning infiltration and causes of minor impact and low malignity. We were stark catering differences and confusions.

Together in our house of safety we were red white and blue identities and green white and gold identities and familiar with Irish diaspora social clubs and we were faithful workers towards the never ending of civil war. We would 2am argue each other towards the viewpoints we were supposed to be only observing and not accepting. We drank Ulster Harp lager and the whiskey with a map on the label that showed Ireland before 1921.

I once re-encountered a graduate of our safe house alma martyr as we each drove our respective brothers to the front. We were attacking and defending a Bristol bookshop with the customary escalations. I punched him before he punched me. We were exculpatory savage with each other.

No one told us that our work had an inbuilt lifespan limit. Deception corrodes well-being and personality with major effects that are psychological spiritual. Mission failure becomes inevitable. We fast or slow realise our labours do not possibly have the advertised effect and are not ever vital in ongoing struggles to shield the weak or to defend the precious realm. Every action is its own defeat.

Graduates of the Squad become permanent cynicism and walk away deep infected by our target sedition. Thereafter they become self-destruction due to their certainty that sin is righteous and righteousness sin.

My subsequent work with Prav and thereafter derives from the justicefury you gave me. I am my own fault but I am also yours.

I became saved by justice and exponentially effective with Prav. I then progressed to my own operations and towards things like Nigel.

Nigel took my days and weeks spent suddenly away from him as proof of magnificent infamies committed beneath the direction of hard-striking men. He would attempt to interrogate me regarding these imagined adventures on my return but I would be sheepish evasions and fear flashes in response. He decided this demonstrated my excellent secret-keeping capacities and this was in a way not wrong. I made repeated shows of optimum silence and mild stupidity when I was close at his side with spaniel affect as he preferred.

My perceived reliability meant he was pleased to take me on several occasions to a bow-fronted semi in New Malden full of prisoner girls from Benin. Prisoner women would be more precise as a term although he habitual avoided their classification as such.

Nigel had sex dominance requirements that relied upon black skin and high-contrast contact and purchased access with accompanying ownership fantasies.

Driving me there on our first outing he would talk in coke rushes and have wild hands. I am not a nervous passenger but have minimum safety requirements which he did not meet.

I quick positioned myself as habitual chauffeur to his brothel of choice. Inside the premises I established an apparent comfort habit of going to Bedroom 4 with a woman whose genuine name was Promise. She had defeated posture and showed effects of poor nourishment although she was also still intent upon small dignities established quietly. She used home dye products and relaxer and had at that time blonde hair in what is called a pixie cut. It made her neck seem long vulnerable. Her appearance in general might have seemed playful daring and high self-esteem in other contexts and with another demeanour. Promise had insufficient African indicators for Nigel to find her palatable. He would make loud insult assessments of her qualities while we sat in the lounge for casual initial drinks as if we were ill-matched strangers at the start of a dinner party and not assessing a selection of forced sex prisoners overseen by a succession of frowning Moldovan and also Essex men.

Promise had her little finger missing from both hands. In Bedroom 4 we did not discuss why this was because privacy is a rare thing and a kind of glory in every circumstance. We sat on her bed and talked about French irregular verbs and where she would most like to live in Paris. After the first time I would bring her the brand of chocolate wafer biscuits that she liked. At a certain point towards the end of each visit she would cry. This would indicate when her fantasy futures exhausted their sustaining energy. We would walk downstairs after the hour and project her symptoms of weeping as my fault and a result of ambitious rape scenarios.

In the sex aftermath period of lounge drinks Nigel would like to sit between women on the white leather sofa and side eye check their compliance and presentation of desire pretences. He would wear and discuss his Derek Rose silk satin boxers and also fully unfastened bespoke Hilditch & Key shirt with the name marked on each button. He would be arms spread and staking his claim over territory and all available subordinates. He would grin and make displays of successful sex sweat.

His repetition of similar behaviours over time offered a scale by which to gauge his decline. His limbs were dying into fat. He grew a belly overhang of fish paleness under black wire hairs. I would glance at him admiring and away and think it would require deep dissociation and professionalism to find him bearable or touch him. His tailors conspired to disguise his nature while he was dressed and therefore amplified his powers in the usual manner of tailors. Without a suit he was this unearthed thing and white like strange rot or unexpected tubers.

In the lounge I would be crouched in the lowest armchair. I would hide myself in buttoned shirt and low-status trousers that were usually from M&S. I was the shyness and self-loathing that Tom dog should be. Disguising muscle tone and readiness and signs of discipline took severe postural modification. I would experience neck and back pain after shrinking and hunching for hours in his company.

I take only ibuprofen for pain and nothing stronger because over-the-counter opiate traps are to be avoided. I had an ulcer once and should not take NSAIDs but I risk it.

I was unable to release Promise from that situation in the ways available to me and I could not make her liable to succeed as a free individual. I have moral purpose but also focus overriding. I am target retention always and Nigel was my target. Sudden poli-cebody arrivals at his favoured disorderly house would have made his paranoia blink. He needed no disruptions or awareness jolts.

I am irresistible progress towards my conclusion and this means I can be the silent joysong from on high. This is my consolation for tasks left undone.

My often role for Nigel became chauffeur. I drove him into Redbridge and Islington and Bexley and Havering so that he could attend poker games in private homes and other impromptu build-ings. The black tie gambling haunts were tired of Nigel and would not have him. He claimed he was tired of them.

Nigel had playing faults that were amusing predictable. He tilted after large losses and was prone to skin reddening at his neck. He was without real-world or work experience and therefore lacked concentration. His character assessment abilities were stunted childlike and when he played with perceived inferiors he was unable to see them in detail. He indulged irrational attempts at punish-ment of his opponents based upon loss grudges. Nigel had minimal probability knowledge and played with divine right attitude. He chased flushes and was easily drawn by transparent bluffs. Pairs could entice him and he was beguiled by river card assumptions and strange obsessions unrelated to his hand. His manly display refusals to ever flop were endless expensive for him and internal satisfaction delight for me.

He played beyond his resources which were by this point part Russian underwritten and part fictional. Had he been a man of complexity I could have viewed his actions as a conscious cycle of transgression followed by preprogrammed Jesuit penance. He was infactly simple and only incompetent and too full of failure to understand his failing.

I never quite begged to join the poker table but seemed crestfallen lonely in various chairs in various corners repeated. I was beaten eyes and sad sips of piss beer always coincidentally opposite Nigel and in very plaintive but uncomplaining view. It took six months before I was permitted to play alongside my purported master owner. Nigel enjoyed attributing my money to fantasy disreputable sources.

Poker is revealing easy for me and those such as me.

I am now structured to fix on victory. I had to build many character defences into Tom so that we could both permit and enjoy his losses. I developed the habit of making a small win I could keep by faking nervous stomach troubles and leaving the table to sit with seltzer tablets signing calls of weakness. It would not do for me to keep on winning, but I could avoid too much loss.

A core Tom Stott characteristic is inability to deal with stress. He carries bicarbonate remedies always along with peppermints and makes jokes against himself about them. He hints at school discomforts and examination failures and romance failures and sex failures because of gastric unreliability.

On one poker evening I did reward myself by winning hurtful money from Nigel.

As recompense I had to make sure to spill piss on my trouser front during a urination break. I returned thereafter with a strong shame presentation and beta-level apology mumbles and falling flat jokes. I should then have reached for my tablets or mimicked intense intoxication and allowed him to gain back advantage. I did not want to.

I liked that I could tug him back and forth with his money and status needs.

I had slowly introduced the truth that I could get better coke and amphetamine for him from interesting secret and hypermasculine suppliers with whom he might one day personally meet.

My drugs were indeed admirable high purity and therefore a bond escalation between us. He began to trust me for his pleasure provision and to upgrade the frequency of his calls and texts.

Addiction need is among the best levers for access and the imposition of dominance. As his use accelerated Nigel would sometimes feel his status being lost. This would provoke small tempers and pouts. I continued to present myself as harmless and household dog faithful while also unpredictably withholding his supply to engineer his pressure levels. My excuses for non-delivery of his substance loves involved underworld narratives that he tried to like and find distracting.

Causing him withdrawal panic was a satisfaction to me.

The conclusion of Nigel was triggered ahead of schedule. As the pandemic washed over their island kingdom there were closures at Stonyhurst and Winchester Colleges and the other better schools so that the better children could ride out the plague in safety. The Houses of Parliament followed suit as befitting those used to obeying significant headmasters. Reference was made to oncoming and inevitable depredations among lesser and unblessed lives. The wider mass of national residents were instructed to fend for themselves while staying indoors for preference along with their fortitude and natural common sense and also their existing and propagating community spread and patriot symbols and goodbyes and turned milk dying slow on unopened doorsteps and so forth.

Disease death reared exponential and MPs fled to second homes and novel fraud opportunities.

The time was unprecedented opportunities.

Predators and scavengers and hunters are born to search for opportunity. We are built to find our luck. If you are preparation efficient and maximum awareness you will have access to your luck. You will be wings in the air uplifted on chance and flying with the currents of the world.

As soon as the country locked down I could lie awake at night and hear the rush of midnight things roaming over the idea of England and feeding hard. Calamities met each other and made more.

I had known when the number of ravens grew more numerous for year on year that a story of large death must be preparing. Ravens plan to always feed their children and have traditional appetites. This is only my superstition and unrelated to facts and ecology. I am aware of this. But a person who lives by waiting for lucks and chances needs their own superstition. Prav began mine because it was necessary. He gave me to the ravens. I am glad to have them and to be among their sons. I have their faith. The nihilists in our craft never last long.

I enjoyed a plague spring of country wildlife and birdsong and the basking gladness of my river. I was also occupied with occasional presentation of high-quality excuses for my lack of drug supplies to Nigel. I rendered myself more and more unreachable. I needed him beyond impatience as any and all sources dried and stopped. I waited for my final opportunity with him in the way any raven waits on the high highest point and watches until the ordained perfect instant and joycalls to the sky and to creation because he has a fine and blithe and perfect life. I am trained to be overview thinking and absence of light.

Nigel yearned for his leisure relaxations while lungs became inadequate across his constituency and body bags rolled past reminiscence murals in care homes he may once have visited for photographed tea and smiling. Lockdown Nigel considered himself

released from all work pretences and was full of schoolboy freedom elations and desires for personal liberties within chemical
entrapment. I then dipped from evasion into silence and answered
not one of his messages for a week. He tight obsessed on the space
where I was meant to always be.

The final call from him came at 9pm on 27th March. He was tight
and wide awake. When he heard my voice he became instant festive energy with need beneath. He was in some way remembering
the tall frown of windows around Front Quad and the narrow flags
underfoot and the so many beams overhead indoors and helping
to crush the new-bug in his first-term shiny shoes. He was needy
unwary and susceptible to dreams of starting over again clean and
reinciting fraudulent happiness as a boy of blissful promise.

They never do grow up.

I breathed to myself before I spoke to him. Inoutinoutinhalfout.

There is an alive feeling that trips and opens when a job truly
begins. It is a variety of pleasure impossible to replicate by other
means.

High-level speed and transgressive mobility was tedious predictable as the most tempting lure for Nigel. I suggested an outing
drive.

I had prepared a narrative for him to track along inside.

He of coursely agreed to a privilege demonstration and power
joy opportunity. Nothing could be finer than to romp like a hunt
across a padlocked nation that was cowed by every order to stay in
place. Nigel delivered himself to opportunity. Nigel delivered himself to me.

At the beginning of February I had taken possession of a nondescript dirty Land Rover with deceptive plates. This was in Devon. I
then used the vehicle to survey terrains and coastal features before
returning it to assigned parking off a quiet street at an outskirt of
Exeter.

I asked Nigel if perhaps we might overnight drive to some sea-
side air.

Nigel can anticipate no danger in the sea. It is only a little blue comforting thing at the foot of white sand beaches to Nigel. He thinks it is a wealth demonstration backdrop. Access to native servants abroad gives him constant interior role-play scripts that feature lying in soft shade with the surf saying innocent far-off whispers. He is no longer quite able for water ski and jet ski exertions but pretends he avoids them through boredom and not incapacity.

He does not know that all salt waters and coasts and coastal skies are mine and places of worship and baptising strength for me.

People forget that ravens are sea birds as much as land birds. We are adaptation made manifest.

From my outset I have established Tom Stott as using frequent and sometimes incorrect seafaring metaphors and terms. His pathetic non-sailor and non-swimmer status have been made also clear.

The absurdity of Tom in comparison to myself is a private comfort.

It is needful to incorporate jokes and pleasing flavours during any long deception as an aid for resilience and ultimate survival in the life. Each smooth sea reference and mention of hands on tillers lets me rejoice.

Tom has been presented as inevitable nervous frail if ever placed in a beach setting. This has left Nigel a clear and so far unexploited bullying opportunity. I know this pulls him.

I suggest that Margate or Whitstable or Frinton or suchlike would be demeaning as options and I volunteer to undertake a long and therefore more forbidden jaunt. I lean Nigel towards the truth that a plunge down from London all the way to Cornwall would offend every regulation and sensibility. Our journey would surely be moved by the true huntsman spirit and full carelessness as if we are wearing our colours and trampling the hedges of ground-walking people and whooping through livestock to make them snap limbs and miscarry. We would be the riotous cornering and tearing of domestic pets and the tearing of them limb from limb and a force to demonstrate good order and natural pre-eminence.

Nigel finds this most acceptable.

My apparent address at this time is a first-floor one-bedroom flat in a pebbledash and red-brick terraced house on Ivanhoe Road in Hounslow. At the front is a garden that has given up and been turned into concrete for parking but which is only weeds in cracks and no cars. It will be more than simple for me to walk out and be ready at the northernmost corner of my road in the quietquiet and under no cameras. From here I could take over driving and steer us easy west.

I cannot visit his house because we are agreed it is unfortunately burdened with oversight security and untouchable sanctity. I have never been near for reasons open to interpretation.

I advocate for seeing the dawn close to waves and being lordly solitary.

There is a glee in his tone that is diagnostic and makes me in my turn private gleeful. He is too intent on cruelty fun to be careful or object that my arrangements put him to much more work than being driven from the first. He is not even moved to correct the idea of Tom being lordly.

I know that Nigel is most likely recalling whatever details he can from one night the previous autumn when I drove him back from a poker game held inside an industrial unit at Mill Mead Road in Tottenham Hale. This journey provided my planned correct time and staging for Tom to confess a boyhood incident involving the Coppermill Stream at the edge of Walthamstow Marshes which were not far from our location. I recalled a push and slithering fall and sad choking death immanence. I added laughter rained down upon me and betrayal by supposed friends. My weak-armed scrabble to conquer the greasy bank and rise to safety was portrayed with intensity and flashback signs. I presented long-term anger about night-time chill confusion and a soaked and lonesome walking back in the long dark to a family home that was poverty and cooking fat as permanent taint and a maisonette on Turnpike Lane.

Nigel was delighted when Tom had to pull in and park for long moments to steady himself inside an obvious trauma resurgence. My hands shook in a way that convinced me. Prior to my latest revelations Nigel had been sullen pondering and withdrawn because of increased debt levels and creditors of St Petersburg origin expressing uncivilised Vasilyevsky Island threats. Now he patted my shoulder with the brisk sympathy of a prefect towards some newly arrived bedwetting prep school beast. I knew he would never forget an appetising fear in a subordinate.

His voice is already warm with malicious thinking.

I elongate the call with apparent slow pondering of fit destinations. He is anxious to rush instantaneous to see me and wheedle for any available drugs. I reference the sea again and fine possibilities of noble cliffs.

I then tack away again and steer his course on another angle.

He needs one more nudge into the carefree youth he pretends he enjoyed so I offer enthusiasm and my own dogged boyishness and let slip that we will have a *Good-day* which is his old school term for an awarded leisure day. Public schools are an inherited disease and Nigel knows his ancient and modern Stonyhurst terms because he is a pupil of the third generation. His family made its money poisoning young women in a mercury vapour lightbulb factory. By the time his great grandfather could afford the country seat and baronetcy he had the same twitch limbs as his workforce and was quicksilver raging as perfectly as any oldblood nobleman.

The family sends boys to a school full of moral principles. Principles thoroughly identified can be more thoroughly avoided.

I need his young and happy self to be predominant. It is all the stronger for being a wish fulfilment fiction.

I say to Nigel that we shall both enjoy a holiday which I call a *Blandyke* because the childhood of the chosen boy from the chosen school is full of useful code words to define his worth.

I tell Nigel that Cornwall will be as good as St Omer for us. This is a sort of kindness to aid Nigel as withdrawal need drags at him.

He easy and easier slips into a favourite version of his boyhood. We are both intent on bringing him back to name tapes freshly sewn in position and itemised and his innocence and prayers to Mary also fixed and the clatter of cricket boots running out to sunshine.

I need Nigel to have hope. Stress is an aid to manipulation but hope is better. Nigel was once unconcerned by treason and unsecured loans as blended income generation and happy with a life of indulged vices. He is now very concerned on a rising scale about involuntary falls from hotel windows in lieu of monies owed. His withdrawal paranoia is hybridising with his national security surveillance paranoia and his fear of significant Whitehall corridor glances. So we must stay calm and warm nostalgic. We will have our Good-day.

He is too far from his last fix to wonder how I would know any part of the Stonyhurst lexicon.

When he hangs up I feel tired because of the long work ahead. But this passes.

I dress Tom in soft plimsolls and a thin cotton shirt and trousers and navy pea jacket. I am not inappropriate for London and 2020 and also not inappropriate for 1947 and Arthur Ransome. Tom has never worn natural fibres before. They make him look more substantial and assured although he bumbles as sadly as ever once he has left his house. It is very reasonable for my driving gloves to be in my pocket.

My walk to the corner is made lovely by the big new silence of the city. The night tastes already different and has more of leaves in it than before. Birds wake in the streetlight and talk to each other for long passages. They will become ambitious in their placement of nests. All it takes to improve anything is an absence of people.

An ambulance siren is howling bad news over to the east and then it fades and does not come near me.

I do not have to wait on the corner long which I regret. I am listening to a blackbird who is awake in the streetlight and singing dawn. There has never been one in Ivanhoe Street that I know of.

Nigel is an interruption. He is keen for gear and possible salt cruelties and so his well-tailored headlights arrive on time. He is driving the new Bentley Flying Spur which is in burgundy with the all-black wheels option and the illuminated radiator mascot.

His standard lateness is thirty minutes. His rebuking delay is an hour and above.

The standard delay on arrivals among the wealthy is thirty minutes as if they have all agreed beforehand.

Nigel opens his door with the correct very minor noise to prove itself expensive and a spill of light that is a particular type of wealth comfort poem. These details are important to him. The little mascot shine shines like a toy out of place or an odd small bit of Christmas.

Nigel emerges untidy and walks across his own headlamp flares so they bleach him from shins to waist. The spirit of adventure has put him into egg-yellow corduroys with a checked shirt and tweed jacket. Each garment is German made and therefore looks perfectly English. His scuff-toed elastic-sided boots are Chelsea pretending to be equestrian.

He is funny in his way.

Before I take over the driving he shakes my hand which is another difference from the normal. His palm is wet. For this moment in Hounslow we could be two men engaged in gentlemanly pursuit as illustrated in a book on national customs. Identity is sixty per cent costume and more so for Nigel and his type. I am remaining Tom but also edging up increased authority and a shift in powers. I am not changing. I am revealing. Tom will simply be more of a very fine fellow than previously guessed.

But I do not rush my alteration and add in a stumble before I gain the leathery calm of the Bentley. This allows a confusion in which I can put on my gloves. They are Beretta close-fit shooting gloves in fine calfskin for good dexterity and pressure comprehension. I struggle with my canvas holdall and have trouble putting it neatly in the passenger footwell while Nigel slips in behind me and rattles at the bottle cooler. He is making his start. Guilt and chemical dependence are rendering him down into strange new substances. Even from here his skin smells like cheap new carpet mixed with fear.

I become lost in apparent fat-fingered beta struggles with his satnav and frequently consult a scrumpled paper scrap and mumble a postcode. The gloves still work with the touch screen and this is one of the reasons why they are good. My fumbling is the demonstration of Tom still being Poor Old Tom.

It also displeases Nigel which is my fun.

He tilts every conversation towards drug acquisition and I am apology anguish.

Nigel swings ice in a fresh glass of something and notices we are not moving. I feel his impatience thickening the dark. I switch to adjusting my seat and the driving mirrors with indecision and botched motor control.

The car interior is dark red leather and piano black veneers and like sitting in a warm mouth full of rotten teeth. I would have preferred burr walnut. That would have softened the pseudo-aircraft instrumentation and let me assume the dignity of a person setting out on water in a proper craft.

I finally pull away smooth with all of the clever cylinders purr working. Driving is a demeaned skill I am allowed to possess.

Nigel sighs and sets Arab Strap singing through the excellent sound system about strangeness and loud eyes. The bass line is unnatural large and deep because this is how Nigel wants it. He needs the night speed window blurs and colour rush alienations and the lightning music touches under his skin and his troubled thought collapsing into rhythm and destination and inexorability.

I always feel that way.

Our best route slips lateral sly away from surveillance and motorway exposures. This speaks of a reasonable secrecy and is nothing alarming. I thread through Feltham and past all the pubs in mourning for their loss of trade and the businesses closed for good and the businesses soon to be closing. The plague is like snow and covers all other disasters in one smooth curse.

Still this might be only a city asleep in normal times. Nothing is on fire. There are no riots yet.

I hear Nigel is clawing at the bar again. He never does know how to pace himself.

The car feels empathetic powerful. It moves unopposed on empty A roads towards Windsor and I have to be careful to keep my speed under the limit. It would not do to trigger camera traps. Nonetheless I am a bullet thing going smooth between golfclubland and parkland and countryclubland and they will never see or know me.

The traffic lights change and cycle to regulate the flow of nothing.

Driving is the key policebody spy tool. Have a van and groups will need you. Have van troubles and you can justify hours away. Have access to multiple vehicles and you will be essential. Be the driver and you know the schedule. Know the schedule and then you can change the schedule and then you can make the schedule. If you can make the schedule then you can make the strategies and then you can make the actions.

I am able to drive left hand and right hand and automatic and gear shift and army surplus and minibus and truck. I have lost my policebody tricks and tells behind the wheel. Now I am just a man who can drive anything.

The suburbs wither behind us and becomes sparse while I thread our route through obscurities. I pretend this is because of policebody checks on illegal movement. There is often undersea thick nothing darkness on either side of my and only my burrow of light up ahead with occasional glimmers from traffic signs. The air conditioning draws in the rise of after-dark life from meadows and the gorse scent remains of yesterday.

Nigel dozing with his jaw slack.

I have space to myself and consider the riotous spring and how it is mockery of people dying in great numbers and leaving grief behind while the bluebells rage so thick and blue. But nothing means us any harm. This is just spring.

Taking a curve I glimpse the eye shine of muntjac. Four of them are small hoof trotting on the far side of the road. They lift their white tails as alarm indications and canter away. I let them. I do not even have to slow because they avoid me. They know what I am.

When I am two hours and more along the journey I pull into a kind of lay-by near the A303 with wide space of country spread around. I stop the engine and the music and this makes the silence slap in. Nigel wakes.

While he is still dry mouth blurry I get out of the car and remove my gloves and walk with my holdall into the headlights. I lift up the bag by its handles and am clever boy pride about it and raising a trophy.

Then I unzip the canvass and dive one arm inside and lucky dip out a white cloth. I flourish it for Nigel before I lay it across the bonnet and make sure not to cover that blue and white shining B because it should see all the fun. I dip again and then stand with my fist round a jar of sun-dried tomatoes and olives in oil. I set it on the cloth.

This gets Nigel awake and fretting about his paintwork. I am arms wide placation and carefulness while I lay out soft parcels of porter-cured ham and Iberico ham and a tiny young Camembert. He reaches me in time to accept a linen napkin and a bone-handled knife in the dim. While I keep laying out dainties he twists the lid off the pickle jar and rams his fingers in.

Our smoked salmon once swam wild off the Orkney Isles.

Nigel likes recitations of provenance which makes him the same as all unrooted and weak pretending men.

I tell him that I am his Minister and that now we are not late but early and that boys who are up at the rattle deserve their bread-and-beer whenever they wish.

There is sourdough bread in tiny rolls here and beer for him which is Marston's Pedigree and mild and round in the mouth so as not to interfere with feasting. This is a guess because I do not drink it.

A Good-day and bread-and-beer.

We sit on the grass and it is fresh growing and has a liveliness I can feel pushing when I press against it and which is a way that life answers life. There is no light from any window and no sign that the land is not ours entirely for all the miles to the sea and this is being a gentleman and at peace.

Nigel ranges away to piss for a while. He comes back windingly and unsteady. I am sure to unzip foolish and early before I shuffle plaintive away and suggest in fragmented sentences that I never can piss when I am close by other men.

He waits triumphant for my return and hums a little of 'Es Zittern die Morschen Knochen'. He taught himself the melody so he could be clever offensive in quiet groups while also growing buoyant at the gaiety of flourishes and implications of territorial ambition and SS dominance fantasies.

He hasn't the balls to mock accidentally hum something more widely known as belonging to the shitfreak deathshead supermen.

He is prone to joking mentions of hanging by piano wire and I smell one is on the way. I begin quick and intervening thanks for his letting me join him in our adventure.

Nigel no longer remembers that our adventure was my idea.

A jovial mood then prevails and I lie back on the turf non-dominant with one arm behind my head and full exposure of neck and torso. Beyond me there are night things doing animal activities along paths we cannot see. I would rather be with them.

Nigel laughs and pours a little beer on my shirt and this is acceptable and not a problem and I open my mouth wide so that next time he can pour it in there. He does so and is surprising gentle with the amount although inaccurate with the placing. I turn to the side and spit it out while pretending to struggle beetlelike.

A fox screams because this is the season for it.

Nigel makes a pantomime of sudden remembering and patting at his jacket until he locates a little stitched black leather folder. He holds it out as if it is treasure and then flips it open the way he must have in front of a mirror repeated. It is a Met Police warrant card.

He is giving me a Met Police warrant card with a not good photograph but definitely my photograph.

A Met Police warrant card.

He wants me to have it.

I sit up and present myself as dog alert for my treat and do not laugh and laugh and laugh.

A Met Police warrant card.

He tells me that I am now under his blessing and may claim the powers and rights of a Special Protection Officer.

The breaking of laws intoxicates him afresh.

I soft my hands together prayerwise with the warrant card between my palms. As if I would want to touch the filth of such a thing when I am risen far above.

He describes thinking the card might aid our journey if we happened to be road halted by genuine policebodies.

It would naturally be a large misstep to ever use it.

A forged warrant card.

Or perhaps a more real than not warrant card from a Met policebody with extracurricular needs.

I wonder what Nigel paid for it.

And I look at the warrant card picture that is my picture and this is a problem because where did he get it.

A Met Police warrant card.

I begin eating the scones to overcome the beer and locker-room taste in my mouth. There is blackcurrant jam and clotted cream in little jars and that will do and I infect the jam with cream and vice versa and eat it all anyway.

The photograph was familiar.

I move on to the Montgomery Cheddar with the fruit pickle. I am not hungry. I am subduing the flavour of beer and the policebody Blue.

Nigel is plainly also not quite hungry but eating to fill other needs left unrequited.

I remember I made a set dressing photograph of Tom with regulation haircut and tight focus to show just enough of a khaki shirt and NATO pattern pullover. My failed military history has been very rarely mentioned but was there anyway in an ugly frame for Nigel to note and approve on the one visit he made to my fake home of the time. He paced about hating my flat in baroque locutions while also inspecting its living room for information and also anticipating coke. I had left him alone for a long enough while to imply that my drugs were hidden with uttermost secrecy and hard to reach and not simply waiting in the second from top kitchen drawer. Nigel must have taken a shot of the picture with his phone. That would explain the blurred and grained iteration of my face in the ID.

I considered it amusing that I had originally used an old policebody photo from my Metropolitan ID as the basis for the fake. Sometimes things are funny and then get funnier still.

I stow the warrant away as if it is precious amazing.

We will not need it.

There were no roadblocks on our way here because public health is of no great concern. Council house parties will be fined and black sunbathers will be chivvied. We and our kind may roam.

I focus Tom on having awareness that the food is very good and that it is in no way strange he eats fastidious with knife and fork and hands still inside gloves.

I ensured a high-quality menu. Nigel is a picky eater. Our contentment builds in flurries and then blows away and then repeats the cycle.

I do not think of insects in the grass and their seething bodies.

It is not dawn but object definition is dialling in by degrees. The moon is no more than a rind and gives no help.

I tell Nigel we must now hurryhurry because of the sun being relentless in its motion and our plan for triumph as we see it rise. He watches me butler away the remaining food and shake out our crumbs and put everything tidy in my holdall. Someone has always cleaned up after Nigel. I make noises of regret over having no further surprises held back for when we eat breakfast. Nigel is magnanimous and begins to tell a story about a prostitute and other manly circumstances. He is angling for revelations from my other lives. I steer him back round to his seat with soft power under his elbow and nodding and chuckles for his mentions of anatomy and fluids. The story is very long because of all his need to dwell on flesh details and because he loses his way in many of the sentences before he can end them.

There are sex conquests that I prefer him not to discuss. He knows I do not share some of his tastes but there are also the red yawning times when he needs to explore and describe them in spite of me and to enjoy narratives that he knows I would rather not hear.

There are photographs other than mine in his phone.

I never want to see them and Nigel mostly always does. He pretends that thrill and exposure risk keeps them in his jacket pocket but it is only simple need and just another addiction.

And the children in the pictures are only Thai or Mexican or from areas of the UK that are equivalent.

It is odd to consider how much effort he and his like have put into making the UK a Third World country. Nigel never does short British stocks or British currency with any enthusiasm. He does love money but his aim has been the creation of mass vulnerability.

Only men such as Nigel call anywhere *Third World* now. The modern term is *developing nation*.

Britain is not developing so perhaps *Third World* will do.

Considering economics is a way to preserve my equanimity while Nigel looks at what he looks at.

I return to the driving seat. Away from the dark and green air the car seems small and smells aggressively new when I twitch the heat up high. I feel that I am chilled.

We are apparent brothers who have broken bread and here we are granted heat and light and horsepower automatic to all four wheels with electronic suspension. I try to project the ways in which we are glory and buccaneering and I pull out to take us further west.

I skirt Wincanton and am of coursely passing other failing businesses that happen to be farms and fields and crops. I please myself with imagining meadows and woods that will spring up when farmers stop trying and activities subside. There will be even more birds. There will be corncrakes walking low and buzzing like electricity inside tall nettle clumps. Every year more will arrive from the Congo Forest.

Nigel wants no more music but only to hear himself and the masculine rhythm of his breathing.

He viewed Parliament as a captive audience even as Parliament viewed him as low-IQ white noise.

I am foot-down speed and my mind is in another country with wolves and bears returned. England would become suitable for safaris. The native folk would offer tourists craft objects and traditional songs and dances and vernacular foodstuffs they cannot afford to eat themselves.

I want Nigel to be shut up quietquietquiet. I am maximum distraction to avoid hearing his sex obsession recitation. I cannot take response action.

I am a person who does not tolerate frustrated violence. I have done nothing to amend this. I am wolves and bears returned to England and ravens who lead them on to prey. I am fingers hard on the wheel and sweating in my gloves.

There is an oblong of far light alone in the deep blue beyond the car and this means a window and a house attached and I pretend that I can live there which is what I always did when I was a boy. I would think of feeding badgers at the foot of a garden and mending injured foxes at my fireside.

I will never know why the Policemind did not send me to infiltrate environmental groups. I would have liked that. I would have stayed and gone native and been perhaps changed in positive directions. Or perhaps I would have added what I always bring and made the cause flourish through fear imposition.

No policebody ever comprehended that inside me is all animals and claws and wings in motion.

While I pass north of Honiton the dawn is very started and the car is moving through grey and silver particles of light. There will already be small singing in the woods. I would like to stop and hear it. I have Nigel instead and his terrible narratives and laughing about vaginoperineal lacerations.

He is exhibiting high-level diagnostic behaviours that I do not need because I know him and his dark triad clichés already. Anyone could know him at a glance.

I am here because I know him. I have made him be here because I know him.

The road signs start speaking of Exeter and I am glad.

And Nigel is mumbling that he is pleased by blood.

Only an imbecile monster is pleased by blood.

The best monsters avoid it.

I am bringing us south of the airport when Nigel rises to minimal situational awareness and asks our destination. I tell him fatherly this is still his surprise. I also say that we have specific vehicle requirements for which I have provided. He is the type to be mostly incurious about detail because almost all arrangements have been made always by others and constant to his benefit.

I wind the Bentley through St Loyes residential streets and he becomes quiet because this is a difference in speed and surroundings that even he can notice. We both feel it change our mood.

Saint Loyes is not the patron of anything that matters to me.

Our designated Land Rover is waiting and dusty unharmful in a small modern development of brick savagery and allocated parking in small courtyards that suggest unneighbourly distrust. I set the Bentley outside a pair of box houses intended to seem Georgian. They have no front gardens but only gravel plots somewhat bigger than a grave.

Now it is time for important tomfoolery and energetic cheer. I exit immediate and rush to piss against the corner of one house. Nigel slurs out of the car and walks to my side. He is dick out boyish chuckles and nudges. I cut off my flow and move a little. He presses me further sideways and is by now pissing hard in some variety of high arcing competition.

I make small alarm discomfort noises while giving more ground until we are both pissing into the doorway of one house. This is of coursely pleasing to Nigel but also not enough. He always escalates. I side eye watch as he flaps open the letterbox and pisses in through it.

My apparent distress at this makes me unsteady. I dismay whimper and move badly in the low light so that I knock him both palms flat against the door and his cock is most likely grazed a little by the metal of the letterbox. He inhales sharp between his teeth.

As retaliation he rabbit punches the side of my head. I tolerate this. It is an additional indication of his weakness and inaccuracy. He is a sad and small rabbit.

I submissive smile and beckon him through an archway that leads to the parking places. This is where we find the 1984 Land Rover Defender with bench seats in the back that would be perfect for taking comrades and brethren to an action. It has nostalgia for me of a type that is not about spaniels and gun cases and hip flask comforts.

Nigel is sudden whining and unwilling to abandon the Bentley. I think this is because he has been able to masturbate in private comfort while I have driven him and this will be less possible now.

He tries to make master and commander yaps at me but only sounds blurred. I am keeping myself too busy to hear him by taking our Good-day supplies from the Flying Spur and putting them safe aboard our next chariot.

I do call the Land Rover a chariot. This amuses me.

Then I pantomime a moment of forgetting which pocket has my keys for the Defender.

He slaps at me and lands with only fingertips on my left shoulder.

I whine react and whisper details that emphasise the way that soon we will be surveying our domain and gorging on dainties and out in holiday mood when laws and decency are against us but we are victorious all the same. Men of a better type must always be proving it with freedom and power demonstrations. This catches him a little and we drive on.

It is important to sweep a target gentle and definite along the required path with enough speed and justification to ease all caution.

I lock up the Bentley and hand its keys to Nigel for his pocket although he will not need them again. While we are closeclose I say there are also more and better treats to come in a tone that lets him turn needy for chemical love sensations and the end of loneliness.

A blackbird is calling to itself about the morning and is saying purrs of laughter and phrases I do not know but also *we are here we are here.* Far down the street there is one sleepless window making a blue TV shine.

The present idea of England is high insomnia incidence. I can taste night worry being endemic habitual and this is the scent and flavour of all failed states. I know this because they are my regular workplaces. They are my preference because sins there remain undisturbed by investigation unless they are overly grotesque. The present idea of England is already much in fashion as a convenience killing field. I smile because I am not often fashionable. But I can always make exceptions. I am my own master.

When I open its door the Land Rover gives me a stale dog and diesel and earth smell. This and its general conformation perks Nigel and fills him with predictable country pursuit memories. This makes him automatic imperious and he snatches the keys before shoving in past me to take the driving seat. I hover like a disappointed child until he beckons and orders me to sit up front at his side as if we are the same species and heading out on a jolly.

This is as I wish. He is as I wish.

My surprise and lovely gift for him is in my pocket and is a gram of coke. His junkie anticipation rush cancels out the way that he wants to be angry because I have not supplied this earlier.

He laughs about how a Christmas has come for only him and the way he is a lucky boy.

I say a gram is all that I could get due to difficulties and he does not listen because he is building fat lines for himself on the shallow dashboard. These are awkward to snort but he manages because naturally he does.

I do not ask him to fasten his seatbelt. He would rather be free and at risk and why would I prevent that.

We jolt off and the contrast in suspension between the Landy and Spur is very stark.

Because he is incapable Nigel mild scrapes the vehicle in getting it though the archway which causes a transfer of brick residue and paint. He is both drunk and on his upward cocaine slope. His two opposite directions are meeting in his brain and becoming one that is upupup.

He steers erratic and cannot locate a reliable or anyway appropriate speed. I talk him alongside routes to conceal his dysfunction and our passing.

As soon as we are approximate in Cornwall I sing out hard with *a good sword and a trusty hand* because it has the mood I need. He knows the words and is braced by the classroom ghosts being taught this as a credible type of folk song. He sounds close to full chemical and his energy is sharp edges and a bitterness in the air.

I watch his forearms show a confidence surge while he becomes a greater danger to himself. I would replace him but it is important that he drives us to our end now.

We manage every verse with some repetitions. We are Western Men raising our voices to sing of death and this is amusing.

I whistle the tune for a long while after we run out of words and he tooth grinds and swallows beside me and rubs his face.

I ignore him and give clear directions in a mock sergeant voice to compliment his sense of officer dash and capacities.

After half an hour approximate Nigel pulls over and takes another pair of lines that are wasteful sloppy. The texture of the dash is ingrained with white powder evidence. I suspect that he already plans to lick it clean.

His heart is apparently audible or else I can feel it knock through the metal of the bodywork. It makes me happy and also I enjoy various place names as they run past us like other possibilities I will not engage. Some of them are Broadwoodwidger and Tregadillett and Hawks Tor and Four Winds and Tregoss and Trevarren. By Three Burrows we are not far from the place.

I am not far.

I am remembering my route for the written record.

Also for my own satisfaction.

Inside the Land Rover I can smell the salt before it arrives in reality and I like that I have this illusion always available in key moments. It seems like a confirmation of my choices.

We pass a palmful of asleep farm buildings. The road shrinks to a track and becomes shoves and bumps beneath us and then just grass. We dribble to a halt proximate to the South West Coast Path which is a picturesque and carefree thing of happy nods and remarks to strangers when it is in daylight. It is a different thing at night and in this earliest part of dawn and lies deserted for me as I wish.

The after engine silence is full of metal expansions and contractions and far waters moving and the breeze that is irregular pawing at the vehicle.

Light is swelling before us with the sun not far from showing. Nigel is unaware that we are facing almost due west here. There will be none of the promised and glad surveying of a sky red and gold with flourishes of cloud and for only us. We have turned our backs on this sunrise.

To reach the bay we will be dropping down in darkness where we belong.

It is very natural to suggest a descent to the beach. Nigel is all verve and acceleration and the need to move.

I say that after our walk we can eat our breakfast. We will have a hearty appetite and be refreshed. There will be enough coke left for another treat. This makes him hesitate because he wants it all nownow but I am egging him on with sea water thoughts.

I say that we are close up above Nanjizal Bay which is a place famous for a cleft stone view and general natural beauty. I do not mention swimming because Nigel must think of that himself.

We walk out between fields that are full of life murmurs and night insects and the animals that eat them.

Nigel begins to talk speedy about swimming races and his proven athleticism. We have reached the time for this.

When the last fence is past I move in behind him and we cross a gentle but increasing slope and the sea breathes up like an animal that is vast and turning in its sleep. The ground has become uncivilised.

I let Nigel keep on finding the path which is obvious pale and tipping into a sharper descent. A heavy and heavier shade moves over us as we sink behind the cliff. Nigel has movement impulses that are faster than his feet on the uneven surface. He totters occasional like an elderly thing and his smooth leather soles are no help to him. This is good.

I walk through the yesterday traces of milk and sweet from the early gorse flowers that are mostly asleep. If I were alone I would cup blossoms between my hands and breathe on them until their perfume wakes. This is impossible without thorns pricking my fingers but I do not mind thorns because they are true to their purpose.

We are stepping in among young heather and tussocks on a path worn to sand and sunk by the wearing and I am very silent and very tight now behind Nigel.

I point out a lonely lifebelt that is set distant but in sight and a useful cue. Nigel will want revenge for the damage reality is

321

inflicting on his poise. He has stopped whooping when he slips and stumbles. The lifebelt will make his mind up without my doing anything.

He tells me we should swim.

I do not laugh outside myself and I tell him that I really am almost unable to swim.

He tells me that I should have learned.

I admit that I will be frightened if I am in water. I say that I almost drowned once as if I have forgotten confessing as much on our earlier occasions.

Nigel has not forgotten.

He calls me a number of pathetic creatures.

I return to silent and we keep walking and his limbs have cocaine timing and clatter about when he trips again.

We run out of path when the cliff sheers straight down with waterfalls singing in the dim to one side of us. There are wooden stairs here and Nigel skip staggers down them to the beach. His feet are odd loud as if they know about scaffolds.

It is occasional hard to know nothing about scaffolds.

I pad quiet in my plimsolls and see the pale gleam of his neck.

And here is louder sea noise being merry in the curve of the bay. The salt air lifts me and lets me be not a land thing any more.

We are under a great height shadow now and it is much colder than on the slope and almost like being already immersed. By my watch the sun is just rising and warming Mousehole and Newlyn and Raginnis. Here the bay is holding itself still secret in night.

The beach is relative uninviting at the first with large stones to navigate and scramble after winter has scoured out the sand nearest the cliff.

I am sure foot and easy progress and silent happiness and my dark wings are wide gliding for the pleasure of it. I am licking my lips and purified.

Nigel falls heavy against a rock and swears. He revenge insists that I swim.

I present as fearful of his anger and promisepromise I will try at least to wade and be in the shallows.

The breeze punches us from all the directions it wants and will be harder and stronger the further we go out.

Nigel tells me I will fucking swim.

I swear glum docile that I will try.

He is asking me to die because he will find it entertaining. I am not mistaken in this. He is making me righteous.

I was already righteous.

Up ahead is a band of white sand shining and laid out right before the water. Nigel is immediate happy when he reaches it. He says praise things about my choice of location but plays with the bully undertone he likes.

For a while he runs back and forth on the soft and smooth and sand. He goes from cliff edge to cliff edge between the jaws of the bay and does not set foot in the water and this is his own sea nervousness. It shows a good instinct on his part. Sometimes in altered states we notice the true risks and blades that hide from us otherwise.

I send myself into a wailing stumble as distraction. I begin to limp.

If we paused and waited the bay would be a kind and afternoon sun place with swimming in the jewel depths of safe pools but we are here now and not for that.

Nigel wants to meet the full truth of the sea which is what no one should ask for.

He walks to the southmost side of the bay and climbs somewhat on to the rocks. The tide is incoming but with hours before its top. I do not mention this because I should not be aware of it. He stands and is instantaneous the schoolboy of quality who is easy with undressing and knows the proper order of items to be removed. He is sudden able to fold and stack and leave all tidy.

When he is finished and naked he stands as if he is still the tight stomach thin leg creature he was decades ago and not this white sag and testament to poor usage.

I think of all the other eyes that have seen his nakedness. I dwell on this for moments. He is asking me what I am waiting for and has changing room arrogance authority.

Tom is programmed to flinch at certain tones without my having to make an effort and so he does. I let him recoil and trip stagger on the sand from trying to walk while taking off one shoe. I present as having a somehow damaged ankle.

Nigel laughs because I intend that he should.

I scurry back to the rocks further from the sea and huddle for shame while Nigel closes on me and hectors. I am not in any way the fine old pal now. I am the limp dick underclass weak body.

He yells while I strip clumsy for him and pile my clothes disorderly on a tall blocky boulder. This is my danger point because I am leanbody fit and mesoectomorph muscle. Nigel should not see me as I am because this would provoke dissonance. I therefore hunch crouch more profoundly in plain embarrassment and also cold. My hands are in a genital shield posture as if I have nothing worth showing.

Nigel laughs more because he is supposed to and shows me his weak back as he brays and run runs to the water and keeps on with display splashes and wide arms and yells that sound like his bad blood chemistry and pretending courage.

A spring sea is the harshest because it remembers winter.

I watch Nigel stall at the cold water pain and then recommit although his progress out is slower. He turns and calls to me when he is thigh deep and will not proceed until I am ankles and then shins and then also thighs submerged and close beside him in the push swirl and backwards drag of live water. Without the coke I believe he would only dip himself now and swim a few strokes before turning back. But he is still dangerous fast in his brain and I am pleasepleaseplease can I get out now begging so he has to keep on.

He takes my arm and walks us deeper. I pant squeal at the point where the chill rushes full up over my genitals and belly and the water takes our feet and Nigel begins to flail into a kind of crawl stroke in response.

And this is when I can reclaim and be myself.

I swim up to be level with him very fast easy although the waves are complex churning and hard to read. Nigel is already not happy with the sea and the muscle it puts into its way of playing. A bully knows a bigger bully.

This bay is not recommended for safe swimming because of contraindications.

Next I begin to present as panic struggling. I grab for him with a momentum that drives him further out as he tries to avoid me.

I am yelling now occasional and also ducking beneathbeneath and he is slapping at the swell up ahead of me in a wallow progress.

Nigel is tiring. This is fine.

I shout once more with arms upraised and create loud struggle impact splashes audible over the many voices of the sea. I then repeat my quick slip below the surface but do not emerge.

Nigel always was a person who would not save a drowning man.

I swim quick and under in the blue dark.

I have a long breath and I hold it.

Nigel inhales water when I rise and grab him and cling sudden against his back with also my one knee hitting his balls so that he chokes again and breathes in additional water while I sink him.

He fights. This is natural. He is a never challenged man and therefore fundamental weak but his body has defence instincts that are superior to his thinking.

I disengage from him with an elbow to his temple and take in another good breath while he wheezes to the surface. This is when I grip his arms full back and trap his legs and down he must go again.

There is a moment in the process of murder when a body asks for comfort and for the usual right and ability to live and keep on living because this has been all that it has known and it is bewildered. Something in it longs for a mother and salvation from bad harm.

All of his limbs are longing and confusions. He is twitches and the trace of warmth that is his urine leaving him. He is almost done.

325

I release him and breathe hungry while I smooth move to his right side so that I can knuckle press his vagus nerve and feel his light go out.

Then it is easy to swim out with him and float him face down until the sea consents to take him.

The waters beyond the bay are spiteful and dislike intrusion. I am heavy exhausted as I turn landward and fight home.

I possibly consider also drowning because there are times when it can seem easier than not.

But then I prefer to keep on and the sea approves and the violence of it is very beautiful to be inside and fatherlike with terrible love.

Once I am out on the sand I stagger fall and lie a while at rest. I feel I am fortunate rescued from a shipwreck. I am very provably alive and clean.

I roll on to my back and do not stand until I am shivering and the increeping tide is licking at my feet. The sky is full blue overhead and this is my day and I am larger in it.

I take Nigel's clothes and put them among rocks far above the high tide line. I check his phone and erase and remove my photograph. I leave my number in his contacts file because it belongs to a name that is not mine and will not work beyond today. He uses habitual a messaging app that vanishes all he sends and receives at will. I burn our last chain of call and response. I leave in place his pleasure pictures and various bad evidences because he deserves shame and shame comes to such as him only after death.

Nigel was born to become an extremely explicable suicide caused by debt and appetites and gross criminality.

Up under the cliff I choose one of the waterfalls to slapdash rinse my skin and hair. I drink from it also because the place seems generous welcoming since I have given it a death. It is good to be natural naked and to stand the way that I stand with my own gait and postures.

Then I go back to the granite block where I left Tom's clothes and dress my own self in them and walk up the slope. The clothes are very comfortable and suit me far better than him.

Where the sun shines the gorse is thick in the breeze and I pause by many of the bushes and inhaleinhaleinhale.

It is only nine or so in the morning and I will go and eat some of the stupid expense food from the holdall while I sit in the lea of the Defender. I will pour out the last of the beer as sacrifice libation for the earth because I do not drink.

I will then put the empty bottles and other remnants in the holdall and leave the vehicle unlocked with its cocaine traces and only fingerprints from Nigel who was so unobservant about my endless wearing of gloves.

I am glad I saved the leather from salty water which is bad for them. They are dry and not a hinderance during any activity.

The Land Rover Defender will be traced back to the one pretend Georgian house with piss in its hallway and DNA traces on the letterbox. Palm prints are later found on the door itself and also a recent impact in brickwork close at hand. Not so far away also is a car belonging definitive to wicked and implicated Nigel with the new revealed unpleasant and complex life.

Inside the house is the owner of the Land Rover who is in both a state of advanced decomposition and a condition rich in bestial torture signs.

There will be indications of hurried attempts at clearing evidence but also one glass with a Nigel thumbprint and three finger dabs that have been somehow missed.

Pornography appealing to vile predilections will be obvious shocking to even the hardened Blue eye.

The clothes left by Nigel will be located and his storm-tossed despicable body. His phone will be a series of headline shocks and suppressed additional horrors that will leak online.

Nobody who knew Nigel will ever have been his friend. His former social circle will declare itself violated and his transgressions heinous. The Met will quietly rally round to dispense forgivenesses.

Nigel was a terrible man.

The owner of the Land Rover was a likewise terrible man.

They met fit ends.

I do not enjoy cruelty. I do what is necessary to create my desired results.

And I take my pleasures in normal ways.

I enjoyed Nanjizal Bay after my swim and slept once I had finished my picnic.

Then I walked from the Defender along the Coast Path until I reached Sennen Cove. That is where I had rented a garage that held a nondescript Vauxhall Corsa.

The journey took something over an hour because I dawdled and sat sometimes and was delighted with the sun and with looking at the blue above and blue below and where they meet.

I waited for ravens and none came to salute me but I could not resent this. I know they have much business of their own.

In the garage I tilted back the car seat and slept for a little while more before I set out and drove gradual back east.

I paused in woods along the way and there were a few hours when I climbed a tree and was joyful boylike. I fell asleep again because I was after all very tired as I always am when a job is over.

Sue died

Dancing Sue.

Lovely Sue.

Sue who saved Corinne from terrible things at home.

Sue who saved Tommy the first year I arrived, saved Idil the year after that, then Darius and Bryaton, saved all the rest of the little souls with no defence in the howling world – the ones who would have been destroyed and wiped away. Instead their photos are up on her wall – leaves on her big, proud oak-tree mural with long, long branches. Her office is still full of them, smiling into the lens and holding certificates, wearing graduation gowns, smart uniforms, waving with babies, waving back towards her and the good she'd done.

Sue who saved me and kept on saving me.

Sue who saved Oakwood and kept on saving it.

Save one life, you save the world.

That's literal, not metaphorical. You never know how many other people you will save by saving that one. You'll never know how many they'll save in their turn.

In the same way, you never know who you'll destroy by ruining just one person, by watching them fall but not reaching out your hand.

Sue knew that.

Sue acted on that.

But she got so tired with the saving.

She did more than all of us, was more at risk than all of us. The meal supervision and the Welfare Checks – she was out every day in a world full of risks.

And Oakwood, the place that tries always to be safe – it's full of risks, too. We do our best with hand-washing protocols and keeping-your-distance protocols, but the tinies don't remember them. We've made air-filtration units, we open windows – but every breath may be against us.

And the parents unwilling to believe anything is wrong, they're against us – the parents very ready to believe in mythical problems, in a country encouraged to do the same. We're all meant to take no care of ourselves, to take no care of others.

It's all so stupid, stupid, stupid.

And what did Sue die of? Preventable stupidity, cruelty, superstition.

Everything she hated most climbed into her lungs and took her – a little virus like a curse.

After the diagnosis, her oxygen level crashed. They moved her into hospital, but she wasn't in bad shape.

We all sat in Big Room together and held hands, watched her onscreen together. Everyone comforted everyone else.

She could laugh and chat. The words seemed hungry, searching for strength, but they were still her words.

We were sure she'd be fine.

We were very cheerful and this would be an opportunity to learn so many things and to have such a welcome-home party.

Then for a few days things seemed serious, but she rallied. This time only the staff room waved to her on screen, there in her hospital bed but jolly and sure that she would be coming back.

Or was she pretending? Was there a new dull metal light at the back of her eyes. I can't recall.

I know I didn't say enough to her. I didn't say the right things – the words that would have been effective spells.

And, meanwhile, Oakwood made her cards. They were the finest and most jubilant and most excellent cards.

There was time for her to see them, too.

I heard myself tell Year Five about how pleased Mrs Delara had been by every single one of them. When she felt better she was going to answer them.

Francis found me swearing in the kitchen.

All the words.

All the ones I don't say.

None of them was right.

I didn't mean *fuck them*. I meant something much worse than that.

To everyone who keeps assuming that only disposable people will die, to everyone who believes there are disposable people, I wish all the worst things there are. To everyone who saves no one, who saves nothing, everyone who looks at us and sees useless meat, noisy meat, stupid meat, I wish you to know what it is to be meat. To everyone who thinks we'll rot later and might as well rot now, everyone who is so suddenly rich while we are so suddenly dying, I wish every curse there is, every bad magic, because all I have is words. And to everyone who is killing us, letting us die in so many, many wildly cascading ways, everyone who smirks through announcing *do this and I'll do the opposite*, I wish you death. I wish you terror, loss, mourning, each possible harm, and I wish you death.

I didn't mean *fuck them*.

Fuck shit dick cunt fuck fuck fuck.

I didn't mean that either – it didn't mean anything. Those are only human words for human things.

I didn't mean *fuck them*.

In that moment when I got the news I meant *kill them*.

And I meant it with all of my heart, with all of my soul and my conscience. I wanted them to die, only them and no more of us.

It is wrong to think that.

Sue was the opposite of that.

Being a teacher is the opposite of that.

Being human is the opposite of that.

And I wanted to just be a teacher and be human and keep the people dear to me with me for a reasonable time, for a reasonable lifetime. But those with the power to care for us – the power we lend them – have stolen my good things and made me die in this small, secret, squalid corner of myself that used to be at peace.

They are making us die in all the ways.

So I can no longer pretend, when I write about Buster, that we are so utterly different.

And so *fuck them and fuck him.* And you know what I mean.

And we'll go back to the PTSD present tense and the misted river and the river that might be beautiful if Buster wasn't here.

I might as well keep on writing about him – Buster who volunteered to be less than human and who prospered as of course he would. Not being human is all the rage.

Along the damp quayside I go and down the ladder and on to his wreck of a boat. I pause when I touch the deck, but not for long. I won't stop now, won't be stopped.

It's ridiculous in retrospect – this rushing towards an unknown, being full of optimistic fury and hopes of final triumph. I don't know what kind of hero I'm imagining I can be. I may be the stupid woman in weak shoes at the start of the book, or the TV episode, the movie – improperly prepared and not the hero, only yet another victim who'll lend energy to the story, make the anti-hero even more charmingly, shockingly, pleasantly dark.

I am beyond sick of anti-heroes. They are not entertaining, sympathetic, a spice of Darwinian thrill. They're a chance to stare into a sewer, a chance to make more of us happy with the onward march of monsters, of Stiltskins, of Buster. With every mass media nudge, down and down we go.

And meanwhile, my thoughts seem to be hurting me in hot, bad rushes. They bang about. I feel spiked like an unguarded drink left on a bar top.

My body doesn't want to go forward, but I do.

And I win.

I walk onwards and down the uneven, filthy steps of a companionway that leads to what looks like a wheelhouse. It has a blackened and weathered goblin door.

I pull at its handle, expecting a lock to halt me, but the doorway yawns open so smoothly that I almost stumble.

Fooled me again.

Inside, the little room is immaculate – and he isn't here.

The air is sticky with him and I want to retch, but he isn't here.

Everything I can see is in desperate, savage good order. I lose a period of time in trying to process the way he has kept the exterior of the boat apparently ruined, but hidden a flawless and functional and aching white space inside her.

So it's the opposite of Buster.

I'm looking at layers of paint, laid over paint, laid over paint – every surface of rough wood layered into a smoothness – like snow over a wicked field. Ropes and charts and signal flags and other things I don't recognise are stowed, neat in compartments, on brass hooks, on dustless shelves. A number of little cupboard doors are snugly closed and may well be hiding more perfect organisation, although I don't check.

This is perhaps some part of the real Buster: obsessive-compulsive Buster, ready-for-inspection Buster, no-real-personal-detail-and-therefore-lots-of-room-for-storage Buster, lies-filed-away-according-to-name-and-date Buster. He is a creature of functions and uses – this is nothing but function and use.

I think I am right about that.

The wheel is immaculately varnished and surrounded by modern dials and screens and levers, each carefully inlaid into some kind of glowing hardwood. It's beautiful. And it would cost money. This is the make-do improvisation we imagined. I imagined. I don't yet know that he's probably some kind of millionaire, but I'm still unsurprised. He always was a man with sudden rolls of cash for blurring reasons.

I can't hear him moving, down on the level below. That's maybe why I'm able to sink down the next steps, further into this place where he's chosen to be, built around himself. As I descend, a heat rises to meet me, as if his breath is everywhere and needy.

He isn't here.

Inside the stripped-out body of the barge there is more deafening whiteness, painted thick over the metal walls and ceiling, the rivets, the wide planks underfoot. The space gives a long perspective from a kind of study here by the steps – an empty desk at least – and then on to a little kitchen with brass fittings and lots of mahogany. Money again. There's a Belfast sink. Beyond there's a lounge with a broad Persian rug, cushions made from ruined kilims, a brown leather sofa and armchair, a dark blue stove with a merry silver funnel.

The narrow boat we planned together was going to have a Belfast sink, a long view, cupboards with handy catches to keep them closed, a cheerful rug.

I always imagined needlepoint cushions – that I would sew them slowly to mark significant dates and sayings, family names, a portrait of the dog we'd choose.

He stole this dream, too.

Filthy, filthy, filthy thief.

His version of my hopes is nearly homely, the touches of colour are almost kind – happy tea towels, one very red vase, a yellow oilskin on a peg, paperback spines faded to pastels – but it all mainly wants to be a hospital, a place where blood can flow and be easily cleaned away later.

I can see faint marks where he's passed, footprints across the serenity of the floor. Next to the stairs is an orderly shoe rack and the pair of felt slippers he probably changes into when he isn't being rushed. I have made him rush.

Nowhere are there pictures, ornaments, the clues a person leaves.

It all smells like his spy police liar skin, his sweat. Also his fear.

The mostly red rug in the living area might mean something to him, or might be left over from an identity, might be set dressing. The wood-burning stove has its implements set ready, log basket poised and full. The old leather of the sofa and single armchair hint they might have been with him elsewhere. Or they might be lying.

So some of my instincts have, at least, improved. Although I am not afraid enough, I'm not pretending this will turn out well.

The big tartan laundry bag he was carrying has been dumped on to the floor – I suspect very carefully dumped. His red wig is shoutingly evident, the better to show me how clever he was to wear it. Scattered on the rug are his expensive London clothes and expensive shoes, spilled in a tangle, along with the expensive brief-case he'd used to suggest executive intentions.

It's a sign of true merit now – buying the best and disrespecting it, trying to show that you're better than all of the skills that combined to make your shirt, your jacket, the pen in your inside pocket.

His jacket pocket is on display – it shows a little tailor's label that reads MADE FOR FLETCHER CURRIE.

I suppose he intended I should read it.

I already know he's a man dressed in lies. I'm sure he's no more Fletcher Currie than anyone else.

I never wanted to know who he really was, not even to try for a prosecution. I wanted him to be over. I wanted to stop being shamed by the thought of him. I wasn't going to parade my wounds, even to reveal what ought to be his shame, my government's shame, the shameful thing that pretends to be our police.

This blunders through my mind while I look round at his ranks above ranks of little doors in all the walls for whatever masses of storage he needs. I don't look behind any one of them, in case they're packed with clotted madnesses.

I remember myself as I stand on the rug. I'm facing two plain bulkhead walls with a narrow passageway between. Somewhere back there is the place where he washes and shits and pisses and makes himself look human. And there will be costume storage. He doesn't have clothes – only costumes. There will be somewhere he sleeps, I suppose. If a thing like him sleeps.

I'm standing still, but feel that I'm out of breath. Too many emotions are cycling and smearing and cycling inside my chest. And I am so hugely tired. An angle of daylight is falling from above the little passageway. About halfway along it there's a gleaming wooden ladder that leads up and out. It seems an invitation and I don't trust Buster's invitations.

But I have to keep on, be the teacher, lead the way. I am very

336

silent as I walk, so silent that I worry I have gone deaf for some reason. Perhaps the air he lives in eats up sound.

I reach the ladder and see the faint marks where his shoes have contaminated every rung. I am pleased that his filth is showing and pleased by the way this will disturb him when he is so clearly intent on convincing himself that he's cleaner than clean.

I begin my climb upwards and make my head and my shoulders emerge and be undefended as they pass through the open hatch and back into the salt marshy air as a bird calls in a long, sad whip of sound.

My scalp tingles with risk.

My instincts are once again being right and useful.

But I am still alone.

I swing out and on to a tiny deck inside the high prow that makes the barge seem more seagoing and effective beyond this strange little stretch of lazy river.

Maybe he really is gone, slipped over the side and away.

I take a step and look down over the side of the boat – and here is his escape route: a small landing stage at the foot of a grimy metal ladder, sitting tight by the hull, a kayak resting there with its paddle, all ready to carry him away.

Only he hasn't gone away.

My hands sweat. They might have been dropped into dirty water, sick water.

He looks like a bundle of dark rags, abandoned clothes, like another discarded identity but with him still inside.

Buster. *Fuck him.*

He's folded over on himself, hunched down next to the kayak with his forehead rested on the landing stage, hands braced over the back of his neck as if whatever flight he's on is crashing.

He may be feeling something. He may be trying to look like a man who's feeling something.

Or he's pretending to cower away from my rage, playing yet another game where I have to feel guilty and let him be the victim.

He always was good at physical presentation – *Look at me being the poor man this crazy woman has pursued and maybe now she'll punch and kick me in her fury.*

This makes me want to try.

Only I'm not like him. I am not like these scarecrow pieces.

And how small he seems – the obsession of my adult life.

And I'm not going down there. He can put on his show for himself.

I'm starting to feel that the whole of today and my hunting and trying and keeping on has been what he's arranged for filthy reasons.

I start to feel stupid. My neck prickles.

I head back to the ladder and climb down as quiet as I can.

Then I stand by his sofa and wait for my hands to stop shaking.

Years of anger are swarming in. But if Buster is so small, then shouldn't the years and the anger feel small, too? Couldn't they be small, too?

I don't understand why, but this makes me smile.

And I go and light the pristine rustic hob under the perfect choice of cheery whistling kettle. I pull open cupboards with innocent, neatly ranked contents until I find a small selection of ideal mugs. A bit more searching and here's an antique tin marked TEA and full of loose-leaf, because that would be right for this fantasy. The tin marked SUGAR has a perfect patina, as does the one labelled COFFEE, which I'm sure holds perfect grounds of high quality.

I won't have coffee here. Coffee belongs to Francis, who doesn't know where I am and has no idea why I would ever have come here.

It surprises me that I want to hug Francis. I want to breathe in deep with my face in his hair and kiss his ears and be nothing to do with Buster. I want to hold the one and real and singular, unified man who is Francis. I realise that I love him and I realise I'm still broken, because I am surprised by it.

But I'm making tea – the remedy for all ills, including the Blitz and Dunkirk and all the mass casualty fun we are now meant to embrace.

My tea will be with sugar, which I don't usually like, but I assume that I'm in shock.

Before I use it, I pour boiling water all over the mug to scald away Buster.

At just the most perfectly logical position on the worktop, his teapot is waiting. I scald that, too. His fridge was pretending to be another cupboard and breaks the Edwardian illusion when I open it. Nothing inside but violent light – no butter and bacon in brown paper, no quaint little jug of milk.

So I'll drink my tea black. And I won't wonder why he needs a fridge, or if he eats.

Is he a thing that eats? Is he a thing that needs to cook his meat?

I make sure to spill tea on his nice cream-coloured tiles.

Then I half-fill my mug, because my hands are still unsteady.

I press my palms in tight around the burn of what I'll probably not drink – it's still a comfort.

An unjudgeable length of time passes.

Then footsteps threaten overhead and the inevitable thing is on the ladder, is coming down, is coming in.

He pauses, head still out of sight, and reaches out his left hand to the hatch frame, grabs it. Sudden, he slips both feet off the ladder, drops for an instant, then swings.

It's a nice effect. I bet he's practised it, rehearsed how he'll take his body weight on one arm, on one hand's grip.

He sways, slowly curling his knees up to his chest and winding his free arm round his shins. I can't see his face, only this giant spider shape, this offence.

He's proving a point about strength, about being nothing natural.

And maybe he's trying to be like Monkey and for that I should pick up his perfectly shiny fire extinguisher and throw it at him.

Hang, hang, hanging like a murderer, like a nightmare and being sure I still don't see his face, not yet. The paint smears on his overalls don't look like symptoms of work, creativity, art – they're signs of chaos.

I do still remember his timing, though. I do wish I can't automatically count – *one, two, three* – between a new tension in his wrist and the start of his head, leaning back and to the side.

So there he is, the monster.

And his eyes are asking a question I can't translate and he seems close to smiling, close to pleased about some secret. His kind always pretend they have wonderful secrets, but they only ever have the one – *I'll hurt you.*

I hear myself tell him, 'You don't need to play the psychopath.' I wouldn't have thought I could.

Then I hate that I flinch when he lets go and drops. The noise when he lands on the boards seems too soft, boneless, and he stays balled up there on the floor, a dark and dead insect in dirty black overalls and an army surplus jacket.

'This is mine.' His voice is muffled, but the water beneath the boat must surely feel it.

He still has the mouth of the man I thought I knew – the one who specialised in being uncanny. 'Boat.' There's a brassy kind of edge about his voice. 'Mine.' He has a different accent maybe – somehow, a Londoner but with a trace of something further west. I'm sure that's meaningless. 'Mine.'

I used to be happy when I heard him.

'What?'

'It's mine.'

Buster slowly stands in the way that a liquid pouring upwards might. 'The case will collapse. The OrKestrA – case against them will be collapsed.' He begins walking towards me in a rush and I flinch again. At some point I have reached back to steady myself against the kitchen counter.

He doesn't come near me, though, only makes for the foot of the wheelhouse steps.

The detail of him confuses: manicure, skin – they all fit a person with time for maintenance, for luxury. Even the Number Four cut is beautifully finished, a minutely longer flare in front, neck freshly trimmed.

He is fascinating, like all venomous things.

His second-hand clothes look shallow, like Halloween, but there's something truly ravaged in him. Behind his left ear there's a thin, pale scar that runs down beyond his immaculate hairline and slips inside the collar of his overalls. It's ragged.

'Collapsed.'

He carefully removes and racks his plimsolls, puts on the slippers, apparently intent on nothing else. 'I am not. To explain myself – I am not. To achieve full accuracy is… The scenario is challenging while soluble.' He returns, soft-footed, staring at the trail of footmarks he's left himself to clean away, acting the saddened butler, the put-upon househusband. He scoops up the mess of belongings he abandoned, carries it away along the passage where, no doubt, he'll stow it somewhere in the dim privacy he keeps there.

I almost begin to think he has forgotten I am here.

He reappears – bad jack-in-the-box. 'The barge is where I do not talk or have to talk or have people.' His motions seem automatic, ratchetted.

He moves like a tin toy, speaks these flat little bursts of half-finished thinking – apparently to no one in particular, or to himself. 'Collapsed.'

Then his shoulders shrug back and he looks at me again. Something behind his eyes engages and his diction flexes, becomes more fastidious. 'The norm for my type is guilt and retirement of chemical and alcohol decline with other dysfunction. I am not the norm. The norm is drunk in a damp cottage and regrets and reckless gun possession. The norm is late-night calls to nowhere and tears and hen runs full of failure in gardens where nothing grows and anger bafflement.' He flexes his accent again, this time towards *Horse & Hound* vowels. 'One might consult on domestic terror and clandestine powers and penetration by overseas influence, mobster sedition influence. One might advise a minister, or two, a government. One might soar and be unscathed above moralities and viewpoints. One might have success. Success blesses all.' His eyes flare whitely towards me. 'I have seen it done.'

And then he droops, becomes the smaller mechanical boy thing again. 'Out of the norm. There is me. Also I am.'

I hear myself ask him, 'What?' I don't know what I mean and neither does he.

'The case will collapse. Things like myself are predictable locatable and I located the provocateur concerned. He led them astray. Should undue provocation influence and suchlike have occurred and should an operative admit it.' He coughs. 'Should a government have provably created an action that it now seeks to prosecute.' He coughs again and this time covers his mouth like a good boy. 'Dynamo, Arthur, Karl–'

'Don't talk about them. You don't know them. You weren't family with them.'

He nods once – *updown* – almost as if it's a tic that aids with processing. 'I was a disease model thing that weakened their immune system to later infection vectors.'

'I don't know what you're talking about. I know you killed Monkey. I know you killed all of us and Monkey the most. You murdered him all the way.' I may be screaming. It feels as if I'm screaming.

'I provoked and led the OrKestrA into actions and meetings with more radical organisations and thereby infiltrated further networks, or rendered them easier to penetrate. I thereby rendered OrKestrA members more vulnerable to influence and easily led.'

'Nothing like it. You stopped us trusting anyone.'

'But the OrKestrA members at the naval base all trusted one of me, one of my kind, and did as he suggested and implied and required. But the case against them will collapse. I located the one responsible and was persuasive and he will confess.' He coughs again – this odd little noise that a human throat shouldn't make.

'Buster, I can't deal with any more gibberish. I'm just here for–'

'Why. You are here for me, for why. I brought you here and am explaining.'

But this is my story and not his. I don't want this to be about the ways in which he's freakish and draws attention.

Still, he does get attention, doesn't he? He is a very modern thing, perfect for the ruined world – a monster that makes you stare.

'I know you, I bring you here and you learn the truth and are mended.'

'You know nothing about me.'

'Untrue.'

'Fuck you.'

'Untrue.' And this slippy shine of light leaks out when he glances across at me. That's when I know he is dangerous, factually dangerous.

But he packs the light away again and continues in a dull, low, unpausing grind. 'The entity who planned the Faslane operation designed it as a maximum discreditable and high-risk action with aspects attractive to the media landscape. The intention was to undermine years of effective and peaceful protest against this base and by extension all other nuclear bases and to obliterate any narrative regarding the illegality or impracticality or unaffordable expense or absent morality or other failures of nuclear deterrence on a global stage. All governmental entities with manifold inefficiencies and failings need a radical narrative of feral and long-term maddened intent with potential religious overtones and fanaticism subplots. That way they always have a contrast that shows them as the better option.'

This time his cough is graphic and seems infested.

'When you see… When you see how easy it is to move people, how magnificent lying is… You understand reality.' He looks at me like a boy who wants his teacher to be proud, before his whole expression blanks and he continues, 'The operative disappeared in mid-operation after assaulting two MoD police. He was left untraced and described as untraceable and perhaps dead. But he was near Llanberis and pretending to dig vegetables and keep bees. It accesses cocaine regularly and has antidepressant prescriptions.

It is very undefended.'

'No one is *it*.'

'I am. It is. And a full accounting of the operation to relevant quarters is underway. I feel it progress. All the charges will go away except the resisting arrest for Karl, which I am unable to amend. He should not have resisted. He is not the kind of thing that can. But this will ease the path for the larger success. The national situation is malevolent toxic and there must be some small sacrifice that will amount to some months in prison. I think only months.'

'And you think doing this will make you a good person? Will make up for Monkey? For anything?'

'No.' He seems almost puzzled. 'I am being tidy. I examined accessible virtues and that is my virtue – I can be tidy. That is a virtue accessible to me.'

And I'm fully afraid now. I'm remembering all of the times a Stiltskin took my dignity after Buster – in a bedroom, in a kitchen, in a hallway, in an office, on a street – all the small robberies, everything else.

He's right. He is an infection, he does weaken you for everything that's after. Every Stiltskin is.

But I have dignity now. It took me years to grow it, feed it, make it strong and see it rise. I'm not crying now. I'm not praying and praying for help, asking a black space over my head for justice and getting silence.

And if I want to, I can be strong. 'You only even need to be a saviour because you left them in harm's way. None of them need ever have been arrested, locked up on remand. Not one of those gentle, beautiful people should have ended up in that courtroom. None of them.'

'I was busy.'

'Busy?' My volume is making my ears sing, but he seems not to notice, just keeps on as before, like someone reciting old prayers from a terrible religion.

'Always busy.' He sits, almost collapses – knees together, head down quick, as though a string has snapped and dropped him in his armchair. 'There was a Syrian in Paris. It was necessary we should meet.'

Then he smiles just the way that Buster used to smile, that Baron Saturday smiled, after we threw a whole household up into the air and took our applause and were examples of love in the ascendent, of little triumphs over circumstance and objects, the victories normal people long to see.

Fuck him.

Fuck him for making that a lie, along with all the rest.

He smooths at his short, short hair, as if he's attempting to steal Francis, too. 'I was in Paris a week after Notre Dame burned and I walked along rue Le Regrattier on the *Île Saint-Louis* and I remember this because I wish to and because I need some things that are my own and I remember everything of how the buildings are so stretched tall and cream, clean elegant and full of angles that are pleasing because they are *comme une vieille femme élégante qui a vu des hécatombes et des roses* and they lean and seem relaxed and not the result of time and forces and the air is the usual sweetness under and all of the quartier wakes up at ten or perhaps later because it wants to and because it has stayed up late and been merry. I reached the Quai and the Seine and walked along inside the scent of water and the way it smells also like an animal. It smells of this strange wet fur and is fastfast and broadbroad and in the wind from the cathedral I could taste wet ash and cinders and I thought that I was inhaling prayers and blessings and a fireplace centuries ago and wood cut new before I had ever existed then which was given to me now by fire and therefore I was more secure alive now and more firm established irremovable and clean…'

He doesn't seem to draw breath.

Abusers do this. They heap up bizarre details to keep you away from anything you need to know or say. They make every story their own. He feels like a headline I might meet any morning – that same narcissist shove of sick priorities.

'And I walked beyond and I sat and drank coffee in the afternoon and the sun shone moderate and I watched the cop divers from La Brigade Fluvial working the river and back and forth and being blue under the blue sky and in the blue water by the Pont Marie and I saw how they each are fastened to the boat so they never get lost.' He stops with a head twitch and swallows audibly. 'You think that I sound like a broken clock and am pitiful and I agree.'

And this is the point when he does seem to recede, to be wholly pitiful in the way he always should have been.

I tell him, 'I don't care.' He gives that tiny mechanical nod again. 'Don't agree with me! I don't need you to agree!'

Buster folds forward to set his head on his knees, braces his hands back round his neck. Now I suppose I'm meant to be the air crash about to hurt poor little boy Buster.

Fuck that.

'What was I, Buster? Did you hate me? Was I nothing?'

I can hear the canal water licking the boat, patting at it as if the river is worried for me.

'What am I, Buster? What was I?'

And this is when I throw up.

I can't stop vomiting. I throw up everything I've eaten since breakfast. 'Fuck you.' There's a moment, too, when the mug of tea that I'm still holding falls and smashes. 'Fuck you.' I keep retching, spitting up spittle and bile. 'Fuck you.'

His barge isn't lovely and neat any more, isn't tidy.

So there's that.

And then Buster springs up, arms tight to his sides and his wet teeth showing.

But I don't step back. My body doesn't do the thing it always has when the Stiltskin comes to get me.

I don't retreat.

And there's a second when he looks at me.

I'm not sure if you understand the way this is – things like this, how they feel.

Then again – you might.

That's why I'm just pausing a little here.

I do hope you've got no idea of the ways people end up crying because of some other time that should never dare visit them again, something that breaks over their heads without asking and covers their face with rancid heat. I don't want you to know about crying that stinks of terror, or how you can find your own sweat gets tainted by adrenaline and cowardice. I don't want you to hate every part of what you are because none of that could be something you deserve.

You shouldn't have to be shivering with a cold only you know, or have that taste of electric metal between your teeth.

But that's just words.

I want you to never have been to that kind of place.

If you have, I'm sorry and I don't want to make you feel it edging back.

That kind of thing leads you to strange places and it leaves you there alone.

After writing that section, I went out to the courtyard for a break, just swung my window open and climbed out.

Paul noticed me first and then Francis, or maybe both at once. They saw the way that I was feeling, and Paul took the paper pad out of my hand – this paper, this hand – and Francis ran down the spiral stairs with a blanket.

There must have been a part before that, one that suggested there ought to be a blanket. I don't remember.

I stopped work for the night. I talked nonsense with the boy I try to save from the terrible places and with a man who's tried to save himself and knows how.

They keep a close eye on me since Sue died.

They keep a close eye, anyway.

They make me no longer alone.

This evening I lay with the back of my head on Francis' lap, because he's a comfortable surface. I am, apparently, also a comfortable surface. So we alternate the heads in laps thing. It's pleasant and one of the small, good things that are meant to join up and slowly build to make a decent life.

We were on the big wine-coloured sofa that I paid for in cash at a weird kind of charity shop that vanished soon after. That's why our household still calls it *The Brigadoon Settee*. Doing this entertains us and we can if we like. That's possible. I loved it and was able to have it and keep it. That's possible, too.

And it's possible to write down my life without the cruel bits of memory eating me up.

Francis never asks much about my generally-in-the-dark hours scribbling. This is part of his general patience. I also don't say much without being asked.

In my defence, if I could talk about all of this stuff, I wouldn't be writing it down.

'Actually it's a cycle of epic verse in Elvish.'

'What is, Anna?'

'The – you know – thing.'

'The thing I stare at every evening with plaintive curiosity?'

'I hadn't noticed.'

'No, you were too busy with the thing.'

'Really? I mean, I'm not being an arse about it, Francis? Am I?'

It's only that I want a record of me to be here – in case. It shouldn't be another way of hiding. Is this another way of hiding? Another evasion?

'No, no… Not, really.'

'What?' I was hoping that Francis would say *No, not at all – how could you possibly ever be an arse?*

He sidesteps my little whine for reassurance, 'Paul and I were betting it's the *Necronomicon*. Or the Old Testament, only this time as limericks.'

'That would be hard.'

'*There once was a man, Shalmaneser*.'

'*Who hurt himself holding a beaver*. No – that's rubbish – too hard.'

'*It clawed at his knees*.'

'*And his Sadducees*. I am not doing limericks. This one's already ahistorical and just no.'

'One can be overly mysterious, though…' Every time he inhales, the deep of his breath presses his pullover, soft at the back of my head. 'I mean, Paul and I've been waiting to read it for ages…' It's not a great pullover – wine coloured: sofa camouflage. Wine camouflage, too, if it comes to that.

'Well, I will finish eventually.'

'It's like tapping out *shave and a haircut* and never adding *two bits*.'

He's not wrong. He is a wise man. I arch my back a little bit and settle again. '*His remains finished up out in Giza*.'

'I didn't mean the limerick – I meant the magnum opus.'

'I know. I do know.' And I can't tell him – *It's meant for you to read when I am dead. Dead like Sue, dead like all the rest.*

Francis cups his hand round one of my ears and squeezes very gently. I'm not sure how this ever came to be a gesture of affection and reassurance, but here we are. It lets me hear my heartbeat and that tiny, creaky roar of muscle and tendon and blood in his hand – here we are, alive together.

He leaves one of his pauses and it does what they always do and swings me open like a window, lets me climb out.

I pat his knee, which is a fine and sturdy knee. 'It's just this thing I need to write. Not notes, or lesson plans. Just this thing.'

'You did mention…'

'Did I mention?'

'You did. You told us *It's just this thing I need to write*, which broke your previous complete silence. We assumed that your vow of silence had weakened. That or you were distracted by the video where those puppies were rescued from dying in a hole.

'I did like that video.'

'It was excellent.' He inhales, long and slow. 'We know something must have thrown you, otherwise you wouldn't have just blurted everything out like that … shocking confession … so many details… And so forth…'

His thigh is tensing and untensing under my cheek. I'm making him stressed.

'Hang on, wasn't it the video where the rescued dog turned out to be a bear?'

'No, it was the one where the couple are out for a stroll in somewhere mildly hellish – ours not to question why they would – and they hear this solitary puppy scrap making *eepeep* noises, but then there are the noises of other tiny scraps and it is revealed that down some kind of utterly inaccessible well there are all these trapped wee beasties and it takes all day for the couple to dig them out by hand without accidentally murdering them instead and then–'

'And then they're free!' I remember, of course I do. Sharing animal resurrection videos got us through some very bleak months apart and continues to do so now we're together. 'Then six months later the couple are lying on a massive rug and the dogs are all crazy with happiness on top of them in a glossy big heap of tails and ears and noses and big soft feet.'

'I don't remember the couple having soft feet.'

'Stands to reason – pets resemble their owners.'

'Fair enough.'

'Grown up and with their owners who went from no dogs to seven overnight.'

'Overday.'

'No one ever says that, Father Francis. I wonder why?' And back swings the window, I feel it shut. I can tell he's not finished exploring where I can't quite let him be – not yet.

Francis tells me, 'It's autobiography. Obviously.'

'Why obviously?'

'The crying.'

And he sets the palm of his hand to hold my cheek and his thumb rests just under my jaw and stays there and it's the right fit.

My body has not always been my friend, but was born with certainties like this, inherent knowledge of the way a hand should touch my face.

Eventually, as a human person, you stop being in too many places at once, stop thinking you'll rip. You rest in one.

When I say *you* I mean *me*.

And eventually I can do something like writing this while Paul scrolls about online, looking for that puppy video, which is much harder than one might assume because typing in keywords like BURIED PUPPIES NOTHING DIES DIGGING ENDS HAPPILY CUDDLES produces enough results to burn out all the XML sitemaps involved. Such is the current need for ENDS HAPPILY CUDDLES. Such is the current need for NOTHING DIES.

And no, I don't actually know what XML sitemaps are, no one does. People like Francis talk about them with people like Paul and then look across at me like Rosicrucians who suspect they've said a bit too much about Atlantis.

Francis is in the usual deckchair beside me and trying to mend all the pieces of a bowl he broke into exactly those pieces, in order to have the chance to reattach them. He's learning kintsugi – the art of highlighting the beauty of repairs, of chips and cracks. Our household appreciates the idea of that. Nonetheless, we remain waylaid by the stage of broken crockery and have not yet advanced even a mug to the stage where our scars become our glories.

Our household is also getting slightly high on all the acetone involved. Acetone comes into the process more than I'd anticipated.

And we have generally caught our second wind with the Plaguetime Projects and Skills Improvement.

I'm learning Gaelic. *Tha mi gu dearbh.* And Paul is knitting a hat – Fair Isle. Leastways, we think it's a hat. Paul says if it doesn't turn out it can be a snood. There's a lot of leeway with snoods. Paul's also the only one of us studying seriously, getting ready for uni, for leaving me.

More properly, I should say he's getting ready to join the world, as he should.

But the world will try to kill him and I don't want him to go.

I don't say that out loud.

I sit here instead.

And I write.

I break the darkness into little bits and then, in the end, I'll have written it all and the ink will have locked it away.

Even Buster in the barge will be only some marks across a page – a little trail of marks and uprights and nothing more.

I hope that.

I'm deciding to be sure of that.

But when I close my eyes I can see how he snapped up from his seat like the night thought he is and I saw the black gloss of his wide dilated pupils and the absence, the nothing behind.

Alone with him on the boat, like a stupid victim.

But I stood. I withstood.

I withstood him.

And the barge didn't pitch up and sink, didn't burn, and I didn't fall, and I didn't run away.

Sometimes not running away is the best option.

And Buster seemed surprised by this. There was a flicker of recalculation somewhere, changing his expression, making him lick his lips. The wet little sound of it seemed far off and like a cheap mechanism operating badly.

And I told him, 'I am going away now.'

His head gave that tiny tic – *updown* – before his concentration seemed to switch. And he stared down at the ruin all over his floor. It made his fingers twitch, undecided.

I backed away until the wheelhouse steps were up against my heels. 'I am going away, and I am going to be happy. You are not.'

By this time – the last time I saw him – he was crouched in the middle of his rug and puzzled, sunk in the mess I'd left him. He glanced round at me once, not angry, not anything easy to define.

He might almost have closed the thought of me away and started to make room for whoever's next. That's how it seemed.

He didn't show mercy – he'd killed me once and had no appetite for doing it again. I was unimportant in the way I always had been. I think that's true, sometimes. And sometimes I think that I forced him back, that being who I am, being the person I have become, kept him at bay.

That seems less convincing.

I know that once I'd climbed the steps back to the wheelhouse I was rushing, beginning to panic. I skinned my knuckles climbing the ladder to reach the quayside and then forgot my route back to Hythe Station. It seemed years since I'd walked from there.

I didn't notice I was bleeding until I was sitting on the train.

And by the time I got home I was very late, and Paul made an act out of being worried. 'It's a *mobile* phone – that's the clue – *mobile* – that means it's a phone you can take around with you in a pocket, bag, haversack, or other…'

Meeting my eyes made him stop and we just hugged.

I told him I'd been sick and that Court 10 had been horrible and I wasn't going back. That was the truth, but incomplete.

He looked at my bloody knuckles and, rather than lie, I simply didn't tell him how I'd hurt myself.

I also didn't tell him there's no closure, because nothing closes – you just move further away from whatever happened and you change. You find out that the damage can be only the damage – but you can be almost anything. You can grow on past the darkness in the way that your bone grows round a break. Or maybe it's more like the way that a tree grows round a nail. The nail never grows – it's stuck, then it's smothered, overwhelmed by life until it rusts away.

You're not the nail, the injury, the harm – you're the one who is out in the world and free.

For once, Buster was honest.

The case against my OrKestrA friends, my family, did collapse. The prosecutions ended in mumbles and evasion. Almost nothing in the papers. The noise a whole country makes while it slides down a cliff in ugly bounces drowned out what might have been an interesting scandal. Plus, there's no real appetite for holding even past authorities to account. I did see one small and moderately spiteful article that used a smudgy photo of the OrKestrA near a picket line.

We rose above it. And after that, we might as well have never been.

For a few days, a shifty bloke in an anorak loitered up and down our bit of Wicklow Street. He looked like someone who wanted to lurk round strangers' houses and thought being in the press corps would mean he'd get paid for it.

Or else he was just an average pervert, maybe a burglar, or a cop pretending not to be a cop. That's all much the same thing, though, isn't it?

Karl got time served, community service and a fine.

Life and Court Number 10 both moved on.

And what's left of the OrKestrA got together again and ate dinner to celebrate, if not victory then survival.

Paul came along, too, because he's an honorary member. He and Mrs Fire are endlessly eager to juggle pencils, bread rolls, glasses, eggs, spare change – anything handy – indoors, or out. They're very good at it, have super-safe hands, and the glimmer of objects and of their concentration is very lovely. They do have a history of making waiters nervous.

And the OrKestrA is older and more sedate and doesn't insist on pyrotechnics with every course. We can be reasonable.

For most of that evening we didn't discuss the trial. We talked about the so many demos flowering in that year – which ones we'd made and which we'd missed. There had been millions on the streets. (Or dozens, if you believed police observers. They never are great at counting.)

I'd got used to feeling claustrophobic in the shoulder-against-shoulder press of bodies, queueing to even enter protests for women's rights, for minority rights, for democracy, for healthcare – and against the fragile sadist Stiltskins and all their vandalisms.

That – probably final – OrKestrA night we were on a rolling high about it. None of us could remember attending so many marches that so regularly swept along Piccadilly, covered Hyde Park and keep coming, kept rolling on for hour after jolly hour, with more still waiting to set off. We seemed to be in a time of peculiar joy: signs, banners, music, jokes, Morris dancers, drums, strollers and players, and separate interest groups finally together, seeing each other, pressing for joint necessities, for life. I thought it was uplifting that so many people wanted peace, equality, healthcare, food, clean air, enough time to make a whole life and be happy in it, enough time to leave the planet habitable – the usual crazy stuff, which seems so indulgent when compared with money. Really, though, it was more of a strong indication that all the paths to life were disappearing; 2019 may have been our last hurrah.

I remember we did believe that life could win, then – that we weren't too late. We were optimistic. Demos are optimistic things – why else bother with them? The fascists were real and here again, like a recurrence of syphilis, rotting the brain, making limbs jerk and throw the old, familiar murder and suicide shapes. The situation was terrible, but not hopeless. Or was hopeless, but not serious – something along those lines – and we were acting as if our optimism might be justified and an effective remedy. We thought what we were doing would be enough.

And we'd begun to get used to docile police, leaning and yawning police, outnumbered and therefore well-behaved police, even after dark. We'd begun to get used to Parliament hearing us right outside its walls, the people being louder than the servants of the people, not storming the palace, but being a reminder of how frail it was. Here was unarmed, unviolent, unimpeachable pressure. Here was a hope to decrease pain, rather than sell it.

It seemed that any neighbourhood, any community might become an OrKestrA.

You can't blame us for hoping – it had been so long since we could.

And here's a day of pleasant details, radical details – I need to remember this.

There was an afternoon, maybe in the early autumn of 2019, and Paul was walking with me behind someone else's genuinely quite adequate drum ensemble. They weren't the OrKestrA, but they were fine. And the whole boom and clatter – with us in tow – was just swinging by that ugly clump of show-off luxury hotels opposite Green Park. Yet another helicopter jittered in to survey us, and we waved up towards the inevitable camera, whoever it was working for. We waved up with thousands of other waves, tens of thousands, in one long, roiling cheer.

Paul looked at me with a smile like Christmas morning. 'Was it like this?'

'The OrKestrA? Sort of. Smaller. But, yes. It felt like this, yes.'

That wasn't a great omen, because we'd lost: the pits closed, the mining jobs were never replaced, more and more of our communal possessions were sold off at a loss. We didn't stop it. We didn't really ever stop anything. We didn't keep the troops out of Iraq.

But this time the marching would keep on. That was our opinion round the big restaurant table. After the one monumental day of Iraq marches, in 2003, Hissy said too many of us assumed we'd been definitive – expressed a remarkable new will. Job done. There wasn't enough follow-up – not to resist the joys of war unbound: the looting, the mercenaries, the torture, the adoring embedded press, the bin bags of cash for the chaos engineers. Even while we carried our placards and felt the wind try to turn them, take them – our country's bombs were already dropping expensively, tipping us into another exciting mistake. It was going to be broadcast gold. Gold in general.

This time, though, we knew better. The people would keep on agitating, reminding, resisting. So the outcome would be different. Really. October 2019 had seemed so remarkable. Almost everyone at our table had been happily caught somewhere in the crush that spanned the width of Whitehall. We'd gridlocked the whole West End on the 19th. We'd cheered and hoped and sang. We'd felt the city shift. I was pretty sure we had.

I certainly said that out loud and believed it, while Mrs Fire smiled at me across the cutlery and dinner plates. (All being used for purely culinary purposes.) She raised one eyebrow the way she always used to when anyone started *being terminally naïve.*

Her hair was still in a naturally upward flare, but bright white. I hadn't expected that – or that she'd be heading so determinedly towards comfy, plump and twinkly, as if she can't wait to be the pensioner who surprises you by swearing, or by innocently hand-cuffing herself to vans attempting deportations. In a story, she'd be the uncanny kind of woman who knocks on your door for a glass of water and looks at you appraisingly with purple-blue eyes, just before your life begins to shatter. Treat her well and she'll lend magical assistance, weave you something better than you had. Treat her badly and you'll sink without a trace. I remember deciding that she always will be burning, it's just that now she has a different flame. She understands endurance.

For a while, Court Number 10 nearly took Dynamo from her and she had no powers to block its way. But she's almost herself again. Almost. And Dynamo has joined Mrs Fire in embracing knitwear and obvious benevolence.

Maybe he seemed too good, too soft, too kind to be true and therefore a suitable target for an agent provocateur. Dynamo was never the kind of activist that breaks into naval bases. He must have been terrified. He isn't a spy, a wrecker, a foreign agent. Of course, he's not. Those people have all of the power now, they own us and condemn us by calling us their names.

I never had been able to work out how Arthur, Karl, Phil, Bill and especially Dynamo would ever have ended up planning and executing something like the ham-fisted midnight disaster Court 10 and the newspapers described. There was a desperation about the property damage, and the use of fire – incriminating, poorly controlled fire.

Dynamo had nothing but respect for fire, he would never have misused it.

That last OrKestrA night, I sat and watched Karl teach Paul one of his complicated clapping and tapping patterns. Then they ran it through together, perfect. Then Karl delayed the whole of his part by a beat and the new set of cascading rhythms was so beautiful it made us applaud.

Karl wasn't a terrorist, either.

Another Buster, a Stiltskin, had groomed our friends, led them on, insisted that paper lanterns with naked flames should fly over parched summer grass and the more and less imposing structures at the edge of a submarine base. Karl and Dynamo and the rest were tricked and then abandoned by a man they never saw again, someone who made sure to harm two MoD policemen.

It had always been unlikely that every member of the raiding party would manage to scatter and vanish into the warm night and the scent of pine. My friends did make it to their cars and waited for the Stiltskin as long as they could before driving back to Glasgow. They hid for a couple of days – all except Phil, who delivered himself to A&E at the Western Infirmary and told them he'd fallen downstairs.

And there were no headlines, not even small mentions of what they'd done. And their strange friend with the good boots didn't reappear. Over the months they relaxed, wondered if official embarrassment had helped them, airbrushed the whole security breach away. They'd gone home, slowly relaxed and not one of them had told the rest of us about the clumsy thing they'd done. Dynamo didn't tell Mrs Fire.

That hurt her.

He looks tired.

In Court Number 10, the prosecution never used Dynamo's proper stage name. They kept claiming he'd called himself *Mr Fire*. They twisted everything they could, the way that Stiltskins do and followed whatever weird playing out of logic suddenly triggers a trap that was first set in motion in 1997.

That's another thing that Stiltskins do – they wait.

In 1998, Dynamo and Mrs Fire became Mr and Mrs Waller-Nye. Both of them took both names and headed out on the road again. Their van life never ended, the tour just became permanent.

They're children's puppeteers. Things are very hard and strange now for touring entertainers, any entertainers, but Dynamo and Mrs Fire are managing, I think. It's always a tough gig: hunching and multitasking inside a booth and offering up magics so that small, demanding people can have fun. Puppeteers are underestimated, but they have to provide the miraculous before they can even begin –to give animation to objects, to make shadows act in three dimensions, to make dead objects live.

I watched them feed each other forkfuls from their differing plates: ravioli for risotto and vice versa. They always did want to be sure they weren't missing out, even back when the OrKestrA was eating what was very much the exact same beans-with-other-beans casserole in each and every bowl.

At the restaurant table, Dynamo took their forks and let them dance with each other in precisely the way that seemed right, round and round on the tablecloth – honest, simple craft and wonder. Everyone needs it.

In what I think might have been April this year, Paul and I found this little film Mrs F. and Dynamo had put online. Trapped at home with no audience in sight, they had made sad and frightened domestic utensils in a kitchen sing to each other from a distance – spoons and a set of whisks, a honey dipper, a tiny butter knife. A corkscrew raised its arms up slowly and became a little metal woman with clear knowledge of how to be happy no matter what and alive, alive, alive.

I cried. Paul cried. Year Five cried when I showed them it. I sent the link to Colonsay and Francis was still crying about it when I called him.

Crying for happiness is an extraordinary thing. Giving that to someone else – it means that you haven't gone wrong. You're operating as intended, as a human being.

That first lockdown was full of terrors. I would never want it back, but it gave the world time to remember why we cry for happiness.

Dynamo and Mrs Fire never forgot.

The OrKestrA couldn't, either. It wasn't absolutely made out of good people, but in the end it made good people out of us. Maybe that's why it attracted vandalism – because beauty does.

That's what I was thinking while Clumsy Mary and the Apocalypses were down at one end of the table, laughing like kids at a funfair. No change there – not different, only older. Their notes were lower and hands brushed hands more often, as if each one of them needed to comfort and to be reassured.

Mary started a podcast in lockdown. It's a mix of politics and the sounds of objects falling, ripping, burning, blowing up. She's doing very well with it.

Mr Kink became a physics teacher, which seemed on odd fit, until I considered how much showmanship and demonstration might be involved and how many bodies would be described in motion, how many forces and reactions with predictable results. I always found the maths part of physics horrifying, but I'd guess the fact that Mr Kink retained his Mr Kink coolness helped his classes tolerate all of that calculus and algebra and whatnot. There has to be a cool teacher. There has to be someone to organise fashion shows and theatre trips, balloon debates, visits from travelling jazz bands – the weird and extra things that mean every child can find their place, at least one place.

Twenty-first-century learning is meant to be this Strasbourg goose process – force in the low-grade corn and keep 'em caged and docile. Harvest what you want, dump the rest of the carcass.

Mr Kink was a blur of fundraising efforts, jamborees and scholarships breaking out on council estates.

That dinner was the first time I met his wife. She was also the slimline and smouldering sort with long hair and a fringe to flick. In fact, she had the haircut that he used to sport when he pounced and prowled and sent housewives into giggles while we all marched by, our very own selves and glorious, the UnRule OrKestrA.

Three weeks after the schools opened up again, Mr Kink got Covid. He survived, but says that he's a little blind now and a little deaf and he seems to feel exhausted all the time.

I picture him healthy at the dinner, balancing a breadstick on one finger's tip, looking like a man who'll be glamourous forever. Phil and Bill sat – naturally – side by side and watched him, too. They bent heads snug together and shared whispered giggles, threw sly glances at the world, because those are the things they like to do.

They no longer see each other much – Phil's up in Norwich and Bill is in Exeter. It takes time to visit. They're both electricians. It suits their personalities, and their personalities are weirdly, almost perfectly aligned. No domestic jobs – although Phil did connect up my cooker as a favour – they work in film crews. The thing is, they never quite manage to work on the same movies. This would be funny if it didn't make them both so sad.

Court 10 seemed to show in their faces only when the table was covered in wreckage and we were checking pockets, ordering last drinks, talking about going home. The OrKestrA used to be home.

Phil and Bill had been set free and all was well, but not really. No one wants to hire an electrician who might somehow be a mad-in-secret firebug and radical saboteur.

Karl and Arthur were more obviously watchful, restless, as if they were wary of being pulled back and transformed again into prisoners on remand – the accused Karl William Maltby, 55, and the accused Arthur Magnus Kerr, 54.

Before the arrests and the trial, Karl was managing a Disability Resource Centre, filling it up with song sessions and poems, musical composition classes to make soundtracks for the therapy biking, painting classes for those with over-reckless arms, relaxation light shows, physio sessions, personal sign boards for the wordless, decent food in the canteen and work experience in the kitchen.

One good person makes many good things and more good people. Karl's good at that, makes one thing fit another and become more. Before the arrests, whenever I'd call him, he couldn't stop listing what was new and what needed improvement and how he could mostly, mostly, at least slightly, manage to help his clients. He did this even though the national aim was to never help anyone, particularly not if they needed helping.

Court 10 destabilised all of it.

Arthur had been consistently delighted by self-employment as a decorator. He'd found the humdrum jobs satisfying but had loved gently coaxing homeowners into marbling, murals, ceilings full of sky. All that early shouting over crowds and open-air singing had left him with a chocolatey rumble of a voice. And his hair was still swept back from his temples, as if he were a cartoon man in the teeth of a typhoon.

They had both been useful and happy.

Then Court 10 caught them, robbed them.

Now Arthur works every hour there is driving delivery vans. Karl is unemployed.

And Monkey Monk – he stayed gone.

I could pretend that I felt him watch us while that evening ebbed and slowed. I could write about a soft space in the air that was pleased by who we'd become, or rather who we'd kept on trying to be.

I didn't feel anything, though.

Gone is gone.

Trafalgar Square:

If Buster can put down locations at headings, why can't I?

This happens in 2019 – in the year of hope and marching.

2020 was going to be more of the same. It wouldn't be bafflement and tantrums in the face of extinction. It wouldn't make me realise that people fear wearing masks because they don't want to ever meet each other's eyes. It wouldn't be Sue waving a hand at us, wearing her BiPAP mask, not quite able to keep her phone from shaking.

Her eyes were frightened.

2020 wasn't meant to be 32 degrees again this afternoon and front pages covered in pics of happy splashing children, with no hints that unprecedented heat and death are underway. August is burning. In Jagoda and Bogdi's delicatessen, some guy was talking about how much he loved an Indian Summer. In India's summers now the birds fall dead from the sky. I wanted to kick him, but there'd be no point.

2020 was supposed to about Paul going to uni soon, sooner. Horribly soon. We're making the most of this last month, clinging on. How any of his in-person learning will be arranged is still unclear.

2020 wasn't meant to be so many changes, not these changes. Soon, I'll be starting to work with my next Year Five, saying hello. That's as it should be, but none of us wants to move past the point where we're in mourning. Beyond mourning there's permanent loss. We don't want to welcome a Year One that will never meet Mrs Delara.

And in 2020, when Oakwood closed for the summer, the staff still met with last year's kids online, but only for an hour once a week. Continuity. Comfort. Need.

We'll have a new Head soon and that'll be yet more change, although I think Claudia the Deputy will probably get the job. She should do. Claudia is organised, effective, charming. It's just that she wouldn't ever lift up one of the tinies and fly him round over her head, or turn Year 6 Geometry into songs and dance moves.

Claudia will be efficient. This is not a time when efficiency is enough – not that it isn't nice.

And meanwhile, I make my share of the Welfare Checks and the coverage for free meals. And 2020 is about not thinking I follow the same route Sue did, visit the same homes, get hugged by the same children, hold the same hands.

2020, the year of terrifying proximity.

And if I go off to Colonsay, start living there with Francis, that'll be yet another change.

Bogdi and Jagoda are leaving already, closing up the shop. When no other customers are in, they make jokes – 'Bad news: there will only be enough food for half the population after Brexit. Good news: the year after that, there will be just enough.' We all laugh, but have sad eyes for separate sets of reasons. By Christmas they'll be in Poland and out of this.

So I need a *pleasant detail*, need it at once.

Make it a large one – why not – while I'm thinking of streets full of people reclaiming their space, hoping for good change, good futures.

I want to remember Trafalgar Square on the 11th of October, 2019.

Westminster was quiet, a hint of its lockdown future echoing in, London cleared of people overnight by some massive swipe of intervention.

I'd walked up from the river past tube stations that were closed for the duration of the ambient peculiarities. I found a Whitehall empty except for crash barriers in stacks and parked police vans. Half-empty plastic water bottles littered the dashboards, creating their own little cycles of condensation and water drops. You'd have hoped they might at least know better than to buy single-use plastic. Or maybe they were making fun of the climate protests.

The police sense of humour always does escape me.

Here and there I could see lamp posts with copies of the XR Rebel Code taped round them: a neat and healthy list of good behaviours, an attempt to prove the cleanliness of their intent.

People my son's age and younger had taken central London. Now they were talking to it about the burning world while the media swirled with dirty rumours about them and the cops tried to reconfigure their response.

The other generations – even mine, which frankly never has been that impressive – seemed willing to join in, too. For days, rebellious newsfeeds had been full of pensioners getting arrested for helping to block the Embankment, disrupting flights, being locked to a giant pink boat at Oxford Circus – very disobedient, very civil.

Of course, others of the various generations were oblivious, having sly pints, eating crisps, listening to *The Archers* or being outraged. Some just wondered why the traffic was even worse than usual.

XR had occupied London for days. Streets had broken out in carnivals, in funeral processions for our future. In certain districts, nothing but emergency vehicles could get through. Our *law and order* government was also a government unwilling to fund publicsector employees like cops and therefore was on the brink of finding its own interior contradictions were self-defeating.

I strolled up level with the Duke of Devonshire's statue. It's the kind of bizarre confection Britons are intended to gaze up at faithfully: cocked hip, knee britches, King Leopold wedge of beard, a cape and a suitably dismayed expression. Behind me, a young man in a brown coat cycled past, one-handed and easy, through all the quiet and country-tasting air. He went free-wheeling down southwards with a hay bale balanced on his shoulder and a small dog skipping alongside and seemed to pull a ripple of alteration behind him. I remember him so clearly because he and I were the only people visible and because he was so casually remarkable. He made it seem this peace and space might stretch on for weeks, for months. He wasn't entirely wrong.

Great Scotland Yard was busy, but in oldnew ways. It was packed with horseboxes and horses – hooves shifting on tarmac and big breathing and the smell of fresh shit were making the whole place seem strange and time-travelled back to the edge of our internal combustion mistakes. A cop made himself an odd focus for dissonance. He was using the old, old gestures of a person calming horses, whispering the traditional soothing sounds and walking a bay mare down a ramp, the way that bay mares have always walked down ramps. But he was still wearing Kevlar, a sniper's baseball cap, tactical fabrics. He was still a riot squad hard man.

And I suppose the men who sit tall in the saddle with whatever kinds of helmets and boots never have been quaint. And possibly being in such a position means you can't help wanting a cavalry charge now and then, a swing at unruly skulls.

At least they don't have sabres any more.

Still, there was no charging that afternoon. Whitehall seemed to be dozing in the pause left after war.

It wasn't until I was nearing the square that I heard my kind of disturbance. It was drums – overlapping and complicated and unruly drums – the OrKestrA. As I hurried up, I almost expected myself to be late for a gig. Surely the OrKestrA must be there already, surely we must be performing and young and together and all alive. Maybe time was actually in flux and I would meet myself, already there by Nelson's Column.

Of course, it wasn't us, wasn't the OrKestrA – but maybe it was something better.

Trafalgar Square definitely looked better than I'd ever seen it. Nervy tourists were taking pictures of it from the nearest traffic island and here it was – New London rising into sight.

The Square was a grove of wooden towers and flags waving from bamboo sticks and branches. Banners hung from the walls north of the fountains and beneath it all lay an encampment with large and small and oldnew and disreputable tents, a floating pink model jellyfish, stilt walkers, a field kitchen hemmed in by garlands of drying tea towels, cooking up something that smelled of the 80s and turmeric. And there was talking and talking and talking and talking – Quakers in handknits, activists in outdoor gear and walking boots, slender young people in layers of cotton and castoffs who could have been from anywhen – talking figures everywhere, hands mobile, explaining the world to each other, explaining the world to clumps of softly-softly cops who shifted from foot to foot and tried out facial expressions without finding one to fit.

A van stacked high with metal barriers was waiting near the shopping arcade that swings round to Northumberland Avenue. As I crossed over the road and entered the square, a strawberry-blond man in corduroy darted out in the opposite direction and ran up on to the heap of barriers like a parkour fox at bay.

The van pulled away, on cue and unknowing. Brer Fox had escaped from something, from someone, and was borne off into the distance, balanced and waving one arm above his head like every hero ever has. A part of the endlessly circulating crowd looked across from the Trafalgar zone of occupation and cheered. He saluted again, very merry and heading south, smaller and smaller.

If Whitehall had smelled a little like the meadow it might once have been, Trafalgar Square was drifting with the familiar fug of damp tents, damp wool, damp wood, hot stew, hot water and warm skin. It all tasted like every peace camp, or long-term picket, or festival changing room the OrKestrA had ever roamed to. It was the scent of our tour van and our communal self – my family.

It takes a lot of parabens and propylene glycol and aluminium and sodium lauryl sulphate and triclosan and so forth to stop anywhere that people gather smelling much like this. I was walking through our past as a species – the scent that used to worry woolly mammoths and ancient bison.

I spotted a cop being casual in a comfy fleece and doing the *friendly and useful* act and wondered how many others were here, but pretending to be activists.

But then I stopped wondering, because – well, it was just this strangely lovely day. Somehow, all my good past, all my kind past, had drifted back into this one small patch of London.

I couldn't walk more than a few feet before I was hugging Canadian Sol who fought for trees – he'd been part of 'Pollok Free State' and the resistance to the M77 when I saw him last. That was 1995, which was only two or three weeks ago, surely? I hugged Scottish CND Ann – I miss fortuitous and free-range hugs – and then I hugged Chloe who was once caught hitting a Trident submarine with her kayak paddle. Hugs from Quaker Fran and Quaker Andy. I hadn't met either of them since we were kettled in Sauchiehall Street protesting the invasion of Iraq. Or no – it was when we were almost kettled much later on in Piccadilly. I think it was the same day people decided to occupy Fortnum & Mason – in as far as a shop and tearoom might ever resist your occupation. Staff members peered and giggled out of windows as yet another broad crowd marched to no avail beneath them.

That day I was wearing my country tweed demo jacket. Wear tweed, leather shoes and look irritated – encircling cops will part for you as if you're Moses and they are the Red Sea's most deferential shallows.

My speedy release meant I was just in time to hear a journalist trying to hand – someone, anyone, please – a brick they might – someone, anyone, please – want to chuck.

Demos – they're an education.

All this history was coming at me and I should have been tearful because we had never succeeded, rarely come close. But, instead, I was elated. We were still working and still hoping – and still trying to act like citizens of another, better country in another, better world.

And the biggest and hardest hugs were from Hissy and Sissy. They couldn't stay away, either.

I remember we hooked our arms, linked elbows and ran like kids. Ridiculous. Faded ladies, starting to be old, worried about the nearing rumours of Court 10, but so delighted in this moment, our moment.

Up beyond the western fountain, Paul was juggling empty oil cans painted with flames. Of course Paul was there.

And we ringed ourselves round him and span and span.

There was nothing wrong with that day.

I did briefly consider that perhaps this was some kind of shiny day that would neatly round off everything before I got hit by a van – or else maybe I had died already and this was my easing into heaven.

Mainly, I just span.

Then we listened to poems being shoutsung through a dodgy PA system in the square, as the dark crept in and it was some of the strangest and finest music I have known. It was spells and promises and as it should be.

Then a wild rain came suddenly and violently in solid sheets. The sheer volume of water was very beautiful and very funny and a few of the Red Brigade appeared as soon as it started and lifted their hands up into the streams flowing down off the jury-rigged canvas, these dim figures, robed in crimson, moving slow and making the deluge seem like something intended and a chance for beauty.

A fair percentage of the audience ran across to the arcade over the street and huddled there on the wet stone flags. We wanted the words to go on and not stop until they'd changed us, changed something.

And new drums doubled and redoubled, low impacts and hard, high snaps loose between the buildings, elbowing their dignity and tall assumptions. More promises, more spells.

I was holding Paul's hand while the crowd recited Blake together, call and response – *Wisdom is sold in the desolate market where none come to buy.*

We tried not to feel the cold and almost managed.

By the time the last voice stopped and we'd given the last cheer, it was late.

We'd done something for the planet, or nothing for the planet, or both. Maybe we'd done nothing yet, but now we were ready.

Rumours were fluctuating in the dark as we left the arcade. As with all information on the Left, each fragment of news was differently despairing. We were told the cops were moving in to reclaim the area soon, truce over and clear the dream away. Or else we were told the occupation might hold longer, another day, but with more arrests and perhaps violence. The square remained steady so far, strung with improvised pinpricks of light: tiny bits of energy returned to us, rising and speaking to the moon. Tents glowed from within like a steady hum of welcome – that old-fashioned idea.

We four – Hissy and Sissy and Paul and I – started walking along Piccadilly towards Green Park and maybe a still-open tube. My back was reminding me that I'm not twenty and can no longer sit on damp stone flags for hours.

The road was still semi-blockaded and therefore clear of traffic, so we claimed it, began to swing along expansively.

But then Paul stopped, tugged my arm.

Before I turned my head, I knew what he was going to do. Before he let go of me and sank to his knees on the tarmac, I was sure.

My Paul, Tall Paul, there he was kneeling in the road and smiling so completely, so absolutely, smiling like my best and only boy as three cops closed around him, solemn and slow as undertakers.

They asked if he was going to move.

He shook his head and told them no.

I knew he'd do that, too.

And I knew that I should kneel beside him. If I cared about him and about his generation and about the burning world then I would do that little thing.

But I am a coward.

Hissy moved to stand tight at one side of me, Sissy closed in at the other, their arms being a comfort, a slight rock of motion, locked snug at the small of my back. They didn't kneel, either. We were what we are – three middle-aged women who never have been radical. Oh, we do our tiny best and we try to be useful and help but we have these pathetic limits to commitment. We defeat ourselves because we have already been defeated so very often by so very many things.

Or maybe it's only me who is defeated and maybe they knew that I would need them.

We watched as they took Paul away, carried him like a very long and very placid roll of carpet because he wouldn't help them, wouldn't walk. We called to him – *I love you. I love you. I love you.*

I was too scared to do anything more.

So my Paul, my son, was alone and lost in the press of those blue bodies and their mildly clumsy, mildly irritated lifting. His height made things unwieldy for them.

I love you.

I knew they would, most likely, do him no harm. He was only very peacefully resisting. He's a white boy with a middle-class accent and witnesses who could say he was taken away.

I love you.

Sissy made a kind of cabaret about calling out the coppers' numbers while I tried to make a note of them on my phone. Not that my fingers were working well.

I love you.

I knew he would probably be all right, but that didn't matter, couldn't. Paul is still the child who swam in to be with me and made me an ocean as he came. I could feel it through the months, his pulling closer, bobbing and shifting. He's the bundled-up small weight against my body, resting there heavy as absolute trust on our first day together. His hair was still damp from his journey and his hands still purplewhite and strange from being so long underwater.

My Paul with the same confiding eyes from that day to this – his hair was wet that night with the policemen, too. All that rain.

I should have gone to kneel beside my son for as long as I could.

I love you.

My Paul with raindark hair from swimming in to do what's right, to kneel in Piccadilly.

But I was too scared for what's right.

I hope I'd do better now. I think I could.

Being locked in somewhere with police, though. I don't think I could do that.

6th July 2005, Gleneagles:

You will have assumed I was there at Gleneagles because of diagnostic elements and signs. It was the kind of mess my type arranges.

I deny that fault. It is genuinely not mine.

I could have told you this aboard my barge which is called *The Sunday* for obvious reasons.

I loved being the Baron and found him a genuine enjoyment recreation. That was true and remains so.

I was hesitant unimpressive during our interaction period. I had only my base personality to speak with which is not effective in communications. Other preparations were possible but I did not make them because I wanted to not hide so you would see the truth of what I am.

Also because a person at times needs a mirror to be functional.

Prav knew me but he is gone now.

When you were aboard *The Sunday* I witnessed a small and transient horror reaction in your eyes that was only partial expected. It was indicative of good instincts and an indication that your survival awareness has developed since our period of interaction prior.

There were impulses on my part. During my climb down the ladder and into my private living room below deck which is a place for only me and very private I did brief consider removing you.

A boat is a collection of ways to die and be lost thereafter.

I refrained.

In a way I have therefore saved you from great harm.

Also if I have a home it is onboard *The Sunday* and I do not want death there.

I do not want struggle.

We both know that life is a Darwin struggle although this is a human construct and human term for something better understood by the animals that are less savage twisted and playplayplay as well as striving.

If I had put on the mask of Tom Stott or of Peter Landau or of

Fletcher Currie or of Albert Lockwood I could have spoken effective fluid about many things and these would have included Gleneagles.

I could not have been Buster because I do not recall enough of him and because you do not like him.

Sixth of July in 2005 I am in Gleneagles and I am long gone from the Blue.

The eight leaders who imagine themselves as select pre-eminent in the world are meeting in a golf spa hotel because this is always the right combination of faked landscape and gossip with a background of curated low-effort high-dignity sport. The wealth power people do not sweat where photographers can see them. They are competence masks with traces of godly celebrity and gameshow smiles. They are humdrum beta male game of posing in bathroom mirrors but raise themselves with demands that all of their mirrors should come with hotels attached.

By 6th of July the Iraq blood pit is well established. Dark prisons metastasise tunnels between themselves and are country to country to country and the way to beat flesh into liquid. Confessions run down walls in sweating little rooms that taste of piss and horror. The anointed eight are happy intoxicated with being in the best club and with meat dreams fulfilled and disappearance and execution fun and swift high-explosive revenge.

You will have driven with others as far as Perth on the demonstration day. The Blue blockade was set up there. I was inside and under the Blue skin by then and a concealed parasite and listening watching. The riot gear and shaven head muscle cops without numbers were flexing in lay-bys beside their vans. I could smell the violence need.

I had seen the camera towers up at dawn and gaggled together for comfort warmth. They were neck stretched above the little houses of little persons and far seeing as the eyes of masters should be. Each of them was unashamed obvious aimed and peering at the point where a predetermined narrow route for marching suddenly opened out and ran beside a broad and undefended meadow. It was soft open for yard upon yard of invitation until it reached the new wealth-protection fence.

This was plan laid out three dimensional unashamed.

Plans need not be secret in fast-asleep countries.

You will recall the groundswell narrative for previous days had been significant cultural disturbance and effect empathy tales of infant and child fatalities and dirty waters and absent education for the poor. There was discomfort association between unlimited missile funding and the mass persistence of starvations. Successful change effectuation was portrayed as non-threat activity.

Marches and concerts and films and talking among people of significance had taken place at high visibility.

Blue briefings around Gleneagles were Molotov anxious for weeks ahead of time. Apparent pacifism had continued consistence and generated fears and legends of darkest dye.

The Blue has no comprehension of the peaceful. The Blue is violence of the fittest and teeth and nails and boots. It is suspicion elevated and made witless obedient to power.

Auchterarder village stood partially boarded against projected mob rampage and despoiling of its treasures and purities.

The new and high grey metal wealth-protection fence was planted firm and moderate effective around miles of high-grade gaming turf with bathroom mirrors and hotel attached towards their centre.

A bomb hoax was made predictable manifest for excellent misdirection provocation. A confluence of action events were in any case preparing. It made my head ache.

In pause forethought opportunities I did consider the OrKestrA. I had not ascertained if it was drivingdriving between roadblocks and golf courses of the lesser kind. Or you were perhapsly parked and waiting to hear if negotiations had succeeded. Delay and apparent bargaining took up morning hours. Tony Benn and Blue authority made their compromise and outrage and stern but fair and other statements. This was efficient in escalating above-average tension to great heights and began the need for satisfaction release.

I do not know if you were rage aware. I do not know what kind of van you travelled in. You perhapsly drove past the parties of men in pastel sweaters standing on dyed grass and being silent outraged. They were funny.

You perhapsly understood Gleneagles to be a music box of large dimensions with parts that were outrage in oppositional orientations and also outside broadcast lenses and also passion and riot shields and love were all there and intended to play one tune which is always the same tune.

When the finally released buses and minivans and cars arrived for speeches and democracy and assembly I was standing presenting innocent wonder in Auchterarder High Street and eating chips on the pavement.

Auchterarder and surrounding territory presented high-degree innocent wonder. A slow march curled about the streets and pathways with a suitable and photogenic banner held across the bodies of the leading rank like the ribbon round a cake. March leaders less famous than those in previous London events dreamed deep imaginings of power and influence.

Blue intervention paused their progress at the choke point location just before the meadow and the cameras observing readiness. Unexplained compression from new arrivals and mild panic was imposed and then removed.

Nothing happens to the front rank of a march at this stage in the fall of a democracy. Politicians and minor influencers are permitted their outing and can then feel satisfied and leave.

I was not in the front rank.

I was behind.

The bad place is always behind.

I was idling pausing backtracking until the cycle of choke point confinement and release had escalated to intolerability and screams.

And I could smell the sharky shark intent and knew a face up ahead of me and another at the right edge of the crush beside a fat girl with blue streaks in her hair who started crying.

More marchers were funnelled into the space with no space. There was a low-level tease of Hillsborough intention.

But we were allowed our wild release.

And then I was happy free running and the first of the riot cop batons was singing down inside the required music. We played on the preordained meadow and we were entertainment and violence porn headline images and the cop helicopter landing for filmic effect with forces LARPing Vietnam D-Day leaps to glory and blood and blood and blood.

I hurt the Blue.

(space break)

I kicked it when it fell.

I was effective efficient and imposed harm and sick days in no way commensurate to my prior wounds.

I was emotional trauma in depth.

I was clean with mayhem.

And they did not catch me because I am slyly fast and know the Blue moves.

I merry strolled from a blithe and diverted direction and put gloves on over my blood knuckles. Then I slow straggled back to the chip shop and ate deep-fried chicken and more chips with a little wooden fork. I was righteous adrenaline hungry.

And the streets got thick quiet with no ID number bluebodies keen for bootsman fun.

An editor from an alleged Left-leaning newspaper was glad dog trotting by them. He was grins and small announcements to himself and random bootsmen of the day and how he found it thus far excellent and *tasty*.

He was fresh in the rush and triumph phase of his compression and release cycle. The choke point had been liberated and his narrative could return to compassion as suspect and a violence precursor and change as risk and war as opportunity stability right ordering. The next morning headlines would sing of Blue nobility.

And later the next day in any case London exploded with new mutilations and limitless justifications of death torture business.

Blue fears had drawn too much Blue attention to the North. London was vulnerable open and its watchfulness blinked.

I heard the marching music for the OrKestrA that day.

I wondered what show you put on and if you marched and if they held you in the choke point. You would have foxed their purpose if they tried. I realise that. You would have brought them the chaos that is light and then all the tension they wanted would have been gone.

There is planned music but it can be overwhelmed.

When you were onboard *The Sunday* I had a small intention to ask if anyone ran the Elastic Rabbit at Gleneagles and if you ever did run it anywhere without me.

It is my act and belongs to me and I took a great deal of time to make it.

But when I saw the open meadow and camera cranes I entertained the wish that you would run the Rabbit there. On the long and grey rough grass it would have been possible to catch the crowd and play the act for them according to its original intention.

That could have been almost possible.

The Electric Rabbit was a happiness and a beauty and truly there for the child who was properly selected by myself and therefore the right child to meet it. They would know they were the one essential and right child.

It was their taste of soaring.

Fuck all the men and all the men and all the men and all the men who want to be congratulated for not having killed me yet.

Fuck all the women who want the same.

Fuck everyone and everything that helps them.

These are some of the things that you can't explain to an estate agent:

Why you're crying and also saying things like 'I'd want someone who'll make sure they look after it.'

Why calling your home 'it' makes you feel even worse for finally, really deciding to sell up this building that is not really a building, but more like a big, old animal that has always hugged you and kept you safe.

Why apparently the room is listening around you, tangibly paying attention and being hurt, or surprised, or offended.

Why you worry the house may be permanently sad now, in the way that you are sad – as if you are two friends about to lose each other.

Why signing the wedge of paperwork that commits you and starts the process of selling your friend makes you feel unholy.

Why sliding your copies of the paperwork into the stiff and aggressively coloured new folder provided makes you feel sick.

Why it is good news that your property has earned more by just standing in place during your years together than you have in all your working life – and why this is information that makes you feel pointless in numerous ways.

Why you are disgusted with yourself for profiteering and for having a home at all when fewer and fewer people do and yet are also frightened that somehow you will slip into the gap between one shelter and another and get lost in homelessness.

Why you start shaking after you let him wander off and take pictures of that living room ceiling rose and all the moulding that was fiddly to strip and paint but worth it – that kitchen doorpost where Paul's growing and growing is still recorded in ascending biro lines, with only one there for yourself and another newer mark for Francis. And that dent in your bedroom lintel that you made on the very first day when you moved in – it annoyed you so much at the time, but it's only a dimple really, a tiny wink exchanged between your home and you.

Why you are relieved when Francis returns, because you seem very alone – your miserable home and miserable self.

Why you shouldn't have contemplated taking this meeting alone when Paul or Francis or both would have stayed with you and helped, because a toddler or even a lizard of average intelligence could have predicted that you would feel horrific.

Why you cling to how neat the estate agent looks with his dapper black mask and his flat-top afro with a tight fade at the sides and his small and brisk tie knot and his very white shirt and his very blue suit, because they make him look efficient but also decent and as if he can pick out other decent people and know them and introduce them to your gentle, friendly, harmless home.

'I'm being silly, it's just a house.'

And this young man with the kind eyes upon which you hope you can rely watches you over his mask while you apologise. He just waits and nods. Then he says that nothing needs to be a rush.

It's a good time to sell, though, he says. People are tired of wherever they've been trapped for all these months and the stamp duty holiday is helpful, he says. People want a change, it's normal, he says. Properties are beginning to swell the market, he says. Londoners are leaving for greener places and who can blame them, he says.

So get out now, before the rush becomes a full flood.

He sounds a little poetic – *a full flood* – and offers the phrase if he has repeated it in similar contexts and is pleased about it in the way that a craftsman is pleased by good equipment.

'This is so silly.' And the heel of your hand is smearing at a new rise of tears. 'I'm lucky to have a house. I'm lucky to have this problem.'

You can't remember what to call him. He did carefully give you his card, which showed his whole name and his even younger and slightly startled photograph. The card is now somewhere in the glossy company folder, which you hate and don't want to touch again for a while.

Something about the gold in his eyes, this small turn of light, and about his patience means you start explaining, 'Me and my boy, my son, we ran away here and it was nice and we liked it and we've kept on. It's where I came to. It liked us back – seemed to.'

You hiccough and swallow in a clumsy way that almost chokes you, 'Silly.'

But he touches your shoulder very lightly for an instant and says, 'Not silly.' And when you can look at him again, you know from his face that he loves his mother and that he remembers a day when she had to run.

Paul and Francis came back with the sunset, found me in the courtyard trying to mend myself with qi gong and *punch in horse stance*, but clearly not looking as functional as I'd hoped. They bowed to each other – *after you; no, after you* – before they came in through the little blue door – both acting the comedy butler now, happy after their latest London Stroll for Manly Bonding.

Francis even started to announce the epic nature of their route, 'Judd Street past Coram's Fields, over to Russell Square Gardens, over to Soho Square, to… Anna?'

And there they were, staring at me as if I matter. Which, in somewhere deep, does still surprise me.

Paul asked me, 'What's wrong, Mouse?' That did it, of course.

I remember the warm soft blur of arms coming in and being held and folded inside this parcel of us – Paul and Francis and me. And that's home and not a place. Inside the parcel, I tried to explain about the horrible brochure and the house, our house, my house and how it's time to go, maybe to go, maybe to run from England since it's run away from us. All of the words are hot and eventually wet against Paul's shirt and, somehow, Francis' hair.

It's always sympathetic, that hair. Empathetic.

'Poor Mouse. We knew you'd decide, but we didn't know when.' Much younger Paul would call me Mouse when I was sad and small-looking and had pink eyes – *like a mouse*. He hasn't done this in years. I suppose he must have stopped when I got happy, stable, content – whatever the states are that stop people worrying for you audibly.

Sorry, I'm describing myself as far more crippled than I am.

There are days, though.

But also there are days when the boys, when Francis and Paul, take me up the metal stairs, which I'm already in mourning about, and I have a bath and they make cocoa and when I emerge we're all of us in our pyjamas and dressing gowns. It's too hot for dressing gowns, or cocoa, but they set the mood, and we set up the speakers and then sit on the sofa and sing along to DVDs of musicals all evening and into the night. 'Mustang Sally' and 'Everybody Needs Somebody to Love' and 'Walking in Space' and 'Let the Sunshine In' and 'Sunshine on Leith' and 'All Over the World' and 'Damn It, Janet' – we dial up our volume and make ourselves feel better.

We love a good musical movie.

And – *important detail* – I can now watch *The Rocky Horror Picture Show* and just enjoy it.

You need this story here. It's an old, deep story, one that stops at the end of a trail I never travel. It's the place where everything stops in the heart of the wood.

You need to know.

Or maybe I need to remember that I know and I need you here with me.

So.

I came late to *Rocky Horror*. Surviving in my mother's house had involved escaping into textbooks and asexual perfection. It meant that every cult classic passed me by – especially a celebration of joyful erotic twistedness and blurred lines. I wouldn't have dared to look at its high kicks and lipstick. Not yet.

But then I reached 1983 and the first term of my first year at uni and many of the eggshells I'd been walking on were no longer relevant. I was free.

And I could taste the change, feel it like fur brushing static into my skin. I was just one anonymous First Year, blundering, prowling and scampering about inside halls of residence, in bars, in breeze-block corridors, round stairwells, over lawns – we were everywhere. And we were deciding who to be and what to love. Grant-aided, fully funded, Sodom and Gomorrah was arrangeable, if you wanted. Or you could head towards applied knowledge, incendiary knowledge, skull-thrumming knowledge, late-night sitting-on-the-carpet-at-the-feet-of-your-pothead-lecturer knowledge. Some of us picked playing sports and shouting, sports and drinking and then more sports. There was even a club for spelunking – a pastime involving almost all of my nightmares. Almost.

We were, in short, just handed many granted-aided freedoms that we have subsequently refrained from passing on. Our children's futures slipped our minds. My generation really did bogart all the good stuff and the fun.

My non-conformism conformed to the usual types – the T-shirts and the edgy books and dodgy haircuts and the societies to join while searching for your adult personality. Pagan macrame, white-water life drawing, politics, satanism – there were too many options, really, but everyone joined the Film Society: cheap movies, new movies, old movies, cult movies, you'd get them all. You couldn't go wrong. There were even all-night marathon showings of movies, movies, movies, movies.

I signed up.

And then the first marathon rolled around and staying sleepless from dusk to dawn for happy reasons seemed intoxicating in itself – for me, anyway. I was already happy as I walked through the damp winter gloom of the main campus towards my first overdose of entertainment and the lecture theatre cinema. Inside, more senior audience members were settled with sleeping bags and varied supplies. They all seemed like wise veterans of something complicated – everyone always did. And I was alone. My nascent OrKestrA family was months away from forming, but I was still happy, excited, relaxed.

I didn't mind being alone. If your childhood house is an embarrassment – clearly has shames and strangenesses that other households don't – then you get used to seeing solitude as safety, as self-defence. By this time, I'd already spent years avoiding birthday party invites, reciprocal hospitality, lifts home. I'd sometimes ask people to drop me at addresses that were not my own and this worked fairly well, until I forgot which lie I had told which person.

I know, I know – *I once went to the pictures by myself when I was a student* is neither a story, nor interesting. But I'm not finished yet.

And now I'll tell you I'm sitting, ready, and the bump-and-grind music begins, in underneath the opening credits and here's *The*

Rocky Horror Picture Show. And I watch Brad and Janet leave a clapboard church after someone's wedding and sing to each other about their uptight love.

I understand *uptight*, if not *love*.

They seem like my sort of people – asking-for-it innocents at the start of a disaster. Even sheltered and nervy me could work that out. I did read books, after all. You can hide a lot of useful information inside books.

I remember the noise of light rain on all sides, which I realised was caused by showers of gently falling rice.

Audience participation.

Apparently everyone else in the lecture theatre really was a wise veteran of that, too.

When Tim Curry in wet cherry lipstick threw his drink at the camera, someone behind me poured water on my head. Or they may have spat the water – it seemed to be at a mouth kind of temperature. Rubber gloves snapped and flew at the appropriate rubber glove moment, slices of toast span and landed on the steps beside me.

It was every kind of mayhem that mother would not have allowed. Also some kinds she wouldn't have heard of.

A gentle buzz of dope smoke spread.

And apparently everyone but me knew all the words.

The same as ever.

Only it wasn't the same.

I'd suddenly met a film where the odd and weird and freakish at heart were slightly victorious – and those were my people. Those *are* my people.

Normal is such a tiny hole in reality and so few of us can live there comfortably. *Normal* is not designed to be an easy, or welcoming, fit.

No one in that lecture hall was being *normal.* My top-button-buttoned virgin self found the pouting and strutting and innuendo and general sexiness and bread frisbees overwhelming. I found it *something*. I found it a *word*. I recall being passingly sad, experiencing this small and beige mumble of bewilderment, as I realised I had no vocabulary for whatever *this* was.

But maybe it was *joyful*.

Maybe I was *comforted*.

I felt both cosy and more free – *They're weird, I'm weird, perhaps life's weird*. I think this began my understanding of what makes *home*.

And I was laughing hard enough and brave enough to hear myself and find the sound convincing. I was someone who had been a good girl and studied hard and got good marks and now I had earned my escape. I had gone to university – a respectable type of flight. Perhaps I could be a happy, possibly sexy person here.

So much about me already seemed impossible – the peace, the smiles, the nights filled with only the kinds of disturbance that had no relevance to me. Maybe I might drag step and falsetto into a future of loving and being loved. Maybe life would recline for me, cherry-lipped and flexible, obliging.

I was having a pleasant night and maybe a small epiphany. That's what imagination's for – to give us a small epiphany, now and then. Human beings make thumbscrews and landmines, but we make better things, too – the films, the books, the jokes, the statues of muscular naked men wrestling snakes, whatever. We build these mechanisms for releasing joy in others, for building paths to carry ourselves away.

I seem to recall myself grinning so much my ears hurt. I could feel time was stretching and tickling around me, prepared to be more generous. I was about to be someone I'd like.

Then we were done, the last movie ending around dawn. My head was singing to me like a pleased kid among friends at the back of the bus – the kid I never was. The final credits slid up the screen and went away. I stretched. I was still successfully more than awake and a newly qualified wise expert in being delighted.

I stood up to leave in this fug of general happiness – a bit of dope, too, but mainly fellow feeling. That's all an audience is in the end, an expression of fellow feeling.

I wasn't used to being an audience of more than one, but thought I'd prefer it from then on. And the next time they showed *The Rocky Horror Picture Show*, I'd know at least some of the words. I'd bring toast.

Little ripples of tiredness made the stairs up to the exit seem slightly taxing now and then, but that was okay. Everything was okay and I thought – *I'll remember this forever. I'll even remember thinking that I'll remember this forever. I'll remember this while I die and by then I will know if my real life began tonight and if 'Don't Dream It, Be It' was actually something I did. I hope I don't disappoint me.*

I was also thinking *'Don't Dream It, Be It', that's a bit obvious, isn't it? Is that art: just giving your audience orders? Is that entertainment?*

But if you've already pleased them enough, most people will do what you ask. They might even feel it was their idea and you just helped them with it. This can be a good thing – or a point where politics and showbiz intersect with optional morality.

Outside, I liked the clean chill of the air and the blue-grey way the day was starting, the first birdsongs. I wanted a coffee but nowhere was open to sell it yet. I could have waited, loitered among the muddy campus lawns and the dozing flagstones and the various departmental buildings that somehow all looked as if they were tower blocks in Novosibirsk. I'm willing to bet that's an insult to Novosibirsk.

I could have gone and hung out in an empty common room, in a corner in the student's union, on this or that greasy sofa. I might have taken a nap. I possibly could have dared to borrow someone's mug from a common room kitchen, sneaked some instant coffee. This was long before the days of entrance security and smart IDs. Unguarded snacks and beverages were fair game – especially to the newly courageous like me. Still, my confidence wasn't quite at the point where I felt that available buildings – or coffee granules – were there for me.

So I kept walking towards my own oblast of student flats.

My quickest route led partly along a narrow path between chain-link fences and ugly shrubs. The women in my seminar groups would avoid it in the dark. We already knew what trouble looked like, no matter how sheltered our pasts. We'd make tasteless jokes about it. We'd walk its long gauntlet in a daylight rush.

Nevertheless, there was an assumption – I made the assumption – that somewhere couldn't actually be as unsafe as it looked, not inside a campus dedicated to guarding and growing the vulnerable young. No one would build a perfect hunting ground, right there among us.

You know now, don't you, where the story goes?

Ten minutes into my walk and I was at the entrance of the rat run.

Just as I didn't pause for a nap or a coffee, I didn't change my mind and take the long way round instead. I pressed on through the almost daylight, the fencing high on either side. And I kept feeling as completely happy as I ever had.

I was dressed unrevealingly. The top button of my blouse was fastened up. I wasn't drunk and I wasn't stoned. I had no bad habits. I had done nothing unreasonable or wrong.

And I know you don't want to be here now, don't want to be trapped between the fences.

But we're together now, inside this.

And there's a moment when I realise something is odd about one of the bushes, something odd about a movement. I spot it very fast, admirably fast.

Still, I am too slow.

Something about my running away doesn't work.

There's a point when I understand that my knees must be skinned inside my jeans now because of the fall. I have fallen. This little girl time from ages and ages ago fills me up – my being a very little girl, and I am crying because I have fallen and am hurt and I can remember that my mum – who was soft and young then – holds me and this seems like love.

I am in confusion.

And the man smells like too many cigarettes and the newspaper and vinegar stink of chips.

He says things – strange mind things, sad and alone things, pathetic pretendman things.

And I'm not afraid, because of the hate. I hate him so much.

But there is the pain, as well.

I've known all my possible pains before and now I have this new pain that is him and which is terrible.

So I go away.

He does his filth pain sickness things and I am a safe little person and elsewhere and I have skinned knees and I am loved and I am way high above my self in a tiny room and holding the door shut because there's no lock.

Only then I know there will be blood and must be blood and there is blood and the tiny room doesn't exist enough to keep me from it.

He puts a stain in my mind, in who I am.

I want to fly up high away again, but my head is very heavy.

I want to be hiding in the tiny room.

I don't want the stain of him.

I think he'll maybe make me die.

And he has no right.

He has no right.

And I try again to be in the tiny room and curled up tight.

I want to be curled up like my dog that had the silky fur.

I want to be closed like a fist.

I try my best, but everything is too much and over and over.

I do my best.

He had no right.

And I couldn't curl up tight, but I pretended.

I didn't get scared until he'd gone and I wasn't dead.

Except really I was dead.

His breathing was still on my forehead and in my hair.

And his pain was there.

And I was sick.

And he had left some little machine thing with me, made it part of me and it would wait and hate me. It ticked.

I wanted to scream, but I never have been able to.

At some time that was later, I was running to the residence block and the stairwell and my front door and that door existed and it had a lock.

And I was scared that he might come back. He stole only everything that mattered and not my money and I was afraid he might want that, too.

It took me a long time – inside my room that was a real room and had a real lock – it took me a long time to stop pressing my shoulder against the door.

Afterwards, I did everything I shouldn't – throwing my clothes away and showering and scrubbing until I couldn't feel my skin and swallowing toothpaste until he was almost gone.

The idea of his taste, I couldn't get rid of that.

Then I was in confusion.

Then there was no one to tell, so I told no one. I had no OrKestrA to help me.

Then a pregnancy test. AIDS test. STD test. Practical tasks are occupying and you need something to do, as if someone has died and you need to keep occupied as a distraction. It's just that you're the one who died..

Still, I did keep occupied.

And I am very sorry to make you know about this, but I am a teacher and we do have to explain. I didn't turn into Annanka Ladystrong by accident.

You already knew that, though. It was easy to guess.

You already knew the world has Stiltskins.

It's not just one Stiltskin, though – it's never just one – that's what I wanted to explain. The first Stiltskin will be too much and over and over, but also he will mark you so that every Stiltskin knows your weakness, seeks you out. They're always more of the same, always too much and over and over.

Buster the Stiltskin thinks he understands the world, but he doesn't know anything, not unless he knows this – the world is a place full of people who live in the over and over. It's not just the harm you deal with, it's the other harm it brings on late, it's the fact that once you're weak, the harm never stops. It's the same thing and the same thing, it's the over and over.

And I spent years inside a story about how every Stiltskin in the world can see my shames and find me.

And it took more years to learn that's not a story – its true name is *lie*. And I don't believe that lie, not any more. Stiltskins made it and nothing they make ever lasts the way that love lasts. They make only mechanisms, little *over and over* machines. And now is not their time – it's mine – it's ours.

And you're reading this now, here with me in my story – mine, mine, mine – which has no shame left inside it.

And I'm no longer alone.

People do their best to stay alive and be ready for when the kindness comes. They're standing, waiting in queues, looking through windows, but inside they're in a fight, they're fighting the war of their lives. They seem to be invisibility and silence, but they are sacrifice and triumphs never mentioned.

That's not an unimportant story.

I'm an Oakwood Primary Year Five teacher and I have a son and I have a lover and I have love. I stayed alive and I was ready and the kindness came.

And I'm out and writing in my courtyard and my honeysuckle flowers are closing down their scent as the birdsong starts – from sweet to sweet while the dark lifts away. And dawn is still dawn and good. I don't mind the dawn. And calling hearts still begin softly with small experiments.

Fuck the Stiltskins.

2020, Gouliot Headland:

This is my goodbye or funeral Anna and therefore I am inviting you to be the sole mourner. I realise you will not wish to. My process of leaving is already begun and I think this will be pleasant to you.

I began to die in Berlin and then continued downstream on the river where you found me. I will finish on Gouliot Headland which is near where I truthfully began as this thing. I am therefore being full circle and neat.

I have certain qualities which are that I am neat and orderly and ingenious remorseless. I assumed that I was righteous with Prav but have only been such relative recently in my solitude and works. I remove undoubted wrongs and have no grey or undefined or debatable mission aims. I am the working of justice and the tending of a choked and clotted garden where the good should gain light and therefore thrive.

Over these years you will have wished me dead at times and I will have agreed at times. I am reconciled to my existence and attempt to be of use. I have more purpose than many human people and there are ways in which I do less harm.

I would prefer if you know that. I would prefer to have told you what matters about me and who I am. I would prefer that you think of me as a gardener.

You may not have read this far.

You may not have read at all and that will mean I am not preserved in the kind of forever that is information spread from mind to mind. I believe in that immortality. The imperfect transmission of detail from person to person may assist me and is how rehabilitation always works.

I would prefer forgiveness after death and you are the variety of person to prefer forgiveness and understand its benefits for those who can forgive.

Also you always used to listen.

I may be lonely. That is probably true.

It is not my fault that I am a thing that does not die.

I am made of messaging and finance and information and useful identity fictions. I am part of the eternal life of money. Pieces of me are password protected irremovable and will become only gradual obsolete outwith a normal human lifespan. I am scattered like guesses and rumours and lies. A scattered lie is unpredictable resilient and resurgent.

Sometimes I imagine a successful thief will take my baseline elements which are properties and funds and materiel and attributes and tools. Then he might build me again in fifty years or a hundred years or longer. He might vampire my name back out across whatever world is left by then. I wonder if he will be better than me at being me. I wonder if he will be useful.

It is unfair that morally better and more genuine individuals do not thrive in comparison to creatures like myself. It is unfair that we slow burn away like lights in abandoned buildings that fail very gradual according to tolerances and stress. It is unfair that another person with dark feathers could reoccupy my building and set it up shining again. Ravens can be scavengers if they want.

Mainly I do not properly end because I did not properly begin.

I have consistent had limited access to the benefits of living as one person. This is very fair to the morally better and genuine people. My varieties of sadness are an example that should reinforce the moral principles of a just and ordered universe and other such comfort thoughts. I assume the morally better and genuine people would want this.

I can of coursely make false deaths for myself. I can vanish and leave behind firm indications of mortality.

This is regular necessary.

Berlin is traditional as a place to disappear but almost anywhere will do. The great and old cities are all gateways because they are built for human beings and the one thing all human beings do is disappear. Homes and streets and parks are full of past vanishments.

My choices have always lain elsewhere but Prav picked Berlin.

His body became inevitable unsuited to our vocation and hesitant slow in impractical ways. So he made himself atoms and blew away.

I had nevertheless an impression that he was moving and disturbing the sharky water in which we both moved and stirring the dark raven air. Certain incidents and styles of work suggest he was not absolute inactive. I felt his eye wink behind certain happenstances. Or perhaps some small horror would be outlined in a hotel newspaper and I would hear him polyglot swearing in my ear like an unsubtle ghost.

I have no explanation for my seeking him out. I was not commissioned to do so and could gain nothing on my own behalf by seeing him again. I spent nevertheless months in navigation of his trick trails and cul-de-sacs and mazes. His slips and his identity smudges and his tells were very faint.

Prav always was very hard to find.

He is almost perfect.

But I am better than him and more.

I find everyone in the end.

And I am his kind of disciple and kind of son. I know him.

And perhaps I am like every disciple and every son in my need to hear an apology for all that has been done. Perhaps I need to hear myself forgiven for all that has been done. A settled account is neat and I may want to be neat.

In my hand luggage I carried a copy of this document and I may have intended that I give it to him although in the end I did not.

Sometimes I do things without knowing why and operate only on instinct like the happy animals.

I hunted out Prav in the manner of something cautious hungry and the looking made me quiet in my mind like carving in balsa or building a jigsaw or any successful stupid hobby activity.

Searching for my type triggers alarms in the dust and sends up flares. This is natural. We retain our predator traits and are never only prey even when pursued. We do not hide without laying down defences. We are hard to trap and the world in its current state aids and nurtures us.

In confirming a Berlin location for Prav I also announced myself to him and suggested my soon arrival.

I understand this in my skin as I walk along a sunshining path beside the Spree. I am not afraid. And the river sings up with late summer lights and shows iron in its colours and is also a washing away of EastWest memories and barbed-wire memories and drowned child memories and cold new freedom memories with blue lips. I am a kind of happy.

This is a pretty day.

And Prav will be waiting. Father and teacher and priest and killer Prav will be sleepless waiting.

I know he is current occupying a sixth-floor apartment with overlook awareness views at the top of a large and optimistic experiment block that hunches into serpent bends between Joachim-Karnatz-Allee and the river. According to the available floorplans he has extensive space and bedrooms although he is only one man with no dependants. He is in his eighties or older according to various records. After so much time a man should have dependants.

I know half of his windows must survey the lawn and shrub area sheltered inside one tight waveform curve of the structure. Prav can then gaze further across the Tiergarten greenery and on towards Zoo Station. His other windows keep an easterly surveillance arc from Carl-von-Ossietzky-Park to the globe at the top of the television tower that stares blue and distant panoramic. The Fernsehturm stares over everything. Television is a constant need for absolute access.

The tower waitandwatches like Prav although it is something like three decades younger and therefore lacks experience. No doubtly as an Eastern thing it continues to somehow benefit from the onward immutable progress of the anti-fascist proletariat. This may be true of Prav also.

The Fernsehturm continues in use but now broadcasts advertisements and compulsion addiction entertainments and partially democratic news information. This makes it a monument to pragmatism.

Prav would understand.

Prav who has come back to his beginning.

This is the cliché habit. When death leans in and begins to see us we want mother comfort and being once more in our first home is as close perhaps as we can get.

My skin is troubled by response awareness of his guaranteed observation. But I do not look up as I approach closer. One does not look at a god and god is what we call the power that made us.

When I press the entry buzzer he responds unrushed and says an old name. I cannot recall if the name was his or mine. His tone is effective merry and implies that we must have prior arranged *Kaffee und Kuchen* for this afternoon and he is pleased to welcome me.

In any situation not entirely foreseen it is possible to rebalance and gain power by reclaiming the scenario as your own and pleasing to you.

This makes me smile. Prav used to say that he hated politicians because they do not earn power but only appropriate it.

He simply despised a lesser class of men who made clumsy stupid use of his own techniques.

All our strongest hatreds return to ourselves. We dress them in rhetoric and delusion but when we fall on the dark waters and are alone we see what is true.

Prav smiles when he opens the door to me and it is almost impossible to tell that he is afraid.

I am snug-fitting shirt and khakis and loafers and grey blue tweed jacket. I might be a US money farmer in town for the latest Staatsoper premier. That is the generalised suggestion I intend to make. For Prav alone I am presenting minimal concealment and relaxed motion and innocence with melancholy overtones.

Prav walks ahead of me into his flat and keeps hands low and shoulders calm. *I baked on Monday. Baumkuchen. I bake now. May I assume that you still like apricot...?*

We are both very smooth and as if we have rehearsed for many years on warm evenings in separate houses. That may be true.

I am no more political than I ever was dear boy. He wears navy corduroys and a black cashmere sweater with a soft grey Fendi scarf wound loose at his soft neck. He has decided on his Eton drawl for me and this is no more or less appropriate than anything else. It is not a symptom of nerves. *We were ahead of our time in being one might say flexible. The political has moved towards me. Towards us. The strength of believing in nothing. Those chaps are trying to corner the market. Yes?*

He never used to ask me questions unless they were intended to make me repeat my shames. Or else he was teaching me our catechism which is now made flesh and dominant religion and perhaps we tried too hard and made it so.

I answer according to our rules that belief is the ultimate strength. Unbelief will triumph temporary through surprise concealment.

But our definition of the temporary may outlive us both...

He turns his head enough to let me see that he is smiling.

I was sleeping. I do that in my afternoons.

This is a lie. It is poorly delivered and hearing himself makes something in him skip a groove.

He reads as the wealthy kind of thin but is truthfully the readiness of wires and whips and instincts hidden in loose clothes and calm posture. For cover he keeps talking and I agree to listen because I am kind and there is love or kind regard here in addition to the other things.

In limited contexts I think I understand love.

Now everyone is anything and nothing. At night I imagine the way they all sit in offices and palaces and listen to the big clock ticking down for them like feet in a passageway. They hope they have just enough time to steal just enough wealth to buy safety...

He is playing the insulated Mitte hipster who maybe met Ulrike Meinhof at parties and who no longer would insist upon complex sex with commune members or manifestos or poems or bombs. His leaf-green felt slippers display him as non-threatening and humorous whimsical. They are a deft and skilful touch and I admire this in a way that is partial strange affecting and has emotional impacts.

We are like the return of a tune played first on transistor radios in parks that were young at the time and full of lovers. It is impossible to listen without the dissonance of hope being overlaid by time. It is impossible not to remember that parks become developments of ugly houses with small gardens and trapped children behind glass.

The joys go. They grow tired.

We were never mobsters.

I pause and let him keep shuffle walking forward because I guess this will irritate him. He constant prided himself on predicting the next move in any interaction.

A mobster is a foreign asset is a politician is a debtor is a pervert is a populist is a drug pusher is an arms dealer is a prince is a spy is a mobster is a foreign asset...

He leaves me behind as if I am student dull enough to sometimes forget how I walk.

We understand the underlying truth. That nothing is real and we are righteous in a time of chaos.

Prav reaches what is surely the doorway to his lounge. I feel him consider where he would like what comes next to happen.

The lounge is as good a place as any.

I walk gentle towards him while he waits and say that we used to be the fastfast shadow blurs in the fabric of reality. We used to be discordant when acting against a democratic backdrop. But the democratic backdrops always liked us and the ways they could inflict us on the wider world. And in the end all shadows will come home. And in the end we are the real things among the blurs and shadow and there is no backdrop.

Prav swallows and his face is very clear and handsome in what must be window light touching his skin from across the room he cannot quite enter yet.

Do you remember in Les Jardins du Luxembourg, old chap? I took you to watch the sails on the boating lake. The flags of all nations pushed about by children with long sticks.

I say that I remember because this is true. He is describing a Paris afternoon early in our association. We were in the soft phase of enticements and seduction.

I breathed in the scent of grey dust from restless footpaths and hot almonds roasting in caramel. It was an excitement to be abroad and free and beginning another beginning again. He told me we are the sticks of clever boys and sometimes we push whole countries farfar. Sometimes we break ourselves short in their hands and keep them away from their fun. Sometimes we become their punishment.

I know he is enjoying the way he stands balanced on the good honey wood of his parquet flooring and shows me his undefended back. His still thick curls of hair are entirely white now and brushed high in a minor pride display.

And which is the stick and which is the boy and which is the boat with the little flag flying to be important? And why is there no one adult anywhere? Do you remember?

Remembering changes nothing.

I pause for him to nod and precede me into his long and calm living room with the creams and fawns and clever paperbacks in multiple languages and fine old ontungwa palm leaf baskets. His set dressing suits him. The scatter of postcards added to his bookshelves implies a proper life.

Only in the target countries intended for decivilisation is confusion in traditional roles encouraged. That used to be the case.

Prav sits in the Eames chair he keeps next to his view. I watch the familiarity of it comfort him.

I ask him if he remembers Sudoplatov, the great spymaster.

Pavel Anatolyevich. We could hardly forget. Not as great as he pretended and yet also perhaps greater. Which is appropriate for his trade.

Sudoplatov the teen soldier facing Nazis and also the KGB man and also the planner who had Trotsky murdered and also the zek in a Soviet Gulag and on and still on in his successive forms.

I think of him often. To be more accurate I often recall his description of the ones who will be traitors. The ones who would always be traitors in some way.

Prav knows his catechism just as well as I do. We speak together and make ourselves a prayer:

Search for people who are hurt by fate or nature,
The ugly,
Those suffering from an inferiority complex,
Craving power and influence,
But defeated by unfavourable circumstances.

There is a short while when we smile together and I feel extremely peaceful. We do not need to say that we were never traitors. We were never that.

Then Prav closes his eyes and tells me *I have noticed your late work and its direction. If there were an army of you then you might amend the world. The traitors have it and they will not give it back.*

The rest of what we do together can be predicted.

I do not die but I am always funerals.

Perhaps ninety-nine funerals and perhaps one hundred. I forget.

I can say that I took my kayak out on a silk day along the river and my path was average beautiful with my paddle breaking into the echoed sky and pushing on.

I was flying.

This was in a dawn perhaps one week after I made a goodbye with Prav. The reed buntings called my way which was *Allsofree Alwayssofree Allsosofree* and they sounded like small knives drawn over whetstones.

The river is good for small disposals.

The river is good for peace.

I pick times without people to join the water because this offers me maximum privacy and efficiency. Also my aloneness can allow me to seem a clean animal to myself.

In this dawn I cut the blue and push against what is an incoming estuary tide. The port and starboard marker buoys are orderly and proper and true guidance. Their colours bleed green and red picturesque over the silk moving surface and fish lurch from under my bow.

Avocets shift and patter but they do not believe I am unsafe, do not fly.

I have this good solace. Even me. I have this reality that is salt and does not change in essentials because it is always changing in all other ways.

I break to my starboard and enter a broad creek. This turns the tide for me and the inrushing water is my friend that pulls me between the green shine of samphire and the height of reeds. The course here leads to a tide mill wheel set in a pool.

But I never do reach the mill.

I let my kayak leaf spin with the currents and I am almost close to drunk with being above clouds and beneath clouds and running the fold of the world between blue and blue. A space has torn open between gathered cloud direct above, and a trace of water vapour left behind is casting veils of colour.

I do not think that this is here to please me or is a fate indication but I am pleased and feel myself fitted in the day.

The country at either bank falls quiet around me while I look up to know which predator has come. It is a marsh harrier which is broad wings and dark fingers and angles and sudden twists and a call of apparent and terrible grief. I watch it rise.

As one bird fades into white cumulus another curves in and calls. Then another. Then another.

Seven harriers ride up and higher and call as they lose and find themselves through the white. There is so much need in their crying that it hurts me.

Their black shapes circle and are invisible and then not. They occasional cross the field of colours that looks so much like sanctity. I could imagine their screaming is for heaven and to be let in. I could imagine they do occasional touch it. I could imagine that when I no longer hear them they have been in some way satisfied or taken in.

That was perhaps my equivalent to mercy.

I am not the worse things in the world.

I am only this thing that does not quite live and does not quite die and that will go to Sark soon and be back where it started.

I will sit on the narrow saddle of turf between the bracken slope and the big granite teeth of Gouliot Headland.

I will taste salt on my lips and smell warm lichen and hear the sea breathe and I will wait until I hear the ravens shouting how alive they are as they dance and roll and dip together while they round the cliffs.

They will make themselves silver in the sun and then turn until they are the dark of nowhere. They will be witch shapes and madness and breasting the future like figureheads and they will be joy.

They will be like a thought that god could move the world beneath me.

They will not recognise me but I will know them.

I know nothing about heaven. I'm sure only that ordinary people are going through whatever day this is – it could be any day – and a fair percentage of them could easily start screaming and never stop, just lie on the ground and not stop howling until there's nothing left of them.

But they don't. They mainly keep on and make sure reality still functions for everyone else. And they're not called queens or emperors or heroes and they don't get help. They don't get a mention.

But they can maybe sit sometimes and rest the way that Francis and I sat in Cable Bay on Colonsay and be entirely where and who they are – all the pieces, all at once.

One of our times like that – *kind detail, generous detail* – was spent watching the slow shift of water and hearing it lapping at seaweed like a sleeping dog licking its lips. We liked the way the rocks lazed in the sand, the way everything seemed old and warm and larger than us in good ways. Nothing about it made us want to harm any living thing. It wasn't a pattern of interconnecting deaths to us. It was somewhere we could feel at peace.

We kissed and – I realised later, falling asleep in the evening – I didn't once hear myself thinking *This is how normal couples kiss when they are in a relationship, but your half of this isn't normal or in a real relationship – you're failing.* We just kissed.

And I don't want to ever again hear from people who want to sit with wildlife because that somehow gives them permission to kill. I have never believed that murder as pleasure, or self-indulgence, or a cure for inadequacy, is some sacred and essential part of nature. I don't think that having an appetite for cruelty is admirable, or natural. Apart from anything else, it's a waste of energy, and nature never wastes that. Those in charge of our national fascinations say otherwise, but they are mistaken.

Weird little Stiltskins might have power, they might be determined to pick apart everything keeping us safe, but they're irrelevant. The ordinary people who can live in this world at this time without screaming – they're stronger than the Stiltskins.

Even if the Stiltskins do seem to be winning.

The broken and filthy Busters can't own us and make us small the way they're small.

How do I know that? Because I remember the terrifying March when the world closed down and we were scared, all scared enough to make the air cloying with panic sweat. In those first few 2020 days, Paul and I stayed awake in the kitchen and ate biscuits and talked nonsense until we knew the sun was coming and it would be safe to sleep. Somehow being unconscious in the dark felt overly reckless.

But out in quiet London, house windows were full of teddy bears and rainbows, as if everybody had worked out that we needed to feel like children who were cared for and to be adults who cared for the young. And the masks and masks and masks were there – *Look, I care about you; look, you care about me: we do this for each other* – and we waved to perfect strangers who waved back perfectly. We were together and were precious.

No one had broken us yet.

I was there. I saw it. I knew it.

I don't recall now how long that lasted, our civilised interval – maybe a week, or a number of days, maybe hours. But we were the ordinary precious people we are now, only we noticed that we're very strong – imaginative, kind, ridiculous and strong. We wept at the thought of each other and the ways in which we can be kind and unexpected. We wept at mercy.

Anywhere those people are could be such a merciful country.

I woke up wrong this morning. Out of sorts.

The sunrise was lovely, which is something – lemon-yellow clouds with geese across them, heading in from over Bevin Way.

My new Year Five is settling. We practice our Brave Waves across our screens and I believe there are genuine benefits – beyond the whole *not dying* thing – to teaching them while they're at home and can feel relaxed. Depending on the home. Added eccentric Wi-Fi and interrupting cats are now standard, familiar elements of any lesson – like my warm and cosy feeling that Mr Simms' efforts last year have very, very slightly let my new cohort down. He seems to have skimped on the world geography again and got even more obsessive about insects.

Of course, Oakwood still has only an acting Head. And, of course, I won't be staying with Year Five that long. The first buyer for my house dropped out in a flurry of mystery and excuses, but the current couple – they are nice, but I hate them, hate them for wanting my home – that couple seems keen and solvent and not mentally unstable in any inconvenient way.

Paul is home from uni. His in-person tuition collapsed almost as soon as it began, infections loping through the student residence blocks all around him. I tried not to seem delighted he was back. I tried not to enjoy that fizz of sparks and feathers in my chest when he says my name, or when I can feel his breath on my cheek. But I love that. Why shouldn't I?

And I love being feet up on my bed with Tall Paul against my one side and Francis against the other. And then we'll adjourn for one last cuppa, beyond which there will be bed, but in under the covers with Francis and his hair. We are almost dull, but also absolutely not. He is the miracle of someone who is in the right place. I am in the right place. We are together. We sleep well. And I love that. Why shouldn't I?

I love who I love and there's almost nothing else. Trap me indoors, lock me down and keep me from busyness and let me think while the whole of a city thinks with me and that's what we know – we love who we love.

My love is almost all there is of me, because that touches everything, changes everything.

If I have the chance, I'll demonstrate that for the rest of a long and happy life. I'll be exemplary.

Soppy, I know – but what else would keep us all going through ruinous day after ruinous day.

It's October, but still mild – unnaturally mild – and we're waiting to hear if we're shutting down again tomorrow – more anxiety over toilet paper supplies, more reliance on delivery vans, more ambulance sirens passing. Or maybe we'll start the new lockdown next week, or at some point further off when someone in an office somewhere marks the right amount of death on a graph, or on a flipchart. Perhaps all of the relevant numbers are just scrawled at the edge of something more important.

Yesterday, Paul and Francis and I drove out to my mad little mum's care home, stood on a patch of damp grass in the garden and smiled and, I suppose, offered her Brave Waves as if she were onscreen and not standing behind the lounge window in her last birthday's cardigan.

She never wore a cardigan in her life before she went there. Now they're the costume I send her, so she'll fit in. Or else they suggest an identity she'll find easy in the absence of her own.

Her eyeline wanders, fast and random, from face to face, so each of us is emphatic in her direction: lots of arm action, big expressions, mouths working away while producing no words. We never do say anything, we just mime. It's too hard to be cheerful if we're yelling across each other. And there's so little to say.

As usual, she responded most to Paul and Francis: coy and then ladylike and then jovial, pointing at this or that about their appearance, seeming to notice changes. I don't know who she feels they are – some composite of male relatives, neighbours, employers, boyfriends, my dad.

For a while she stood and held her carer's hand as if she were a schoolgirl landed with a lumpen companion in the lunch queue. Then she reached into her pocket and took out a postcard – not recent and slightly distressed. I send a fresh one every week, fill them up with neutral well wishing, rubbish about the garden, the weather, the bad parking and rude behaviour I see when I walk to the shops.

She held the card up for Francis, who duly made sure to bend forward and pay great attention. Then she smiled and I watched her mouth very carefully enunciating – *From my daughter. She's a teacher.*

I'm not wrong – that's what she said.

She looked proud.

I love who I love and that includes unexpected people.

She was proud.

And it's past midnight here and I should stop. When I write sitting up in bed, Francis does sort of doze, but I know he's not properly resting. His hair stays awake and watches me and tickles him in his brain – that's what I tell him.

There's not much left to write in any case. You have it all now.

I love Paul.

I love Francis.

I love my mum.

That won't change, even if I'm not here.

The beautiful things and the funny things are important.

And please do look after the things and the people that are beautiful and funny, both at once – they're much more than important.

And I gave you the information about scones – so whenever you make one, or come across one, you might think of me. Small domestic comforts are underrated.

And I do try to live as I would in a merciful country. I still hope for that. People do. Many ordinary people do.